"A [...] for. *The Red Bikini* is a winner!"
　　　　　—Jennifer Probst, *New York Times* bestselling author

"I love this book! . . . A fantastic debut. Charming and funny and a totally great read . . . And I have a new favorite hero. Fin is amazing!"
　　　　　—Susan Mallery, *New York Times* bestselling author

"The easy charm of fictional Sandy Cove, California, sets the scene for a sweet romance . . . Christopher's writing is crisp and her characters are strong, and readers will look forward to the next installments in the trilogy."
　　　　　—*Publishers Weekly*

"A great debut and a fantastic start to a series."
　　　　　—*RT Book Review* (4½ stars, Top Pick)

Berkley Sensation titles by Lauren Christopher

THE RED BIKINI
TEN GOOD REASONS

Ten *Good* Reasons

Lauren Christopher

B

BERKLEY SENSATION, NEW YORK

THE BERKLEY PUBLISHING GROUP
Published by the Penguin Group
Penguin Group (USA) LLC
375 Hudson Street, New York, New York 10014

USA • Canada • UK • Ireland • Australia • New Zealand • India • South Africa • China

penguin.com

A Penguin Random House Company

TEN GOOD REASONS

A Berkley Sensation Book / published by arrangement with the author

Berkley Sensation Books are published by The Berkley Publishing Group.
BERKLEY SENSATION® is a registered trademark of Penguin Group (USA) LLC.
The "B" design is a trademark of Penguin Group (USA) LLC.

For information, address: The Berkley Publishing Group,
a division of Penguin Group (USA) LLC,
375 Hudson Street, New York, New York 10014.

ISBN: 978-0-425-27449-1

PUBLISHING HISTORY
Berkley Sensation mass-market edition / April 2015

PRINTED IN THE UNITED STATES OF AMERICA

10 9 8 7 6 5 4 3 2 1

Cover photos: Marina © Arief Rosa / Getty Images;
Couple © Reggie Casagrande / Getty Images.
Cover design by Sarah Oberrender.

For my loving and supportive children—
Ricky, Rene, and Nate:
Thank you for all the cheerleading and understanding.
I couldn't have written three better kids.

ACKNOWLEDGMENTS

There are always a lot of wonderful people to thank for their help in writing these books.

For this one, very special thanks go to Gisele Anderson and her husband, Dave, of Captain Dave's Dolphin and Whale-Watching Safari in Dana Point, who gave me answers, tips, and advice regarding whales and dolphins (not to mention inspiration for Drew's awesome boat). Captain Dave (and "Mrs. Captain Dave") boast an incredible knowledge of whales and dolphins, and I'm so appreciative of their time and enthusiasm in answering my e-mails and phone calls.

Also thanks to Dana Wharf Whale Watching in Dana Point whose boat, the *Dana Pride*, first inspired me to write about whale watching. When I went out with my kids one spring many years ago and saw three grays and a dolphin stampede myself—all that beauty in the ocean—I just knew I had to write about it someday.

All the whale-watching captains of Dana Point are true stewards of the ocean, and I have the utmost respect for all the work they do for marine life. Any errors I made in trying to bring this work and beauty to life are my own.

Thank you to my critique partner, Tricia Lynne, who critiqued this book as I was writing it and always offered the most amazing help. You are a true friend, confidante, and a talented writer, and I'm lucky to have you in my life.

Thank you, too, to so many people who read this book at various stages and gave me great advice and feedback: beta readers Debi Skubic, Michelle Proud, Crystal Posey, Kristi Davis, and Mary Ann Perdue, who helped shape this story; writer friend Tamra Baumann, who keeps me motivated and on schedule in our almost-daily e-mails; Mark and Lauran Lansdon, who helped me with some of the sailing lingo; and my mom, Arlene Hayden, who helped copyedit and proofread (and cheer me on).

Thanks, as always, to my awesome agent, Jill Marsal: Your encouragement, dedication, and patience are lifelines to me.

And thanks to my editor, Wendy McCurdy, and to all the staff at Berkley, including Katherine Pelz and Jessica Brock, who do such great work. (And special cheers to the copyediting staff and cover designers!)

Behind-the-scenes thanks go to friends and talented professionals Shawn Oudt for my author photos and Carli Krueger, who does all my newsletter, website, stationery, and logo design.

And last, but certainly not least, I want to thank my incredibly patient husband, Chris, and my three kids who have been so supportive. Kids, this one's dedicated to you!

CHAPTER

One

Lia's rolling briefcase bumped over the wooden dock slats as she rushed down the ramp in her high heels toward Drew's boat. The rhythmic thumping of the broken wheel on the left echoed the relentless thump in her chest, especially when she saw the empty wheelchair parked at the end of the dock, a seagull perched haughtily on the handle in the late-winter sun.

"Drew?" She pulled her case to attention and peered up and down Drew's enormous white catamaran deck. Long shadows darkened the back end.

When she was met with only the quiet laps of the harbor water splashing against the hull, she mentally measured the leap from the dock to the three small steps at the back of the boat, then eyed the deep Pacific below. She took a tentative step with her toe, but the catamaran pitched a little too wide for her pencil skirt.

"Lia!" Douglas's gruff voice, rasped from at least five decades of smoking, preceded him as he hoisted his bearlike body through the narrow cabin door.

"Douglas! Glad to see you. How is he?"

"Churlish."

Douglas wiped some kind of potato chip grease from his

fingers onto the belly portion of his T-shirt, took the steps down to the catamaran's low stern, and hauled Lia's briefcase into the boat. He reached out his weathered hand to help her make the leap, but his eyes slid to her shoes.

"Where are your boat shoes, sunshine?"

"I came straight from my last client when you called."

"On a Saturday?"

"No rest for the promotion bound." She threw him a tired smile for proof. Her boss, Elle—real name Elvira—whom Lia not-so-affectionately thought of as the Vampiress and who regularly used phrases like "I'll hold your feet to the fire," had been running her ragged.

"Here." Lia undid the straps of her shoes and handed them one at a time to Douglas, who stared at them curiously before chucking them onto the bench seat that ran along the edge of the boat.

He jutted his chin toward the main hull. "Enter at your own risk."

Drew's galley was clean and sparse, mostly bright white with splashes of nautical blue and meticulously shined stainless steel. Lia was always surprised at how spacious it seemed, even when the catamaran was filled with the forty-five guests he usually had on a whale-watching trip. But today it was eerily empty, with just Drew sitting at the small galley table, twisted so he could unload a tiny cupboard that was part of the curved bench seat. He slammed paperwork and small canisters onto the tabletop, then hauled out three or four folded plastic table-cloth-looking items that looked like some type of covers. Beneath the table, two bright white, slightly bent casts covered both legs, his toes poking helplessly toward the narrow walkway.

"Drew, I'm so—"

"Save it, Lia." Without a glance back at her, he continued stacking things onto the table. "I know you're sorry. Everyone's sorry. I'm sorry. But I just don't want to talk about it right now."

She pressed her lips together and tore her eyes away from the casts, then sidled in toward the table, lugging her briefcase behind her. The case was filled with two hundred new color brochures, plus two hundred colored tickets and passes she'd had made up for his new whale-watching business. She really wasn't supposed to be doing free marketing work on the side for her friends—the Vampiress would screech into her twenty-third-floor ceiling tiles if she found out—but Lia's friends had terrific businesses, and Lia always had marketing ideas for them.

"Drew, I think we need to talk about this and come up with a plan for what you're going to—"

"I don't *know*, Lia." A small vinyl bag landed on the table next to the canisters. It seemed to be the main thing he was looking for. He turned slightly in the dinette seat. "I guess you didn't understand the part, 'don't want to talk about it right now.'"

She tugged her briefcase closer to the table and edged around his casted feet to take a seat. "Drew, as your friend, I would honor that one hundred percent. And I would come here and make you soup in your lucky bowl from college and pour you a nice, neat scotch and we'd sit here and get plastered. But, buddy"—she cupped his wrist—"I have to come to you today as a marketing manager. Because I just booked the Vampiress's most important client on *your boat*. Because you needed the business. You need to come through for me on this, Drew. *Please*."

Drew stared at the table. "I don't see how I can make that happen."

Images of the Vampiress and her rage floated through Lia's head. Lia was not much more than a glorified administrative assistant right now, and had been for the last four years, but she was on the cusp of a promotion—a huge promotion to open the new office in Paris—if she could pull this off. She could feel it. It had been a dangling carrot for the last three years, but now—finally—it looked like it could happen. And just in time, too. Turning twenty-nine and still hoping she got the coffee right for her boss was not exactly what she'd had in mind for herself when she'd stepped into the hallowed glass walls of the most famous ad agency in Southern California.

"Drew," she started again. She kept her voice calm. "I just spent two whole vacation days helping you sell a hundred freaking tickets for excursions over the next six weeks, and you launch Monday. I know you're feeling frustrated. And I know you're feeling desperate. But you need a plan. And I need that promotion. So we need to figure out how to run this boat for a couple weeks, and how to run that charter next week. Let me be your free PR person and help you come up with something. And then let me be the friend who's going to help you through all this." She stole another glance at the casts.

"I need the friend who will sit quietly and let me brood."

"Then you should have called Xavier."

Drew smiled and stared at the table. They both stilled, listening to the gentle marina waters lapping the sides of the boat and Douglas's distant whistling of "Daydream."

"I wanted you to come," he said quietly. "I knew you'd know what to do. I just don't want to keep rehashing the accident."

She gave his forearm a gentle squeeze. She knew her friendship with Drew was strong. And knew he'd come through for her. Their friendship had undergone a subtle shift in the last six months, when she'd become his public relations manager. He was the fourth friend from Sandy Cove she'd started helping with marketing. It probably wasn't smart to give up her measly leftover time off to help friends for free on the weekends, but she enjoyed it. She helped Drew and their friend Vivi, who ran the cute little vintage clothing shop on Main Street. She helped her next-door neighbor Rabbit who ran a surf camp for kids, plus their landlord Mrs. Rose when she needed to advertise for new residents. And Lia just started helping Mr. Brimmer who opened a wine-and-cheese shop on Main and didn't know how to start a website. She was really proud of some of the campaigns she'd launched, and proud of all her friends for starting such brilliant businesses. Until today anyway.

Drew was flexing his fingers, staring at them on the table. "We need to find someone for at least the first week," he said.

"Yes." A breath of relief escaped Lia's throat. "Do you know any other captains we can call?"

"No one I can trust."

Lia listened to the waves lapping. "What about Douglas?" she asked.

"He doesn't have a commercial captain's license."

She figured as much. Otherwise he'd have been the clear choice. Her mind raced. "Kelly from the marina?"

"He's fishing boat only."

"What about want ads?"

Drew scowled further. "This is an expensive boat, Lia."

She nodded and touched his arm again. Drew was more of a control freak than she was, with touches of OCD to boot. She couldn't imagine him giving up his boat to anyone. It cost more than his house.

He gingerly began putting the items from the table into a box that was wedged onto the seat next to him.

Her mind wanted to stay focused on business, but it kept drifting to the motorcycle accident she imagined. She'd just flown in from a trade show in New York that the Vampiress had sent her to, gotten dressed this morning, threw everything into her car to start visiting the Los Angeles clients she'd missed this week, then received the call from Douglas. The horror of the accident—Drew sliding across the freeway off his motorcycle—and the fact that they could have lost him, played over and over in her mind all the way to the marina.

"Does it hurt?" she asked.

"I'll be okay. Painkillers help. No talking about it right now."

Lia nodded and eyed the neat stacks in the box. "Need help?"

"I got it."

They sat in silence again, Drew organizing the items in the box in his fastidious way, his movements slowing as he seemed to think.

"I thought about calling my dad down here from San Francisco," he said, "but his heart's been bad. My mom thought it best we not tell him yet."

Lia's mind raced back through everything she knew about Drew. They'd been friends for six years—part of a small circle of really cool people here in Sandy Cove that had all become like family, really. Until recently, anyway, when she started working eighty-hour weeks. She and Drew had even tried to date once, eons ago—he'd picked her up to take her to a nice restaurant near the Sandy Cove Pier, but when he'd leaned over to try to kiss her, they'd both burst out laughing.

"Oh! What about your old first mate, Colleen?"

"Maternity leave."

Lia slumped back. Colleen would have been perfect.

"There is . . ." He stared at the table, as if trying to decide whether to mention it or not.

"Who?"

"I don't know. Maybe not. It's probably too risky . . ."

"Who?"

Drew shook his head.

"Look, if this person can sail, and knows anything about whales, and—whoever this is—let's consider it. This is both of our careers we're talking about. . . ."

"My brother."

Lia frowned. "I didn't know you had a brother."

"He just . . . showed up."

Behind her, Douglas took a step down into the cabin. "He just washed up on shore, is what you mean. Need anything more, boss? Want me to get you loaded up?"

"In a minute. Here, take this." Drew shoved the box across the small galley table.

When Douglas stepped back into the sunshine, Drew glanced up at Lia. "My brother's a wild card."

"Where is he? Why haven't I heard you mention him in all these years?"

"Well, 'just washed up on shore' is about right—he sailed in yesterday. He's a little messed up. Been sailing the world."

"Well, that . . . that sounds *fortuitous.* Sounds like perfect timing." Lia's heart began racing. Maybe this was an easier solution than she thought.

"Did you not hear the 'messed up' part?"

"What do you mean, 'messed up'? If he can sail the world, he can certainly sail in and out of the harbor. Does he know anything about marine life?"

"Oh, yeah. Former U.S. Coast Guard. Naturalist. Environmentalist degree."

"What are you waiting for?" Lia scooted her hips around the bench to reach into the briefcase for her cell. "He sounds perfect. Let's call him."

"Lia." Drew grabbed her wrist. He looked up at her through the bangs that fell across his forehead. *"Messed up."*

"How messed up? You mean on drugs?"

"No, not drugs."

"You mean, like, crazy?"

Drew shrugged. "He went through a lot of tragedy over the years. He's just kind of . . . on his own. Just stays on that boat and anchors wherever the winds take him. He rarely even talks. He won't agree to a tourist boat, no way."

"Can't you ask?"

"He won't agree."

"Drew!" Lia brought her head down to try to get him to look at her again. "You *need* him. You don't have many options to keep your business alive in this most-important week, and I *really* need that charter. He's family. He'll do it for you. Just ask."

Drew looked away without answering. He scanned the cabin, as if searching for anything else he needed. Beads of perspiration lined his forehead.

"Drew!" Lia couldn't believe he wouldn't consider this. It was an easy solution to a problem they needed to solve by Monday. Family would do anything for you, right? Granted, she sometimes missed phone calls or important gatherings with her own mom and sisters, but that was only because she worked a lot. If Giselle or Noelle or her mom really needed her, she'd be there. "I think we need to come up with a plan," she said softly.

"Let's talk about it tomorrow. I need another painkiller. Douglas!" he hollered over his shoulder. He turned back toward Lia. "So how's your boyfriend, anyway?"

"He's fine. But Drew, let's discuss this. I booked some impor—"

"Did he leave for Bora Bora?"

"Yes, but let's stay on task, here. I think—"

"I thought you guys were getting serious. I can't believe you let him go to Bora Bora without you."

"It's not serious, and I don't think 'let' should be a phrase in any healthy relationship . . ."

Drew threw a grin at that—it was an argument they'd had time and time again—but then he turned and looked frantically for Douglas.

". . . but I think we need to come up with a plan, Drew, for who's going to sail your boat Monday. It's booked solid for the first three weeks, and my client wants to show up to inspect it before the big charter next week, and—"

"Doug!" His yell had a twinge of desperation.

"Let's just ask your brother. It would be a simple solution, and you trust him, and—"

"Asking my brother would *not* be a simple solution. In fact, the more I think about it, the more disastrous it seems. So let's get that idea off the table. Let me think of another plan overnight, and we'll talk tomorrow."

"But we're running out of time."

"Give me until tomorrow. Maybe Doug and I can handle it—he can lift me up to the captain's bridge every day." At the sight of Douglas lunging down into the cabin, Drew gave a weak smile and began maneuvering out to the side of the dinette, his casts clunking along the deck floor.

Doug lifted him with a loud exhale—about 240 pounds of man lifting 160—then lumbered out of the galley, staggered down the stern, and hoisted their weight back up onto the dock. The wheelchair was waiting, set with its brakes on, now with three boxes next to its wheels and the seagulls scared away. Douglas plopped Drew into the chair with a grunt. Both men were already drenched in sweat, and their faces had gone white.

A daily lift into the captain's bridge was out of the question.

What were they going to do?

Drew made eighty percent of his annual income in the six weeks of whale-watching season, including the festival weekend. He and his new girlfriend Sharon were struggling as it was, trying to launch this business, trying to make ends meet. And Sharon had a special-needs child that Drew said he didn't help pay for, but Lia knew he did. And now these new medical bills . . .

And man, Lia hadn't even told him the part about the first two clients she'd booked for Monday and Tuesday—she didn't want to make him feel guiltier than he already did, or cause more worry to spike with his pain. In addition to the client she'd booked for the Vampiress, she'd found two potential investors for Drew, which he'd said he really needed. And both were showing up this week. If they showed up to a boat that was inoperable . . . well, not only would they run from investing in such a thing, but Lia's reputation would be shot.

She gathered her shoes from the blue-cushioned bench seat and tugged at her rolling briefcase. Douglas lumbered back on board to secure the cabin door.

"Douglas, wait." She jerked her case back toward the galley. "Tell me about his brother," she whispered. "Could he operate this thing?"

Douglas gave her a sympathetic glance, but then his allegiance shifted back toward the dock. "His brother's trouble, sunshine."

"We need someone, Douglas. Full tours start Monday."

"Can't you refund them?"

"For *six weeks*?" Her whisper rose to a panic. "These are really important clients. And Drew's already spent half that money, I imagine. And the other half is probably going to new bills after this accident."

Douglas's silence told her she'd probably guessed correctly.

"Where does his brother live?" she pressed.

Douglas fiddled with the lock. When his silence lengthened, Lia let her shoulders fall. He wasn't going to answer. She turned away from his weathered hands.

"Slip ninety-two," Douglas finally mumbled under his breath.

"What?" She turned her head slightly. Drew was staring at them.

"Guest slip. Ninety-two. Far north end," Douglas said without moving his lips.

He turned into the sunlight, heading back toward the stern, and Lia followed. As they stepped back ashore under Drew's watchful gaze, Drew shot them both a suspicious look.

But Lia was going to have to betray him.

Drew wasn't thinking clearly, and she was going to have to make this right.

For him.

For her.

For this promotion.

And for about five other relationships she couldn't seem to get right lately.

Guest slip ninety-two was nearly at the end of the marina. Dusk fell in light purple, and a lamp sputtered as she passed. There were no liveaboards allowed at this end and, with a cool February night that threatened rain, there weren't many people out, even on a Saturday. Lavender-colored water lapped against the empty boats that lay still and quiet at day's end, all packed together like sleeping sardines.

Lia glanced again at the piece of paper where she'd written the number, pulling it back from the breeze that tried to curl it, then slid it into the pocket of her skirt along with the dock key Douglas had slipped her. She concentrated on not getting her heels caught in the weathered wooden planks.

When she reached slip ninety-two, she pushed her wind-strewn hair out of her face and peered around the deck. It was a small sailboat, about a twenty-footer, dark and closed up for the night. The sails were covered, the ties set, the cabin lights off.

"Hello?" she called anyway.

Nothing.

Her footsteps sounded obnoxious in the otherwise-peaceful night as she headed down the side dock along the boat's port side.

"Hello?" she tried again. "Drew's brother?"

Dang. She didn't even know his name. Her heels rang out as she wandered farther. The only other sound was the familiar creaking of the boat's wood against water, and one rope hanging off a mast that clanged lightly as the boat pitched and slightly rolled. The sailboat didn't have the gleaming OCD-ness of Drew's catamaran, but it was neat, the teak floors swept, the sails covered, the ropes in perfect twists. A jacket and an empty bucket sat on a glossy teak deck bench.

"Hello? Mr. Betancourt?"

A slight shiver ran through her. Maybe she'd rushed into this. She should have asked more questions—at least his name, and maybe more information about what, exactly, "messed up" meant. As an image began to take shape in her head—ex-military, maybe posttraumatic, older, bigger, bearded, crazy, loner—the light on the dock snapped and buzzed. She turned on her heel and her pulse picked up. She wasn't one to scare easily, but this probably wasn't one of her brightest moves.

But then . . . a flicker of light in the cabin.

She turned nervously.

The cabin door creaked and a man's shadow emerged, buttoning a shirt as the tails flapped in the night wind, as if trying to get away from him.

He twisted his shoulders to clear the cabin door and stepped slowly toward her while the boat pitched, moving across the deck with all the assurance of a man who is used to the sea.

He was bigger than Drew—nearly half a foot taller, and broader in the shoulders. He had the same dark hair, but his was much too long, and he swiped at it as he looked up at her on the dock. Although his face was in shadow, she could see a week's worth of facial hair darkening his jaw. His dead, gray eyes narrowed as he studied her and finished the last two buttons. "Whadoyouwant?" His voice was like gravel.

"I'm um . . . a friend of Drew's."

His eyes made a quick sweep of her—not out of interest, seemingly, but in the way you'd assess a dirty floor, deciding how much work it was going to be to deal with.

While he continued to wait—probably for a better answer—Lia fumbled with her purse. "I um . . ." For some reason, she checked the piece of paper again. Ninety-two, right? But certainly this was him. She could see a vague family resemblance in the straight, narrow nose, the hard-edged jaw, the dark eyebrows. Though this man's brows seemed much more sinister than Drew's, pulled into a deep V beneath a lined forehead as he waited for her to say something.

"I uh . . . I came for Drew. He needs . . . um . . . Well, he needs a favor."

The boat creaked and rolled under the man's spread legs, his knees giving way in the slightest movement to make him as sturdy as the mast.

"Doesn't seem like Drew would send you to tell me that."

Lia licked her lips. He had her there. She tried to give him one of her friendliest smiles—they usually worked on everyone—but he seemed unfazed. He narrowed his eyes and waited.

"I um . . . well, yes, that's true. You're *absolutely* right about that." She laughed just a little, flashed another smile. Normally men didn't make her nervous. She'd learned a long time ago that an optimistic attitude, a great smile, and a positive view on the world could do wonders and get her almost anything she wanted, with men or women. Or hide anything she wanted.

But this man seemed too robotic to care.

"He's uh . . . well, you know about the motorcycle accident, right?"

Nothing.

"Well, after his accident, he's a little stuck. He's got whale-watching season right ahead of him, and he needs to run his business. This is *his* season. It's the biggest season. I mean, from February to April, it's—"

"I know when whale-watching season is."

"Yes, of course. Then you know. It's huge. And he's booked every single day for the next four weeks, and I could easily book the additional two, and—"

"*You're* booking him?"

"Well, I help, yes."

He didn't seem to like that for some reason, but he gave a slight shift on his leg that somehow indicated she should go on.

"So I'm . . . I'm just so worried for him, and he needs a captain, since the accident and everything, and he just needs someone who can sail his cat, and who knows about whales, and who can take on the business for him for just a few weeks, and—"

"Sounds like this is your problem, not his."

"Oh, no, it's *his*."

Well, *too*. But Lia's own personal problems didn't need to be part of this discussion. "He's . . . the *money* . . . you know. This is the majority of his income. And medical expenses now. He's . . . He's in trouble, Mr. Betancourt."

He scanned her again—some kind of assessment—and blinked a slow blink of a man unimpressed. "I'm not your guy."

"What do you mean?"

He turned and started back into the galley.

Lia found herself stumbling toward him across the dock, although she didn't know where she intended to go or what she intended to do once she got there. "Wait, Mr. Betancourt. You can't help?" She couldn't control the incredulousness in her voice.

"No." His deep voice gave the word a feeling of cement. He wandered toward the jacket and snatched it up.

"But . . . you . . . you *have* to."

"No." He turned back, giving her high heels a strange glance. "I don't."

He scanned the deck again, seemingly to see if anything else needed to be crushed in his fist the way the jacket was. "If Drew wants to talk to me, tell him to come tomorrow. But I have a hard time believing he sent you."

He lumbered across the deck, and the brass rails of the galley door glinted as the door slammed shut.

Stunned, Lia closed her mouth, her protest swallowed.

The dock light flickered again behind her with a loud pop, sending her into an embarrassing jump, then began an ominous hum and flutter. She glared at it, trying to figure out what to do as darkness fell. She'd thought she'd be able to simply solve this problem, but apparently she was losing her touch.

Not that this guy was an ideal solution. Drew was right. He'd be a nightmare with the guests, especially the Vampiress's client, looking more like he was going to slit their throats and steal their bounty than tell them the gentle breaching habits of blue and gray whales.

But at least he was a start.

As the lamp began its death hum, she glanced down the long dock toward the main part of the marina. She only had one minute left of any kind of light at all, then she'd have to find her way back in a sliver of moonlight, which was being shadowed now by black-tinged rain clouds.

With one last glance at the now-darkened cabin, closed up apparently to fool the harbormaster into thinking there were no liveaboards there, she headed back along the dark, narrow planks.

For the second time that day, and about the fifth time that week, she felt like a complete and utter failure.

Two

Sunday morning, Lia leaped out of bed at six. She had a lot of work to do.

She cleaned the desk area in her bedroom, pushing aside the three garish bridesmaid dresses that hung near the closet—she couldn't believe she had *three* weddings this year, and all three of them in blue, which was not her favorite color to wear. Her oldest sister Giselle was the first, with a wedding in July, followed by two girlfriends who were getting married in August and September.

Lia was really happy for Giselle—she was marrying one of Lia's best buddies, pro surfer Fin Hensen, and Lia was thrilled for both of them. But her sisters and mom thought Lia was purposely avoiding the wedding plans. She hadn't helped pick out the bridesmaid dress. She hadn't gone to the florist to see the centerpieces. She didn't go out the night the three of them—Noelle, Giselle, and their mom—and their dates went to see the DJ. She overheard her mom and Noelle whispering one night in her mom's kitchen that she might be jealous, which bothered her more than anything. Nothing could be further from the truth. She just worked a lot. Couldn't they understand that?

Lia cleared a space at the antique desk in her bedroom, pushing aside her Eiffel Tower lamp and the ring dish that looked like a French postcard, then fired up her laptop while she headed to the kitchen to brew the strongest pot of coffee she knew how. Her cat Missy slinked a figure eight around her pajama pant legs, waiting for her own breakfast.

"Let's eat then get to work, Miss," she said, lifting the calico.

Like every morning, Lia sipped her coffee while staring at the framed crayon drawings her six-year-old niece, Coco, had colored for her. Giselle and Coco had lived in Lia's apartment until they were ready to move in with Fin and, during that time, Coco had decorated the whole place with crayon drawings. The three still hanging in the kitchen were of cats and zebras, and the four in the living room were of sunflowers and tire swings.

When Coco and Giselle had moved out, Lia thought it would feel wonderful to get her space back again so she could work in peace. But, the truth was, she missed her sister and niece terribly. The very same week they left, Lia went to the rescue center and found Missy.

By ten o'clock and four cups of coffee later, still in her pajamas, Lia had scoured all the seafaring want ads online and placed twelve calls to the Sandy Cove marina to see if any of the shop owners or the sportfishing place knew of anyone looking for a job. The prospects were bleak. Anyone who knew this business had his own boat or crew ready to go for the season. Lia clicked off her phone with frustration. She might have to go back to Drew's brother.

She sighed. To do that, of course, she'd have to go through Drew—admit that she'd gone behind his back, then ask him to go down to the marina and beg his brother himself. Neither seemed like a happy ending. But she was losing time. And getting desperate. She took a deep breath and dialed.

Her first four calls went to Drew's voice mail.

That was odd, that he wasn't calling her back. But she tamped down her worry and worked on other projects—the new website for Mr. Brimmer, and a YouTube contest for one of Elle's clients.

She answered the door for the postman, who was dropping

off the first two pairs of many shoes she'd ordered for the weddings, in every shade of blue imaginable. These first two were a pump and a heeled Mary Jane—she didn't like either—so she stacked them against the wall. Around noon, she punched in Drew's number a fifth and sixth time.

By her seventh call, at two, panic was setting in.

She started to leave a message, grabbing her jeans out of the neat piles of laundry folded on the purple velvet chair in her bedroom. "Drew? Sorry I keep calling. I just need to talk to you, as you know. I think I'll just swing by your house, actually. I called a few East Coast marinas, but I'm having trouble. Call me."

The jeans still in her hand, her pajamas halfway off, the phone rang back. Drew's number displayed.

"Drew, buddy, I've been trying to reach you, I—"

"Lia, this is Sharon."

"Oh, Sharon! Hi! Is Drew okay? I'm sorry I keep calling, but—"

"Yeah, the thing is, he's *not* okay, Lia," Sharon snapped.

Lia's heart began to hammer. Sharon had been dating Drew for about six months now, but Sharon and she had gotten off to a rocky start as friends—Sharon had felt, right from the start, that Drew spent too much time with Lia, and too much time working, and she accused Lia of exacerbating both.

"I took him back to the hospital this morning," Sharon said in a whisper that sounded accusatory. "He was having some trouble breathing, and the doctor wanted to keep him overnight and check for blood clots and deep-vein thrombosis."

"Oh my God." Lia yanked her jeans on faster. She didn't know what deep-vein thrombosis was, but it sounded dire. "Is he at Sandy Cove Hospital? I'll be right there. I just have to—"

"Lia, *no*. Stop. He's comfortable. I'm going back in an hour. He'll be fine. But really—you have to stop calling him. And talking to him about work. The stress is getting to him."

Lia halted. "Oh, Sharon, I'm so sorry. I don't mean to cause him stress. I just want to help." She moved more shoe boxes aside and dropped into the purple chair. "He needs a captain for the next several weeks, and—"

"Let's just let him *recover*, okay?" The snap in Sharon's voice felt like a slap across her face. "Can you just handle this for the next few days without involving him? Maybe cancel the first day or two, and then we can reconvene and come up with a plan? His health is more important than work right now."

"Of course!" Lia said when she got her breath back. "Of course. I *know* that. But this business is everything to him right now, and—"

"It's *not* everything. Deep-vein thrombosis could stop his heart. There's more to life than work, Lia."

Backhand slap.

"Please," Sharon continued in Lia's stunned silence. "Give him a few days of rest. You can call on Wednesday." And she hung up.

Lia stared at the dead phone in her hand. It shook as she steadied herself back to her desk, tears pricking her eyes. She stared at her laptop screen, which began blurring.

How could Sharon say such a thing? Of *course* she knew there was more to life than work, and of *course* she cared about Drew's life. She poked at several screens, shutting them down, feeling sick. She wasn't a workaholic or anything. Or maybe she was. A little. She just knew that financial security was everything. Growing up the way she had, she knew that to be all too true. And these people in Sandy Cove, or even her own mom and sisters, didn't seem to realize that, to be a success, you had to think bigger. You had to be "on" all the time, like they were in L.A.

She slammed her laptop closed. She was worried for Drew, but she knew Sharon would take good care of him. Sharon was a nurse herself, and he couldn't be in better hands health-wise.

But to handle Drew's business herself? With Sharon hijacking his phone and holding her at arm's length? And the investors showing up—unbeknownst to Drew—throughout the first week? And the Vampiress's client Kyle Stevens showing up on Monday morning to check out the boat for the charter?

Lia studied the Eiffel Tower lamp, letting the clean lines blur into muddy ones, but she knew what she had to do.

She needed to pay another visit to Drew's brother.

The guest slips looked less intimidating in the day. Lia's hopes lifted as she skittered down the marina stairs and made her way past Sandy Cove's gleaming white boat masts that stood as tall as the palm trees around the harbor, all profiled against a bright blue sky.

She was better dressed for the boats now: white Keds and blue jeans. She'd wondered how much time to invest in her appearance for this particular encounter—usually marketing herself was half the job, the Vampiress always said (usually while eyeing Lia's sometimes-messy topknot with disdain). But Lia wasn't dealing with a Fortune 500 business owner here. She knew it wouldn't matter. She'd wrestled her slithery hair into a simple ponytail, took two swipes with a mascara wand, tugged a light sweater over her jeans, and called it a day.

"Hello?" she called. "Mr. Betancourt?"

The boat looked much the same as she'd left it last night—still closed up, with the bucket sitting on the bench and the same rope clinking quietly against the mast. The late-afternoon sunshine glinted off the teak floors and well-worn captain's wheel, the wood faded where the owner's hands must rest. The boats on either side had vacated their slips for the day, leaving Drew's brother's boat to look even more isolated and quiet. She didn't know if he'd slept aboard—she assumed he had. And, in doing so, he was breaking the rules. She glanced around and hoped she wouldn't see the harbormaster anywhere nearby.

"Hello?" she called again in her most cheerful voice.

The cabin door swung open with a bang, and Lia flinched.

Drew's brother stepped out much the same way as he had last night: looking too big for the door frame and none too happy to be called through it.

In the light of day, she could see him better, although it didn't improve matters. He had the same scowl, the same hard lines around his jaw, the same bad manners. He squinted angrily at the sun, and tried to look up at her as the sunlight streamed over her shoulder.

"Hello, there!" She gave him her warmest smile.

"You're back," he said in the same tone of voice you'd use to describe the return of the measles.

"I am! I thought we could talk again. I was going to bring you coffee but I didn't know what you liked. Can I buy you one at the marina shops?"

"No thanks."

"I can buy you a tea? A soda? A beer?"

"No." He grabbed the rope that had been clanging against the pole and tightened it.

"I hoped we could discuss how we can help Drew, Mr. Betancourt."

He gave the rope a violent tug that caused Lia to want to step back. "I told you to send *him*," he mumbled without looking at her.

"He ended up back in the hospital this morning and couldn't make it."

She thought she saw a flash of some kind of emotion in his face—not exactly worry, but perhaps some kind of surprise—but then he turned away before she could tell. He mumbled something and moved toward the helm.

Lia sighed. This wasn't going to be easy. She followed him along the dock and shaded her eyes from the sun. The light was cold and bright in February in Southern California—an abrasive white. The brief rain last night and today's wind had cleared the air into a crispness, but it left the sun to shine in a fierce, unfiltered way.

"Since his accident, you know, he's in a lot of pain," she went on, "and I really want to handle this for him. Can't we talk, just you and I?"

He bent behind the helm at the back of his boat and started the motor. He had on cargo shorts today and a long-sleeved white shirt, cuffed at the forearms. The ocean breeze whipped the fabric around his menacing frame. She wondered, again, how old he was. Drew was twenty-nine like she was, but his brother looked a little older. His trim waist and muscled back made him look young—possibly in his early thirties. But something about the way he moved—like he was dragging himself through life's motions—made him look older.

"I won't take much of your time," she said. "I can explain everything quickly."

He snapped his hair out of his eyes and headed back in her direction. Hope soared in her chest. He bent a muscled leg onto the dock near her and hauled himself off the boat in a strangely lithe move. She hadn't realized how tall he was. But instead of looking at her, or inviting her down, he barreled past her and began undoing the stern line at the last cleat.

"Are you leaving?"

"Yep."

"Can't we talk?"

"I'm busy."

"Can I come with you?"

He shot her a look of exasperation. "No."

A stab of panic set in as Lia watched him toss the line into the boat, then amble down the dock to untie the others. Three more lines, one swift turn out of the harbor, and her chance would be gone.

"When are you coming back?" she yelled.

His hand went into the air as if to dismiss the question.

Frantically, Lia scanned the side of the boat. Could she jump in from here? She'd certainly been known to resort to desperate measures before. One didn't keep the Vampiress happy without being bold, that was for sure.

She watched him step into the boat at the bow, following the last line he'd tossed. The sailboat tottered under his weight as he turned, coiling the line around his arm. Lia flipped her purse strap over her head and shuffled toward that end of the boat, which was still hugging the dock. She had only seconds to think. While his back was still to her, she took a flying leap—of faith and on air—and plunged to the deck behind him.

"Ooof." The sound escaped from deep in her belly as she found herself against the cabin windows, a hand breaking the crack of her head. She didn't know what had hit her. But, when her eyes flew open, Drew's brother's body ran the length of hers, his thick forearm against her neck, her chin forced upward. He weighed about a million pounds. She squeezed a breath through her windpipe, but he spun away within half a second and lifted his hands in surrender fashion. *"What the hell?"* he growled out.

Her heart continued to hammer. She closed her eyes and tried to suck in as much air as possible. The "ex-military" and "former Coast Guard" part of Drew's description came back to her in a rush, and she felt the heat of embarrassment creep across her cheeks.

"Don't ever, *ever*, do that again!" he spat.

"I'm so sorry, Mr. Betancourt," she whispered, still trying to draw some air into her lungs. "I'm—"

"And stop calling me that!"

"Wh-what should I call you?"

"Call me Evan." He turned away, snatched his dropped coil off the deck, and glanced back at her, clearly unsure what to do with his anger. "What the hell is wrong with you? Why would you do that?"

"I'm—I'm just really desperate, Evan. I need your help. Drew needs your help. I really need to talk to you." She was still plastered against the slanted cabin windows, her hands still raised, still trying to catch her breath.

He motioned her toward him. "Get off there. Stop looking like that. I'm not going to hurt you. I'm trained to react that way."

"I know. I'm so sorry." She stood on shaky legs and straightened her sweater. Her purse strap had practically cut off her breathing, and she loosened it against her collarbone. She couldn't get her heart to stop thundering. The gentle roll of the boat wasn't helping her shaking, and she grabbed a pole next to her and leaned forward, hoping she wouldn't throw up, trying to clear her head, clear her lungs. "I forgot you were Coast Guard before," she said on a few deep breaths.

He looked at her suspiciously. "How did you know that?"

"Drew told me."

Maybe he really hadn't been sure she knew Drew. He kept glancing at her while he shifted his weight and finally threw the line back at the metal cleat on the dock. "*Never* get on an occupied boat without asking permission to board. I'm surprised Drew didn't teach you that."

"We're . . . we're really not that formal."

He glanced at her again but didn't say anything. After wrapping the line around the cleat a few times, he put his hands on his hips and took another deep breath. "Who are you to him?"

"A friend."

"A good friend?"

"Yes."

"He must be doing okay, then, if you're here and not at the hospital."

"Yes, he'll be okay. They're checking for deep-vein thrombosis."

He looked away, as if processing that bit of information. "Does he know you're here, asking me this?"

Lia considered lying. It seemed a lie could get a "yes" much sooner. But her intuition kicked in and told her that a lie with these two brothers could come with a host of other problems.

"No," she admitted.

Evan took another survey of the ocean's horizon. "What else are you to him?"

"What do you mean?"

"Anything more than a friend?"

Lia nodded. She'd have to come clean. "I do some marketing for him. For free."

That didn't seem to surprise him as much as she thought it would. "Anything more?" he finally asked.

Lia didn't know what he meant by that—like, romantically? But she shook her head. "That seemed like enough."

The line of his mouth quirked up in the slightest way—it might have been a smile on a normal human being—but before she could tell, he turned and started tugging at the line to secure it further. His irritable movements made her think she'd hallucinated it.

"Well, I'm not taking you with me." He gave another angry yank. "I'm going to have to ask you to disembark."

The boat obeyed him, the bumpers rubbing up against the dock as if pointing the way for Lia.

"Listen, Mr. Betan—er, Evan—I know we got off to a bad start here. I'm very sorry. I don't know what I was thinking. That was a stupid move. I just feel very, very desperate. Drew really needs your help. He can't take care of the *Duke* alone."

Evan whipped around at that. *"What?"*

She took a step back. For such a huge man, he sure moved fast.

"What did you say?" He took a step toward her.

What *did* she say? Did she say something wrong again? "I said . . . uh, that he couldn't take care of the *Duke* alone."

Evan's lips parted—she'd finally caught him off guard. Although she didn't know why.

"His boat," she offered. "The *Duke* is his whale-watching boat, and—"

"I gathered. When did he name it?"

Lia couldn't imagine why this mattered, but she searched her memory. "It was . . . I believe it was . . . let's see, it wasn't last January, but the one before. . . . Two years ago?"

Evan's gaze slid to the deck floor. He hung his hands on his hips again, but his ferocity was gone. His shoulders slumped, his forehead lines disappeared, his hair fell over his eyes like a dark curtain. He stared at the shiny deck tape for a long time, sparkling in the sun. Finally, he reached for the line again. The only sounds around them for a full minute were a lone seagull squawking overhead and the water slapping against the dock pillars.

"I'm only here for a week," he mumbled.

Lia wasn't sure she heard him correctly. It sounded like a reluctant agreement, but maybe she'd hit her head in the scuffle. She was too hopeful to ask him to repeat himself, so she just held her breath.

"Okay," she said. "We could find someone else after that." She waited for him to correct her. When he simply walked away, back toward the stern line, she went for the assumptive close: "If you could help for just the first week then, that'd be great." Although she was bursting with relief, she tried to keep her voice calm. She had the sense of talking down a tiger who hadn't decided if he were going to pounce or run. "I'll have Drew write out a script for you."

"I don't want to talk."

Didn't want to talk? How was he going to give the whale-watching narration? "Okay . . ." She was determined to think of a way around this. "Um . . . We can work something out."

"You can do it," he said, leaning forward to grab the stern line. "Have Drew write it out for you."

"Well, I don't usually come aboard for these things. He has a deckhand named Douglas. Maybe he can—"

"The deckhand's fine." He tugged on the tie. "So we're done here?"

"Um . . . yes." This seemed too easy. Could she trust him to show? The Vampiress's client was too important to take any chances. If the client arrived with his entourage on Monday, and no one was there . . . "So you know how to sail?"

He threw her a quelling glance and finished tying the line.

"A cat, I mean?"

"It has a motor, doesn't it?"

"Yes."

"It's a cruise cat, then. I think I'll manage."

The sarcasm in his voice let her know that was probably an insulting question, but she didn't mean to insult him. She just needed this to go off without a single hitch.

"So you'll be at Drew's boat? At nine? Do you know which one it is? Here, let me give you a business card."

"I know where the commercial vessels are. And you just told me the name. And the time. I'm good."

She shoved a business card at him anyway. "The first tour is at nine."

"So you said."

"It's *very* important. The first client is—"

"I get it."

"There are two tours a day."

He didn't respond to that, but indicated with the business card where she should step off the boat.

Should she mention the dress code? They needed to make a really good impression. "Can you wear something like this?" She waved her hand in his chest area. He really did look good with the dress shirt on. "I can have a polo shirt made up for you with the company logo, but you're quite a bit bigger than Drew, so I'll have to ord—"

"Listen, lady." He turned, exasperated again. "I'm about two commands, three eyelash bats, and four seconds away from changing my mind. If you want me there, you'd better quit now and disembark."

Lia pressed her lips together and nodded. Yes, definitely. She struggled up the edge of the boat and gracelessly flung herself back to the dock, stumbling ashore. Evan didn't help her, just stood with his hand hanging off his hip and frowned at her disembarking technique.

"Nine, then?" she couldn't help but reiterate.

"*One* command away . . ."

She nodded and clutched her purse closer to her body, then walked away with what little pride, and few take-charge skills, she had left.

Evan finished tying the last line and went to the back to cut the motor. He'd been planning on taking the boat out for a short spin, to see if his work on the motor had improved matters at all, but now he didn't feel like it. That last bit he'd done just to get rid of her.

He threw his jacket across the bed and glanced at the card she'd pushed his way—*Lia McCabe*.

Damn, her relentless cheerfulness had worn him out. How could anyone go through life so perky? She was a tiny little thing, but hard to look at—it was like staring at the sun.

He slid the card under a bottle of scotch along his sideboard and glared at it. He supposed he'd have to show now. What had he been thinking? Problem was, he *wasn't* thinking. He'd been feeling. Always dangerous. Her saying that name again—the *Duke*—had torn another rip right into his chest, right there above his heart. She even said it like Renece used to.

His hand found its way to the tiny drawer, right along the side of the bed, and before he could remind himself it wasn't a good idea, his fingers felt around, past the handgun, past the box of bullets, and curled around the small frame he knew was in the back. He pulled it out and started to look at it, but had to drop it onto the countertop when his hand began to shake.

Minutes later, he mustered the courage to turn it over. He winced. There they were: Renece and Luke. *Luke the Duke.* Renece had her head bent toward their son's, her brown curls falling against his cheek, both of them with that same bow-shaped smile they shared. Luke was on the verge of a laugh—Evan remembered that look well—and his front tooth was missing, which he'd been so proud of. *Daddy, do you think the Tooth Fairy will come?* Evan had assured him the Tooth Fairy would, but he and Renece had both forgotten until about two in the morning, when Renece had awoken him with a start, and they'd rummaged through their jeans on a chair next to the bed, and then through Renece's purse downstairs, until they found a dollar bill and four quarters. They'd snickered as they crept past the moonlight rays through the window, taking turns sneaking the money under Luke's pillow while he slept, teasing each other about their terrible ninja skills. The whole escapade had ended up back in the bedroom, where Rennie had laughed and fallen on top of him, snuggling against him in the dark. He'd remembered appreciating the moment—he'd been on leave, which was when he appreciated every moment—but he couldn't have possibly appreciated it enough.

How could he have known those moments would be forever ripped from him in just two more days? How could he have known his little boy with the missing tooth would take his Tooth Fairy money to get a milkshake at a fast-food place that would be taken over by a crazed gunman? He wondered for the millionth time if Luke saw the machine gun before he was killed, if he was scared, if Rennie was afraid before she turned to face her own fire, if her face was contorted into agony as the realization hit her? And, most importantly, why he couldn't have been there to protect them.

The rip pulled harder against his chest. He shoved the photo back into the drawer and pulled the gun forward, then slammed the drawer and spread both hands wide across the cabinet, taking deep gulps of air.

He scowled at the business card, half under the scotch bottle, already mad at himself for agreeing to such a foolish thing. Giving whale-watching tours to a bunch of happy, spoiled tourists seemed about the last thing he wanted to do. Describing whale migration patterns and dodging cotton-candy fingers from kids whose greatest concern was what brand-name T-shirt to wear that morning . . . while his wife and little boy lay buried in the ground, riddled with bullets, their bodies so devastated the caskets had to remain closed. . . .

God, he would never make it.

But . . . damn. Drew had named his boat after Luke.

Two months after it happened.

He'd thought Drew would have never forgiven him, but there it was: the *Duke*.

He pressed his hands into the cabinet again and let his shoulders sag, glancing again between the bottle of scotch and the business card, not sure what to do.

Right now, it could go either way.

CHAPTER

Three

As Lia rushed through the morning fog down to the Sandy Cove marina on Monday, she whispered positive mantras to herself under her breath and hoped everyone would show— Douglas, the cook Coraline, maybe their part-time steward, and, of course, Evan. But, try as she might, her hope kept slipping at the Evan part. Somehow he just looked like the kind of guy who disappointed people for a living. And she didn't have a Plan C.

She'd left a message with the Vampiress, as she'd tugged on a casual sweater and tennis shoes that morning, that she was going to spend the day on the *Duke* to make sure everything went well with Kyle Stevens's pre-charter check. She knew Elle would like that. Kyle meant everything to her.

Kyle Stevens was one of the wealthiest men in Orange County, a descendent of one of the area's founding fathers. The founding fathers had made their wealth in ranchland and oranges in the eighteen hundreds, while Kyle—two centuries later—was making his on oceanfront property and lavish clubs that catered to Hollywood celebrities and Southern California elite. At twenty-eight, he'd become one of the youngest multimillionaires in Orange County. And at thirty-two, with his good looks and fortune, he'd become one of the most eligible bachelors. He had a lot of mover-and-shaker friends, and Elle wanted to make him happy. Though, ultimately, she wanted to make his *father* happy. She wanted his father's business, which was currently going to her competition in New York. Elle found it embarrassing that this famous Southern California family wouldn't keep their business with the largest Southern California firm. And she meant to correct that.

Kyle was a good client, running his club and two condominium high-rises straight through the Vampiress. He was very hands-on and often visited their ad agency in person. Elle knew he'd made a couple of favorable reports to his father, and her black glossy bob would quiver in anticipation as she announced this to the staff.

The day he called about a whale-watching tour threw them, though. They'd never set up such a thing. But Kyle loved the ocean. He loved to hang around pro surfers, famous deep-sea divers, local scuba nuts, and folks from the American Cetacean Society. He asked Elle if she could set up a charter for him and forty-five of his closest friends, who were all wealthy and famous, to go whale watching in the spring, and Elle saw dollar signs. When Lia heard this, she'd blurted out that she had a friend, Drew, who could run the charter. Elle had looked at her with long-overdue, and much reserved, interest— someone from *Sandy Cove*, who had a boat that could impress *Kyle*? Lia had nodded her assurance. She'd always had a mouth that skipped ahead of her, and now she'd been a bit sorry she'd let it run away. But she could do this. Drew could do this. In fact, it would be a boon for Drew, because his boat might have its picture plastered all over the society pages.

Over the winter, Drew upgraded in preparation. He spent a fortune on custom glass-plated viewing pods unique to the *Duke*, underneath the two hulls; another fortune on new nylon nets at the front of the boat so people could look straight down at the water; another fortune for new seating for the front of the boat; a fourth fortune on educational posters and hands-on exhibits for the kids; and paid cost for all of Lia's marketing materials she'd created. They were ready.

What Drew didn't know was that Kyle himself had booked a tour for the first excursion of the season to check things out and make sure things were ready for his charter. It was weird for the client himself to check things out ahead of time, but Elle chalked it up to Kyle's sea love and told Lia not to question him. She repeated her constant refrain: *Do whatever Kyle wants.*

Lia was going to tell Drew about the uber-important first client as soon as she returned from the trade show, but then she got the call about the accident, and the news seemed as if it would stress him more than cheer him.

She took a deep breath.

She could do this.

Lia headed down the familiar dock, where Drew's wheelchair had been before, and a sigh of frustration escaped her lungs. The area was empty.

"Evan?" She climbed aboard Drew's boat—maybe he was waiting aboard. "Cora? Douglas?"

Silence.

She walked all the way around the deck as her heart began to hammer. Cora and Douglas would be bumps in the road if they didn't show—she'd called them awfully late, and Douglas was probably halfway to Vegas already, considering he thought he had the week off and zoomed out there whenever he could. But Evan wouldn't be a bump: He'd be a block. No Evan, no tour. She imagined the look that would be on Kyle Stevens's face. And then the Vampiress's.

And then she wanted to throw up.

"Evan?" Her voice quivered in the early stages of panic.

She started to unlock the cabin, but didn't want to have to lock everything back up if she had to go find him, so instead she twisted her rings while standing at the back of the boat. Luckily, she was a bit early. Maybe he just wasn't a punctual guy. Good thing she'd told him an hour before the first actual tour.

She waited five more minutes, checking her cell. She had so much to do. If she had no deckhand, she had to pull the covers off everything, and she wanted to set up the cabin for guests the way Drew always did. And dang, she sure could've used a coffee. She glanced longingly up the dock through the morning fog, hoping Cora would show. Although Lia could probably figure out how to use Cora's French press if pressed.

Desperate times, and all. Her cell phone told her only two more minutes had passed.

She headed back into the cabin and rummaged through a drawer for the small chain that Drew sometimes used across the stern. Her hand flew across a piece of cardboard in her neatest, most professional Sharpie handwriting, which still came out a little too bubbly, but it would do: *10 a.m. Whale-Watching Tour: Wait Here!* She hung the note and the chain at the stern entrance and dashed down the dock toward the guest slips, twisting her ankle at the bottom of the dock.

Dang. Even her body was betraying her. . . . She rubbed it and hobbled on.

Evan's sailboat looked the same as it had the other days. She couldn't tell if he had slept onboard or not. That would drive Drew crazy. He was a stickler for rules, and was friends with the harbormaster, Harry James.

Lia glanced around for Harry and kept her voice down in case: "*Evan?*" she called in a loud whisper, limping along the port side.

Fog left a quiet pall along the harbor as she scanned the deck for any clues, but the white February sun was starting to break through, glinting off the boat's brass rails. From her ten-foot distance, she tried to peer into the cabin windows. Some kind of brown paper covered or blocked most of them from the inside, except one, which had a torn curtain pulled back enough to take a peek.

"Mr. Betancourt?" she tried again, louder. "*Evan?* It's me, Lia."

She eyed the deck. Should she take her chances and jump down? Knock on his door? After what happened yesterday, she didn't want to risk it. But time was ticking here, and she couldn't just stand around and wonder where he was.

"*Evan?*" Louder.

Nothing.

She glanced at her phone for the time. Tentatively, she poked her toe against the hull. The boat rocked gently, but not enough to wake him. Finally, she went for it: She threw her weight into a leap and flung herself onto the deck. A sharp pain skewered through her ankle, but she'd live. She regained her balance and rapped on the cabin door.

"*Evan?* It's me, Lia," she called before he thought it was an intruder again. "Are you in there?"

She got only to the second rap when the cabin door flew open and Evan scowled outside.

Seemingly half-awake, he stood, half-bent, with only jeans on, his arm casually dangling a gun at his side. His other hand came up to shield the morning sun from his eyes, and he squinted to bring her into focus, then—when it finally seemed to register who she was—he murmured an obscenity and whirled back into the cabin.

Through the half-ajar door, she watched him snatch up a shirt from a bed that seemed to take up the whole back of the cabin and slide it over his muscles while he opened a side drawer and tossed the gun inside. Behind the gun, he shoved some type of small, silver-framed picture, then slammed the drawer. Two empty scotch bottles teetered, and one tumbled onto the floor as he swore again and threw it on the bed, which was covered in discarded clothing.

Lia was still blinking her shock at seeing him so scarcely clothed, an unbid intimacy with a man she thought of as scary and strange. But . . . wow . . . with a crazy-hot bod. She forced herself to turn away as he cast angry searches around his cabin for something, then disappeared into the little bathroom, where she heard the water running. While he was behind the door, her curiosity stretched tighter, and she poked her head in.

The cabin was almost all cedar and navy blue, with clothes strewn across the soft surfaces, and tools, wires, plastic bags, and some kind of varnish cans taking up most of the hard surface space. A low cabinet in the back of the galley was opened, revealing some kind of motor, with three kinds of wrenches sitting in front of it. Lining the main galley walkway were boxes filled with canned green beans, canned peaches, and other pantry items. Torn plaid curtains covered a couple of the windows, while others, which seemed to have the curtain rod missing, were blackened with paper taped around the edges with loose duct tape. A depressing darkness clouded the whole space except for where Lia was letting the light in.

When the water turned off, the door banged open and she leaped back. He snatched a pair of aviator sunglasses off a tabletop and barreled past her, his damp hair brushing his cheekbones as he threw her a withering glance.

Out on the deck, he found his shoes under one of the side benches. He shoved the glasses on and stalked off the boat without looking back, trudging up the dock, his shirttails flapping in the morning wind.

Lia darted after him. What had started out as surprise and maybe a little pity began to simmer into a low anger as she scrambled to climb out of the sailboat and keep up with him, her ankle throbbing now. Granted, he was doing her a favor. But he'd *agreed*, right? Man, Drew was right. This guy was a wild card. But her desperation—along with his murderous scowl and punishing pace—kept her from saying anything.

He buttoned his shirt as they walked. Or practically ran— he had long legs, and she needed to take a few steps for every one of his. She couldn't help sliding her eyes to that smooth, tan, muscled chest that was disappearing before her as she hobbled along, but she riveted them away while berating herself. This was Drew's crazy, hungover, scruffy brother, not some cover model.

Except *wow*. Just wow.

She glanced sideways one more time, but he was all buttoned up now, tucking the shirt in as they trudged forward. He refused to look at her. He was still unshaven, sporting a five-o'clock shadow that was edging closer, perhaps, to eight o'clock. His hair had received a finger combing, the ends damp near his collar, but jagged slices fell forward around his face. He was going to be a PR nightmare. But she didn't care at this point. She'd just hide him and his rogue-pirate look up in the captain's bridge and hope Kyle Stevens didn't notice him.

"Will you need a little time to look around?" she finally spoke, once they were on the other side of the marina and she was nearly out of breath.

He grunted some kind of response, then slowed as Drew's boat came into view. From here, the boat looked beautiful. It was backed in, the scrolled name *"The Duke"* clearly visible, every curvaceous edge sparkling as the early morning sunshine broke through. There were already about forty tourists in line in front of her sign and chain. There were two young couples, standing with their arms around each other's college sweatshirts; three families, with about six kids among them, all scampering along the dock and playing with the chains; two mothers with umbrella strollers; and a separate group of five teenagers who leaned against the dock wall and pointed down to the rocks below, probably spotting crabs. Behind them squirmed a slew of first-graders—about fifteen of them—a field trip from L.A. that Lia had booked last week. She scanned the crowd but didn't see Kyle Stevens yet.

Evan swung his neck toward her. "*Kids*?" he demanded. He said it as if she'd booked a boatload of cockroaches.

"Well, one class." She frowned back. "Do you not like kids?"

He didn't answer, but forced himself forward, his feet dragging across the wood planks.

"Let's get you on board so you can learn your way around," she said in the most cheerful voice she could muster. He'd probably love the boat once aboard, and the captain's bridge was so elevated—he'd be alone on the roof of the boat—so all the kids and tourists and whatever other people he hated would be long forgotten.

She hustled the rest of the way down the dock ahead of him and undid the chain, striking up a conversation with the first few people in line so maybe they wouldn't notice him slipping in behind her. In front was a pretty young mother with soft brown curls framing her face; she drew a boy to her side who looked about five. She said she was the mom-blogger Lia had booked several weeks ago named Avery.

"Oh, nice to meet you, Avery," Lia said, pumping her hand.

"Is there a best place to sit?"

"You'll be comfortable anywhere," Lia assured her with a smile.

Lia could feel Evan stalling behind her, and she watched Avery's eyes dart over her shoulder. Lia bit her lip. She hoped this mom of such a small child wouldn't get too nervous about a hungover, long-haired, bearded dude as her captain. *Please don't mention this part in your blog*, Lia willed with her eyes. Evan hesitated, glancing between the woman and her child, then finally—thankfully—ducked behind Lia and hopped onto the stern.

"Is everyone excited?" Lia asked the crowd.

They responded with the enthusiasm of a football stadium,

especially the little kids. Normally, Drew was great at this part. She scrambled to remember how he did all this.

"We're just going to get a few more things set up for you, then I'll come back and we'll get everyone boarded," she said in her tour-guide voice. "Kids, start thinking now about how many whales there are in this part of the ocean, and I'll tell you the answer when you get on board."

Lia undid the chain and limped onto the stern.

Evan was in the front of the boat, frowning next to the new blue lattice nets.

"Where's your crew?" he asked in his deep rasp.

A wave of embarrassment washed over Lia for some reason—as if she'd lost the crew herself. "I don't think they're coming."

"No one?"

She shook her head.

"How many are there usually?"

"Four. Drew is captain and tour guide, Cora is the cook, Douglas is the deckhand, and Drew has a part-time steward named Stewey."

"His steward is named Stewey?"

"Not his real name."

Evan ran his hand down his face. "And no one's coming?"

Lia bit her lip. "No."

"Who's giving the narrative?"

"I probably could."

"Do you know anything about marine life?"

". . . if you could write things down for me."

He stared at her, hands hanging off his hips. He glanced around the deck, perhaps trying to imagine how they were going to pull this off, and looked as if he were going to jump overboard. But finally, slowly, he turned to inspect the life vests under the bench seats.

"What's wrong with your ankle?" he growled from behind a bench door.

"I think . . . I just twisted it a bit."

"Get some ice on that. Where are the fire extinguishers?"

Lia pointed, and Evan moved to the box, glancing inside. "Does Drew keep any firearms on board?" He was moving back toward the galley. He seemed to have gone into Coast Guard mode.

"Um . . . no, not that I know of."

Evan gave a curt nod. "How many passengers will there be?"

"Forty-five."

"We should get him another fire extinguisher, then. Does he have a first-aid kit in there?"

He waited for her to get the cabin door open, then followed her inside, his head barely clearing the ceiling, while she looked for the first-aid kit. He leaned against the countertops while she checked the top row. It took her a few tries, but she finally found the kit in a top cabinet. She pointed it out for Evan's mental checklist, but he motioned for it with his fingers. Taking it from her, he rifled through, snagged four Advil packets, then withdrew a long white plastic thing.

"Emergency ice." He held it out for her. "Put it on your ankle. And here." He rummaged for another Advil packet and shoved it at her. He snapped the box closed and tossed it back into the cabinet. "Do you need help with the covers?" He inclined his head toward the bright blue ones Douglas had put across the bench seats.

"Yes, thank you."

He held out his palm for the keys.

As Evan lurched away with the ignition key, Lia stared after him. There was so much she wanted to know—why he slept with a gun, why he and Drew were estranged, what was going on with all the simmering anger, why his Coast Guard career ended—but she wouldn't ask. She didn't really need to know. She couldn't keep him after this. Drew wouldn't like it. And he looked like too much of a wild card to keep around.

She glanced back out for Kyle Stevens, but still no sign. Quickly, she ducked back into the galley and set things up the way she remembered Drew kept them, pushing all thoughts of Evan out of her mind. They had five minutes before boarding.

She set out their new pamphlets in an acrylic holder; straightened the new poster Drew kept of various dolphins for kids to see the difference in their sizes; propped up a framed picture he kept of all the different whales; and found his new models of whale teeth, which she spread across the countertop. She tried to remember where Drew usually placed the little stuffed whale he called Willy and finally settled on one of the blue-cushioned benches out on the rear deck.

When she went out onto the deck, Coraline was waddling up the stern with two large shopping bags in her arms.

"Cora! I'm so relieved to see you!" Lia unburdened her of one of the bags.

"Sorry I'm late, sunshine. Didn't think we'd be heading out this week."

"I know. Douglas hasn't shown."

"I don't think he's coming, sweetie, but he called to make sure I'd be here for you. He said you found a captain?" Her eyes went up to the bridge. "Drew's brother?" she whispered.

Lia ushered her into the cabin. "Yes. He seems a little cranky today, but I hear he's good." They plopped both bags onto the countertop.

"Maybe he needs coffee," Cora said.

"That would be *great*."

Cora patted Lia and waddled her way behind the galley counter. "I'll get right on that."

Lia blew out a relieved breath. At least one person showed. She checked her texts again and thought maybe she could get Stewey for at least the second tour. Once she sent another quick message, she headed up to the bridge. "Are you ready?"

"Yep." Evan was at the helm, adjusting some dials and fiddling with the radio.

"Our cook showed up," she offered hopefully.

He glowered but didn't look her way. "Could use a deckhand more."

Yes, I get it, Mr. Negative. But she dismissed his scowl and looked him over. He looked really ragged. The hangover and anger and deadness in his eyes made him look like he might actually end up overboard before the end of the day. "Are you sure you're going to be okay?"

"I'm ready." He looked out toward the horizon with a finality that indicated that's as far as that conversation was going to go.

Lia turned and descended to the main deck. It wasn't worth it to press him—to ask him how hung over he was, why he didn't take her request seriously, or whether he'd drained those entire two bottles of scotch alone in one night. They would just get through this day, then she would reevaluate. Maybe she would insist that Drew rethink the want-ad idea. For now, though, she had clients to impress.

"Hello, everyone!" she called in her most lighthearted voice.

Evan ran his hand down his face, cursed Glenlivet for at least the hundredth time, and turned his head slowly so his eyeballs would stop throbbing. He scanned the dock for Tommy. Clearly, Tommy was a no-show. Bastard.

Evan had called Tommy late last night, an hour after Lia had skipped away and a half hour after he knew he absolutely could not face her and her painful cheerfulness again. She was like some kind of Cinderella cartoon, with singing cartoon birds floating around her yellow hair. He didn't want to deal with her, didn't want to deal with Drew's boat, didn't want to see the name "*The Duke*," and certainly didn't want to deal with a bunch of strangers, kids, or even sunlight. He just wanted to be left alone.

But he said he'd help.

So his midnight call to Tommy Two-Time, after three seductive glasses of scotch, was, admittedly, a little desperate. Tommy might not be the most reliable guy in the world, and had spent more than a few nights in jail around these parts— which might have been where his nickname came from, although Evan wasn't sure—but he could sail with his eyes closed and knew how to find whales. And Drew knew him as well as Evan did—they'd all sailed together around here when they were kids. So that was a plus. Evan was surprised to get ahold of him at all—he wasn't even sure Tommy was still around—but, after a strange exchange of information that might have been tinged with too much scotch, Tommy had agreed to navigate Drew's boat for a fee, which Evan agreed to pay, up front, through the entire week. He'd do that much for Drew.

But when the knock reverberated on his cabin door this morning, and Cinderella stood there looking wide-eyed and expectant, Evan knew Tommy was back to his unreliable ways.

Bastard.

So now he had a full day of stinging sunlight, throbbing brain, nausea, Cinderella, a boatload of kids, and a passenger who looked way too much like Renece to deal with.

He rubbed his face again and wondered if he could get through this day. And if he could stop his eyeballs from throbbing. But—as he'd always told his crew—anyone can do anything for a day.

". . . type of killer whale?" he heard from behind him.

He opened one eye at a time, peering back over his shoulder. There were no sunglasses on earth dark enough for him right now. "Wha?" he managed to croak out. His tongue felt like it had fur on it.

"Is there only one type of killer whale?"

His questioner was about four feet tall, the stripes on his shirt providing an assault to all of Evan's senses. Once Evan was able to open both eyes, and come to some semblance of focus, he realized it was *the kid*. The one with the Renece look-alike.

"What do you mean?" He couldn't handle this right now. He could barely keep his head screwed on.

"Are there lots of killer whales or only the black-and-white ones?"

Evan pressed on his temple so his brains wouldn't spill out and glanced behind him in hopes that someone would save him. "Actually, the real name for that whale is an orca, and it's not really a whale but a dolphin—the biggest of the dolphin family."

"But does it kill people? Will it kill us if we see him today?" The boy plucked at his shirt.

"No, no, kid." A sharp pain right behind his eyelids had Evan gripping at the bridge of his nose. "No, he's—"

"*Conner!* What are you doing up here?"

The soft voice had Evan's head snapping up, and the vision had him on his feet in half a second. But the movements were all too fast, and he swayed embarrassingly and gripped the wheel. *Renece. Damn, she looked so much like her. . . .*

"Hi, I'm sorry. I'm Avery." The woman thrust out her hand.

Evan didn't know what she was apologizing for, but he cut himself some slack for slow brainwaves this morning and gave her hand a swift shake before pulling back into himself. She was beautiful, the way Renece had been, but the fact that she reminded him of a ghost left him feeling more repelled than attracted. He took another step away and thought he might hurl.

"Captain *Betancourt*." He heard another woman's voice from behind him.

He couldn't take this. His head honestly felt like it was going to come off and roll down the stern. He forced his eyeballs to shift in the other direction. It was Cinderella.

"I see you've met our captain," she said merrily to the Renece look-alike.

Cinderella had two steaming Styrofoam cups in her hand and a water bottle tucked under her arm, and unloaded all of them onto the captain's table before looping her arm around Renece Look-alike and steering her away. "He's going to get us off to sea in just a couple of minutes, so I'm going to ask everyone to take a seat." Cinderella threw a megawatt smile to the little boy. "I have a special place for *you* to sit. Right next to Willy the Whale! Would you like that?" The boy bobbed his head maniacally, and Cinderella guided them both back down to the main deck.

Evan let out a breath he hadn't realized he'd been holding and eyed the bottled water. Without another thought, he yanked off the cap and took four long gulps before tearing into the Advil packets.

"Yes, that was for you," Cinderella said, returning to the bridge and eyeing the nearly empty bottle. "Want another?"

"That'd be great."

"The coffee's for you, too." She scooted the Styrofoam cup closer. "Cora makes amazing coffee—you might rethink that deckhand remark."

As irritating as she'd been with her excruciating cheerfulness earlier, she now seemed like some sort of angel. One who could flit around with bottled water and strong brew.

"Thanks," he said, keeping his voice low enough to protect him from reverberation in his head.

She reached for her own cup. "As soon as we get out to sea, can you jot some notes about what we're seeing?"

He squinted in her direction. Damn. He'd forgotten about that part. This day was just getting better and better. "Can we keep it to a minimum?"

"What, the narration?"

"The noise. The narration. The microphone. The kids. And our"—he swung his finger back and forth between them—"interaction." He slid another glance at her. He was being an ass. But he needed to keep her glib conversation and perky attitude from causing his head to roll into the sea.

"Sure," she said, her voice faraway. Finally, she turned and left.

He sighed into the empty space she created. He was a jerk. He shouldn't have accepted this request. He wasn't fit to inter-act with normal human beings anymore, even if it meant pos-sible forgiveness from his brother.

He pushed his hair out of his eyes and concentrated on the cat's controls.

He would just get through this one day. Then he'd call Tommy Two-Time again and double his price.

If he survived today, that was.

CHAPTER

Four

Lia stood at the boat entrance and welcomed the last of the passengers aboard with her friendliest smile. They milled about in clusters in their blue jeans and tennis shoes, some sitting on the bright blue cushions along the back of the cat, some jogging toward the front where the blue lattice nets were, their cameras bobbing against their sweatshirt-clad stomachs. A family of seagulls squawked overhead and landed at the highest point on the catamaran, chests puffed, as if waiting for their ride, too. The sun broke through the gray sky and cast spotlight rays along the deck.

Lia took the last ticket and craned her neck toward the wood-shingled shops at the Sandy Cove marina to see if she could see any limos that might belong to Kyle Stevens. A limo would certainly stand out in Sandy Cove.

But he hadn't shown. They were two minutes late now, and she didn't know if she should wait. When a young multimillionaire booked a pre-charter check for himself and two guests, were you supposed to give him special treatment? She bit her lip. *When he was the Vampiress's favorite client, and the son of her dream client, you did. . . .*

She let the passengers find their places while she fumbled

with the main-deck microphone. There was another one up in the bridge, but she didn't want to use the one next to Mr. Grumpy. While she waited, she rummaged through the drawers in the galley until she found what she was looking for: one of Drew's whale books. As she flipped through, she scraped her mind to remember anything Drew had told her about whales, or how he usually started his presentation. She'd been on this ride with him several times, sometimes on business so she could give him marketing tips, and other times on private outings with their friends because Drew loved it so much.

Baleen. The word jumped off the page. He always explained that to them, and how whales were divided into baleen and something else. . . .

"Welcome, everyone!" she began into the microphone. "We hope you enjoy your visit today on the *Duke*. My name is Lia, and I'll be narrating for you today. We have Captain Evan Betancourt navigating our ship, and Coraline Jones offering coffee, soft drinks, popcorn, and other sundries in the galley. . . ."

"And chocolate-walnut cookies!" Coraline yelled.

Lia had to bend down from her perch outside the galley door to peer inside toward Cora's voice. "What?"

"I brought homemade chocolate-walnut cookies!" Cora said in a stage whisper. "One free per passenger."

". . . And homemade chocolate-walnut cookies," Lia said into the microphone. "One free per passenger."

Giddy claps erupted from the first-graders.

The motor gave a funny rev right then, like an impatient boyfriend gunning his V-8 in the parking lot, and Lia wondered if that was Evan's weird way of communicating. She glanced up the steps. She didn't want to extend their interaction any more than she had to—he'd made his request pretty clear—but she clicked off the microphone and jogged up to see if everything was okay. On the second step, though, she winced and grabbed her ankle. This thing was going to swell like crazy once she got off it. She remembered the Advil packet and emergency ice sitting on the galley counter and gave two small points to Captain Betancourt.

Up at the helm, Evan had found a pair of Drew's binoculars and was adjusting them with another scowl.

"Are you signaling me?" she asked, trying to throw enough indignation into her voice to let him know she didn't like to be summoned with engine revs.

"We ready?" he drawled.

The view from up here was pretty spectacular—she never came up here with Drew. The entire north end of the marina was visible, a thicket of white masts sticking up like matchsticks against the jewel-tone blue of the ocean. On the other side, palm trees and Cape Cod–styled buildings surrounded a brick-lined patio to make up the small Sandy Cove marina: two gift shops, a tackle shop, a high-end clothing shop, a sandwich-and-coffee shop, and the ticket office. Lia took a split second to take it all in, along with a deep breath of salt air. Navigating from up this high must be pretty life affirming.

"We're missing a few people," she said, taking one last sweep of the shingled shops and hyndrangea-lined parking lot. "But it *is* past ten."

"Do you know how to cast off the lines?"

"Oh . . . not exactly." She glanced down at the cleats on the dock. "I can probably manage if you show me. How many are there?" From up here, she could see they crossed one another like a game of cat's cradle.

"Four." Evan ducked under the canopy and lumbered down the stairs and through the crowd of tourists.

So much for keeping him hidden from the guests.

Lia followed, leaping off the boat where he did, watching him unravel the first line from the cleat. His movements were natural and forceful, despite the hangover—like some kind of machine on autopilot. "Get that one down there."

They made their way down the dock, untying all four lines, tossing them onto the boat, then Evan stepped lithely on board, looping the lines around his arm and stowing them with quick, deft movements. Lia tried to mimic him, peering down the deck to see how he wrapped them around his muscled arms, but he finally strode in her direction and took the rope from her. "Go talk," he murmured.

She went back to the microphone and flipped through Drew's book to the section on baleen. "So I asked all of you if you knew how many types of whales were in this part of the ocean today. Does anyone know the answer?"

The little kids from the field trip all shot their hands into the air, waving wildly, and Lia fielded answers, watching out of the corner of her eye for Kyle Stevens. Her gaze kept sliding, though, toward Evan, as he wrapped rope through his biceps and avoided eye contact with any of the passengers. And then her line of vision incorporated Avery, who had Evan securely in her sights. Avery's lips parted as she watched Evan move down the port side. Fear didn't seem to be part of her perusal.

Lia forced her attention back to the book.

"Whales are divided between baleen," she announced, scanning the copy, "which means with sievelike teeth made of keratin, like our fingernails; and toothed whales, which are whales with real teeth."

Evan glanced back at her, and she wondered for a second if she were getting the info right. His expression—especially behind the sunglasses—was inscrutable.

"We'll be seeing mostly gray whales today, and possibly some blue, which are both baleen."

At one point, Cora came out and finished stowing the last line. Evan gave Cora a deep nod of thanks in about the friendliest gesture Lia had seen from him so far, then he trudged up to the helm. Avery twisted in her seat to watch him from behind.

Huh.

So Avery might be attracted to Evan. This was good, right? At least Lia wouldn't have to worry about a blog write-up going out to thousands of readers a month discussing the scary captain aboard the *Duke*.

Lia took another look at Evan. Maybe the pirate thing was some women's cup of tea.

As the boat began motoring away, making a slow, wide turn to point them out of the harbor, Lia took a deep breath and thumbed a few pages forward.

But then she glanced up and spotted Kyle Stevens jogging his way down the dock.

"Captain Betancourt! Captain Betancourt!"

Evan glanced over his shoulder to see Cinderella hobbling up the bridge stairs, but he riveted his concentration back to the turn. He had to give his little brother a lot of credit if he did this every day. Sandy Cove's harbor was tricky, seemingly designed more for folks who wanted to hide behind its cliffs than for those looking for an open welcome mat.

"Captain Betancourt!"

He rolled his eyes. He wished she'd stop calling him that.

"Whaddaya need?" He eyed the distance to the jetty and calculated how wide he could make the turn. The sun glared off the water.

"We have to go back!" she said when she got to the top of the steps.

He frowned. This chick was crazy. "We're halfway to the jetty," he said calmly.

"There's a passenger we left on the dock." She stopped short and took a deep breath, her hands fluttering over the controls as if looking for a "back" button. "We have to get him. He's here with four others."

"Seems he's here late."

"But he's important. We have to go back."

"He should be here on time."

The glance she threw made it clear he was no one to talk. But he chose to ignore that and forced the throttle instead.

"I'm serious!" She gripped his wrist.

When he glared at her hand, she yanked it away. She needed to stop doing that. She was clearly one of those touchy-feely types. But he wasn't. And she needed to knock it off.

She stepped back, as if to give him some personal space, but she definitely wasn't backing down.

"We *have* to go back." Her fingers spread as she stared at the console. He could tell she was dying to control this—the vessel, the situation, him, *something*.

"We'd have to make the turn all the way back in, ready the fenders, loop the lines," he said. "We'll be twenty minutes off schedule."

"It's worth it."

"To you?"

"To Drew."

He ground his back teeth. Of course. She knew how to get to him already.

"And to me," she added reluctantly, although she said it as if she knew it wouldn't make any difference to him.

Her gaze drifted over his shoulder at this mysterious Big Deal Passenger, waving from the dock.

He threw the throttle again and maneuvered the tricky turn back. As he calculated the distance, he wondered again how Drew knew this chick. She had crazy written all over her. Her cheerleader exuberance wasn't something Drew would normally be attracted to, so dating was off the table. Plus she'd said as much. And Evan had been damned sure to check. The last thing he needed was to get tangled in one of Drew's relationships again.

"You'll need to loop the stern line," he grumbled. "Loosely. I'll take the bow."

She headed down while he concentrated on pulling back in. He did a stellar job, if he did say so himself. Especially with a hangover. The glasses helped keep the brightness down, from Drew's squeaky-clean white deck, to the winter sun glaring off the water, to Cinderella's tourism smile.

When the boat was snuggled tight, he headed down the steps and checked to see who garnered this type of attention. Must be some rich fat cat. Probably in a suit and tie and shiny shoes.

But all he saw was a youngish-looking dude in cargos and a T-shirt, with an Ivy League haircut and a watch that probably cost more than Evan's sailboat. Cinderella was fawning all over him, so this must be the guy. Two beefy men stood behind him in dark shades—they could only be bodyguards. As Evan watched Cinderella dropping her head to the side in the universal sign for *I find you attractive*, he wondered what this asshole's story was.

"I'll get them," he mumbled, stepping in front of her. They could do this without retying the whole vessel. He secured the back end, enough to let them step aboard, and reached out to help them by the elbow. The bodyguards, as expected, didn't want to be helped. Mr. Big Deal Passenger allowed Evan to help him, though, which made Evan lose his last four millidrops of respect.

"Mr. Stevens!" Cinderella beamed. "It's so great to have you aboard."

"Aw, call me Kyle, Lia." He cuffed her shoulder.

Evan rolled his eyes.

"Thanks for stopping for me," he added.

"No problem," Cinderella said. "Drew's not here today, but this is his *brother*, Evan Betancourt!" She said it like being brothers was the most stunning coincidence in the universe.

Stevens turned, as if surprised that Evan was still there, and looked him up and down. "Nice to meet you." He shoved his hand forward, and Evan finally shook it.

"So where's Drew?"

Cinderella jumped in: "He was in a terrible motorcycle accident."

That caught Stevens's attention. "Motorcycle?" He said it with the kind of wonder that Evan associated with rich, entitled young men who were entitled to everything but risk.

"Yes, but he's on the mend."

"And you're running the business in his absence?" Stevens gave Cinderella a quick once-over that seemed to hold some dubiousness. For some reason, her breasts and hips seemed to be an important part of his perusal.

Evan stepped into Stevens's line of vision. "We've got to get going," he said, taking the line from her. This Stevens character was rubbing him the wrong way.

"I am." Cinderella moved around Evan. "We don't expect any kind of bump in the road for the business. Come aboard." She motioned with her hand, the model of efficiency. "Be sure to check out the underwater whale-viewing pods on the lower level. Your charter guests will love them."

Stevens moved to one of the back benches with his body-guards, who looked huge and uncomfortable in dark jackets. They didn't exactly blend in. Cinderella got back on the microphone.

"We see several types of whales year-round, but at this time of year we see an abundance of gray whales . . ." she continued.

Evan jogged back up to the bridge and repeated his exit, watching the turn again and listening to Cinderella discuss everything she knew about gray whales. She was doing a pretty good job, he had to admit. She had a nice voice—not overly exuberant like her personality, but strangely calm once she was on the microphone.

". . . The gray whales migrate from Alaska to Baja,

Mexico, between December and early March, where they stay in the warmer waters, have their calves, then migrate back up from February to April or May, right along this coast. . . ."

They were a half hour late, but he could finally see some open sea. Stevens and his boys had moved well away from Cinderella, which felt like a strange relief. He didn't know why that Stevens character was so important, and he certainly didn't want to have a full conversation about it with Cinderella, but something wasn't right about that guy.

Lia gave her overview of the gray whales' migration, glancing around the boat to see where Kyle Stevens landed, and took a nervous sip of water between her narration.

She hoped he liked the trip. And hoped he didn't have a lot of requests or changes for his charter next week. And hoped Evan could be a charitable-enough captain.

Clearly, Evan wasn't going to help much. While Drew was friendly and personable, Evan all but had a "closed" sign hanging from his forehead. Whatever. She reiterated her plan in her head to keep Evan away from all passengers, especially Kyle Stevens. This trial-run tour had to go off without a hitch.

". . . So take a look around the boat, be sure to take a peek at our viewing pods right down the stairs, check out some of our educational materials, and we're going to go find some *whales*!" she said into the microphone with a positivity she didn't feel.

The catamaran picked up speed right on cue. Drew did this, too—sped out to sea once they cleared the jetty. He knew they might have to look around for a while to see any whales, and they only had a couple of hours, so he always flew over the waves in the first part of the tour. Despite her skepticism about Evan—or maybe because of it—the similar style gave her hope.

Lia pulled a few strands of hair out of her lip gloss and turned into the wind. The couple in the matching college sweatshirts leaned against the rail, taking pictures of the Sandy Cove coastline. The fifteen first-graders were corralled along the starboard side, all holding hands in twos and threes, eyes barely clearing the rail.

Some of the moms introduced themselves to one another, wrapping themselves in their jackets against the wind, and Avery was—

Lia glanced around. Where was Avery?

Her gaze flew up to the bridge, where, sure enough, Avery's sundress rippled in the wind.

Man, she sure hoped Avery wasn't married. That was some dogged determination.

But she really wanted to keep Evan from the passengers.

She trudged back up the steps, wincing at every left step, and threw her most polite smile toward Avery as soon as her head crested the rail, but Avery wasn't paying attention. At least, she wasn't paying attention to Lia. Or her son, who was standing at the edge of the bridge. She was paying attention to Evan.

Evan was standing at the helm, the wind blowing his hair back, his mirrored glasses directed straight ahead, as if he didn't know Avery was standing next to him. But of course he did: She was at his shoulder, talking nonstop. Words like "divorce," "two years," and "bastard" floated back toward Lia.

"Hey!" Lia greeted.

Evan looked back over his shoulder with such a sense of relief Lia actually felt sorry for him.

But his attention went right past her.

"Hey!" He shot forward, grabbing Avery's little boy and yanking him back from the edge of the steps.

Evan's deep voice, the sudden lunge, and the unwanted attention must have met in a terrible swirl for the little boy, and he burst into tears.

"I'm sorry," Evan said, dropping the boy's arm. "I just didn't want . . ." He turned his ire on Lia. "Didn't we discuss this?"

Lia didn't think it was fair for Evan to turn on her, but he was right. A child didn't belong up here. At least not with two adults who were so inattentive.

"Avery." Lia turned to her calmly. "We like to keep children away from the captain's bridge, and we prefer that adults stay on the lower decks, too." She guided Avery back to the stairs as she talked. "Do you have questions, though? You must have a ton of questions to make your posts as accurate as they are. I can answer almost anything for you. And what I can't answer, we'll throw back to Captain Betancourt after the tour is over." She flashed her best smile back at Evan, as if they were the closest of friends. Evan just stared at her, looking incredulous. "Maybe we can sit down in the galley. Did you get your cookie from Cora yet? Conner, did you get your cookie?"

In no time, Avery and Conner were smiling at her, Avery's pride intact, as they made their way down the steep stairs and back toward the galley.

As soon as she got them settled with their free cookies, and Cora started telling them tales of sailing the Pacific, Lia sensed another passenger heading toward the bridge steps. Dang, she really needed to put that chain up.

"We're going to let our captain concentrate on getting us out to sea," she said, steering the two passengers in "*Go Wisconsin!*" sweatshirts away. "If you have questions for him, pass them along to me, and I'll be sure to ask." Marketing smile. Gentle touch to the elbow. Free cookie. Problem Two diverted.

Lia hustled back to get the chain rigged up across the bridge stairs. Just as she secured it, she heard a strange clicking over the speakers. Then the same series of clicks, repeated.

She sighed, undid her chain, and climbed back up. Her ankle was killing her.

"Are you *signaling* me?"

"On the radio, they said there were some grays just off Table Rock." Evan pushed his hair back off his face and peered through the binoculars. "I'm going to head just to the west of them. We should be able to see them starboard, against the coastline."

Unsure what to do with so many words from him, especially in a series that didn't involve grunts or scowls, Lia staggered toward the console. "What should I tell everyone? Stand at two or three o'clock?"

"Let me get there first."

He began heading in that direction, then glanced her way and frowned.

"Do you not want me to stand here?" she asked, unable to keep the aggravation out of her voice.

"You're fine."

As simple and uninviting as the words were, they felt like some kind of a welcome mat coming from him. Lia let her shoulders relax.

"You should get off that foot," Evan said.

"Too much to do."

"Where's the ice I gave you?"

"Downstairs. I'll use it when we're done."

He shot her another look of annoyance. "Where downstairs?"

"On the counter."

He reached just past her knee. "What's your cook's name again?"

"Cora. And she's not just a cook; she happens to be a very fine friend of—"

"Cora," Evan said into the microphone. "This is Captain Betancourt. Would you bring up the white tube of ice that's on the counter, please?" He clicked the microphone off and put it back in place.

Lia blew out an aggravated breath. She was used to being the bossy one. She and Evan might very well throw each other off the boat if they spent too much time together. Good thing she was getting rid of him. As soon as her mind formed the thought, her memory flashed to him that morning, standing there with the gun in his hand, looking like some kind of derelict. And then . . . to his beautiful bare chest, his muscled shoulders . . . She pushed her hair behind her ear and shoved both images out of her mind.

"Here ya go, Captain," said Cora, just cresting the steps.

"Thanks, Cora. Give that to her, would you?" He motioned with his head.

"Did you hurt yourself, Lia?" Cora asked.

"I'll be fine." Lia snatched the emergency ice away, embarrassed. She didn't like people fussing over her. "Thank you."

Coraline headed back down the steps while Lia calculated her getaway. She just needed a few notes about the whales—what kind they were encountering, which side of the boat they'd be on for sure—then she could use the microphone downstairs. "Are we almost there?"

Evan glanced at the navigation screen. "Five more minutes. Have a seat."

"Are they grays?"

"Won't know for sure 'til I get there."

White water formed a froth beneath the cat as they skittered over the waves. If she sat down and took her weight off her ankle now, it was going to throb and swell like crazy. It seemed best to stay on it until the tour was over, then she could relax. She shifted to make it more comfortable.

Evan did a double-take over his shoulder. "You don't take orders very well, do you?"

"Not my strong suit."

With one quick shake of his head, he yanked the emergency ice stick out of her hand, snapped it in two, then handed it back. It was turning ice-cold immediately.

"That's not going to last long, and it's the only one we have, so sit down and put that on your ankle."

His constant string of orders was getting on her nerves. But, with a huff, she sat on the captain's bench and wrapped the tube around her ankle as best she could.

"You can give the narration from up here," he said.

"I thought you wanted this area cleared."

"I did. But you can stay. You're like bug repellant."

Lia blinked and finally closed her mouth.

The ice did feel good against her ankle. And it did feel good to get off it for a second. Frustrated that he was right about everything, she strove to think of other reasons she needed to go downstairs: "Kyle Stevens wants a tour of the boat," she remembered aloud.

"Kyle Stevens can wait."

The boat made a slight arc farther out into the ocean, still skating over the waves. Lia turned her head into the wind and pushed her hair over her shoulder, giving up on fighting and just enjoying the momentary feeling of being "off."

Up here, with Evan, she had no one to impress. Obviously, she wasn't impressing *him*—she'd given up a long time ago thinking that would ever happen, even though she generally liked people to like her—but, she had to admit, it was kind of refreshing. He clearly didn't want to talk. She loved to talk, and probably talked too much even for her friends and family, but it was kind of nice to be silent for a while. He made it feel oddly comfortable.

"And would you look at that?" He lifted the binoculars, breaking his own silence. Though his voice had sounded angry and curt all day long, right now it sounded strangely reverent.

His hand brushed her knee again and loosened the microphone, handing it to her. "Get ready, Cinderella. We're ready to roll."

CHAPTER

Five

"Four," he said, heading northwest in a slow arc. "At one o'clock."

Lia clicked on the microphone, wondering why he just called her Cinderella, but replacing the question quickly in her mind with whale factoids.

"If you'll all look at about the one o'clock point from the boat, you'll see we've come across four whales. . . ." she announced.

Evan gave a swift nod. "Grays."

". . . They're all gray whales, part of the migration from Baja to Alaska. . . ."

"They sometimes travel in pods of two or three like this," he said, fast and low.

". . . Grays sometimes travel in small pods . . ."

"I'm guessing two mothers and two calves."

". . . and it looks like we've got two mamas and two calves, making their way back up the coast."

He cut the motor and coasted the cat into a better position. In the quietude of the ocean, Evan fed Lia lines in his deep, low monotone. He mumbled information regarding the usual length of the female, the fact she was usually larger than the male, notes about mating, and how the females were identified each year by their length and their calf companions as they returned up the coast. He told how to look for the whales by looking for a slick in the water, then waiting about a minute for the whale's back to emerge, then the flukes, flipping over before the whale dove back down.

"The flukes?"

"The two sides of the whale's tail—left fluke and right fluke."

She repeated that into the microphone. She didn't recall Drew ever telling her that. Maybe he didn't know she liked to learn these things.

"We'll stay twenty minutes," Evan concluded. "Grays will come up four or five times in that span of time."

Lia clicked off the microphone. After seeing him look so sullen all morning, it was nice to hear his voice take on a tranquil rhythm, see him lean into a feeling that looked like peace. She studied him as he maneuvered the boat's position. The brick wall he'd been building seemed to be lowered all of a sudden, replaced by something that seemed more like an opaque sheet, flapping in the wind and letting her glimpse behind.

"Why did you call me Cinderella just now?"

He didn't turn, or even budge an inch—just kept staring through the binoculars. "Did I?"

"Yes."

"They're going to come up soon." He put the binoculars down and revved the boat forward.

She wasn't going to give up that easily. The sheet was still pulled back, just a little, and her instincts—some kind of misguided, fact-finding, must-have-the-answers instincts—read it as opportunity.

"So what was with the gun this morning?" As soon as the question was out there, flapping in the wind like the sheet, she felt like biting her lip off. What was the matter with her? Why couldn't she just leave him alone? She didn't need to know this. She had no right, or reason, to be interested in him.

If the question insulted or surprised him, he didn't show it. His eyes remained on the spot from which he expected the whales to emerge, and he leaned farther into his turn, pulling back on the wheel. "We don't have to talk, you know," he murmured.

"I know. . . . Just trying to make conversation."

"No need."

She acquiesced and turned back toward the ocean, resting her cheek on her knee. She was an idiot. He was going to be as closed down as Drew said, and this was none of her business. But some crazy thing made her see his secrets as a challenge, an opportunity to change something dark into something light, and she couldn't seem to stop her mouth. "So you're not much of a talker, huh? Drew mentioned that."

Silence followed as the boat bobbed on the ocean.

The passengers made their way around the boat to the one o'clock position to watch for the slick.

"Tell them one more minute," he said quietly, staring through the binoculars.

She repeated the advice into the microphone, trying to bring her voice down to the reverent decibel Evan was using.

The quietude of the ocean pressed in around them as they waited, the only sound the gentle lapping of the waves.

"What else did Drew tell you?" he suddenly asked.

The question sent her head whipping toward him in surprise, but she did her best to remain calm. He was like a wild animal—no sudden movements or he'd leap. "He said he hadn't seen you in a long time."

She tried to remember the rest of the conversation and how much to say. "He said you'd been sailing the world . . . that you docked wherever the winds took you. That you were . . ." She shrugged, hesitating over the next part. But she liked to be honest. "That you were a little messed up."

The corner of Evan's mouth twisted into a wry smile, and he stared at the horizon. "About sums it up."

"What did he mean by 'messed up'?"

Evan didn't look like he planned to answer that, but instead steered the boat farther north and tilted his chin toward the ocean. "Watch," he said, indicating the slick that had just emerged on the ocean's surface, a large oval of concentric circles. "Tell them ten o'clock."

Lia instructed the passengers, then watched Evan staring in that direction.

"And . . . *now*," he said.

Two water spouts rose into the air on Evan's cue like fountains, right in front of them, followed by two gargantuan gray whales' mottled backs cresting—first both mamas', then their babies'. And then—in a slow, fluid movement—the enormous flukes popped into the air iconically then dove back down.

Lia's lips parted as she rose, her ice pack sliding to the deck. The sight of these giant mammals never ceased to amaze her, as many times as she'd seen them with Drew. But, as soon as she rose, the pain on her ankle forced her back down with a wince, and she yanked the ice tube back on, keeping her gaze firmly on the whales.

Cameras clicked along the deck below. The first-graders huddled together and pointed and squealed each time the flukes flipped. One passenger set up an underwater sports camera and leaned forward to get the camera into the water. Avery ushered her son to the side and pointed things out to him, taking notes in a narrow notepad she carried. Even Kyle Stevens looked impressed, leaning against the rail in the back with his entourage.

Lia clicked on the microphone, but then changed her mind, deciding to let everyone enjoy the moment in peace. She wrapped her arm around her knees, rested her chin, and waited another five minutes for the whales to come up again with their spouts, thinking about that wry smile Evan had given at his brother's assessment.

Evan was right.

Talking might be overrated.

Evan pulled the boat farther forward to keep the whales in everyone's ten o'clock range. The tour was already a half hour late, thanks to Stevens, and he wouldn't be able to stay long, but he loved seeing the two mother whales traveling together; something about it warmed his cold heart. Nature continually amazed him. It was good to get out of his sailboat, get out of his head, get out of his shitty down spiral of a life for a day, and come out here.

"*. . . herd of dolphins, traveling southwest. . . .*" the radio crackled.

Evan lifted the microphone. "This is . . . uh . . . Captain Betancourt on the *Duke*. Could you repeat that?"

"We've got a superpod of dolphins traveling southwest, should be just south of Newport now."

He checked his coordinates again. Score. He'd give the passengers another few minutes with the whales, then catch the superpod, which was always something. Even though he'd have to cut everything early because of the half-hour setback, these passengers were getting quite a ride.

"Tell them we'll head back in five," he told Cinderella. "They'll see the grays come up one more time, then we'll head north to catch a herd of dolphins."

Cinderella repeated the information, then clicked off the microphone and held it by her knee.

It was best he get out of this quietness with her anyway. Did he really call her "Cinderella" out loud? And he couldn't believe he shot off that question about Drew. What the hell had he been thinking? He was never the type to do that—he always played his feelings close to his vest. But Drew had him confused right now, and nature always made him stupid.

The wildness of the ocean was good for him—it made him feel small and insignificant in life, reminding him of his place—but it also made him divulge things. His last major fustercluck happened out in nature, too, also on a boat, a sailboat he and Drew shared with their father, when he'd suddenly felt the need to blurt his feelings to another of Drew's friends. One with beautiful brown curls. All it took was one day out on a vessel, some salt air, and a feeling of being one with nature, and there he was, telling her he thought she was pretty. Which, for a shy, nerdy nineteen-year-old, was a fucking overture. Little did he know what he'd been unraveling. . . .

He glanced at Lia's ankle and refocused his thoughts. She should push the ice up, but he didn't want to tell her what to do anymore.

He wanted that ankle healed, though. He already felt bad about Thomas Two-Time not showing up this morning; he didn't need to be responsible for a broken ankle, too. But it wasn't broken. He knew that. He just wanted it healed. He wanted to be absolved of any pain he caused Drew, any of Drew's friends, or any of Drew's women. He wanted to be absolved for stealing Drew's girlfriend. He wanted to be absolved for marrying her. He wanted to be absolved for fathering the child that maybe should have been Drew's, and he wanted to be absolved for letting them both die.

"Here they come," Cinderella whispered into the ocean breeze.

They both watched as the show repeated itself from four minutes ago: two enormous spouts of water, almost side by side; two vast gray backs; and two tremendous tails, slowly heading back down. Then closely following were the calves: spouts, backs, flukes. . . .

Evan waited for the last splash, then reluctantly turned back to the wheel. They'd have to jet it out to catch the dolphin herd.

Drew's boat behaved beautifully. He had to give his brother another dose of credit, picking out a vessel of this size that still did what you wanted her to, right under your hands. He made a wide arc farther into the ocean, watching the coordinates on his console, sucking in the salt air that spoke of promise. You didn't really ride with dolphins—they rode with you—so he'd have to create a certain speed for them, near enough, that they'd be attracted to his bow waves.

"Tell the passengers we're heading toward the dolphins," he said.

"We're heading out now," Cinderella said into the microphone, sweeping her hair out of her face. "We have word that a herd of dolphins is coming this way, so we're going to see if we can find them."

Her microphone clicked off. "It's a herd, right? Not a pod?"

"When it's big, we call it a herd."

"So this one's big? Which side will they be on?"

"You'll know." He couldn't help but crack a small smile at what she was about to see.

He fed her information about the common dolphin, saying this area had the highest density of common dolphin per square mile than anywhere on Earth, up to 450,000 along this shoreline alone, and that they sometimes traveled in herds of hundreds or thousands here, often working together to hunt for fish, or just play. He told her, line by line, how they were called "common," but were anything but—they were a beautiful, graceful creature that deserved better.

Cinderella paused over that part for some reason, but then continued to repeat all of his lines into the microphone, making them sound better than he did.

She was good at this. Her sunshiny, overoptimistic attitude was perfect for this kind of thing. When you were staring at whales up close, or swimming in a stampede of hundreds of dolphins, optimism was finally valid.

"Here we go," he said, as the superpod came into view.

He created a perfect speed, and nearly a thousand dolphins caught his waves on both sides of the boat. Cinderella's mouth dropped open at the stampede—he couldn't help but steal a glance. She was silent for a second as she glanced all around. The dolphins leaped out of the water all around them, creating beautiful arcs and foamy whitewater everywhere, as if the dolphins were carrying the boat themselves.

"Stay off that ankle," he reminded her.

She complied, which surprised him, and clicked on her microphone, but she suddenly seemed at a loss for words and lowered it. He couldn't help but smile at that. He hadn't seen that one coming.

Oohs and aahs rose from the deck below, along with the happy shriek of the children as they clustered together and peered over the side rails.

"Tell them the boat's proximity doesn't hurt them," he said. "They come to us—they like to ride the wake."

After Cinderella told them, she turned the microphone off again and stared at the mammals, eyes wide, a small smile playing along her lips.

He let himself be riveted by her for a second. Her lips were full and beautiful. He didn't want to notice that, but he did. And had. Several times, in fact.

But he turned away. Not only was she a friend of Drew's—and he wanted Drew to forgive him, not think he was here to steal another girl—but his wife was dead only two years. Every time something happened to let Renece or Luke slip away from him an iota more, the guilt made him want to pull that gun closer to the edge of the drawer. And thinking about Cinderella's lips seemed like one of those things.

The dolphins followed the boat for another mile, and he concentrated on them instead. He studied their slick beauty and watched their hypnotic rhythm. The ocean and its beauty had always been an escape for him.

It sure as hell was a welcome escape now.

"Thank you all for coming," Lia told the passengers as they disembarked, shaking some of their hands. Some slipped her a tip, which she put in her pocket to split with Cora and Evan later.

Cora was out of the galley now, helping Evan stow the lines. Lia had wanted to help, but Evan told her to stay off her ankle and lean against the back rail to keep an eye on the passengers as they stepped off the boat. Cora was doing a pretty good job anyway—Evan was showing her a way to tie a simpler half-hitch knot, and she seemed to be getting a kick out of it.

"That was amazing," Avery said, shaking Lia's hand. "What do you say, Conner?"

Conner squirmed under his mother's arm and threw Lia a huge grin: "Thanks! I saw the dolphins!"

"Weren't they something?" Lia asked.

"They were going like this." He made a motion with his body like a dolphin leaping into the air.

The two boys disembarking behind him laughed, and soon all three were mimicking the motion.

Kyle Stevens stepped between them.

"That really *was* something," he said.

"Can I sit down with your captain and ask a few questions?" Avery asked.

Lia glanced at Evan, who was up by the bow now, securing the lines.

"Um . . . we have another tour after this, and we'll need to get ready. Maybe we can make an appointment to talk later? I can answer questions for you on the phone."

"I'd love a tour of the boat," Kyle said.

"Me, too!" Avery added, trying to wrangle Conner closer.

"Well," Lia interjected, trying to head them off, "as I said, we have another whale-watching tour after this, so—"

"I can come back tomorrow," Avery offered.

"I can swing that, too," Kyle added. "I'm flying out

Wednesday, but I can come by tomorrow—around nine? Maybe take a quick tour of the boat, then do another ride?" He looked at Avery. "I'll pay for another ride for you, too, if you'd like."

A trickle of perspiration ran between Lia's breasts. She hadn't prepared for a repeat visit for Kyle, or a walking tour of Drew's boat. She aired out her sweater and strove to look professional. "I don't know. We're booked for two tours tomorrow. I didn't plan on private tours of any kind."

"How about after the last one?" Kyle said. "I'll even pay for forty-five extra tickets, but it'll just be me." He smiled at Avery. "And you, if you like. Is four o'clock okay?"

"Yes!" Avery said.

"Wait," Lia held up her hand. The Vampiress had said to do whatever Kyle wanted, but she needed to think this through.

"What's going on?" Evan's gravelly voice came over her shoulder.

"We're setting up a private tour for tomorrow," Kyle bulldozed in.

Kyle's casual clothes and boyish grin made him look fun and easygoing, but he had a sharp bark of intolerance that reminded Lia that he was old money. "Miss—" He turned up his palm toward Avery.

"James. Avery James."

"Miss James, here, and I would love to get a private look at the helm and maybe some of the things you've outfitted the catamaran with here."

Lia stepped in front of Evan. "Well, since Drew's not here, Mr. Stevens, it might be best if we waited until—"

"Remember, call me Kyle. And I just have a few questions before the charter next Monday. Of course, you and I could meet *privately*, Lia." The smile he threw her, and the quick assessment of her breasts, which now had a river of perspiration running between them, threw her off guard.

"We can do the tour," Evan interjected.

Lia looked up at him, unable to hide her surprise.

Lia glanced between Evan, Kyle, and Avery, the panic setting in. Of course, she could call in tomorrow, too, and tell the Vampiress she needed to be on the boat again. Elle would be irritated, but at least Lia was following her anything-Kyle-wants edict. And

Evan *did* know the boat. He'd know it from a commercial-business point of view, too, since she was pretty sure the Coast Guard did the commercial-captain's training anyway. But he wasn't good for PR. . . .

"Okay," Lia finally said, desperation winning over logic.

A boyish joy crossed Kyle Stevens's face. Lia almost expected high fives to follow.

"Four o'clock. Tomorrow," she added in a voice that pretended she had control.

Kyle disembarked with a satisfied smile, followed by Avery, two big bodyguards, and a dolphin-leaping boy.

CHAPTER

Six

Before the next tour, Lia, Evan, and Cora wiped down counters, seats, cushions; put the whale artifacts back; swept cookie crumbs; restocked coffee cups; and checked the fuel and lines. It was a lot to do for just three people—especially on a bum ankle and with Evan's constant growls to get off it—but they managed to finish everything moments before the next tour began. Cora ran to the marina market for lunch, coming back with two double-cheese burgers for Evan, which he snuck away to eat alone, and for her and Lia, egg salad sandwiches, which they wolfed down together in the galley.

"He's good," Cora said, her eyes lifting to the deck above them.

Lia broke open a salt packet. "He's okay, I guess. He's not Drew."

"He's more fun to have around than Drew."

"*What?* How can you say that?"

"He's more fun to watch on deck." A small smile played around Cora's lips.

"What are you talking about?" Lia asked.

Cora just shook her head. "If you're not noticing, you're blind."

"You think he's *attractive*?"

"You *don't*?"

"He sort of scares me."

"That man could scare *me* anytime."

"Cora!"

Cora laughed and gathered their paper bags, doing a double-take at a bright blue flyer stapled to the side. She yanked it off and spread it out on the counter with the heel of her hand. "Oh! It's Valentine!"

Lia wiped the corner of her mouth with a paper napkin and leaned over to see the flyer. "A valentine?"

"Not 'a' valentine, *Valentine*—a humpback who's come by here for years with her calves. Her flukes have a perfect heart on them, outlined in white." Cora pointed to the picture of her tail on the flyer. "But a fisherman in Mexico thought he saw her tangled in some fishing lines this year on her way up. It looks like they're asking everyone to keep their eyes peeled to make sure she's not in danger. She's the model for a lot of logos around here, including Drew's." Cora twisted her shirt to show it off.

Lia was aware of the logo—in fact, she was the one who had it designed onto the polo shirts she suggested Drew's staff wear—but she hadn't known it was modeled after a real whale.

Cora pushed the flyer to the side. "So what's going on with your nice accountant man, anyway?"

"He's fine. Still traveling." Lia tapped her jeans pocket for her cell phone. She must've left it on the counter again. She'd have to see how Forrest was doing. His last voice message had been oddly clipped, but he was leaving uncharacteristic philosophical messages all around social media. The last one was something about the sky meeting the sun. Lia was starting to wonder if he'd been hacked.

"Oh! They're here," Cora whispered, glancing out the window.

Lia leaped off the barstool on her good foot and hobbled toward the window to take a peek. My goodness. Another forty-five tourists. This crowd looked similar to the first—another first-grade class, more young couples, a few families, another mom-blogger. Lia fumbled beneath the counter for her purse to freshen up, bending toward her tiny compact to check her teeth, smooth her hair back, then touch up her lipstick.

"Do I look okay?" She whirled around to check with Cora, sliding her lips for one last glossy coverage, and came face-to-chest with Evan. His sunglasses dropped to his side as he blinked at her in the darkened galley. At her question, his gaze slid across her face—into her eyes, along her nose, then down to her puckered mouth. It lingered there, and he took an uncomfortable swallow. For a brief second, Lia wondered what it would be like to have this man kiss her—this enormous, strong man who didn't seem like he suffered fools, who would kiss her decisively, holding both sides of her head, pressing for more, wanting to possess—

Evan cleared his throat, thankfully breaking the spell, then stepped back and rearranged his features.

"Cora, do we have"—Evan motioned with his hand, as if he didn't have words to finish the thought.

Cora smiled up at him. "What is it you *want*, Captain?" She threw Lia a funny smile.

"Ah . . ." He motioned behind the counter. "Do we have . . ." His hand waved around again. ". . . any more Tylenol or Advil or anything back there? And I'll take another water. Or two." He cleared his throat again. "We ready to go?" He threw the question back over his shoulder at Lia.

"I think so," Lia said.

His nearness, his size, his mounded shoulders, his sandlewood-and-cedar scent, and the memory of his deep voice rumbling in her ear all morning were causing her breath to come in strange, short rasps, which in turn irritated her. She didn't want to be attracted to him—he wasn't even close to her job-holding, briefcase-toting type. She just wanted to get through this day with her pride and sanity intact.

"Um . . ." What had she wanted to ask him again? Oh, yes. "About tomorrow—"

"Let's get through today first," he said, tearing into another Advil packet Cora found. Without looking at her, he shoved his sunglasses back on and twisted his shoulders through the galley door.

Lia met Cora's amused glance.

"He *likes* you." Cora's broad grin made her look like she was in high school.

"What?" The idea seemed so preposterous, she dismissed it immediately. Evan had seemed to not want to react to her at all—and had slipped into immediate irritation every time he did—so the thought was beyond ridiculous. And the idea that her own out-of-control reaction might have been visible to Cora embarrassed her to no end.

She wiped a sheen of perspiration from her forehead and turned away, leaning forward to look out the window again. Pain scorched through her ankle as she shifted her weight. *Dang.* She sucked in her breath and sat back on the stool. Well, this would keep her mind from straying off into unchartered territory. Only a few more hours to get through, then she could get off this foot and put it up for the evening. She took a deep breath and began hobbling.

Their passengers were waiting.

Round Two.

The next set of tourists boarded faster and smoother than the first, and Lia went through her routine again, this time remembering to mention Cora's cookies right up front. She and Cora got another round of applause.

The mom-blogger Lia had booked for this tour was named Janine, and she was there with her two little girls. She held her camera high in the air to videotape, spinning slowly to get the whole boat while her girls swung around her legs like she was a Maypole. The field trip was a local Orange County private school, with eighteen first graders and five chaperones. The potential investor on this trip was Jimmy Chow. He was an ex-pro surfer from Central California and would be a fun partner for Drew. Lia greeted him warmly and made sure he had a good seat.

Then she dragged herself toward the stairs. She didn't really want to sit on the bridge with Evan on this trip, but she needed his cues for the narration. The electricity that had ricocheted between them in the galley had left her feeling uncomfortable, as if she shouldn't have been flying her kite so close to the storm.

"Cora, I'm heading up," she called nervously.

Cora smiled some kind of weird, knowing smile.

Lia sighed. All right, she'd sit farther away, stay low-key, stop asking personal questions, and filter whale info only. End of story.

When she pulled herself to the top, Evan was standing at the helm, scouting the ocean for slicks, the wind rollicking through his hair. Lia balanced herself against the captain's bench, then took a seat with the microphone in her hand. The paper bag from Evan's lunch was crumpled and left on the console in a way that would've given Drew a heart attack. Lia threw it in a hidden waste tray, earning her a nice, irritable glance from Evan that relaxed her in its familiarity. The blue Valentine flyer from his bag was folded neatly, the photo facing outward, tucked under one of the levers.

They sat quietly as the boat zipped over the waves, the salt air refreshing. About seven miles north, Evan slowed, staring through the binoculars at a point due west.

"There's one," he said. "Or . . . wait, two. Mother and calf. Grays."

He killed the motor and they went through their whole routine again: he fed her lines, and she repeated them, adding info she learned last time. They fell into an easy rhythm, staying quiet between the whales' spouting. Lia kept her head averted so she wouldn't be hit with any stray pheromones.

After the first twenty minutes with the beautiful mama whale and her baby, Evan drove northwest and spotted another. They repeated their process: low lines, Evan leaning languidly against the bridge rail, the steady and rhythmic timbre of his voice vibrating in her veins. . . .

At the end of the two hours, they sailed past a buoy weighted down by sunning sea lions, and Evan delivered more information about the mating habits of the flippered pinnipeds.

When the tour ended, Lia couldn't escape the elevated bridge fast enough.

"Thank you for coming. . . . Thank you. . . . Hope you had a good time. . . . Thank you for coming. . . ."

Evan watched Lia say good-bye to all the passengers as he

secured the stern line. There was a lot to do to close the cat up for the night, but he was going to send her home. She needed to get off that ankle. The way things were looking, it might not even be healed by tomorrow.

He glanced inside the galley and wondered if Cora could give the presentations. Or maybe he could. He didn't like putting on a false face—pretending enthusiasm he just didn't feel—but he might have to. Or at least raise his voice to an octave suitable for the land of the living. Drew's cat crew was obviously dwindling. And there'd be the private tour tomorrow for Stevens and, damn it, the Renece look-alike.

He yanked the knot as hard as he could.

"Hear back from any deckhands?" he asked Cinderella as she waved to the last passenger. "I'll even take Stewey the steward."

She touched her pockets, then looked around as if her phone had just fallen out of her clothes. "Just a sec." She hobbled into the galley.

He headed for the hose, and did his best not to watch her walk away. He didn't want to notice her body. Her shapely legs, her pouty lips, combined with her Brave-Little-Toaster attitude, were all generating some weird attractiveness that was doing a number on his libido. Or reminding him he had one, anyway.

"No, no one called," she yelled back out.

When she reemerged, she headed for the blue cushions to retrieve the stuffed-toy whale that the kids had been playing with, then started straightening the cushions. He took the toy from her. "Go home."

"What?"

"You're not going to be good to me at all tomorrow if you can't walk. Ice that ankle tonight, and if you can't come in tomorrow, see if you can get me Stewey or that other deckhand."

"Douglas?"

"Sure."

She looked around uncertainly. "I don't know if I can get them."

"Try."

Her eyes narrowed as she studied him. "You sure are bossy."

"I just want your ankle healed. Can you drive home?"

"Yes."

"Do you know how to wrap an ankle?"

"I think I can figure out how to wrap an ankle."

"Then go do it." The edge in his voice was unwarranted. He was suddenly finding it easier to stay silent or speak roughly to her than acknowledge where his thoughts were going.

And it was easier still to just get rid of her. "You know any other deckhands around here for tomorrow?" He glanced up the marina. "Maybe some kids who want to make extra money?"

"Drew's pretty particular about his boat," she said hesitantly.

" 'Particular' is probably putting it mildly."

When her lips quirked, he was sorry he'd said it. One, because he really shouldn't be talking about Drew and his crazy OCD behind his back; and two, because Cinderella's lips were now drawing his attention again.

He put his sunglasses back on so she couldn't see his eyes. "Well, go home. Cora and I can get this." He held out his hand for the keys.

"I can't *leave* you here."

"You can."

"I can't."

"You can. Keys."

She eventually gave in, looking sorrowfully at Cora.

"She sure is stubborn," he mumbled to Cora as the two of them watched Cinderella make her way up the dock.

As he turned to start rinsing the windows, Cora mumbled some kind of response and he almost turned back to hear what she said. But he changed his mind. He didn't need to know. He didn't need to know anything else about a woman who made him forget about Renece for almost half a day.

Lia shuffled toward her car, eager when she saw it through the parking lot, and wondered how she could get someone else to do this tomorrow. She wasn't normally one to give up, but the challenges were stacking against her. The pain shooting through her foot was bringing tears to her eyes. Plus she was exhausted—the salt air and bright sun had sucked every molecule of energy out of her. What sounded great right now was a long, hot shower; her most comfy pajamas; a *Real House-wives* marathon; and Missy purring in her lap. . . .

She sighed. She couldn't afford that. She still had work to catch up on.

As she drove, she ran through her mind all the people who might serve as deckhands tomorrow. Then she ran through possible narrators. Taking tomorrow off would give her ankle time to rest, allow her to catch up on work, and keep her away from the frustrating heart-skitter of Evan Betancourt standing too close, with his muscled body and cedar scent. But she couldn't miss the tour with Kyle Stevens. The Vampiress would kill her. Especially if something went wrong.

Her thoughts went back to Evan. What *was* that earlier? And why did she keep wanting to revisit it? Having his eyes slide toward her lips that way—as though he were thinking of kissing her, this huge, quiet man who had been so devoid of emotion just moments before—was one of the sexiest stares she'd received in a long time. But he wasn't her type in any way, shape, or form. Slender men in slim suits who could run businesses were her cup of tea. Forrest was one of those. He had his own accounting firm, and worked hard every day of the week. They had been seeing each other for almost six months. Sometimes he would come over late at night, and they'd sit on the couches with their laptops, working away. She would rest her head on his narrow shoulder and he would pet Missy with his tapered, manicured fingers while they worked.

Forrest understood her need for alone time, her need to stay on top of her career. They gave each other the space they needed. She didn't even mind that he left for Bora Bora three weeks ago, even though he *did* know she was dying to travel the world. He probably just didn't want to interrupt her work.

Main Street was bustling on this Monday evening. She hob-bled down the street from where she parked, visited with Mr. Hickle at the olive shop, showed him her idea for a company Facebook page and how they could have a contest to launch it, watched part of *Antiques Roadshow* with him because he missed his wife who had died three months ago, then limped back to her car as night began to fall. Mr. Hickle was so sweet, but by the time she got back behind the driver's seat, her ankle was nearly twice its normal size. She sped home.

Once she pulled herself all the way up her apartment patio stairs, she saw another three shoe boxes from the postman piled on her porch. She sighed, reached for her apartment key in her purse, and realized . . . her *phone*. It wasn't there. *Damn*. She plowed through her purse, hoping it would miraculously appear. *Damn again*.

Her eyes drifted closed and she dropped her chin to her chest as the realization hit her: *the galley*. Her phone was sitting *on the countertop in the galley*. Would this day never end?

She *had* to get her phone. She needed to check for any messages from Elle, and communicate with Douglas and Stewey.

Moaning at the thought of saying good-bye to her hot shower and comfy pajamas, and trying not to think of the size her ankle must be by now, she headed back down the stairs.

By the time she arrived at the marina, night had fallen. Music drifted from one of the restaurants that had patio lights strung across the back—a pretty, jazzy number on guitar. Lia hobbled past, wincing at every-other step, and headed down the wooden planks of the boat docks, feeling for her extra dock key. Normally she could focus on the beauty of the music, making a miserable evening into something that had some merit, but she was at her wit's end right now.

Drew's boat looked dark and unfriendly at night, the cheerful blue cushions replaced with dark tarps that protected the boat from tossed beer cans and used condoms. She maneuvered through the tarps—which required a few un-snaps and re-snaps here and there—to the galley door. Cora and Evan did a great job closing up, she had to admit. At the door, she fiddled with the key the same way Douglas had—the thing always got stuck—and opened the door into the darkness, shuffling down the galley stairs by using both hands. When she got to the bottom, she fumbled for the light. As her hand made its way along the wall, a low sound came from the back of the galley:

"I'm here," a deep whisper told her.

Her scream probably shattered the next song of the guitar player.

CHAPTER

Seven

"Damn it! What are you doing here?" Lia's whisper shot into the stillness.

She'd recognized Evan's voice right away. A full day of listening for it and repeating it had left the footprint firmly in her mind.

"Resting," he said.

Her hand crawled upward, grasping for the light. An image of him with the gun in his hand from this morning flashed through her mind. Blackness enshrouded her as she scrambled between wanting to look for the light and wanting to keep an eye toward him through the darkness.

"Could you not turn that on?" he drawled. "And not scream anymore? The harbormaster is patrolling. Your eyes will adjust in a second. I can see you perfectly. And don't look so terrified; I'm just sitting here."

Her breath returned in short gasps as she strained to see even an outline. He didn't sound drunk. That was good. He sounded like perhaps he'd just awoken. She peeled herself off the wall as a bright searchlight crashed through the window—probably Harry James's patrol boat—and swept the galley. As it bounced off the opposite wall, she caught a quick glimpse of Evan, sitting on the edge of a cot across the room that had been pulled down like a Murphy bed. She hadn't even known that cot was there. Huh. The light caught his posture, leaning forward with his elbows on his knees, before it swept out of the room.

"Wh-what are you doing here?" she managed to squeak out.

"Resting. Seriously. Come off that wall. You look like you're trying to claw your way out of here."

She forced her breathing back under control and stepped away. As her fear dissolved, the adrenaline crashed and her ankle pain spiked again, along with a healthy dose of anger. "Why are you resting *here*?"

"You didn't wrap your ankle." His voice was calming, quiet, the one that had described the whale calves earlier today.

"You're not answering my question."

"I'm here because the harbormaster was sweeping tonight, and a guy in a neighboring slip said I should make myself scarce if I didn't want to get kicked out."

"So you're sleeping *here*?"

"No, I was going to head back around one. The guy said the sweep would be done by then."

Lia opened her mouth to respond, but then pressed her lips together. Okay. So he was using the boat for a few hours. It *was* his brother's boat, after all, and he *was* doing them a favor. Maybe this could be their way of paying him back.

"What are *you* doing here?" he mumbled.

"I forgot my phone."

An outline of his nod started to materialize. The sound of the water lapping the side of the boat was the only sound for a minute.

"Sorry I scared you," Evan said.

The simple sentence was the most empathetic thing Lia had heard from him, and seemed filled with so much sorrow. Sorrow that probably belonged to a great deal more than just scaring her tonight. Through the dark, Lia could vaguely see that he had his hands clasped in front of him, between his knees, and was staring at them. A lump formed in her throat for some reason, as if she knew a story here that she didn't really know. Something that bespoke of enormous pain.

"Apology accepted," she whispered. "So do you need a place to stay? Maybe we could ask Drew. He has a—"

"No," Evan interjected. "I'm only staying a couple more days. Just until I get my motor fixed. They're just a little strict here in Sandy Cove about liveaboards. You won't need me past Thursday, right?"

She didn't know. Early today, she'd wanted to get rid of him as fast as possible, but he'd actually pulled through for her. Now she sort of wanted him to stay. Someone would definitely have to cover Kyle's charter next week. But clearly Evan wanted, and needed, to move on.

"I'll keep working on finding another captain," she said. Her disappointment caught her by surprise.

She moved toward the counter where she could see a few objects forming in the dark, including her phone. She snatched it up and punched in her screen code, but the phone began powering down. "Damn it!"

Lia always tried to keep upbeat, feeling like life was so much easier when you were, but this day was crushing her. Her skin was tight and uncomfortable from salt and sunburn, her eyes burned, her ankle throbbed, and her limbs hung heavy and sore. And now she'd need to drive home another ten miles to plug in her phone, learn what the Vampiress might need tonight, figure out how tomorrow would go and who may or may not show up—and all this before feeding Missy, showering, then crawling into bed. The fact that that could be hours away weakened her legs for a second.

"Why don't you have a seat?" Evan asked.

"If I sit, I won't get up."

"I think you need to relax."

"I need to get home. I still have work to do."

"I think you need to relax."

She threw her phone in her purse. Her head fell against the cabinet. A guy like Evan would never understand.

The light slashed through the window again, revolving in the opposite direction. Harry's patrol boat must be looping the marina. She sighed. Now she'd have to at least wait until the patrol boat left, or be prepared to answer a dozen questions about why she was slipping out of this catamaran with the lights out this late at night, and why she had a stowaway aboard. Who had nowhere else to go. And she sure didn't need Harry calling Drew about this.

She slumped against the counter. The patrol boat purred softly as it rounded theirs.

"Let me get you an Ace bandage," he said gently. "I'm getting up, okay?"

"I can see you now."

He nodded and shifted toward the counter where the first-aid kit was. As soon as he moved closer, threatening to overtake her space, she remembered why she needed to avoid him. His cedar scent drifted toward her, much stronger now, combined with freshly shampooed hair. She could see damp clumps hanging against his collar.

He rummaged through the cabinet until he found what he was looking for. "Have a seat."

"I really don't—"

"Rest, ice, compression, elevation—Since you refuse to rest, and you only allowed the ice for fifteen minutes, let's at least try a little compression." He motioned toward the dinette.

"I can do it at home."

He shot her a look of impatience.

Finally, she gave in. She'd be strong. She'd pretend the cedar scent wasn't sexy at all. And she'd refuse to look at his muscles. Plus, maybe he really did have some magic bandage-wrapping technique she didn't know about: She couldn't remember ever actually wrapping an ankle before, except once, a paw, for Missy when she'd skidded off a dresser.

Lia plopped at the end of the dinette.

Head bent, Evan knelt in front of her and rested her foot against his thigh. Lazy light from the marina came in through the window and cast a quiet, blue halo in his wet hair as it fell across his eyes. He unlaced her shoe, his fingers gripping the soft, swollen skin around her ankle both firmly and tenderly at the same time. As he pried off the shoe, he let her ankle bend ever so slightly.

She swallowed a few swear words.

"Sorry," he mumbled, glancing up from beneath his bangs.

When the shoe was tossed aside, he gently replaced her foot against his jeans. His thigh muscles were warm and firm, shifting beneath her bare foot. She swallowed hard and directed her eyes toward the ceiling. He unraveled the bandage.

"Come toward me." He motioned with his fingertips, watching the angle of her ankle against his leg. He cupped her heel in the palm of his hand and began wrapping, cradling the arch of her foot with one hand and sweeping the bandage down in a figure eight with the other. His fingers were warm and intimate, pressing into her soft instep. Her stomach quivered.

Lia weakened immediately. She stared at his flexing forearm, bulging on the downward sweep, then becoming roped and taught as he pulled the bandage up. She didn't know if it was the beauty of that uber-masculine muscle, the gentleness of his fingers, the warmth of his palm, the scowl of determination on his face, or simply her own fatigue, but all conspired to set a low heat simmering in her belly. It was a settled sort of warmth, the kind you feel when you're cared for, wholly. It was a feeling of excessive vulnerability. It scared the hell out of her.

"I need to—" She yanked her foot away. The euphoria was making her light-headed.

"Wait," Evan murmured, gripping her calf. "Almost done."

She wriggled away.

"Seriously. Cinder—*Lia*, stop a sec."

Cinder-lia? She squirmed again while he secured the bandage with two small latches, then she wriggled out of his grip and launched herself in a lopsided hop across the room.

He let out an expulsion of air.

"Too tight?" He inspected his handiwork from across the room.

Part of her wanted to say yes. Part of her wanted to give an excuse that would allow her to sit back down, have his warm hands back around her foot, have that wave of euphoria tingle back up through her scalp again. But another part of her pointed out that she was crazy. *This was Drew's "messed up" brother.* That feeling of euphoria should *not* be coming from this man's deft hands on her. He was not her type. He was some ne'er-do-well who traveled the seas alone and without purpose. He didn't shave. He didn't cut his hair. He slept with a gun. She had a *boyfriend*. Or . . . well, not exactly a serious boyfriend, but a man who might make decent serious-boyfriend material someday. A man with a job at least.

"It's fine." Her voice sounded funny and tight.

Evan glanced at her suspiciously and rose to put the first-aid kit away.

"Why are you calling me Cinderella?" she blurted.

The anger that lay in the accusation was misplaced, she knew, but creating a simmering anger was better than allowing a simmering heat.

He paused for a minute to glance at her, then set the kit down on the countertop and began rewinding the remaining bandage. "Did I?"

"Yes, for the second time. And you're very good at evading questions. But I just want to know why you're calling me that."

"Slip of the tongue."

"See? You're evading again."

He stuffed the leftover bandage back into the box. "Maybe I'm just not good at answering a lot of questions."

"All that sailing around the world by yourself, maybe? It's made you a curmudgeon?"

He gave a tired smile.

"Can you give me *one* straight answer?"

He seemed to think that over as he reached for the cabinet doors. "Shoot."

"Why 'Cinderella'?"

Balancing the box above his head, he rearranged a few things inside the cabinet. "Just me being an ass."

"So it's not a compliment?"

"It wasn't. But maybe it should have been."

"What does that mean?"

"It means originally it was because of your overoptimistic attitude—you seemed like there should be birds singing at your shoulder—but now I see you're tired, and your foot is probably throbbing, but you're still hanging in there. And I'm kind of impressed. So now it's a compliment."

"You were making fun of me?"

"I'm an ass. Let's just get that out of the way."

Lia bit her lip and peered at him through the dark. So that crazy moment in the cabin wasn't attraction after all. Cora was wrong. But this made more sense.

Even though her head settled this, though—and told her it was a good thing—some crazy part of her felt disappointed. But, just in case—

"I have a boyfriend," she blurted next.

Oh, God. Did she always have to blurt out every thought she was having? It worked with the Vampiress, who seemed to have an appreciation for directness, but with everyone else it just left her embarrassed.

Even through the dark, she could see his eyebrow rise. The side of his mouth followed in an upward quirk. "Is that so?"

"Yes."

"So . . . is this boyfriend able to come pick you up right now? It might be best if you didn't drive. You should try to elevate that foot."

"No, he can't. He's . . . well, he's out of the country."

The darkness couldn't hide Evan's next frown, as he was probably trying to figure out the strange turns this conversation was taking.

"I . . . I need to leave," she said. She'd embarrassed herself enough. She couldn't figure out why her heart was pounding, why his tenderness a minute ago settled a euphoria over her shoulders, why his smoldering look through the darkness was making other body parts come alive, and all while she didn't want to be attracted to him. Had she *no control*?

In her haste toward the door, she banged her hip against the dinette. When had she ever thought Drew's galley was *spacious*? Right now it seemed like a closet. Her hand was on the brass handle, the door already ajar, when the overly bright patrol light came crashing through the window.

A megaphone blared through the silent harbor. *"STOP! Come out slowly with your hands up. . . ."*

Panic shot through her as she sucked herself back into the galley. The searchlight stopped right in front of the door, illuminating the covered deck, trying to capture her in its beam.

"It's okay," Evan said. He pulled the curtain back at the window. "Just do what they say. You're not doing anything wrong."

Lia's heart thundered. He nodded his encouragement, and she hobbled into the searchlight beam, her hands up, squinting forward: *You're not doing anything wrong. It's going to be okay. It's going to be okay* . . . But the blinding light and surrounding darkness made her body shake. The patrol boat puttered up beside the cat.

"Put your bag on the deck," the voice, still disembodied, shouted at her over the laps of the harbor water.

She shakily set her purse down.

"Move to the edge of the deck, toward my voice."

She scooted closer, squinting into the light, dragging her bad foot.

Blinded, she felt the back end of the catamaran dip and heard at least two sets of footsteps, then tensed in case they grabbed her. But, at the same time, she sensed Evan coming through the galley door. Hands still over her head, heart pounding, she glanced back over her shoulder to see him, caught in the beam . . . um . . . *buttoning his shirt*? His hair was mussed in a way she hadn't seen before, standing up on end.

"Officers, sorry." He shaded his eyes.

"Put your hands above your head!" The officer's voice came fast and excited, now directed at Evan.

Evan complied, stepping in front of Lia. "I can explain. . . ." he told the beam of light.

A half hour later, Lia and Evan sat side by side beneath a bright floodlight Evan had thrown on for the deck.

Out of the corner of his eye, he could see Cinderella shiver, and another flash of self-loathing went through him. How had he managed to jack up another woman's life in such short order? He needed to just stay on his damned boat and head back out to sea. He wasn't fit for civility.

The harbor patrol officers clicked their pens and put away their clipboards. They were about to let him and Cinderella go. The fact that Evan's last name matched the registered owner's name ("Yes, he's my brother."), and that Drew was apparently friends with the harbormaster did wonders. As did the fact that Evan had the ignition keys, Cinderella had a galley key, Evan still had a Coast Guard card in his wallet, and Cinderella had a business card with her name and *"The Duke"* on it. It all made their story aboveboard enough for the harbor patrol. The officers inspected the galley, found the first-aid kit and missing bandage on her foot, saw the open cot, matched it with Evan's just-had-sex look—the only part of the story he had to fake—and seemed satisfied.

He felt bad about the just-had-sex thing—as bad as he did for Cinderella's shivering in the late night, her drop-dead fatigue, and her massively swelling ankle. But, from his own Coast Guard days, he knew that it was a common story for why people were caught on vessels late at night. The sympathetic and knowing glance from the youngest officer let him know it worked. Cinderella didn't seem to notice. And it sure beat having the harbor patrol call Drew. And it sure *as hell* beat the real reason he was here: Tommy Two-Time had shown up this evening, looking wasted and in need of a fix, and Evan was sorry he'd given out Drew's boat information. He'd shooed Tommy away, but something in the way he'd lingered, eyeing Evan as he jiggled the difficult galley-door lock, had made Evan nervous. The last thing he needed was to get Drew's boat robbed.

"Okay, you guys can go," the youngest one said, flicking his flashlight back and forth between them.

Cinderella squinted silently.

"Ya' got a place to stay?" He directed that at Evan.

"Yep."

The officer slid a glance toward Cinderella. It must have been her sullen glare that made him look back at Evan dubiously. "Ya' sure?"

"Yep."

Evan didn't dare look at her. He'd find a place. The officers would walk them both out of the marina right now, past the locked gate, but he could find a cheap motel nearby. He'd be caught for sure if he used his marina key to get back in to his own slip right now. But now that the harbor patrol had its eye on this boat, it would be safe from Tommy Two-Time.

"All right, let's go," the officer said.

Evan stood. Cinderella looked a little panicked. "He wants to walk us out," he mumbled, helping her up. "Lean on me."

She stiffened, but she was at a point now where she couldn't help it. That ankle had turned black and blue. And she looked exhausted and all-around beaten down. Even more than she had when she first stepped into the galley tonight, which was really saying something.

Evan was probably the only person in the universe who could bring down such an overly sunny woman—it must be a talent of his. He mentally swore at himself, then pulled her weight slightly onto his so he could get her off the boat. He resolved to ignore the feeling of her soft hair falling around his collarbone.

Next step, for sure, was to get out of her life.

Lia leaned into Evan. She didn't want to be weak but his bolstering body felt so good. Her head lolled against his firm chest, and she could feel his biceps bulge against her shoulder blade. She had an incredible urge to turn around and strip off his shirt so she could see that chest one more time.

They followed the officer up the dock ramp. The jazz guitarist at the restaurant had quit and the twinkle lights had gone out. The few people who were still out glanced at her being walked out of the marina like some kind of perp. She hoped they were tourists and not Sandy Cove residents, or this news might be all over town the next day. She just wanted to get home and into her pajamas.

At the top of the ramp, Evan let go. She realized her arms had slipped around his torso like octopus tentacles.

"Sorry," she whispered.

"No need." He cleared his throat.

The officer asked a few more questions, verified they both had a place to go, then left them at the top of the marina parking lot.

"So where are you going to stay?" she asked.

"I'll find a place. Which car is yours?" He was already scouting the lot.

"*Where* are you going to find a place? And how are you going to get there?"

"Let's just get you home."

"Look." She stepped in front of him to stop his trajectory. He looked tired. He'd had a long day, too, helping her and Drew. She was swept with gratitude, and made an effort to focus on that instead of her rampant lust. "I can see you don't like having people fuss over you. But why don't you stay at my place?"

As soon as the offer was past her lips, she questioned its wisdom. Her skin was prickling with awareness of him now, especially the way he was looking down at her through the dark, with a testosterone-driven sort of protectiveness. She had read that look as attraction, perhaps, but now she could see he was probably just the kind of guy who felt protective of everything in his sphere. The whole Coast Guard thing and all. But it was translating into something her body found attractive, much to her surprise. She'd always been one of those women who rolled her eyes at muscle-bound men who acted like they needed to save damsels in distress— *Cinderellas*. She didn't need a man to save her. But her body clearly had a mind of its own where this one was concerned. And having him too nearby was not going to be a smart move from here on out. But, on the other hand, she couldn't just leave him here in the parking lot.

"Or I could bring you to Drew's?"

"No," he said. "I can find a motel."

"Sandy Cove doesn't have very many motels, but there is one up by the freeway; I can drive you."

He considered that for a second. It was the first suggestion that didn't make him frown. "Okay. But I'll drive *you*. You can put that foot up for a minute."

The dark cab of her little Dodge felt as claustrophobic as Drew's galley as Evan hunched his shoulders and adjusted the seat. He drove slowly in the direction she pointed.

"You look a little uncomfortable," she said.

He peered out the windshield at the motel sign, which suddenly loomed through the dark. "It's been a while."

"Driving?"

He pulled into the parking lot, his mouth quirking up. "Yes, driving. What did you think I meant?"

"I just meant . . . yes, driving." Heat rose up through her cheeks. *Driving.* Of course she meant that.

"You sure you'll be okay getting home?" he asked gruffly, pulling up on the emergency brake.

"I'll be fine." At this point, she just wanted to be in her bed. Alone. With her thoughts. And Missy. And maybe a bottle of wine.

He waited next to the driver's door for her to hobble all the way around the car and get settled behind the wheel, readjusting the seat, then he leaned against the top of the door and stared down at her. The warmth of his taking-care-of-you attitude tried to settle around her again, but some inner strength helped her shove it aside. She couldn't be attracted to this kind of man.

"I'll pick you up tomorrow at nine," she mumbled into her steering wheel, waiting for him to close the door.

"I'll take a cab."

"No, I'll get you." She reached for the handle and wrestled the door from underneath him.

Her wheels screeched out of the parking lot.

The next morning, Lia's tires thunked over the old asphalt toward the Spanish-tiled Sandy Cove Motel. She turned the car off, then ran her hands down her white pants and took a deep breath. The brightness of the morning cast a sense of realism that had been missing last night, seeming to enlighten the situation now. After a good night's sleep, the events of yesterday—not to mention her rampant attraction—seemed positively absurd. She had had a stern talking-to with herself this morning as she got out of the shower. *No more crushing on Evan.* It was silly. She was just missing Forrest, and maybe feeling too much nearness to Evan on a boat all day. But whatever it was, it was going to stop.

Satisfied with her pep talk, she swung her door open just as a figure in faded blue jeans sauntered toward her through the morning mist. It took her a second to recognize him. Clean-shaven, Evan had slicked his hair back—revealing two bladed cheekbones; a strong, set jaw; and, as he approached the passenger side, eyes that were rimmed in dark lashes. And were clearly blue, not gray. They took her in with something that looked like embarrassment.

"Don't say anything," he mumbled, crawling into the car.

He tossed in two packages that he had been balancing in each hand—heavy enough to make the veins in his forearms pop where his white shirtsleeves were rolled up. But she could hardly take her eyes off his newly revealed face: such pretty eyes, such a full bottom lip, and—heaven help her—a *dimple* on the left side of his cheek that appeared when he shot her that grin of embarrassment.

When he glanced her way, she diverted her attention into one of the bags. A fire extinguisher head popped out of one, and the other appeared to have a full first-aid case in it.

"Restocking," he said, slamming the door. His eyes went straight to her foot. "How is it?"

"I re-wrapped it," she managed to get out. "And it does feel better."

He gave a curt nod. A strand of hair dropped over his cheekbone again. The dimple threatened as he seemed to fight back a smile, avoiding her eyes.

"Why did you shave?" She could hear the gaga factor in her voice, but her mouth had a mind of its own. So much for the pep talks.

"Saw an old acquaintance of mine yesterday evening, before you came, and he reminded me what a drug addict looked like. I thought I might be coming close."

She started the car, forcing herself to look away. *No crushing on Evan.* For the first time, she wondered if he'd ever been married. He obviously wasn't married *now*—no ring, and that sailboat cabin didn't look like something that had ever had a woman's touch. But now, seeing how handsome and almost vulnerable he was under all those layers, she could see a woman swooning for him.

But pep talk number thirty-six: *No crushing.* Asking him now if he'd ever been married would just solidify her slide.

Lia revved the engine and pulled out of the parking lot. This day might not be as easy as she'd hoped.

The sea was choppy under gray skies, and Evan was glad for Drew's good taste in motors. The wind whipped about as he carted their first tourists out, keeping his eye on the incoming clouds. He figured the tours could continue until about four, then the rain might drive them back to the marina. From his own experiences around these parts as a child, he knew that song was true: It never rained in California; it *poured*. Especially in February. For now, he'd just look for whales and enjoy Cora's coffee.

He had come up with an excuse to send Cinderella to the marina when they arrived so he could inspect the vessel before they boarded. It didn't look like Tommy had been around. Having the harbor patrol on high alert after they'd left last night was a good thing. But it was reckless of him to have called Tommy. He'd put Drew's boat in danger, and possibly even a woman—it hadn't occurred to him she might come back for something on the boat. What the hell was becoming of him? A year or two of depression was one thing, but losing his touch was another. He'd finally decided to shave and clean up his act, at least for the next four days. And no more drinking. If he was going to help Drew, he'd do it right.

Mollified that Tommy hadn't been around, he'd helped Cora and Cinderella do a quick opening. Cora landed into the galley and stared at the opened cot as if she'd never seen it before. Evan stepped around her to raise and lock it. Cinderella had blushed for some reason.

Neither deckhand had shown up, which sucked, but apparently Stewey had called and said he could make it tomorrow. And Douglas was going to make it back from Las Vegas. So there was that. Things were looking up. Now Evan just needed Cinderella to find another captain.

"Coffee?" Cora asked.

"Did anyone ever tell you that you make the best coffee on the West Coast, Cora?" he asked.

"Did anyone ever tell *you* that you look like a male model?"

A rusty laugh escaped his throat. Renece had. It was a nice thing to hear when you were a twentysomething biology geek, but it wasn't anything he cared about now. "Somehow I think your skills will take you much farther in life than my looks ever did."

"I don't know," Cora said, getting out her French press. "We'll probably get great tips today."

He broke a smile again and headed up to check the fuel. Cinderella was setting up the blue cushions.

She'd said she'd be "allowed" to call Drew tomorrow to discuss hiring another captain, which didn't make much sense to him—the "allowed" part—but he didn't press. Something told him he didn't need to know more than that—whatever her and Drew's relationship was, it was between them, and he wasn't going to cross any lines there.

But when she mentioned visiting Drew at home after Wednesday, he had mulled that over. Maybe he would, too. Not with her, but right after. Sometime before he left. This help he was providing was a peace offering, but a good man-to-man talk was in order. As was an apology.

He took his place behind the helm and did a quick check on all the gauges.

"Are we ready for the passengers to board?" Her voice came from behind him.

"Ready." He focused his attention back on the console. His head was clearer today, and he was ready to do his job. He wasn't going to let Cinderella distract him today, or her lips, or even those white pants she was wearing that gave him a sweet glimpse of a light-pink thong band when she squatted down to reach one of the cleats. And he was definitely going to forget about that dream he'd had about her last night. It had started out as a dream about Renece, which didn't alleviate any of his guilt right now. Then Renece had turned into a whale, or some such eff-ed up, dreamlike thing, and then Cinderella had ended up on the cot with him in Drew's boat, first wearing some bright yellow Hazmat suit, and then letting him strip it off her, running his fingers down every exposed strip of white skin, and the whole thing was very hot except for all the guilt he felt this morning. He probably should've been the one blushing when they'd lifted the cot today.

But he was forgetting about all of that.

Today was clearheaded business.

Focus.

He was relieved her ankle was better. Another slight guilt he could let slip away. She went back downstairs to attend to the guests while he got ready to pull away, then he dropped to the lower deck to cast off the lines.

A half hour later, the American flag was snapping above his head and the blue paper on his console was rippling in the wind. He secured it under a different lever. It was a picture of Valentine, the humpback whale the community was looking for. He remembered her from his Coast Guard days down in San Diego. Her appearance every year had become legend, her heart-shaped tail often showing up right around Valentine's Day. He remembered taking Renece and Luke out to see her one year when Luke was five. They'd packed a lunch and set out on the sailboat he'd rented for the day. Luke had brought along his notebook and crayons so he could "draw" the whale's tail when he spotted her. They'd spent a whole afternoon looking, and finally saw a few other vessels in the distance, hanging. Sure enough, Valentine spouted then, along with her calf, and Luke got busy with his little crayons. The picture Luke drew that day was still in Evan's drawer on his boat. It was one of the few things he'd kept when he'd sold everything and bought the sailboat to flee.

Evan pinned the blue paper more securely, Valentine's bent tail visible, and steered northwest.

After another mile out, something caught his eye through the binoculars. He started to signal, but paused, wanting to make sure he was seeing what he was seeing. . . . *Damn* . . . He pulled up farther, wondering why no other boats were around, but a huge slick was clearly up ahead of them. Much bigger than for grays. Once he was sure, he sent three clicks.

"Are you seeing something already?" Cinderella asked, pulling herself up to the deck.

"I think we've got a blue," he said, not taking his eyes off the slick.

She scrambled for the microphone.

"Just explain the slick and tell everyone ten o'clock. I want to be sure," he said.

She dutifully gave the narration, but then, just as he suspected, the huge animal—the largest mammal on Earth—broke the surface and spouted. He could hear the crowd gasp, and everyone moved to the side of the cat.

He couldn't help but smile. The smile came from a place that seemed like it hadn't been tapped in a long time, somewhere deep and pure, somewhere that reminded him there was still joy and majesty on Earth, in quiet places like this.

"Blues are the largest mammals that ever lived," he

mumbled over his shoulder. "Baleen. Usually travel alone." He steered carefully so as not to get in the blue's path, and then realized there was a calf.

Cinderella excitedly added that to her narration as Evan navigated the boat.

"This is early for the blues," he added. "They usually travel in the summer."

The whale and her baby kept pace alongside them, traveling about twelve miles an hour. They spouted every now and then, and Evan could hear the clicks of cameras below and the excited squeals of kids. He thought about how much Luke would have loved to have seen another blue. His knuckles ached as he gripped the console. Sometimes the pain was so sharp. But Cinderella spoke then and brought him out of the dark.

"How big do they get?" She had a book in her lap, but the wind whipped the pages all around, along with her yellow hair.

"Seventy, eighty, ninety feet. Almost a football field. This mother's close to eighty, I'd say. Baby's about twenty, twenty-five."

The whales stayed close to the surface, making them easy to see, and then slowed. Evan kept a safe distance and brought his motor down. The sun broke through the clouds, casting diamonds across the gray water.

Then, to his surprise, the mother turned and came straight toward the cat, dipping gracefully and twisting her body. Evan couldn't help but suck in his breath. The crowd downstairs oohed as she rotated just beneath the surface, changing the water to light blue, then blue green, showing off her belly, then disappearing into a glide just feet from the boat. The children on the lower deck squealed and ran to the other side. Evan and Cinderella, too, turned to watch her engage in her underwater ballet. As the whale skimmed the surface on the starboard side, she seemed to be watching them, then dove into a curve that was incredibly graceful for an eighty-foot body.

"Watch for the tail," Evan whispered.

The whale's slow descent caused the tail to take a while to flip, but when it did, the crowd below cheered, and cameras clicked. The baby followed.

Evan took a deep breath and sat back against his chair.

Remembering his dream last night, with Renece as the whale, he had a lump in his throat.

The second tour of the day went as smoothly as the first, despite the rougher waters. Although they didn't find the blue again, they spotted two more grays and one humpback. But Lia would never forget that blue. Having the largest mammal on Earth float right underneath their little boat had been surreal.

After the last of the passengers was gone, she, Cora, and Evan cleaned up the deck and galley. The skies were a dark gray now, lined with ominous clouds, and the squawk of seagulls was decidedly absent. It felt like storm weather.

Lia pushed her hair out of her eyes, turned into the wind, and split the tip money. She handed Cora hers.

"Told ya'," Cora said to Evan, holding up her fistful of bills.

His dimple came out in full force as he stowed the last line. An embarrassing pang of jealousy shot through Lia that Cora could make Evan smile like that. He hadn't smiled once to her that way, or laughed at a single thing she said, or seemed generally happy to be around her. In fact, he seemed to avoid her as best he could.

Not that she should complain. It made her plan easier, of course, to stop her schoolgirl giddiness and focus on the work at hand.

But still. It was a little disappointing.

And she was just pathetic. . . .

"Lia!"

She whirled around to see Kyle Stevens approaching the boat with his two bodyguards, or business associates, or whoever they were. He looked fabulous—he always did. He had thick, blond hair, neatly combed, that almost glowed against the gray background, and a trim figure, which was usually draped in some kind of Italian-cut suit. Today he showed off a pair of khaki trousers and an expensive-looking shirt that had hand embroidery up the sides. This was the kind of man Lia *should* be attracted to.

"Mr. Stevens." She smiled politely.

"You *have* to call me Kyle."

He leaned forward and gave her a European air-kiss, which she usually found pretentious. For him, though, she cut extra slack.

"Kyle, then."

She ushered the three of them aboard, and offered them soft drinks from the galley, wishing she'd thought to bring wine and cheese from Mr. Brimmer's store.

"You don't have anything harder?" Kyle asked. "I want to celebrate."

"Celebrate?"

"I think this is the beginning of a wonderful new relationship. Tom?" Kyle summoned the bodyguard with the shaved head and sent him back to the limo.

Within minutes, Avery yoo-hoo'd from the deck, and Lia helped her aboard. She came sans child today, wearing a beautiful coral-colored sundress that seemed inappropriate for this weather, but did look pretty.

"It might be chilly," Lia warned, watching Avery step aboard in high-heeled coral espadrilles.

"I always run a little hot, if you know what I mean." Avery giggled, glancing up at Kyle. Or maybe looking around for Evan.

Lia frowned and wondered what the hell she was in for this afternoon.

The sky darkened as the four of them circled the deck. Evan pointed out the cat's safety features and maneuverability, while Lia chimed in regarding the whale-watching upgrades Drew had installed.

Kyle was at her elbow every time she turned around, swirling his second glass of vodka, sometimes touching her at the small of her back. Avery joined him for afternoon cocktails and giggled while standing too close to Evan. To outside observers, they might have looked like two couples on a double date. Except, of course, for the way Evan kept frowning in confusion at Avery and stepping away. At one point, Avery reached up and touched his shaved face, smiling and saying something close to his chin. He'd laughed and his face had gone ruddy.

At the front of the boat, they stopped at the blue net Drew had installed that summer. Kyle tested it with the toe of his loafers.

"Will it hold me?" he asked.

"Absolutely," Lia answered.

A childlike grin swept over Kyle's face as he handed Avery

his glass, then crawled onto the net, flinging himself backward as if he were landing in a hammock. Although Lia usually saw him in the most professional contexts—often coming out of the Vampiress's office in his Armani suits—right now, with that half-inebriated smile, she could see the man the gossip papers described: one who was in a state of arrested development, partying since he was fourteen, courting women, nursing vodkas, and dancing to the edge of the danger his family wouldn't let him near.

"Come here with me." He patted the vinyl net next to him and grinned up at Lia.

Elle's words—*anything Kyle wants*—charged through her head as she eyed the sunken net. When she glanced at Evan, he looked irritated.

She tested the net with her toe and tottered toward a corner, but Kyle reached up and grabbed her wrist, yanking her down almost on top of him. She couldn't help but laugh at the childishness of it all, but, before she knew what happened, she was lying beside him, his arm around her, both of them staring at the sky.

"Can you imagine lying like this all night?" he asked breathlessly, waving his arm to sweep the vastness of the sky. "Have you ever?"

"No," Lia said, struggling to sit up. She straightened her sweater.

"Lie here with me," Kyle begged.

"Kyle, I think we need to finish the tour."

"C'mon, just until it—" Before he could even finish the sentence, the first raindrop hit his forehead. Another hit the back of her hand.

"I think our sky gazing might be over." She gave him a smile to soften the rejection, certain he wasn't used to it.

Evan offered a hand and yanked her to a standing position, then leaned toward her ear. "You don't have to do whatever he says."

Anger came up fast and furiously for Lia. She had never liked having men tell her what to do—probably why she never tolerated a boyfriend for very long and kept soft-spoken Forrest around. Bossy men—or, worse, *reprimanding* men—made her crazy. "I'm sure I know that," she hissed.

Before Evan could utter another word, she yelled to Kyle and Avery: "Let's try to see the pods before the rain hits."

They followed her under the sprinkling skies, Kyle with his arm around Avery, rubbing her arms and laughing.

Evan hesitated at the rail, but finally followed behind all of them toward the pods.

The rain began falling in earnest as the four of them crawled into the pods. There were two—one in each hull—tiny viewing stations that could each fit two people standing. The pods allowed a 180-degree view of the underwater world. This was Drew's pride and joy, and it had taken quite a bit of engineering genius—and almost all of his savings—to make it happen.

While Avery and Kyle stood in one, Lia and Evan crouched on the stairway to give them room. Kyle spun in a circle, his face alight with wonder.

"This is"—he waved his vodka toward the portholes— "*incredible.*"

A squid floated by, with a school of golden fish following. Avery gasped.

"I didn't see this before," she gushed. "I wish I'd brought Conner down here."

"Kids love it," Lia agreed.

"I think I could stay here all afternoon," Kyle said, staring in wonder at a tiny ball of krill going by.

The four of them eventually ducked back to the galley, hustling inside just as the first deluge came. Avery giggled and snuggled up to Evan in the doorway, and—even though his arms started around her in a reflex—he looked a little mortified and stepped away.

"Do your bodyguards want to come in?" Lia asked Kyle, trying not to stare at Evan and Avery.

"They'll be fine," Kyle said.

Evan lifted his eyebrow at Lia as their glances met, but Lia headed toward the galley counter, shaking the rain out of her sweater.

"Does anyone want coffee?" she asked.

"No, but I'll have another drink." Kyle reached for the Ketel One. "Miss James?"

"I'd love one." Avery finger combed the rain out of her hair. The rain made her brown curls fall in tighter ringlets around her face, and Evan seemed transfixed.

Lia was furious at herself. *Why couldn't she stop staring at him? She needed to think of Forrest. He was her type.*

As she rounded the galley counter, she snuck her phone out onto the counter and took a quick peek for any messages.

"Is everyone sure they don't want coffee?" Lia asked. "Evan?"

He shook his head, eyeing Avery's glass uneasily. He hadn't sat down—instead, he leaned against the cabinets, his arms crossed over his chest.

Lia scanned for e-mails from Forrest while Evan answered Kyle's technical questions about why catamarans are made with fiberglass hulls. The rain pounded the windows, covering the portholes in rivulets, creating a soothing sort of music in the small cabin. There were no personal e-mails from Forrest, but he had left a very-public social-media update quoting the Dalai Lama. Lia frowned.

". . . and it won't rust," Evan was saying as Lia reapproached the table, a bottled water for herself and one for him. She shoved it into his hands, and he took it with a nod of thanks.

Avery moved her reporter's notepad off the table and scooted to make space for Lia. "So how long have you been sailing, Captain Betancourt?" Avery turned her face toward Evan.

"Ah, I'm not answering those kinds of questions. This is Drew's vessel."

"But I want to describe the tour I had this week—how do you know where to spot the whales?"

"Whale-watching captains look for signs in the water— krill balls, gulls overhead. You can spot the spouts and eventually the slicks. Plus other captains radio in and help when they see something."

"So even though this is Drew's boat, you've done this professionally, too?"

Evan's eyes flicked toward Lia. She could tell he wasn't sure how much to reveal. She thought about jumping in to rescue him, but then changed her mind. She was still miffed about his reprimand earlier. And besides, she was sort of curious to hear his answers, too. She crossed her arms and stared back at him.

Evan shifted uncomfortably. "My experience comes from studying environmentalism in the Coast Guard. Drew's the pro."

"You were with the Coast Guard, man?" Kyle lit up with interest.

Evan nodded.

"How long?" Avery asked.

Evan glanced at Lia again for help, but she just gave him a small, tight-lipped smile. *You're on your own, buddy.*

He threw her a quelling look before turning back toward Avery. Lia noticed that he never looked Avery directly in the eye.

"Eight years," he finally said.

"Were you stationed on this coast?" Kyle asked.

"San Diego."

"Is that how you know the Pacific whales so well?" Avery asked.

This he answered with just a nod. He seemed to want to escape out the galley door.

"But don't you travel all over for the Coast Guard?" Kyle leaned across the table. "Alaska, maybe?"

"I was in Alaska, yeah."

"But you know Orange County, too?" Avery added.

Evan shifted against the cabinetry. "I grew up near here."

"In Sandy Cove?" she asked.

"A little north."

Avery's face lit up. "I did, too! Where north?"

Evan cleared his throat and looked like he wasn't going to answer, but finally: "Dana Point," he mumbled.

"I did, too! What high school did you go to?"

Evan's glances at Lia looked more and more desperate. "This can't be interesting to your readers."

"It's interesting to *me*." She flashed another smile.

"I didn't finish there. I ended up going way up north."

Lia fidgeted with her water bottle and pretended she wasn't listening. She knew Drew had finished school down here, so they must have been separated. She tried to remember if there had been a divorce or something in Drew's family. She remembered his parents had separated, then gotten back together. She wondered if the brothers were split up in the middle somewhere.

"And what do you do now, Captain?" Avery asked.

Evan cleared his throat. "Your readers aren't going to find this interesting. Do you have questions about the mammals?"

"How do you spot the whales—do you use underwater instruments?"

"Binoculars. Whale-watching captains don't use underwater instruments—their job is to keep the environment safe and natural for the whales to live. Sonar and things like that mess with the whale's natural communication and sense of direction."

"I sure hope you continue working with ocean mammals, Captain Betancourt. You know a lot about them." Avery's smile grew broader. "Is there a Mrs. Captain Betancourt who shares your interest in environmentalism?"

Lia turned toward Evan. Avery was good.

He squirmed again against the cabinetry. "Again, this can't be interesting to your readers."

"You'd be surprised." She beamed.

He crossed his arms tighter against his chest. "There *was* a Mrs. Betancourt, but there is no longer."

Lia lifted an eyebrow. *What?*

Both the reveal and the information surprised her. He seemed too secretive to reveal anything like that, especially to a woman getting too drunk to remember any of it and to a man for whom he held a barely veiled contempt.

And even though Lia had seen the brief glimpse of bright blue eyes and handsomeness this morning, now his hair jags had fallen back over the mask he wore, making him seem much too sullen, too dark, to have ever proposed to a woman and made a promise of happiness for a lifetime.

"Oh." Avery dropped her voice into a flirtatious coo. "*Divorced?*" she whispered.

"Dead."

They all whipped their heads back toward Evan. Lia swallowed a gasp.

"Let's leave Evan alone," Kyle interjected, slamming the galley table with a conjured enthusiasm. "I know, with what we know now, I feel comfortable having you as the charter captain on Monday—you're going to be there, right? In Drew's absence?"

Evan glanced again at Lia.

Lia opened her mouth to answer, but she was still reeling from that last bit. *Dead?* If she hadn't seen "previously married" coming, she definitely didn't see "widowed." She wanted to wrap her head around that, rewind through a few conversations they'd had, think about that framed photo he'd shoved into the drawer on his sailboat, but Kyle was pressing for an answer.

"That's one of the options," she said carefully.

"I insist." Kyle topped off his glass. His speech was becoming more labored. "I'd only feel comfortable with Drew or Evan."

Lia nodded weakly. *Whatever Kyle Stevens wants. . . .* She'd figure something out. Whether Drew was better or not, whether Evan was leaving Thursday or not, whether Sharon would let her talk to Drew tomorrow, whether her heart was hammering inappropriately for this strange man she didn't want to have feelings for, she'd figure it out.

"We'll make it happen," she said, forcing her trademark smile.

"Then what are we hanging around here for, drinking coffee?" Kyle banged the table with another breath of overenthusiasm. "Let's go out! My treat."

"Well, no one's actually drinking coffee, Mr. Stevens, and—" Lia began.

"*Kyle,*" he corrected.

"Kyle, you don't have to take us out. I think we can wrap everything up right here, and we'll have everything ready for you when your charter guests arrive."

"No way," he said, slipping into his boyish, spoiled persona. "This isn't about my charter. This is about three people I like, and who I want to take out for drinks. Evan, you in? I want to hear more about your Coast Guard service." His tongue seemed to have trouble getting around the *C* and *G* in "Coast Guard."

"It's been a long day," Evan drawled.

"How about you, beautiful?" Kyle turned to Avery.

"I'll go if Captain Betancourt goes." She threw Evan a smile that looked carnivorous.

"Buddy." Kyle grinned up at him. "Don't leave me hangin'. We've got two of the prettiest women in Orange County right here, and I want to take us all to my new restaurant, and feed you a steak dinner. C'mon . . ."

Evan shook his head.

"Lia? I guess it's just you and me, then?"

Evan raised an eyebrow.

She was caught. The Vampiress's words, *anything Kyle Stevens wants*, were warring with Evan's, *you don't have to do whatever he says*, and she stood frozen. In reality, she didn't want to go. Kyle had clearly had too much to drink, and some of the stories she'd seen in the gossip magazines had begun to float back to her.

She knew the restaurant he was referring to. She'd done the marketing for it. It was more of a nightclub than a restaurant, and she knew there were fourteen private curtained areas along the back that were half bedroom, half dining—several round ottoman/beds draped in purple velvet, with techno sounds, tray after tray of Grey Goose, and just enough food to keep guests from passing out. She wondered if this was where Kyle meant to bring them.

"I can't," she said hurriedly. There was only so much she was willing to do for the Vampiress.

"*Leeee-yaaaa*," Kyle admonished, low, like he was speaking to a naughty child. He pulled his phone out and began punching numbers.

"I have a lot to do here," she rambled. "We have to close the boat up. Right, Evan?"

Evan was studying Kyle.

". . . And we have to get ready for tomorrow," Lia continued, "and—"

"Yeah, Elle?" Kyle said into the phone.

Elle? Lia's heart flipped in her chest.

"I've got Lia here in front of me, and I'm inviting her to my club, but she says she has too much work to do. Can you give her the night off?" He winked at Lia.

Lia wanted to kill him.

If Elle didn't kill her first.

"Yeah, yeah, she's right here. . . ." He handed his phone to Lia. *Oh God.*

Lia took the phone and turned away from the group.

"Who's Elle?" she heard Evan growl as she stepped toward the back of the galley.

"Hello?"

"Lia, what's going on?" Elle's voice was already in its trademark note of intolerance.

"We're on Drew's boat, and—"

"He sounds *drunk*."

She glanced back at the table. "A little," she whispered.

"Can't you give him what he wants?"

"I really can't. He wants to go out, and we have to close up the boat, and—"

"I thought you said your little Sandy Cove friend was going to take care of everything. For the love of God, Lia, if you screw this up—"

"No, no. It's going fine. It's going great. It's just that—"

"I'm getting a *full report* from Kyle tomorrow, do you hear me? I want him telling me you were the most *gracious* hostess, and that Sandy Cove is not a hovel, and that I gave you the night off, and you were able to deliver. You said you could handle this. And this is *easy* compared to the Paris work. His father just set up a possible meeting with me in two weeks. So show me you can handle it. *Do this for me. Now.*" The phone went dead.

Lia stared at it in her hand.

Would Elle really demand that she go *out* with Kyle? And do whatever he wanted? A sickening thud fell into her stomach. But she'd figure this out. Deep breath . . .

"So whaddaya say? I know you have the night off." Kyle grinned as she handed back his phone.

She glanced up at Evan. He was waiting for her answer, too, with cocked eyebrow.

"I can't, Kyle. Evan and I have a lot to do here."

"Whaddaya need?" Kyle scooted out of the dinette. "I can help with any business work, and my guys out there can help with any deck work. But damn, it's raining!" He bent to stare out the porthole. "Whaddaya gonna do? Wash the deck? C'mon, let's lock up and we can all go. Maybe we can talk more about this boat."

He was a whirlwind of energy, sweeping his vodka bottles, collecting the glasses, touching Avery on the shoulder.

Talk more about the boat? Would he consider *investing*?

Even so, a sober conversation would be smarter. "I can't. My ankle is still healing, and—"

"*Leee-yaaaa.* Nonsense. We can make this work. Avery, Evan—I want you to join us."

In the manner of a man used to getting what he wanted, he took over the room, shouting for his guys to help Evan with anything he needed, looking around the galley for anything he could put up or clean. Avery gathered her notebook and looked ready to go, apparently forgetting her earlier conditions regarding Evan.

Evan hadn't budged.

"She doesn't want to go," Evan said into the whirlwind.

Kyle looked back with something that looked like amusement. "I think Lia can speak for herself."

"I think she has."

The two men regarded one another carefully.

Lia gaped. She'd never had men speaking for her in such a way, as if she weren't in the room. But, for some reason, right before the flash of indignity came a thrilling tingle when she saw Evan's jaw muscle dance.

For that, she hated herself even more.

"Are you guys *kidding*?" She stepped between them.

She had to get a handle on this situation. She had to get a handle on *herself.* She had to stop ogling this man's biceps and stop being attracted to someone who thought he needed to save her. Men like that were trouble. Men like that thought of women as "the fairer sex," dainty flowers that needed to be saved. They thought of women as . . . well, as *Cinderellas.*

Lia whirled on Evan. "I'm *fine.* Stop speaking for me."

Evan held his arms up in surrender. "Then tell him you don't want to go."

Some perverse thing in Lia reared its ugly head. It was the same seed of rebellion that had always gotten her in trouble as a kid: that need to think independently of whoever was in front of her. And maybe it was born of some fear of what Evan was making her feel, and what kind of woman she was when she was around him.

"Maybe that's not how I feel," she found herself blurting.

Evan lifted his eyebrow. "Is that so?"

Of course that was not so. But the perverse part of her that wanted him to be wrong, and wanted to remind herself that he was a caveman, kept talking: "That's so."

"I guess I misunderstood."

"I guess you did."

Kyle clapped his hands in front of him. "Well, good, then. That's solved. The ladies and I are going. I'll have my guys swing the car around."

"I'll go too, then," Evan mumbled.

"What?" Lia whirled on him again.

"If you're going, I'll go."

"No! You don't need to go. You said you didn't want to."

"Great! Everyone's going." Kyle stepped up and threw his arm around Evan's shoulders, barely making it across, steering him away from Lia's protest. "I can't wait to hear about the Coast Guard. Were you there in San Diego when they rescued those marines whose Hornet crashed in the ocean?"

"Which time?" Evan murmured.

Kyle waved the bodyguards in so they could hold their umbrellas over Avery and Lia as they all stepped out, and Evan moved out from Kyle's bro-hug and ushered everyone in front of him so he could lock the door.

He refused to meet Lia's eyes as she stomped through the doorway.

CHAPTER
Ten

E van had no idea how he ended up in the back of a limo with a spoiled playboy, the ghost of Renece, and a cartoon-Disney-princess-come-to-life, but here he was.

And the cartoon princess was wreaking havoc; all kinds of old parts were waking up.

They were the parts that made his blood course faster when a spirited woman challenged him; the parts that made his blood boil when he saw a playboy jerk pushing her; the parts that made his heart pound when he saw a stampede of dolphins through someone else's eyes for the first time; and the parts that stood at attention when he caught a glimpse of a thong band on a pretty body crawling across a viewing net.

But he didn't want those parts to come alive. He wanted to keep everything dead, the way they had been. The way they should be. Guilt was gnawing a pit in his gut. . . .

He ran his hand down his face as the limo pulled into the next parking lot, then stared out the rain-soaked window. He was in deep crap.

But as much as he didn't want to be around the temptation of Cinderella, he couldn't let her go alone in this limo, into this night, into a club with a guy like Stevens who was getting more sauced by the minute.

"Is it this one?" Kyle leaned forward to look out the window.

"Yes," Cinderella said as they pulled alongside the palm-tree-lined, '60s-style apartment complex and next to a pebbled staircase that must have led up to her place.

Evan clenched his jaw. He'd hated that she'd given out her address so freely, but Stevens had offered to let them run into their respective homes to change after such a long day on the boat. As they'd snaked through the tiny streets of Sandy Cove, Stevens kept humming about how "quaint" it was.

Evan had showered on his boat in two minutes flat and had changed, although not into anything dressy—just a clean pair of jeans and a shirt. He wasn't the type to have "clubwear" on hand. Or even decent shoes. He had one suit—the one he'd worn to Luke's and Renece's funeral—but it was shoved into the back of his closet, never to be worn again. He only kept it there for his own funeral, which—when he'd put it there—had felt like it could come any day.

"Take your time, sweetheart," Kyle said.

Both men turned to watch Cinderella's ass exit the car as the limo driver held an umbrella for her, but Evan hated himself for it and lowered his eyes.

Stevens did a double take, then turned toward Avery.

"Hey, beautiful, why don't you go help Lia? Evan and I need to chat."

Avery bobbed her head in her pliant way—even her pliancy reminded him of Renece—and let the limo driver open the door for her.

"You look like you need cheering up," Kyle said once they were alone in the silence of the car.

"I'm fine."

"Sorry to hear about your wife." He grabbed two highball glasses out of the drink rack. "Did it happen recently?"

"Two years ago."

Kyle held out one of the glasses but Evan shook his head.

Before Kyle spoke again, vodka splashed into his glass, along with his favorite tonic. "Must be hard."

Evan looked out the window. He didn't bother to answer.

People had tried to tell him the "right" way to grieve—that he must feel this, or should feel that—but it was all bullshit. He felt how he felt. And it took as long as it took.

"Seems Avery might want to cheer you up." Kyle's smirk was probably meant to be friendly. "I think you and Avery could have a good time together. Or I could set you up with someone else if you want."

"I'm not a charity case, Stevens."

"I'm not saying that. It's just that my place is filled with beautiful women. And I want to give you one. Any one. And it's not just the women—these steaks at my place, they're"— he kissed his fingertips. "Anything you want, it's on me. I admire you Coast Guard guys."

Evan lifted an eyebrow. So that might be why he was being so friendly. Evan had met men before like this—adventure-seeking guys who were never able to find their own adventure, for whatever reason, and hung around rescue guys, or guys who courted danger in some other way, asking for stories.

"I always wanted to join the Coast Guard," Kyle confirmed, "but my parents would have killed me. My dad is J.P. Stevens." He looked up to make sure the name rang a bell.

It did. "J.P. Stevens" was on every building site in Orange County.

"They were pretty protective," Kyle said. "Wanted me to stay clean and safe and in one piece to take over the family business."

Evan nodded slowly.

Kyle looked out the window at the rain for a minute. "So which girl do you want?"

The leather creaked under Evan's weight. "I don't think the women are here to be divided up like playing cards."

"I think you're wrong. Avery's a sure hand, if you haven't noticed. And I think I could get a flush with Lia, if you don't want to . . ."

A flush shot up around Evan's collar. Why he felt so protective of a woman he barely knew, he had no idea, but there it was. And it's not like she was the type who needed protecting. Or wanted it. Her flashing eyes and thrown-back shoulders earlier had been clear on that point. But, embarrassingly, her toughness was exactly what was turning him on.

"What do you want with her?" he finally asked.

Kyle studied him. "*Are* you?"

"What?"

"Interested? I can't get a read on you two, if you're"—he made a coupling gesture with his fingers.

Evan's first instinct was to reach over and smash Kyle in the face, but then it occurred to him that Kyle's confusion might work to his advantage—or Lia's, anyway.

"It's complicated," he mumbled.

"So you *are* . . . oh, hey, man, I didn't know. I didn't understand. . . ." He laughed nervously. "I'll take Avery. I like her, too. I just wanted us to all have a good time tonight, but if there's some history with you and . . ." He made a helpless gesture with his hand.

"What do you want with the boat?"

"The boat?"

"Yes. Drew's boat."

"Well, I . . . I was thinking I might like one. When I saw it today, I thought, yeah, man, I might want one of these. I can't believe that awesome vessel is hidden in a little place like Sandy Cove. But I'd just call Hobie and have them design one for me. I don't need to buy your brother's."

"Lia thinks you want to invest."

"*Invest*? Nah, I don't need to do that. Unless . . . do you *need* investors?"

"I think Drew's interested in that."

"Oh. Well . . ." Kyle stared out the window. "I would consider that."

"You can discuss it with Lia."

"I will. Maybe tonight." His smile, still sloppy from all the Ketel One, was hard to read, but it didn't look like it had good intentions involved. Or even business.

"Not tonight."

Kyle smirked. "You don't look like you're planning on closing any deals yourself, Captain."

"She has a boyfriend."

Kyle laughed. "Doesn't seem like a small problem like that would get in your way. But how about if I take my cue from you? If you seem interested in Lia tonight, I'll stay away. Just send me a sign. Otherwise, I might like to see where things go."

The door opened abruptly and Avery slid in next to Evan, a new scent swirling around her, something claustrophobia-inducing.

Lia took the space next to Kyle, but Evan noted she sat farther away, some space between their knees. She'd changed into a dress, but it didn't look like a club dress. Looked sort of like a work dress, actually. Evan blew out a relieved breath and struggled not to notice her legs any more than he already had. Kyle was watching him carefully.

"And we're off," Kyle said, toasting his drink and throwing his smarmy smile around the limo. "It'll take us a half hour to get there. Who wants a drink?"

The sound of the pounding rain gave way to pounding techno tunes as the four of them made their way through a back door off an alleyway into what looked like a concrete hallway.

Lia shook the rain out of her hair, while Kyle swiped drops off his Italian loafers, then turned to the rest of them. "Ready?" His grin was filled with anticipation.

The shaved-head bodyguard swept them past a velvet curtain.

The *boof-a-boof-a-boof-a* techno rhythm pounded in her head as Lia's heels clicked across the floating floor. The room wasn't crowded—it was still pretty early—but tiny clusters of young women and men were already at the bar, most clad in black, the women with tight, short skirts and long silky hair that only the under-twenty-five crowd could pull off.

Lia tugged at her own sensible work dress and felt, for the first time ever perhaps, stuffy.

She shifted her attention to the décor: Here's where she could be proud. She'd suggested half of this color scheme when Kyle first came aboard with their firm, and it played out beautifully. Purple lights danced across the floating floor, patterning out the word "Plush." She'd seen it in photos numerous times, especially when she was putting together Plush's website, but seeing it in person was stunning.

On the other side of the dance floor was a raised, half-circle stage made up of hologram trees that stretched to the ceiling—all in shades of dark green and dark purple, with white lights touching their tips like snow. Some of the trees changed color and throbbed to the *boof-a-boof-a-boof-a* beat. Some of the young women danced through them.

"It's beautiful!" Avery exclaimed.

"Lia had a lot to do with it." Kyle smiled at her.

Avery threw Lia a new wide-eyed look of admiration.

Evan had gone back into sullen mode, acting as if they were taking him to prison. He looked around at the room as if he'd just stepped out of solitary confinement and was seeing civilization for the first time—a mixture of wonder and horror. He hadn't said a word to her since they'd left.

"Some of these areas open at ten," Kyle yelled over the music, pointing to a series of back rooms closed off by curtains. "Although I guess Lia knows that."

"The Den at Ten," Lia said, offering a tentative smile and trying not to imagine what probably went on back there. The models for the design of those alcoves were pictures of old opium dens from the eighteen hundreds. He'd had fourteen circular, tufted, velvet ottomans installed in each one that guests could use as tables, or sitting areas, or beds. Seven of the dens were outfitted with hookah pipes, and Plush boasted fifty flavors that Lia had detailed on the website.

Avery's fingers hooked around Evan's biceps as they made it past the last hookah den. Lia pretended not to notice.

Kyle ushered them through the next curtain, where a bar made entirely of ice sprawled for fifty feet. "Plush" was carved into the front and sides, with ice sculptures positioned every ten feet that took on the shape of female torsos, reaching toward the lavender lit ceiling. Lia knew that Kyle had this bar carved by a team of ice sculptors every night. Rumor had it he requested his most recent lovers—whoever the current cluster was—to stand in as models for his sculptors, and the bodies were always changing. Licking was encouraged.

"Why don't you guys get a drink?" Kyle said. "I'll have my table set up for four." He called his bartender over and ordered something into the bartender's ear, pointing to the three of them. "I need to check on something. Avery?" Kyle held out his arm, and Avery switched from holding Evan to holding Kyle. Lia wanted to roll her eyes.

"We'll be right back," Kyle said, snaking Avery through the bar.

Their disappearance left a gap between Lia and Evan at the bar, but Evan didn't close it. Instead he seemed to be counting the exit doors.

"You didn't have to come," Lia shouted over the music.

Evan nodded once. He looked like he wanted to be anywhere but there.

An old-fashioned cigarette girl with a pillbox hat and bright purple feather dipping down over fake eyelashes approached with a box of electronic cigarettes. She struck a pose in ridiculously high platform heels and fishnet stockings and thrust the box that hung around her neck toward Evan. She was dark and elegant, with long hair slicked into a loose ponytail down one side of her body. He shook his head and forced his gaze away. She seemed to find that amusing, and reached out to touch his chin and bring it back to her attention. "Are you sure?" she seemed to say, if Lia read her lips correctly.

Evan nodded, and she strutted away with a flirtatious smile.

"Why did you?" Lia shouted. She was suddenly hyper-aware that her loud voice and demeanor were not at all as cute and flirty as the pillbox girl.

A bartender slid two drinks toward them, some kind of dark red wine that almost looked like blood.

Evan stared at the drinks but didn't touch his. "Why did I what?"

"Why did you come?"

Lia brought the drink to her lips. It smelled like port, perhaps—sultry and rich. It slid down her throat, thick and silky, with a warm aftertaste. She closed her eyes to enjoy it.

When she opened them, he was staring right at her. "That, maybe," he said.

"What?"

He shook his head.

The music pounded behind them for almost a full minute before he spoke again. "I don't trust him."

"You came because you don't *trust* him?"

"I wanted to come for you and Avery, to make sure you'd be okay with him."

Fury flooded her veins again, but this time it was joined by a warmth through her scalp and cheeks that could have been the wine.

She leaned forward so her harsh whisper could be heard above the music. "Evan, *I don't need you to protect me.* I thought I made that clear."

"You did."

"This is my *client.*"

"I understand."

"I do this for a *living.*"

He nodded.

"But you still came?"

"Didn't change my distrust."

She leaned back and took another sip of the racy drink. The wine filled the back of her throat and slid down into her stomach again, warming her all over.

"Why is this any of your business?" she asked.

He stared at his fists for a second, then shook his head. "It isn't."

"Exactly."

She leaned back. Another sip. Fire in her belly . . . fireworks in her brain . . .

"I'm experienced with him," she went on. "As a client. I know what he wants, and what my boss wants him to want, and we know how to handle him."

"Got it." Evan was frowning at her curiously.

She took another deep sip. Swirled her glass. "We've gotta . . . My boss . . . She *knows* him. And *anything he wants,* you know?"

The lines in Evan's forehead deepened and he lifted his own glass. Sniffed it.

"She wants me . . . to do *anything* . . . I mean, *anything* he wants. . . ." The thoughts were getting muddied in her head for some reason. Wasn't that what Evan had told her? That she didn't have to do whatever Kyle wanted? And didn't the Vampiress say the opposite thing? So why was she telling Evan this? And were those ice sculptures moving? Maybe they were just melting. "I mean, I know you said . . ." She strained to remember if she was arguing a point or not.

She reached for her glass again, but he slid his hand over it.

"Let's hold off on this a minute. Bartender?" He motioned for two waters.

Before she could voice her indignation, or even snatch her glass back, he leaned forward and locked her gaze with the eyes she forgot were so blue.

"Listen." He dropped his voice. "He might want to invest in Drew's boat, so you don't need to convince him of anything tonight. Why don't you just stick with me, and we can enjoy dinner, then I'll get you home."

"How do you *know*?" Her mouth had a hard time getting around the *n* sound. Dang, what was she drinking?

"He told me in the limo. I asked if he was—"

"E-*van*!"

He had the decency to look sheepish.

"Stop *speaking* for me! Stop *protecting* me. Stop doing my job for me. Stop taking my wineglass away. Stop talking to my client about my business. I'm *fine*."

He studied her for a second, then shifted uncomfortably and looked away.

"You got it?"

His jaw muscle danced as he nodded, but he didn't meet her eyes.

"You need to stop this caveman behavior."

"*Caveman* behavior?"

"Yes, caveman behavior. This overprotectiveness. It's unbecoming."

He flashed her a quick, angry look.

"Why do you feel the need to do those things?" She really wanted to know. Not just from Evan but from all men.

He shook his head and looked away. Lines crossed his forehead.

"No, I really want to know. Do I seem stupid to you? Too 'Cinderella'?"

He switched his scowl to the bar and stared at his fists.

"I need some words here."

He reached for his water glass, not seeming like he was going to answer, but finally he took a deep breath. "I don't think you're stupid."

"Then what is it?"

"I think you're trusting."

Ah . . . *Now* they were getting somewhere. She knew a euphemism when she heard one.

"You mean gullible, don't you?"

"Did I say gullible?"

"No, but maybe you don't say what you mean."

"I say what I mean."

"So say more. You think I'm trusting and what?"

He looked away.

"Trusting and what?"

"Optimistic."

She leaned back in her seat. She was getting good at this. Interrogating Captain Betancourt. It was kind of fun. And, for some reason, she was starving for these answers.

"So is that bad? Optimism?" she asked.

"It can be."

"Why is that bad?"

"It can make you look at the world with unrealistic expectations. Make you think it's filled with good things when really it's filled with bad."

"So you came tonight to protect me and Avery from being too optimistic?"

He shrugged.

"Too trusting of Kyle?"

"Probably."

"You're going to *save* me from Kyle?"

"It's possible."

"A successful, wealthy, Armani-wearing Harvard grad? You're going to save me from him?"

Evan sighed and stared at his glass. "None of those things makes him necessarily trustworthy."

"Maybe you're just too suspicious."

"Maybe I am."

The richness of the wine, or maybe the intense look in his eyes, or maybe the sudden loneliness she saw around the lines of his mouth made a heat simmer low in her belly, and she took a step away from the conversation. Some kind of intensity was building between them, and it made her feel like she was coming too close to a flame.

"Listen, I don't want to make you mad," he said.

She had to lean in to hear him. It sounded almost like an

apology. And also like something that didn't fall naturally from his lips.

"Maybe I'm concerned about Drew, too," he added.

She talked her heart back into a normal rhythm and took a deep breath. Okay. That could be true. He could be overstepping all kinds of boundaries because he was a naturally suspicious person, *and* because of his brother. That made sense, right? She struggled to organize a few columns of logic in her head.

While she waited for a hopeful return to sobriety, she checked Evan out. Although maybe checking him out with a slight buzz wasn't the best idea. His hanging hair was looking sexier and sexier, especially the way he snapped it out of his eyes with some kind of vengeance. His dark lashes, now lowered to his water glass, were longer than she'd first noticed. Through the darkened room, through the sultry music, he looked like passion personified.

He had changed into a dark button-down shirt, rolled up at the sleeves, and a pair of darker jeans. She liked the vague rebellion of the jeans. It felt almost like what she was doing, with the work dress. Forrest would have been ultra-respectful in Kyle's swanky club—probably a bit over-the-top, in fact—wearing a pressed shirt with some kind of stylish, unbuttoned vest. And Lia probably would have complimented him on his good taste. But right now, for some reason, all she wanted was to run her hand up Evan's irreverent jeans and lick his insolent five-o'clock shadow.

"Hello." A strange-looking host suddenly arrived at Lia's shoulder. "Mr. Stevens and Miss James are having dinner in a private den in the dance club. He said he'd love for you both to join them. They're in Den Thirteen."

Lia lifted her eyebrow at Evan, but he didn't seem surprised.

"Your steak is already served, sir." The host bowed slightly. "Come with me."

"You already ordered steak?" she whispered as they left the bar.

"Stevens seemed insistent on enjoying his club's specialties, including the girls and the steak. It *has* been a while."

"Eating steak?"

The corner of his mouth crooked upward. "Yes, Cinderella, eating steak. What did you think I meant?"

Eating steak. Of course. Of course that's what she meant. . . .

She cleared her throat and concentrated on following the host. She wanted to turn and make more casual conversation with Evan—ask him more about sailing, about why he was away for so long, about his dead wife, about his relationship with Drew. But the clip with which they were walking, along with the loud music, made conversation difficult.

Besides, he seemed more interested in a good meal right now than in her.

And besides that, she was too buzzed to keep her wits about her with a man who was causing a tingling between her legs.

She didn't know whether to dread or look forward to Den Thirteen.

Eleven

Evan dragged his feet all the way to the den, keeping his head down and his hand in his pocket as they carved their way through the nauseating beat and the crowds that had suddenly filled the dance floor.

Cinderella peeked behind Curtain Thirteen and then waved him in. His stomach clenched. This was not going to go well.

For one, Cinderella was drunk. Well, not drunk, but leaning toward it. He didn't know what the hell kind of wine Kyle had ordered, but it was knocking her on her ass. And he didn't want her to have so many defenses down if they were going to see Stevens. Especially with her willingness to trust anyone with a Harvard degree and nice shoes.

Two, Stevens was probably smashed. And capable of anything.

And three, Evan was completely turned on. And he probably shouldn't be trusted with her, either. He didn't know if it was all these waitresses in short skirts, the women at the bar licking the ice sculptures, or his memory of Cinderella's flashing eyes when her anger was riled, but he'd been aroused for the last half hour. And these ice sculptures weren't helping.

"Lia! Evan! Come in!" Kyle held out his arm and motioned to two spaces around a purple ottoman that seemed to be used as a dining table. Candles in colored-glass jars covered the room. In the center of the ottoman sat two more bottles of the same wine Kyle had sent to Evan and Lia. "Meet Sara and Holden," he said.

Lia and Evan nodded to each of them. Sara's pretty face was illuminated in candlelight. She seemed to be in her early twenties, and smiled at Evan before she turned back to young Holden, who seemed about her age.

Lia lowered herself to a bright pink pillow with gaudy fringe all around it, and Evan took one beside her after scooting it away a bit. The techno dance music drifted through the curtain. Avery had her eyes closed and bounced a bare foot. She pulled a tube from a three-foot-high bejeweled hookah pipe that sat just behind her and giggled as she sent a series of smoke rings into the air. They glowed a sort of yellow against the burning candles.

Kyle wasn't paying much attention to Evan or Lia anymore, having turned his attention back to Avery's mouth. Maybe this wouldn't be so bad. Evan could pretend this was a normal dinner, then get the women out of here.

He took in the steaks and small bowls of food and candles across the ottoman. "Strange way to eat," he said to Holden, who was the only one looking at him.

"It's meant to engage all your senses," Holden said, throwing a grin toward Sara. "You can touch one another while eating, eat with your hands, lean in together, feed one another. . . ." His explanation was lost as he found Sara's mouth.

Shit.

Evan glanced at Lia, who was gaping at the couple, but then she adjusted her gaze toward the dinner.

"Have something." Kyle slipped his cell into his pocket and leaned toward Cinderella, letting poor Avery slide off his shoulder. Avery laughed with undue hilarity. Her toes kicked elegantly to the music. Evan ran his hand down his face. This was going to be an adventure.

Kyle called a few more waitresses in and made sure everyone had what they needed. Holden continued to feed Sara. Evan wolfed down his steak with a singular focus. Although the steak was the best thing he'd had in months, he really just wanted to get everyone out of here. He glanced at Lia's plate a few times. She was hardly eating. He wished she'd eat faster to offset the booze and so they could leave, but he didn't dare say anything. She'd called him a caveman one too many times already.

"The band that comes on at one is amazing," Kyle announced. "Have you guys heard of Indecency?"

"I love to dance!" Avery said, offering a short shimmy to prove it. "Are they a dance band?"

"They are," Kyle said. "You'll love them. And the girls start dancing at one—the go-go dancers in the holograms. You have to see it. I want to find one for Evan."

Cinderella lifted her head.

"I can go-go for Evan!" Avery said, giggling.

Kyle laughed. "Can you get your babysitter to stay later?"

"I could call and—"

"No!" Evan interjected. "No, we need to get home."

Kyle looked at him as if he were the crusty old dean, then motioned for another waitress. "Send Kendra in, will you?" The waitress nodded and left.

Kyle turned toward Lia. "So did you and Evan have a romantic drink at the bar? Or maybe a dance?"

Shit.

"*Romantic*?" Lia laughed. "No, but it was delicious. Decadent. And we didn't dance, but we enjoyed your bar. It's beautiful, by the way."

Kyle slid a glance at Evan.

Shit again.

"Well, our DJ is fabulous," Kyle said. "His name is Master X. I don't think you can leave without one dance." He stood and held his hand out to her.

"We really have to get going, Kyle," Evan said, pushing his plate back.

"No, look, I ordered dessert for everyone." Kyle motioned to the waitresses who entered with lavish dessert trays, piled high with all kinds of cakes and chocolate-covered tall things. Avery, Lia, Holden, and Sara all leaned forward and let out small exclamations.

Kyle's eyes met Evan's. "Just stay long enough for dessert."

Crap. Kyle leaned over and said something into Lia's ear.

"We'll be right back," he said, lifting Lia gracefully in the candlelight. She gazed up at him. Evan couldn't even look at them. It occurred to him that he'd never made her look that happy once in two days. . . . Except maybe when she'd been looking at the dolphins . . . But he hadn't brought her that; nature had.

Kyle dragged Cinderella through the curtain, and Evan felt a crushing sense of defeat. He simply stared at Holden and Sara, who were going at it now across four colored pillows, grinding to the techno music. Avery had moved back to a fainting couch in the back of the den, taking another drag on the pipe. She lay against the cushions, eyes closed, a deep grin on her face.

Evan glanced at the curtain with increasing unease.

"Avery?" he called. "Where are your shoes?"

"Captain Betancourt, this is the most incredible place." She rolled onto her stomach, tucking her fist under her chin. "Don't you think?"

"How much have you had to drink, Avery?" He looked under the ottoman for her shoes, hoping they hadn't slid underneath the energetic young Holden and Sara.

"Just a little. But this drink . . . the food . . . the banana hookah . . ." Her hand waved across the room. "It's incredible. I haven't felt this delicious in *years*."

Another cigarette girl came through the curtain into the den, this one with the same hat and feather the last cigarette girl wore, but a different color. Her long blond hair was twisted into some kind of promise down one side of her breasts, which were being pushed upward in an almost cartoonish way from the tight dress she wore. The candlelight played across her skin, but Evan's attention was diverted to a deck of cards she pulled out of her box and shoved beneath his nose.

"Mr. Stevens wants to know if you're ready to cut the deck yet."

Evan frowned for a second, staring at the deck, then clenched his jaw.

That fucker . . .

Evan managed to pry Avery from the couch, supporting her as she crumbled against his shoulder, and finally found her shoes behind the fainting couch.

She leaned against him like a sandbag as he helped her across the blinking floor, which was shoulder-to-shoulder people now. Couples bumped into him from every direction, and the *boom-qua, boom-qua, boom-qua* tune pounded through his head as Avery kept slipping down his hip. "Avery, keep moving. Like you're dancing," he shouted.

Damn. Getting her through this crowd, out to a car, and into her own front door was going to be a miracle tonight.

He finally got out to the concrete hallway and was relieved to see one of the bodyguards he remembered. This was the shaved-head one.

"Hey, uh—Tom, right? Remember me? Whale-watching boat?"

"Oh, hey, man."

"Your boss called a car for me and Avery here, and Lia, who was on the boat with us."

"Oh, yeah. It's here." He guided Evan toward the front door, past the line that still wove through the velvet ropes and into the rain.

Evan pressed back. "No. I need to wait for Lia."

"You and your lady here can take the car, and we'll call another one."

Evan blew out a breath. There was no fucking way he was leaving Lia here with Kyle.

The car pulled up, and Evan made an attempt to keep Avery from tripping over the complicated shoes he probably didn't buckle right. One of the straps flapped in the rain, and she stepped into a puddle and squealed. Her shoe toppled off.

It took what felt like an eternity, but he finally unloaded her into the backseat of the car and got her address deciphered.

"Your boss will be grateful," he told the driver. "He's been with her all night, but he wanted me to take her out here to you." Evan hoped that was enough culpability to put on Kyle to ensure this driver got her home. He slammed the door, tapped once on the roof, and turned back toward the club.

Now to get Lia.

The music throbbed low in her belly as Lia leaned against the metal rail that surrounded the now-crowded ice bar, staring at the nearest melting torso. Kyle was swapping her drink out for "something else."

She took a deep breath. Maybe this wasn't the best idea. Maybe Evan was partially right: Kyle probably wasn't above trying to get her into bed. On the one hand, she was flattered: He could have anyone in the county, surely. But on the other hand, she was insulted: She wanted him to admire her for her work and her brilliant marketing plans. She wasn't another body to be commemorated with one night of dripping ice water.

"Here we go," he said, sidling up to her with a huge glass filled with a dark burgundy drink.

"Is this what I had at dinner?"

"You said you liked it." A worry line dipped his eyebrow.

"I did. Is this it?"

"Yes. I wouldn't be a gentleman if I didn't admit it's a little strong—it's a tawny port. We found it on a vineyard in Portugal."

She took a sip. The richness filled her throat again. "It's fabulous."

His grin took up his whole face. "It pleases me that you like it."

It didn't go to her head quite as quickly as before, thank goodness. A full stomach helped. But it still swirled more than most. She'd have to watch herself. Small sips. Checking Evan out while buzzed—who would never in a million years make a move on her—was one thing, but losing herself around Kyle would be something different.

"So you travel to Portugal?" she asked.

"I travel all over. Have you ever been?"

"No, but I'd like to. I'd like to go to France. And Spain. And Italy."

"Where have you been?"

"Nowhere."

"*Nowhere*? Lia, say it ain't so."

"Sad, huh? Elle has me working like a coal miner. I told myself I'd do a different country every year on my birthday, starting right after college. I wanted to just show up to an airport every year and choose off the board. But that plan never materialized, since I started working for Elle as soon as I graduated."

"When's your birthday?"

"December."

"I'm calling Elle tomorrow and insisting she give you time off. And I'm taking you to Portugal in December."

Lia smiled. If only life were that easy.

"So what's this I hear about a boyfriend?" He stepped closer, his arm around her back, half trapping her.

Lia took another sip of wine. "Where did you hear I had a boyfriend?"

"Your boat captain mentioned it. Warning me off you, I think."

A warmth slid through her body. Easy, girl. She didn't know what to react to first—that Kyle was clearly flirting, that he and Evan had been discussing her behind her back, or that Evan had been thinking of her somehow in the context of dating.

That last thought—or maybe the richness of the port—sent the warmth from her stomach to her thighs, and settled right between her legs.

Damn it. She didn't want to have these reactions to Evan.

She put the wineglass down.

"So where is this boyfriend now?" Kyle's breath blew the tendrils at her hairline.

She inched away. "Bora Bora."

"*Bora Bora*? He's got a beautiful girlfriend who wants to see the world, and he's alone in Bora Bora? I don't think that's very smart."

Lia refused to be egged on. She stood straighter, but the wine caused her to lose her balance and she gripped the rail, her hand slipping and touching the ice. Kyle watched all the movements but didn't lean in to help.

"He can do what he wants." Her mouth was having trouble forming *W*s now. "We have a very mature relationship."

"Mature?" Kyle's mouth twisted. "Maybe you need something that's more fun than mature."

"No, mature is great."

"Mature sounds boring."

She laughed against her better judgment. Maybe it was, a little. She'd certainly never accuse Forrest of being too exciting. And they'd never had wild sex. In fact, they'd never had sex at all. She'd never even had great sex before, with anyone—always chalking it up to her inexperience or her trepidation with the partners she'd finally picked. She assumed it was something on the horizon for her, like the promotion to Paris. Maybe when she was finally relaxed, settled, had climbed all her ladders. Forrest, honestly, didn't seem like the most likely candidate, but she was hoping.

"I want to make you happy, Lia. I'm starting to see you as a challenge. You've done a lot for me, with this club, and the charter you planned—I want to pay you back. What will it take? Portugal in December?"

She shook her head. She didn't need anything from Kyle. She needed it from the Vampiress. Paris. The raise. The final feeling of "success."

He smiled sadly. "Okay, I see you're too 'mature' for me. How about investing in your friend's boat?"

Lia's head snapped up. The quick movement caused the room to spin, but she was pretty sure she'd heard what she thought she heard.

"You'd *invest*? In Drew's boat?"

"Sure. I was going to buy my own, but if you guys need an investor, why not just do that? Then I don't have to concern myself with the upkeep."

"That would be . . . *great*." Lia couldn't believe her luck. "Can we discuss it on Monday? Get all the details straight? I'm not in the right mind for business right now, to be honest."

He removed the glass from her hand and set it on the ice. "What are you in the right mind for?"

"Kyle, this isn't—this isn't what I mean. You and I have a *wonderful* relationship right now. I admire you and love working with you, but I want to maintain our professionalism."

"Of course. I respect you immensely. And I respect your mature relationship." He threw her a smile that suggested otherwise. "But how about a kiss? Your mature relationship certainly has room for a kiss between friends, right? We can just say we both had too much to drink."

A sickening taste rolled into the back of her throat. *Did she just sell a share of Drew's boat for a kiss?* Part of her wanted to laugh at herself for thinking it was a big deal, but the other part was sending warning bells through her head.

Kyle turned to the bartender. "Hey, get me one of those, too." He cocked his head toward her drink. "And give mine an extra boost, Cole."

"What's the extra boost?" she asked. The sickening feeling in her stomach continued.

"Ah, don't make me feel bad, Lia. I'm not as mature as you. I like my recreational drugs. Helps me sleep at night, anyway. Let's go back to the den."

"Kyle, I don't want to do that."

"We'll get something more private." He pulled his cell phone out of his pocket and started punching in numbers.

"Kyle, no. It seems inappropriate to sell—"

"*Lee-yaaaa.*" Kyle scowled at her. "It's just a kiss. Don't be silly." He turned to his phone. "Salvador? What dens are open?"

She felt a blush heat her cheeks. Maybe she was silly. He didn't want to *marry* her for goodness' sake. And it wasn't *sex*.

"*No*, Kyle."

He raised an eyebrow. Paused. Without another word, and his eyes trained on her, he hung up on Salvador and slipped his phone back in his pocket.

"All right, beautiful. You're a challenge. I like that about you." He reached for the two wineglasses and nodded his thanks to Cole. "Let's go back, and see if Avery and Evan are ready. Who knows what the hell the two of them are doing by now? I imagine Avery's pulling her dress back down, and Evan's getting all zipped up. . . ."

The words hit Lia like a punch in the gut. She remembered Kyle leaving them there so hastily, with Avery pretty much smashed. Had that all been planned for Evan? The image of Evan, stomach exposed, forearms flexing over a zipper, hair swinging—sent another sickening feeling through her stomach. First she thought it was disgust. Then she thought it was anger.

But finally, as Kyle motioned with his head to follow him, she realized it wasn't either of those things. It was jealousy.

She followed Kyle through the throngs of beautiful people, inhibitions tossed aside with their flailing arms. But somewhere in the center of the dance floor, near the *Pl* in the "Plush" logo, she swayed, and a guy near her caught her elbow.

Kyle glanced back. "Are you all right, Lia?"

He handed her one of the drinks and used his free hand to help her by the elbow. "Easy. And don't take another sip until we get back to the den."

His smile was easygoing, but the reprimand was there.

And Lia, buoyed now by strong wine, misplaced jealousy, and her ability to dissuade him from a kiss she didn't want, felt the rising power of rebelliousness: The drink was at her lips in no time.

But six steps in, she realized her mistake. The ground shifted her as the room began to spin, and the throbbing notes receded into a far dark corner of her brain.

Two steps after that, Lia thought for sure the ground was coming up to meet her.

Twelve

Evan had never seen a more crowded dance floor. But by the time he'd convinced Tom to let him back in, and had taken one sweep through the room, he was sure Lia wasn't on it.

The ice bar was his next target. Black dresses, spilling breasts, high heels, black shiny suits . . . *so many people.* It had been a long time since he'd been in the middle of such a throng, and he was remembering why he'd stayed away. Distrust swelled every cell in his body.

He crushed through with his shoulders. But no Lia. He called the bartender over. Sebastian, his nametag said.

"Have you seen Kyle Stevens? I need to talk to him."

Sebastian shook his head. "I just started my shift, man. Haven't seen him yet."

"Can you call him for me?"

"No can do. He contacts the folks he wants to see, not the other way around. Sorry, man. You can wait here for a while. He'll probably be here two or three times tonight."

Evan glanced at all the doorways. Would Kyle have left out the front while Evan had been in the back? Would he have taken Lia back to his place? Would she have called someone to get a ride home?

Evan cursed himself again for not having a cell. He'd gotten rid of his when he'd decided to step out of society. He ran this curse through his head a couple times a year—usually because of some unforeseen storm that was causing black waves to rise before his boat—but this time seemed even more dire. *Stupid*. He ran his hand down his face and whirled to stare at the other three exits.

Maybe the den? Would Kyle have brought her back there?

His heart raced double-time to the music as he scanned the back dens. From here, he could see they'd been designed with backlighting so figures could be watched peep-show style.

He zeroed in on Den Thirteen. The silhouette of a woman reclined on the ottoman, candles set on the ground, man on top of her. . . .

His blood pounded through his veins as he charged across the room. Bodies separated for him as he raced. When he got there, he yanked the curtain practically off its rod.

Sara and Holden both swiveled their heads in his direction. Holden reached out and snapped the curtain back into place.

Evan stepped back and took a deep breath. *What the hell was he doing?*

Even if Kyle *was* a slimeball, Cinderella didn't seem to think so. And that was her prerogative, wasn't it? To crawl up the body of any man she wanted to? Evan didn't need to be some kind of avenging angel trying to right the wrongs of the world. He didn't even know this woman. And he shouldn't feel anything for her. And if she wanted to have hot sex in a curtained den in a nightclub with . . . Evan loosened his collar. Damn. He was burning up. It must be a thousand degrees in here.

He considered making a hasty retreat, maybe heading back to the motel for a cold shower and some common sense. But a shadow in Den Ten caught his eye.

A woman in silhouette, prone on the fainting couch. Her arms and legs hung over the edges, unmoving. Her head lulled to the side, long hair of Cinderella's length dripping toward the floor.

And a man standing over her.

Who was clearly Kyle.

* * *

The fear that filled Evan's veins propelled him across the room in silent flight. A ringing in his ears replaced the music as he threw himself past the curtain and slammed to a halt inside the den.

It was her. Her unconscious body, her heavy limbs, her closed eyes, her parted lips—all hanging lifelessly off the edge of the couch.

The panic that gripped him sent him flying to her side. He snatched up her wrist. Her pulse was weak, but it was there. His first thought was Rohypnol.

Although Kyle was trying to say something, Evan could only hear a rush of blood as he lunged for the smaller man. Fistfuls of material were in his hands as he slammed Kyle against the wall and cocked his fist.

"... *wrong drink!*" Kyle was squeaking, throwing his hands in front of his face.

Evan didn't care. His fist made glorious contact with Kyle's face, sending his head snapping to the side. They both fell against a flimsier curtain in the back of the room, sending a potted plant toppling across the floor.

"She drank the *wrong drink*, man! *Stop!*" Kyle yelled.

Kyle's shoulders hit the floor next, his body bouncing, and Evan got another punch in before he was lifted bodily by two muscled men who appeared out of nowhere.

"What the hell?" Kyle spit upward. Blood covered his nose and mouth. "She drank the *wrong drink*, I told you!" Kyle spit into his palm.

"What'd you give her?" Evan found a guttural voice that didn't sound like his.

"I didn't *give* her anything!"

"What's in her system, then?"

Kyle motioned for the guys to let Evan go. A door creaked shut behind the back wall of the den—probably where they'd come from.

"It's a muscle relaxer," Kyle said. "It was in my drink. She drank the wrong one." He touched his fingers to his nose and peered at the amount of blood. "She'll be fine. I know how much is in there. My bartender makes me one every night."

Evan glanced at Cinderella looking dead on the couch. That looked stronger than a muscle relaxer. But he couldn't prove anything right now, and Kyle was probably used to this story, which he probably used all the time and had made airtight.

"If she's hurt, man, I'm going to—"

"Cool down, Captain. I promise. She's fine. I'd never hurt her. She's my *employee*, damn it."

That wasn't exactly true, but maybe he was saying it for the burly guys. The bouncers bookended Kyle to make sure he was okay. He swatted them away.

Evan went around the side of the couch and scooped Lia into his arms. He couldn't leave her here another second. He didn't care if this guy had *five* Harvard degrees. They probably just helped him get out of jams like this.

Lia's head rolled into his chest as he lifted her, then fell back, her hair all around her face. Her limbs fell over the side of his arms.

"I'm taking her home."

"We'll take care of her." Kyle scowled. "I have a doctor on staff, and I can bring her to my place and—"

"No." Evan started for the curtain toward the dance floor.

"Hey, hey, hey! Not that way."

Evan turned, and Kyle indicated the back door. "We've got a hallway here. Take her all the way down, to the right. Tom will be there. He'll bring around another car." He pulled out his cell phone.

Evan didn't wait for the call. He kicked the door open with his foot and charged into the hallway, which was narrow and cinderblock sided. He followed it all the way to the end, cold air and muffled music pounding through, where it opened into the concrete hall at the back entrance.

Tom's face screwed into anger when he saw him. "Damn." He shoved Evan back into the hallway. "Don't hold her out in the open like that!"

He marched Evan toward a separate exit farther down. When they all stepped out into the sprinkling rain, the car squealed up immediately. "Get her out of here," Tom said, yanking the door open.

A light drizzle of rain covered Cinderella's hair as Evan

slid her into the backseat, then landed in behind her. He told the driver the address he remembered, and put his arm around her, letting her lifeless body slump against him.

Before they'd even pulled away from the curb, he ran a shaky hand down his face.

As images of Renece's ravaged body floated through his mind, and as the familiar sense of helplessness filled his body, he stroked Cinderella's hair and let himself cry for the first time in two years.

CHAPTER

Thirteen

ight assaulted all her senses as Lia slammed her hand against the screeching alarm clock that bounced along the table. It toppled to the ground, its screech muffled into the white shag rug beneath the side of her bed. She tried to peel her eyelids off her eyeballs, but it felt like they were attached with fur. Her fingertips went up to check.

Every millimeter of movement caused another sharp pain. She gave up on the alarm clock and kept her eyes closed, trying to remember what day it was, what time it might be, how she got here last night. She could hear rain against her window. Last night wouldn't even come into focus.

Then—oh, yes! Kyle's club! She remembered the rain, the darkened bar, the ice figures. She had flashes of Evan's forearms along the bar top, his intense blue eyes underneath black eyebrows. She remembered the cigarette girl, Evan with Avery— was that right? And then . . . *Kyle*? . . . at the bar again? . . . And then . . .

She strained for more details. The clock's muffled screeches continued. The rain came down harder against the panes. She struggled again for memories. And *then* what happened? . . .

Nothing came to her.

Her hand slithered under the sheets to her body. Her dress was off. She seemed to have some kind of . . . She wriggled to see what she was wearing, but the vise around her brain tightened. It was some kind of . . . Oh, okay, her camisole and slip . . . Was she even wearing this last night? Her bracelet was still on. And she had a . . . Dang, she had a cotton ball taped to the inside of her arm. Did she give blood? Her shoes . . . She made a small movement with her legs. Yes, her legs still worked. Her shoes seemed to be off. Did she just fall into bed last night, without—?

"Mornin'," came a deep voice from her bedroom doorway.

Adrenaline shot through her as she snapped her head toward the door. The sudden movement sent fireworks off behind her eyeballs, but she could barely make out Evan leaning against the frame, wolfing down a bowl of cereal.

"Want me to turn off that alarm for you?" he drawled.

"Wh-wh—*What are you doing here*?" She snatched the sheet up to her chin.

He set the bowl down on her dresser and sauntered into the room, keeping his eyes averted but snaring the alarm clock off the floor and snapping it off. Then he returned to the doorway and his cereal.

He had on the same clothes from last night, but the navy shirt was untucked, partially unbuttoned, and even more rumpled than last night, if that were possible. The stubble was back across his jaw, and his hair fell in disarray. While he resumed his cereal shoveling, Missy rubbed against his jeans and bare feet.

"Who's Elle again? Did you say she was your boss?" he asked.

Elle? Oh, God.

"Did she *call*?" Lia croaked. She struggled to sit up. "What time—" She yanked the clock off the nightstand with an arm that felt dead. The tape around the cotton was itchy. "What *is* this?" She tried to peel it off.

"I've got a lot to tell you, but honestly, you're not going to be feeling very well for the next few hours, so I recommend you go back to sleep for now. I just need to understand who Elle is." He gulped down another spoonful of cereal. "And I need to know if that boyfriend of yours might be coming through that door anytime soon. I don't need another fist in my eye."

"Fist in your . . . ?" Her mind made an attempt to put all the pieces together, but it just wasn't happening. "What—what *time* is it?"

She held the clock in front of her face.

Eight o'clock! . . .

She sprang upward, but as soon as her head changed elevation, her stomach roiled. Her sights landed on a trash can by the side of the bed that seemed to be there for that very purpose, and she yanked it to the side of the bed, clutching it toward her chin.

Her head and eyeballs pounded as she listened to the rain against the window and waited for the waves of nausea to go away.

"You all right?" Evan said softly.

She closed her eyes and rolled back into bed. "I want to die."

"I'm familiar with the feeling."

"What happened?"

"Important thing to know is that you're all right. We just need to keep you hydrated. Drink some of that water by the side of the bed." He leaned forward, but seemed to refuse to step into the room again, as if it were filled with snakes.

She kept her eyes closed and stretched her memory again to the night before. She was at the bar with Kyle, right? Then what happened? She strained to remember music, conversation, anything, but kept drawing a blank. A strange metal pole stood next to her bed.

"What's that?" she asked, staring up at it.

"I'm serious about the water. That glass there . . ."

"I see it."

"Drink it."

"I will. I just . . ." Her arm felt like it weighed a hundred pounds.

"Now."

The last thing she wanted to do was move, and the second-to-last thing she wanted to do was put anything in her stomach, but she had the sense he wouldn't drop this. She moved her hundred-pound arm and took a tiny sip.

"I have to go to work," she croaked out.

"I don't think that's gonna happen, Cinderella." His voice was almost a whisper.

She willed herself to sit up, to find out what was going on, to get to work, to remember what happened with Kyle—did he . . . Oh, wow, did he *talk to her about investing in Drew's boat*? And then . . . Oh my God . . . *kissing* . . . Did he ask her to leave with him so she could kiss him? . . . Did he . . .

Her hand ran up her camisole. . . . *Did she do more than kiss?* . . .

"Did I . . . Who did I come home with?"

"Me."

That didn't make her feel any better. The satin shorts that matched her cami slid to the left. She was naked underneath. She felt sick again. "I don't remember anything," she whispered.

As soon as she said it aloud, the reality of the situation hit her, along with the fear such a statement should bring, and tears sprang to her eyes.

"Hey," Evan said gently.

She wanted to look at him, but couldn't. She wanted to ask a million questions, but couldn't. She wanted to know if she still had a job, if Kyle was still a client, if anyone was manning Drew's boat, who took her dress off, why Evan seemed afraid to come near her, if she did anything . . . she gulped . . . *if she had sex* . . . if she would ever work in advertising again, if Drew would ever forgive her, and how she could have let absolutely everything, *everything*, slip through her fingertips. . . .

But she couldn't.

All she could do was let the tears slide down her face toward her pillow and fall into the horrible, hopeless sleep that claimed her.

The second time Lia awoke, the light was against her east wall. It was still raining. Two aspirin lay on her nightstand with another glass of water and a hastily scrawled note.

Drink this. Whole glass, it said. *Evan.*

She took the aspirin, drank half the glass, and succumbed

again to sleep. It was better than analyzing her life, which was clearly in its last few hours.

The third time Lia awoke, the light was gone from the room entirely, but the rain continued. Her nightstand lamp had been turned to the lowest illumination, a T-shirt she didn't recognize wrapped around the shade to darken it even more, so there was just enough light to see the note below it.

Good job. One more glass. Whole thing. Evan.
P.S. Fed the cat.
P.P.S. Met your sister Noelle.
P.P.P.S. What's with the shoes? Daily arrival.

She took the next two aspirin, drank half the glass, petted Missy who came to curl up in the crescent her body formed, and even took two of the orange segments that lay peeled for her on a paper napkin. She listened for any movement from the front room, but heard nothing.

Sleep seemed better than addressing her life right now, and she let it claim her.

The fourth time Lia awoke, it was the middle of the night. The rain had stopped. The vise was no longer squeezing her head. She was able to twist her neck all the way to the side to see her alarm clock. *Two a.m.*

She managed to stumble out of bed. The metal pole that had been in her room was gone. Instead of her zombie-walk to the bathroom, she shuffled out to the front room to make sure life was still as she knew it. Somehow, she half expected to walk into a different time-zone, a different era, a different life. But everything was as she remembered.

Except Evan's huge form stuffed into her love seat.

He looked ridiculous on the small piece of furniture, the pillows lined up on top of his body like a desperate blanket. His shoes were off. He had different jeans on, and a different shirt, this one a gray tee that showcased his arms. One of his tanned forearms was thrown over another of her white-brocade fringed pillows. A white bandage was wrapped across his knuckles and through his fist like a boxer. She stared at it for an unreasonably long time, marveling at the cross between his masculine arm and her feminine pillow.

She knew a normal reaction here—upon finding a man you barely knew sleeping on your couch without your permission—would be fear. He obviously had her key. He'd obviously been here awhile. She'd obviously been passed out. But fear didn't even enter her veins. Instead, she was flooded with a warmth, that a man she barely knew was sleeping on her couch because he was probably taking care of her. All of her annoyance earlier at Evan's crazy protectiveness slid away, and she was now filled with gratitude. Along with that damned warmth that started in her scalp and oozed like honey through her body.

He sucked in air and growled a bit, then turned his body as if he were trying to get more comfortable. Three of the pillows he'd been trying to balance tumbled to the floor.

Lia stumbled into the kitchen beneath what felt like cinderblocks on her shoulders and saw that Missy's water and food bowls had been filled. She poured a glass of water and shuffled back toward the bedroom.

On the way, she stopped at her linen closet and took a blanket off the top shelf, then went back and laid it over Evan.

Almost back in her own bed, she realized she forgot her cell phone. She spun back for it, but her stomach violently rolled and she rushed the other way to her bathroom. She threw up the orange and the water. Wiping the sweat from her brow, she got up, brushed her teeth, splashed her face, and crawled back into bed.

She still forgot the cell. But it wouldn't matter anyway. Her life was over.

The next day was a repeat of the last. Notes from Evan. Glasses of water. Aspirin. Updates on Missy. A note that her mom called, and her sister Giselle. Oranges followed by small bowls of broth. A small roll. Lia ate everything but threw up everything.

Her cell was missing.

Missy curled up with her, and Lia pretended to die.

* * *

When the light hit her next, she rolled over and marveled that she felt human.

The rain had stopped and was replaced by sunlight through her window. Morning sun. It must be mocking her, lovely light for a woman whose life was now darkness.

The vise was gone from her head. Her brain felt normal-sized. Her stomach didn't feel like it was going to heave, and her mouth—while dry—didn't feel like it was coated in cotton. Her eyes opened of their own volition.

But she didn't want them to now. She could explain to the Vampiress if she were dead. The Vampiress would forgive her for that. Might even send a wreath of flowers to her funeral. But if she felt fine, she'd have another thing coming. Worse than death—failure, her desk packed up, a sense that the last decade of her work was for nothing. . . . Humiliation.

She stumbled into the front room, where the shades still seemed to be drawn. Someone had put socks on her feet. She had no idea what day it was.

She gripped the living room doorway as she rounded the corner, tumbled into the next room, and let out a shriek.

There, in the middle of her living room, was a naked Evan. He was hopping into his jeans—full frontal nudity. She threw her hands over her face.

Apparently, he went commando.

Who knew?

He spat an obscenity under his breath, and she could hear him hop in a circle and yank the jeans up. Zipper. Button. She could hear the belt clinking.

"Coast is clear," he mumbled. "Sorry."

She peeked through her fingers. He had his back to her now, looking down to fasten the last of his belt. His back was wide and tan, filled with the valleys and hills of muscles across the shoulders, the same back she'd admired that first morning she'd seen him in his sailboat galley. She watched his triceps flex as he finished the belt, then he leaned over to snatch his shirt off her ottoman. He still had the bandage wrapped around his hand. She flashed back to her peek at his privates, and a blush ran up her cheeks—Evan was strong and bullish *everywhere*, apparently.

He slid the shirt on, then turned and looked for his shoes, snagging them off the floor. "Sorry again." He glanced up at her. "Gotta run. Tours today."

"What is today?"

"Friday."

"Today is *Friday*?" The blood that had rushed to her cheeks drained.

He straightened, and a corner of his mouth tilted up. "Maybe I should have been calling you Sleeping Beauty instead of Cinderella." He buttoned his shirt from the bottom while he glanced around for his other belongings. "But I'm glad to see you upright. You look great."

Great? Her hand went to her rat's nest of hair that hadn't been washed for, apparently, three days, and glanced down at the slouchy socks, taking in her wrinkled camiso—

Crap!

She threw her arms around her body to block the view of her puckered breasts, now standing at attention beneath the champagne-colored top.

"Oh, I've seen more than that." Evan lifted an eyebrow. "Sorry, Cinderella, we might have passed the modesty stage."

His cell phone and wallet drew his attention, and he shoved everything into his pockets and turned to grab a jacket he'd hung by the door. "Who did all the drawings here?" He thrust his chin toward one of Coco's crayon tire swings.

"My niece," she answered absently. But she was still on "seen more than that. . . ."

"Nice. Well, you look good," he said. "Compared to before, anyway. This is the first time I've seen you with any color in your face."

Seeing a muscular, naked man in your living room will do that to you.

"I . . . um . . . where . . ." She had so many questions she didn't even know where to start. "Do I still have a *job*?" she whispered.

He grinned while he shrugged his jacket on. "You just slept for two days straight, had an IV in your arm, had Kyle Stevens and his whole crew here in your apartment, woke up to a naked man getting dressed in your apartment, and your first question is about *work*? You *are* a workaholic, Cinderella. Hey, what's with the shoes, by the way?" He cocked his head toward the six shoe boxes stacked by the door.

She steadied herself in the doorway. *An IV? Kyle Stevens? . . .*

"Did I . . ." She swallowed. "Who changed my clothes?"

"No worries there. Kyle sent a nurse home right behind us, and she came in and took care of you. She had you on an IV so you didn't dehydrate. And she took care of . . . you know, all personal things. She put on your skivvies there, and took care of . . . well, you were doing a lot of vomiting."

She winced. "Why did Kyle send a nurse?"

"He felt responsible."

"For . . ." She waited for him to fill in the blank, but his lips tightened.

Her mind was whirling. It was *Friday*? "How's Drew?"

A shadow crossed Evan's face. "He's fine, health-wise. Legs are healing. He uh . . . fired me, though."

"What?"

"It's okay. I didn't expect anything else. He said he'll have another captain by Monday. He asked me to just run two tours on Saturday and Sunday. For a festival?"

Lia closed her eyes and groaned. *Oh God.* "The Whale Festival," she verified. How was Drew going to cover all this?

"Oh." Evan's forehead crumpled into wrinkles as he stared at the floor, seemingly lost in memory. "Yeah, I remember that. Lots of people. Anyway, he asked me to run those two tours, and then leave. But it's all good. Douglas came back from Vegas. Stewey's been on board. Cora's cooking. She's been sending you the broth and the rolls. Hey, I tried to feed your cat. She doesn't eat much."

"I leave out an extra bowl of dry food in the laundry area for when I work late." She motioned lamely, her mind still whirling. "She knows it's there. What about the charter on Monday?"

He glanced up at her through his bangs. "I don't think the charter's gonna happen, Cinderella."

"What?" No. No. No. No. . . . "Who canceled it?" she managed to get out.

"I guess I did."

"What?" She gripped the wall.

"Not technically. I mean, Stevens and I didn't discuss it. But I punched him in the face, and—"

"You *punched* him?" Her mouth fell open as her eyes drifted to the bandage.

"Yeah. I'm not sure he's going to want me to run it, and I doubt he's going to want to face you again after possibly drugging you, and—"

"Drugging me?"

He glanced up at her. "Listen, Cinderella, the whole night was a mess. I feel you were drugged, but his story holds water. And he did send his private medic here, and they kept you hydrated and checked you out, and he apologized a billion times. Those are from him." He straightened his jacket collar and pointed his elbow in the direction of a vase of about fifty white roses that were sitting in the kitchen, behind the wall. "I told him you wouldn't press charges. He said he'd pay for anything you need. I promised to keep it out of the paper until you woke up and I could . . . oh, hey, you're losing your color again. Here, sit down."

He reached for her elbow, but she stepped around him and sat on the edge of the couch, pulling her elbows close to her body and rubbing her arms for warmth. *Drugged? Private medic? Press charges? Evan punched him? Keep it out of the paper?* She leaned forward. She might be sick again. This was a thousand times worse than she'd thought.

She could barely get the next question through her throat. "Do I still have a job?"

"I talked to Elle and told her you'd be out through today."

Lia shook her head. That wouldn't work. She was fired, she knew it. She'd return to her desk, and everything would be cleared out. Maybe even out on the street. Maybe they wouldn't even let her back in the building. She'd ruined everything with Kyle, had ruined Elle's chance to get J.P. Stevens's New York business, had embarrassed the agency. . . . She'd have to start her life over next week. She probably couldn't even work in Orange County again. She'd have to move. . . . She'd have to leave her sisters here, and her mom, and Coco. . . .

"Listen, I know this is a lot to take in. But it's going to be okay. Let me take you—"

"Just *go*." Anger coursed through her as she realized what a mess this was, and *why the hell was Evan Betancourt trying to handle it for her?* She was done for. She'd never work in Southern California again. "Just go," she said again. "I appreciate everything you did, but I need to be alone."

He stood uncertainly and stared at her for a minute.

"Please. Leave."

He nodded, his jaw muscle clenching. "Got it," he said.

The door finally closed, and Lia dropped her head in her hands.

And cried for everything she'd lost in the last seventy-two hours.

CHAPTER

Fourteen

Evan squinted through his sunglasses as he steered the cat back past the jetty and into the tight harbor. Douglas's scratchy voice droned over the microphone, finishing the narration for their last Friday tour. The bright winter sun sat high, streaking through a clean, cloudless sky. Evan pulled back on the throttle with his bad hand and ran through, one more time, Cinderella kicking him out of her place.

At first he'd been surprised. Then pissed. But ultimately, as he'd made his way down her front walk, he'd felt relieved.

He didn't like how his blood had begun pumping again in a dangerous way this week—a way that made him feel out of control.

He didn't like how he'd been turned on—the first woman to make him feel that way since Renece.

Cinderella just stirred up too many emotions, emotions he was no longer interested in. Emotions about caring, loving, investing, worrying. He'd checked out of all that. And planned to stay checked out.

The evenings had been the hardest. He'd come in to see how she was after the whale tours were over each day. He'd stay over just to make sure she was breathing. He ran into her neighbor Rabbit on the first morning, who eyed him suspiciously when he left around five. He'd met her younger sister Noelle—beautiful girl who looked just like Lia only with long brown hair and a hipster beanie on her head. Noelle had looked him up and down when he'd opened the door and demanded to know what was going on. He'd explained at least most of the story, and she'd sworn him to secrecy if their mom called, and then pushed her way in and agreed to stay with Lia all day.

The next day, he and Noelle found an older neighbor named Mrs. Rose, who had said she was the landlord. Noelle asked if Mrs. Rose would check on Lia, and the older woman had bobbed her head and seemed happy to help.

The nights, though, he had covered. He'd nod to Mrs. Rose, walk in, and peek inside Lia's bedroom to make sure she was still alive.

He never went in. Except to leave quick notes. But mostly he wanted to dodge the bright red bra he'd seen out of the corner of his eye, the lacy things draped near the hamper, and the three enormous blue ballroom-looking dresses she had hanging near the door. He didn't want to be near so much satin, or any more things to remind him that she was a very feminine woman and he was a man who'd begun to notice.

But, even though he aimed to keep his distance, his heart was splitting open and starting to bleed again. The spillage came in a rush the morning he realized she'd put a blanket on him. That about killed him. And then seeing the crayon drawings all over her kitchen and living room—she obviously had a little person in her life like Luke. He didn't want to open up again, let the blood flow out.

Having her kick him out was good. He would finish this last tour, handle the two over the weekend during the festival, then sail away on Monday. He wouldn't even see her again.

"Cap'n, a couple of the kids want to come up and meet you when the tour is over," Douglas said from the bridge stairs.

Evan glanced back over his shoulder.

"Is that okay?" Douglas prompted.

"I guess."

Douglas's white hair disappeared.

Evan still dreaded the kids. A couple of them had asked for his "autograph" yesterday and it had about crumpled him to the ground. It was so hard to talk to them anymore, any age. If they were younger than Luke, all he could think about was what Luke did at that age. If they were older, all he could think about was what Luke would have looked like and sounded like if he'd been able to grow to that age. And if they were the same age— about five—that was the most painful of all. Because he couldn't help but think of the roll of the cosmic dice that made *his* kid the one who was gone, while this other kid stood in front of him. And, for thinking that, he felt guilty.

The light bounced off the water as the cat made its way in, making it hard to see the dock. Douglas, thankfully, had already set up the fenders. He was a good deckhand. Evan peered toward the pillars, lining them up, while they made their way through, but another sight on the dock caught his eye.

Was that . . . ?

Damn.

Was that who he thought it was? He snapped his hair out of the way and pulled back on the throttle as the cat puttered in.

And, as he blocked the sun from his eyes, he had his answer.

It was.

Lia began stitching things back up one at a time. After a long morning, sitting in the bathtub in lavender baby wash, watching her tears create bubble craters, she decided to pull herself together around three o'clock. Enough pity.

She wasn't the kind of person for whom things unraveled. Normally she had all the stitches straight, all in a row, tied at the edges in tight knots. But this morning, she had panicked. Her breath had come faster and faster when she listened to her messages after Evan left: three from the Vampiress on Wednesday morning (which Evan must have answered, because they suddenly stopped); three from Drew on Wednesday afternoon (*"Where are you?"* *"What the hell is Evan doing on the boat?"* *"Are you okay?"*); four from her sisters and mom (*"Are you okay? Why aren't you calling us back?"*); and two from Sharon (*"Drew is working again. I heard you're sick. I'm so sorry. But now I wish you were handling things again. Can you help me get him to stop? He's been on the phone trying to find captains all afternoon. . . .*"). None from Forrest.

Her breath had also come fast when she saw the note from Kyle in the flowers (*I'm so sorry, beautiful. I fired my bartender.*).

She didn't believe Kyle had drugged her. Evan was crazy. Evan had already admitted he was too suspicious, and that whole cop/Coast Guard behavior—watching the exits, being so protective—she had no idea what drove all that, but Drew was right. He was a wild card.

But when she saw that Evan had organized Missy's food, folded the blanket he'd used and set it neatly on the floor behind the couch, and left a razor blade and a pair of scissors on her guest-bath sink with clumps of his hair in the wastebasket, her breathing came in a halted shudder, meshed with the threat of tears. *He took care of her.*

After three o'clock, after the lavender bath, after her hair was dried and she felt human again, she took a deep breath, sat on the couch, and started restitching her life.

Her first call went to a frazzled assistant named Courtney who sometimes took Lia's place when Lia had to be out of the office or in New York. Lia had to figure out if she still had a job. Courtney put her on hold to get rid of three other calls for the Vampiress and then came back to the phone.

"She's freaking out," Courtney whispered. "I can see her through the glass, and she's throwing folders into the trash while she's on the other line. But I've got a guy on the phone from Germany who wants to speak to her, and I don't know if I should let him through. She said to hold all her calls."

"That's Markus," Lia said. "Yeah, put him through. She's wrapping up a deal with him that needs to go through by next Wednesday."

"Thank you!" Courtney said, her voice cracking. "When are you coming back?"

"Do I still have a job?"

"Y-Yes! You'd *better*! I . . . I can't . . ." Courtney's voice cracked, and she burst into tears.

"Courtney, it's okay. I . . . I'll swing by this afternoon. Just hang on."

"Is that Lia?" Lia could hear Elle's screech. *"Put her through!"*

"Lia," Courtney whispered back into the phone, "Elle wants—"

"I heard her, Courtney."

Lia took a deep breath and wished she'd asked more questions of Evan. Like who did he say he was when he talked to Elle? And what did he tell Elle that Lia was sick with? And how much did Elle know about what happened with Kyle?

"Lia, *what* is going on?" The Vampiress's whisper into the phone was filled with metal fragments and impatience.

"I'm working on ironing everything out today," Lia said vaguely. "I'm going to swing by the office in an hour to help Courtney and—"

"Don't bother."

Lia's breath hitched. She fumbled for her end table, her heart pounding, when Elle continued:

"Let's fix this thing with Kyle first."

Lia let out a whoosh of air.

"Courtney will be fine," Elle said. "Here's what I need you to do: Tonight is the VIP reception to kick off the Whale Festival. Kyle bought almost all forty-eight tickets for the people he's bringing on the charter. I need you to go. Apologize to him. Bring that captain, that friend of yours, and I want him to apologize, too. You need to fix this, Lia. The tickets are at will-call under my name. Just show up. Dress up. Don't look 'Sandy Cove'; look 'Newport Beach.' Make a huge donation on our behalf and say whatever you need to say to Kyle to assure him the charter's on. Don't screw this up."

"I . . . I don't know if I can get Evan there, I . . ."

"Do what you need to do. J.P.'s going to be on that charter, and so am I, and I want him and Kyle both thrilled with everything. I trusted you to set this up. Are you saying I can't trust you to pull things off?"

"No, I'm not saying that at all, I—"

"Then get it done." The phone went dead. Lia stared at it in her hand.

She wondered if she could just call Kyle and get things straightened over the phone before tonight. She knew him well enough now, right? They'd sort of crossed the bridge into friends, sometime between his limo at her apartment building and his lips at her temple. She dialed his office, her heart pounding, but got another frazzled assistant.

"Would you like me to leave a message?" the assistant asked.

"Yes, tell him Lia McCabe called and I'd like to talk with him before the event tonight."

"Oh, Lia McCabe," she said, as if she were describing something you needed to scrape off your shoe. "He said you might call. He said if you did, to tell you he was looking for another charter. But thanks anyway." A dial tone ended that road.

Lia pressed her fingertips to her temple. She had to convince him to stay with her and the original plan. Unless . . . *could she find another charter for him?*

She fired up her laptop and started scouring. Drew would never forgive her, but her job was on the line now. She called the first two tours she found, and discovered they couldn't accommodate that many people on such short notice. She found a third, but the boat wasn't very elegant—more of a fishing boat sometimes used for whale watching. Kyle's multimillionaire friends wouldn't like that, but it might be her only resort.

Her phone buzzed in her hand with an incoming call. Dang, it was Drew.

"How is it I get this crazy call the other day from Douglas?" Drew fired in his angriest voice, which she didn't hear very often. "And Doug is telling me my *brother* is captaining my boat because *you* asked him to? And now you're home with some mysterious illness? When I know you never call in sick? What the *hell*, Lia?"

"I know. I'm sorry, Drew. I needed to run the tour the next day, and Sharon told me to handle it myself and not involve you, and—"

"Wait, *Sharon*? She told you to do this?" A string of swear words followed.

"No, don't get mad at Sharon. She was just worried about you, and she asked me to handle it for you for a few days so you could get well, and—"

"So you went to my *brother*? Who I told you specifically *not to ask*?"

"Drew, he was a fast, short-term solution to a problem that

needed to be solved overnight. Kyle Stevens was on the first tour."

"Kyle Stevens?" His voice held both incredulousness and awe.

"He might want to invest in your boat."

That shut Drew up. A long silence followed.

"So Evan, he . . ." Lia tried to think of how to explain all this. "He really helped. Kyle likes him. I think he has a little man-crush on him or something. So he brought us all to his club, and we—"

"Evan went to Kyle's *club*?"

"Yes, it was a crazy night. There was a blogger there, too, Avery James, and we all went together, and Kyle expressed a couple of times that he might want to invest. Once to Evan, and once to me."

Another long silence followed. "Evan went to a *club*?"

"Yes."

"How did he look?" Drew asked quietly.

"I don't have anything to compare him to, but I guess he looked okay. A little scraggly. But he shaved one day, and . . ."

"I mean his *disposition*, Lia. Was he sober? Was he functional? Did he scare people away?"

"He seemed fine."

Drew blew out a breath. "Okay, let's talk about Kyle. What are our next steps?"

"Well, he had a charter planned for Monday. I'm not sure . . ." She hesitated, not sure how much to tell Drew. "Anyway, I'm still ironing out the details, but he wants Evan to captain it, and . . ." She paused. Could she say that Evan refused to run it? That he *punched* Kyle? She sighed and tried to figure out how to word all this.

"And I fired him," Drew filled in.

That would serve for now. She decided to cut to the chase: "We need a captain for it. Can *you* do it? Will you be well enough?"

"I'm not supposed to get out of bed for another five days. I found a captain starting Wednesday, but he's tied up until then. Maybe I can unfire Evan. If you say he's been doing okay, I guess I can live with him navigating my boat for a few more days."

Lia sighed. *Might not be that easy . . .*

"Tell me what happened between you two," she said.

Another long pause. "It's a long story. But I'll call him. And unfire him. Or maybe I can go down there and talk to him. If Sharon'll let me." He chuckled.

"I see that hospital didn't sew you in some bigger balls."

His laugh grew into a loud bark. "Man, I missed you."

Lia smiled. It was nice that Drew was coming around with whatever the problem was between him and Evan, but she didn't know how to break it that the problem involved Evan taking things into his own hands and canceling Kyle's charter . . . and only because he was pissed at Kyle . . . for possibly *drugging* Lia. It all just sounded too sordid and embarrassing. And she knew Drew would worry. And rail.

"So you won't be able to make it to the festival, either?" she asked. "Didn't you have a booth and everything?"

Drew groaned. "Yes. I should be there. I wonder if Cora can sit at the booth for a while?"

"I'll handle it," she said.

"No, you've done enough already. Really. You're the best, Lia. And it sounds like you need a few days off, too."

"I'm fine. I'll set up the booth and coordinate with Cora and Douglas—would they each be willing to work it for a few hours?"

"Absolutely. But let me set it up with them."

"No." Lia's mind drifted back to her warning from Sharon again. "No, you rest."

"Then I'll at least call Evan."

"*No.*" Her response to that sounded a bit too emphatic. "It's um . . . complicated," she corrected. "Let me talk to him first."

Drew paused. "Something tells me there's more to this story."

"There is. But I can handle it."

"Lia, he's my brother. Tell me what's going on."

Missy crawled up into Lia's lap while she contemplated, for a second, what Sharon had said days ago, about leaving Drew alone. Letting him forget about business for a few days. Not causing undo stress . . .

"You two aren't getting close, are you?" Drew added.

Lia petted Missy down her back. The fear in Drew's voice didn't seem warranted. "Why would that be so awful?"

"Oh my God, Lia. Tell me you two aren't getting close."

"Calm down. What's the problem?"

"Just tell me you aren't."

She buried a kiss onto Missy's head. Having Drew tell her what to say just made her not want to say it. Plus . . . well . . . it might not be true. At least on her end.

"You know that bossing me around gets you absolutely nowhere."

"I know. It's just . . . this is important to me. I don't want you to get close to him."

Missy dove off her lap to find food. Lia followed her into the kitchen. "It's fine. Really. You don't need to worry."

"Promise?"

"You know I don't promise. But I'll tell you this—if I need you, I'll call."

"Promise?"

She laughed. "If Sharon doesn't confiscate your phone, that is."

"Go away."

"You could have used those balls, you know."

"I'm hanging up."

"Okay. Get some rest."

They hung up, and Lia stared at her phone. *What was this issue with Evan?* But she didn't have time to dwell or decipher. There were more stitches to mend. She couldn't let more things unravel.

She made one call to her mom. One to Giselle. She was able to leave messages, thankfully. Assurances she'd be at Giselle's bridal-dress fitting. Assurances she'd find the right bridesmaid shoes . . . She hung up and stared at the stacks of shoe boxes. That part would have to wait, though.

She attempted to leave another message with Noelle, but Noelle snatched up the phone as soon as she heard Lia's voice.

"Oh my God, *who was that man in your apartment*?" Noelle squealed into the phone. "*Please* tell me you're sleeping with him."

"What? No!"

"Oh, c'mon, Lia! Why not? He's the sexiest thing I've ever seen cast a shadow across your doorway. Well, besides Fin, maybe."

"Noelle! Fin is about to be your brother-in-law. And I have a boyfriend."

"Oh, Forrest isn't a boyfriend. He's just someone you think fits inside the lines."

"What?"

"Forrest just fits your long list of things you think you want in a husband. But sometimes you have to think with your heart, not your head."

"Says the woman who's been serial dating through her twenties?"

"Oh, you flatter me."

"I didn't mean it as a compliment."

"I know. But I'm certainly more of an expert than you. And I say go with your heart, not your head. Or, you know, when that fails, your libido. Damn, tell me that guy doesn't make your mouth go dry."

"I'm hanging up."

"Someone needs to speak truth to you, girl."

"Hanging . . ."

"No, wait!"

"Up . . ."

Lia clicked off the phone. Noelle always called back if she didn't get to say everything. But the phone didn't ring back.

She shrugged off Noelle's ridiculous words of wisdom and pulled a sweater over her head.

She still had some stitches to mend. And right now, she had the biggest stitch of all.

A visit to pay.

CHAPTER

Fifteen

As Evan pulled into the dock, she was still there.

He wasn't 100 percent sure he was the reason for her impatient pacing, and he gave a halfhearted hope he wasn't. But when she eventually caught sight of him, then beamed and tossed her hair like some kind of perfume model, she "yoo-hoo'd." And waved. To him.

He groaned.

After all the passengers had disembarked, after he answered a few questions for the kids, after the chaos of the leaving passengers, Douglas came back for him.

"Pretty lady here to see you." Douglas wriggled his white eyebrows.

Evan pulled his sunglasses off. "You can send her up, I guess."

"I'd think you'd be a little more enthusiastic, considering what a looker she is."

Evan tried to smile and hooked his shades to the front of his shirt. "Thanks, Douglas."

Avery flounced up the last of the steps and gave a coy dip to her head when she saw Evan.

"Hello, Captain Betancourt. Are you still speaking to me?" Her curls fell across her left cheek.

"Why wouldn't I be speaking to you?"

"I was a little flirty the other night, and don't know if my behavior put me on the permanent 'Banned' list."

"You're not on the 'Banned' list."

"Good to hear." Her fingertip ran along the metal rail that rimmed the bridge, her eyes never leaving his face, and Evan wondered what the hell he'd just said. He wasn't very good at this.

"Regardless," Avery continued, "I just wanted to offer an apology. I don't usually get that . . . tipsy. And flirty. Really."

"It's okay. It was a weird night for everyone."

"I also just wanted to say thanks. For getting me home. You were a . . . a real *gentleman*."

Evan nodded awkwardly. He hoped she'd go away now.

"I wondered if I could . . . Oh, what happened to your hand?" She scooped it up like a baby bird.

He pulled away. "It's fine."

Her eyes drifted back to his face. "Well, I wanted to repay you. By inviting you to dinner."

"You don't have to do that."

"I know. I want to. I want to take you to a restaurant I love. Tomorrow night, maybe?"

"I really can't."

"Do you have another hot date?"

He made an attempt to match her smile. "I don't really . . . date. Or go out much."

"Well, maybe you should."

"You may be right, but for now I'm not."

Over Avery's shoulder, he could hear another female voice talking to Douglas. He was surprised at the rush that went through his veins when he recognized it.

He peered over the rail. Cinderella looked great today—rosy color back in her face, strength back in her shoulders, her movements calculated and purposeful. She spoke to Douglas and gave him a grin that lit up her whole face.

Avery followed his gaze. "Well, there ya' go," she said quietly.

"What?"

"Nothing."

Lia had on a loose sweater over bright, tangerine-colored pants. He couldn't help but notice that the sweater came down too low to allow him any more glimpses of thongs or thong bands. He rubbed the bridge of his nose and forced himself to look away.

"Oh! Avery," Lia said, climbing the stairs.

The captain's bridge was small, and Evan never felt more trapped. Part of him wanted to bolt off the edge—maybe dive into the Pacific—while the other part wanted to simply stare at Cinderella and her long sunshine hair, and try to figure out how this pint-sized, overly perky, overly optimistic, too-talkative woman could have been the one to make his heart start beating again.

"I was just apologizing to Captain Betancourt here." Avery moved to one side of the bridge to make room for Lia, blocking his view. Probably for the best. He needed to stop staring. He shoved his sunglasses back on and pretended to attend to the controls.

"I should extend the apology to you, too," Avery gushed, touching Lia's arm. "I don't usually get that tipsy and act so brazen. I hope I didn't embarrass anyone."

"It was a weird night for everyone," Lia said.

"That's exactly what he said," Avery said with a note of wonder. "Anyway, I'll leave you two alone."

Evan's arm shot out toward her, maybe to help her down the stairs, maybe to stop her from leaving him alone with Cinderella—he couldn't tell at this point.

But Lia helped Avery down the steep steps herself. At the bottom, she put Avery in Douglas's care.

Evan watched all of this from the platform, knowing he should make his escape. But something made him hold his ground. Something made him want to stand there in this cramped space with this particular woman. He watched her climb back up the steps.

He was a mess.

"I'm here to offer an apology," Lia said. She was out of breath and a little light-headed, maybe not quite well enough or replenished enough to be out here climbing steps, but she knew she had to do this.

"Lots of that going around, it seems," Evan mumbled.

"What?"

"Never mind." He leaned against the rail. "What are you apologizing for?"

The boat pitched, and Lia gripped the opposite rail. She'd rehearsed this speech a million times on the way over, but she'd forgotten to factor in how sexy Evan was going to look, with his mirrored sunglasses staring down at her and the wind tossing his hair around.

"For, um . . . telling you to leave. Especially before I thanked you. And found out more about what happened."

His eyebrow shot up over the glasses rim.

Dang. She didn't mean to blurt out that part.

"But mostly the thanking part," she said quickly. "I was just . . . overwhelmed. There were so many things to think about. It was a weird night."

"It was."

"And a weird couple of days. Especially for you. From what I could tell. How's your hand?"

He lifted his bandaged fist slightly. "Almost healed."

"Let me see." Some strange instinct made her reach for it, even though it wasn't in her nature at all. She was as far from Florence Nightingale as anyone could be, never knowing how to respond to broken bones, twisted ankles, or even scratches. But something made her want to soothe Evan.

Reluctantly, he ventured his hand out like a huge lion with a thorn in his paw. She took it gently. The bloody dots across the knuckles on the one side were gone from this morning, and he had a fresh bandage. "Who re-wrapped this for you?"

"Cora."

His hand was huge and heavy in her own, his skin dark and weathered where the bandage ended. She stroked it lightly along the edge, knowing she wasn't helping, but wanting to acknowledge this singular vulnerability she'd seen in him so far.

"I just wanted to thank you, really." It was easier to talk to the bandage than to him. Lia had a long history of blurting out thoughts, but not when it came to emotions. Snarky responses? Check. Personal details no one needed to know? Check. But when it came to being able to give sound to actual, real, need-to-be-heard feelings—whether to her sisters or friends or dates—she was embarrassingly silent.

She took a deep breath and tried again. "I appreciate your taking care of me."

It wasn't Wordsworth, but it would do.

Evan nodded awkwardly and took his hand back. He shifted against the rail and seemed to not want to look at her.

"As for finding out more about what happened, I do need to know some things," she added, slipping back more comfortably into checklist mode. "But I . . . uh . . . I don't know if I really want to know everything that happened."

A small smile played around his lips. "Probably not."

"Now, see? That makes me nervous. What do you mean by that?"

He shook his head.

Lia pressed her lips together. Dang, this was embarrassing. *Did she vomit all over him? Did she strip in front of him? Did she flirt with him? Did she flash him?* Any of those things seemed possible, unfortunately.

"Did I, um . . ." She tried to think of which answer she wanted first, and how to delicately phrase it. "What did you mean this morning, exactly, about us passing the modesty stage?"

"I don't think we need to go there, Cinderella."

"I just want to know how much to be embarrassed about."

"Well, I'll put it this way: You don't need to be embarrassed about that."

That wasn't helping.

"Did I . . . Did I reveal myself *willingly*?" she whispered.

"Is that what you're worried about? No. You were just . . . flung openly when I came in one morning, and I didn't mean to look, but—"

"Flung openly?"

"Spread-eagle."

"I was sleeping *spread-eagle*?"

"Yeah. Is that a habit of yours?"

"So you could . . . *see things*?"

"Well, your skivvies were twisted, and I, uh, didn't mean to look."

"You shouldn't have!"

"No, I shouldn't have." He seemed to be trying hard to come up with a contrite expression.

Lia took a deep breath. Okay. At least she wasn't openly flirting. God, she was a mess. *What was happening to her?* Why was she so attracted to . . . *this* guy? Why *him*? This was Noelle's type, not hers.

She toed the deck tape with her tennis shoe and tried to figure out how to proceed. She needed to get him to agree to the next part. She needed to play this cool. Then—and *right* then—she needed to knock this off. She had an almost-boyfriend, damn it. Who had a job and a future. She shouldn't be getting all tongue-tied in front of Captain Betancourt.

"Well, I came to ask you a favor," she said.

"This appears to be a habit of yours."

Lia decided to ignore that. Her sales experience had developed her into someone who was really good at buttering up. Usually. But with this particular man, she knew she'd lost the meter to accurately gauge where appropriate compliments ended and drooling might begin.

"You look good," she attempted anyway. "I like the shorter hair. Are you cutting it for the captain's job? I'm sure Drew would appreciate that. I know you're taking this job very seriously, and we really appreciate it. And you're very good at it."

His arms crossed tighter in front of his chest. "You can just cut to the favor if you'd like, Cinderella."

She sighed. "The charter. Monday. We really need you. Kyle wants you to run it."

A family of pelicans flew overhead and squawked. But Evan never took his shaded eyes off her. "I can't believe you still want to work for that guy."

She shook her head. "What I want is my job. And a promotion. And to get away from Elle. And I have to do this charter to get those things."

Evan watched her carefully. The water slapped the sides of the catamaran hulls. "You really need this charter to get all those things?"

"I do."

"How does that make sense?"

Lia slumped against the rail. She was so tired of fighting for her job, and worrying about it. But she felt like unloading.

"Elle is wooing J.P. Stevens, Kyle's father. And she wants to make Kyle happy in every way. I'm the one who offered Drew's boat for the charter, and she thought Drew and our 'little Sandy Cove' boat couldn't pull it off. So now I have to make sure he does. She's been holding a promotion over my head for years, and I think this could kick me into her good graces if I can do it. And I think it could get me fired if I don't."

The boat rolled gently beneath them. Evan stared at his shoes, crossed in front of him as he leaned against the rail. "What's the promotion?"

"I'll get to head up a campaign for one of her clients in Paris, and live there for a couple of years."

"You want to live in Paris?"

"Yeah, who wouldn't?"

He shrugged.

"Have you ever been there?"

"I docked there for a few months."

"Was it wonderful?"

He smiled, maybe at her breathlessness. But he didn't seem to be making fun. "It was what you make of it, I guess."

"Were you too curmudgeonly to enjoy it?"

His grin widened. "I suppose. So you need to make the charter happen to get your Paris?"

"That's what I'm told."

"And all it takes to convince you Kyle's on the level is a dozen white roses?"

"I think there were four dozen, actually."

"I stand corrected."

"But no. I can't be bought off with forty-eight roses. I just don't think he drugged me."

He threw her a look of irritation. "I see we haven't made any progress on the 'too trusting' front."

"I just . . . I believe the best in people."

"I've noticed."

"He apologized profusely."

"I'm sure he did."

"And he said his bartender just switched our glasses."

"Of course."

"Evan! Why would he drug me?"

"To *get into your pants*, Lia."

She snapped her head up at his raised voice.

"Sometimes people take advantage of you when you're always trying to be nice," he added.

"I'm not always trying to be nice! I'm doing my *job*."

"But you come across as too nice. Too . . ."

"Gullible?"

"Trusting."

"Oh, that's right. Here's where your caveman behavior comes back in."

"Damn it, it's not caveman behavior. I'm just aware of human nature. And I know what men are thinking. And men like that feel *entitled*. To do whatever they want, to whomever they want, however they can get it. They're not used to hearing 'no.' They don't know how to accept it. And those are dangerous men to *be around*, Lia."

She blinked back his nearness, his anger, the passion in his voice, but she didn't feel afraid of him in the slightest.

"You called me by my real name," she marveled.

"That's because I'm pissed."

"So you're going to use my real name whenever you're yelling at me?"

"I suppose so."

"I think I like it."

His Adam's apple worked a few times, and he stared at her for what seemed like ten minutes. His gaze dropped to her lips, and his head lowered slightly. She thought for a second he was going to kiss her, but then he dipped his head lower still and stepped away.

She tried to resume breathing.

Evan ran a hand over the back of his neck. "All right, let's bring this conversation back."

"You were yelling at me."

"I didn't mean to yell; I just worry about you. Or women like you."

"Now, what's *that* supposed to mean?"

He blew out a breath. "I'm just saying men like that are dangerous, if you're not willing to . . ." He waved his hand as if to fill in the rest of the sentence.

"To *what*?"

"To do whatever they want."

"You mean like blow jobs? Lap dances? Sex?" Now that he had her all riled up, she was ready to spar. She liked seeing so much passion play across his face—it was a huge improvement to the man she'd first met, with the dead eyes. Plus it was something she never got out of Forrest, that was for sure. This man was intriguing, sexy, hot, and filled with emotions that lay simmering just below his surface, that he'd been trying to keep tamped down for some reason. Lia was finding it intriguing to bring him just above that surface, like the whales spouting.

"You said earlier that you say what you mean, right, Evan? So spit it out. You mean blow jobs, don't you?"

He pinched the bridge of his nose. "Lia, please."

"He's my *client*."

"I'm not arguing that point."

"But it's purely business. Are you one of those men who think women just sleep their way to the top? They don't actually work for their positions? I worked *hard* for that position, to be the lead marketer on his account."

She'd closed the gap between them again, and his lips drew into a straight line, the color gone. He clearly didn't want to step back, but didn't seem to want to get any closer, either. His Adam's apple bobbed again.

"I work *really hard* for him," she added.

Evan visibly swallowed, but didn't take his eyes off her.

Okay, she was flirting now. She didn't need to say "hard" like that, twice in a row, with a sultry drop to her voice. She'd lost all sense. This guy was hot, with his muscled arms, and his square jaw, and his jaw muscle dancing when she got him worked up. . . . She didn't care if he was Drew's brother. She didn't care if she had an almost-boyfriend. Noelle was right: Evan was the hottest thing that had stood in front of Lia in a long time. And she suddenly wanted him to kiss her with all that passion she could see simmering below the surface, right this very minute.

But he moved farther away—or as far as he could, anyway, until he bumped into the rail in the tiny space. He blew out a breath and propped his arms up on the rail behind him. "Tell me he didn't proposition you in some way," he said.

She took a deep breath herself and pushed herself

away—away from his lips, away from his passion, away from temptation.

"What did he ask of you?" he asked, still apparently trying to make some point.

She tried to focus. *Ask of her? Proposition?* She scoured her memory and dug up some of the details of Kyle she'd maybe let slip from her mind in the last several hours, information she didn't really want to face, or acknowledge. She remembered Kyle's lips in her hairline, his leaning in, his smelling like cologne, his asking for a kiss in a private den. . . .

Damn, maybe Evan was right.

"I, um . . ." She couldn't bring herself to admit it. "I really don't remember much of the night." There. That was true, at least.

"I think he wanted more than you're telling me."

Another point for Evan.

But still, he didn't have to take it to the next not-necessarily-logical conclusion, did he? That Kyle wanted to drug Lia? Why would he risk his career, his livelihood, to do something so illegal in his own club, in public? He was one of the most powerful men in Orange County—why would he want a kiss, or a boat, or sex, or whatever, from *her*? That was preposterous.

"Well, I'll be sure to make things clear with him, if it'll make you feel better." She'd acquiesce that much. "But I really need you to run the charter. He wants you to run it. He likes you. He wants us all to be friends."

"I don't think we're all going to be friends, Cinderella."

"Okay, so we won't be friends. But can you just run the charter?"

"There's the issue of Drew, too. He doesn't want me to run the charter. Or even the boat."

"I talked to Drew."

"So did I."

"I talked to him later."

He crossed his arms again and squinted at her.

"That's the other part of the favor. When I told Drew that Kyle might want to invest, he said he would 'unfire' you."

"He doesn't mind my running the boat?"

"He needs you."

Evan looked away and thought that over. "He was pretty

pissed when I talked to him." The sadness and failure in his voice made her chest hurt.

The water made peaceful, sloshing noises against the resting hull. "What happened between you two?" she asked quietly.

He shook his head. "It's a long story."

She let him have a pass on that one. Clearly, neither brother wanted to talk about it. Plus, there was the other favor she needed. . . .

"So what are you doing for dinner tonight?"

He crooked an eyebrow.

"I, um . . ." She fidgeted against the boat rail. "I have two tickets to a huge shindig at the Ocean Museum tonight—wine, appetizers, desserts, that kind of thing. You can eat really well. Let that be our thanks to you, for helping us out through Monday."

"No thanks."

"But it's right down the marina. About a hundred yards from your boat. And you have to eat anyway. They get some of the best local vintners and chefs for these events."

"Doesn't really sound like my thing." He turned back to his console and tucked the binoculars underneath.

"There's live jazz, and . . . they raise *lots* of money for the marine mammals." There. He'd like that part.

"Seems like something you and your boyfriend should do together."

"It's not a *date*. It's a . . . well . . ."

He folded the Valentine flyer and stuffed it in his pocket.

". . . you know, a . . ." She shrugged. "A charity event. Part of the business."

"Another favor?" He headed down the steps.

"Well, all right, if that's how you want to look at it." She followed him down. "I'd go with Drew if he were running the boat this week. But Kyle's going to be there, and the Vampi— um, I mean, *Elle* . . . wants me to go. And make nice with him. And apologize. And make sure everything's good for the charter."

She almost bumped right into him as he whirled around. "I haven't even agreed to do this charter for that slimeball, and you're already asking if I'll go and make nice with him at some charity event involving wine and jazz and *more people*?"

"And apologize."

"And *apologize*?"

"There's good food," she offered weakly.

Evan headed for the galley.

"Really, the food is fabulous." She followed him as he gathered up his things and lifted his hand in good-bye to Douglas and Cora. "I saw how much you like to eat. This food will be just as good. There are desserts from Sandy Cove Dessert Company, and—"

"Lia, *please*." He turned around. "I don't want to go. I'll run the two tours on the weekend, and then the charter on Monday if you want, but I don't want to go to a big event tonight. There are at least ten good reasons why I shouldn't."

"Well, I have ten good reasons why you *should*. So let's tell them to each other over bacon-wrapped shrimp, and if yours cancel mine out by dinner, you can leave."

He squinted down at her. She could see him warring with something in his head, but he still hadn't said no.

"What were you going to have for dinner tonight?" she asked gently. "Green beans out of a can?"

"I like green beans."

"Bacon-wrapped shrimp is better."

He stared out at the marina. She wished she knew what the final thing would be, to kick things in her favor, and almost started rattling off ideas, but something told her to wait.

Finally, slowly, as the boat pitched gently and the seagulls squawked overhead, he shrugged.

"All right," he said. "Ten reasons. Before dinner. Where is this thing?"

---CHAPTER---

Sixteen

He was clearly insane.

Or maybe just a glutton for punishment.

As he pulled the funeral suit out of the closet and threw it on the bed, he told himself it was the food that was bringing him to this thing, but he knew it was more.

It was a pair of flashing blue eyes. It was a pint-sized ball of energy who was making him feel again. It was a pair of quivering breasts that got his blood pumping to his groin, and a vulnerable admission about keeping a job and wanting to go to Paris that got his blood pumping to his heart. It was the thought of the thong beneath her clothes; the memory of the body he saw under her champagne underthings that first night; and her sweet, dangerous breath on his cheek when she said phrases like "I think I like it."

And *did he almost kiss her*? He couldn't believe he almost did that. Not only did she have a boyfriend—although the jerk was nowhere to be seen, not even a phone call when she felt like she was at death's door—but she was another of Drew's friends that he absolutely couldn't move in on. He was still begging forgiveness for the first one.

Renece had been introduced to him on his dad's sailboat

when he was nineteen. He'd been a scrawny, nerdy kid—out of high school for just past a year, and restless. He'd been a science geek in high school, and had studied hard, especially biology, spending too many hours in the lab where he could be his introverted self. But, despite his scrawniness, he hadn't been afraid to fight. He'd loved it, for whatever reason. And when he was teased in the halls, his first reaction since first grade had always been to take a swing, which landed him in the principal's office at least once a week.

In high school, he hadn't dated much—he'd been terrified of girls—except to go to a dance once with a neighbor girl who'd asked him because his mom had begged her to. He'd gotten to second base once with another girl who'd all but come on to him at a football game one night, despite his braces and weakling status, but that was about the extent of his female experience.

In his junior year, his parents had separated abruptly, and his dad had flown to northern California, dragging Evan along with the promise that he could go to a specialized school that focused on biology. Only when Evan arrived did he realize it was a military school. That was when Evan had started resenting Drew, who got to stay in their hometown, stay with their mom, stay with the way things were.

Twelve hours after he graduated, Evan looked into joining the military. He went with Coast Guard. He figured he could still study biology that way. His dad had been a little shocked by the Coast Guard thing, but Evan could tell he'd been proud, too. It was the first time Evan ever felt he was worth anything.

Before enlisting, though, Evan began working out. He went to the gym every day, without fail. He'd started eating better, loading up on protein, doing push-ups and pull-ups three times a day, punching with a punching bag, and—before he knew it—he began filling out.

That was the summer he met Renece.

She'd boarded the boat with a girlfriend, both in their summer dresses, both looking like movie stars as far as he was concerned. The boat had been set up for Drew's eighteenth birthday, and all of his friends were on board. Evan stood in the back shyly, loading fishing lines in case some of Drew's buddies wanted to do some catch and release, glancing at the pretty girls, but mostly watching Renece.

Drew had sauntered over and introduced Renece to Evan about halfway through the trip. He'd made a special trip, even. He'd left the two of them alone, and Renece had perched on the edge of a bench and giggled at everything Evan said, asking him questions about his studies, what he liked about the ocean, what kind of biology he most enjoyed. At one point, she reached toward his arm and ran her finger along his brand-new biceps and told him he was easily the most handsome boy on the boat. And he'd been a goner after that.

The day after the party, he'd summoned the nerve to call her. He'd flattened the piece of paper she'd handed him with her number on it, and finally dialed. They'd made plans to meet on the beach, and he'd gotten as far as holding her hand. He'd braved it enough to kiss her on the second date. And on the fourth date, because he was so afraid of her, she'd taken it upon herself to undo his zipper and finally take his virginity. He hadn't gotten used to his new body yet, and hadn't fully accepted all the compliments Renece had given him on his muscles, his size, his looks, but she'd made him feel manly and in control for the first time. He knew he'd never forget her.

Three weeks later, after he'd slept with her eleven times and had decided he was completely in love, Drew invited him out with some of his friends and revealed he was dating Renece Peters. Evan had about choked on his hamburger.

"Since when?"

"Well, I might be jumping the gun. I've only gone out with her once. But I've been in love with her since kindergarten, and we've been friends since junior high. I make sure I have at least one class per year with her so I can sit next to her and walk to class with her. I'd marry her tomorrow if I could."

Evan had coughed up a lettuce leaf lodged in his throat. "Why have I never heard you mention her?"

"You've been away too long, bro." Drew had punched him in the arm—his favorite new activity since Evan had finally surpassed him in weight.

"She's hot," one of Drew's buddies had verified with a lecherous grin.

Evan had glared at the friend but finally returned his attention to Drew: "When did you go out with her?"

"About . . . two nights after my party?" Drew had popped a fry in his mouth. "You remember her, right? I introduced you. She was the one in the purple dress."

"I remember."

If he'd just blurted out, right then and there, that he'd been dating the very same girl, all might have been okay. But his secretive nature had bitten him in the ass. He'd gnawed the end of his straw, ignored the morons high-fiving Drew, and tried to slurp some soda down. "And you haven't dated her since?"

"No. But I called her last night and asked her out, and she said she has a boyfriend, but she thinks they're going to break up. He's going into the service or something."

Evan had felt the blood drain from his face.

He'd choked down his fries, choked down his hamburger, and contacted Renece as soon as he could get away.

"Are you dating my *brother*?" he'd asked.

Renece's lyrical laugh had drifted through the phone. "No. He's been in love with me all through school, I think, but I only went out with him once. To be nice. I didn't even hold his hand, or let him kiss me good night. I like you much, *much* better. . . ."

Evan hadn't heard that line very often, and it filled him with warmth. And strength. And the feeling of worth. But still . . . It was his brother.

"He thinks you're breaking up with your boyfriend because he's going into the service."

Silence had filled the other line. "I was worried you were going to break up with me, Evan. Are you?"

"No! I mean . . . I hadn't planned on it. Is that what you want?"

"No. I want to marry you. But you have an exciting life ahead of you, and I wasn't—"

"Let's do it."

"What?"

"Let's get married."

"*What?* When?"

"Before I leave."

"Evan, we can't . . . *Can* we?"

"Of course."

When he'd announced the next day to his family that he was marrying Renece Peters, he was met with a round of silence. The silence was broken, about three seconds later, by his mother's soft sobs, his father's barked question if she was pregnant, and the whoosh of Drew's fist as it punched him in the face.

Renece's family hadn't given them a much warmer send-off.

They'd ended up getting married at the San Diego courthouse with two sets of crying mothers, two suspicious-looking fathers, a bouquet of daisies, a barely healed black eye, and a two-hundred-dollar ring Evan had hardly been able to afford from his scraped-up savings from cleaning labs at night. Drew hadn't come at all. . . .

The sailboat now pitched as Evan tucked his tie under his collar and bent down to look at his reflection in the small stateroom mirror. He tightened the tie around his neck.

So he couldn't kiss Lia. Or touch her. Or even look at her as much as he wanted to. He would allow himself to spend one more evening with a woman who made him think of life instead of death, but then he was done. She had a boyfriend. And he wasn't in the game of inadvertently stealing anymore. And she and Drew had some kind of connection, even if they couldn't identify it. Cinderella kept saying she and Drew were friends, but that's what Renece had thought, too. And Evan wanted to make one last attempt to *apologize* to Drew—it wouldn't help matters if he was having feelings for another of Drew's friends.

He straightened the knot in the mirror and gave it one more tug.

Glutton for punishment, for sure.

Lia stood on the sidewalk in front of the Ocean Museum and stared at the night-lit entrance banners billowing in the breeze, with artwork splashed across the center heralding the start of the Whale Festival. Her first thought was that the artwork was beautiful—a minimalist sweep of blues and grays, depicting a whale spout—and her second was to wonder who the ad agency was.

"Lia, hello!"

"Hello, Mr. Thompson." She shook hands with the owner of one of the most exclusive hotels in the area, who she'd done some ad work with.

"This is my wife, Linda."

Lia was almost always one of the youngest people at these kinds of events, but she knew how to hold her own. She always stayed on top of the new openings, changes in county politics, and the overall who-was-who in the area. She easily slid into conversation with Linda, admired her sequin-rimmed cocktail dress, and nodded in agreement at the beauty of the Ocean Museum's new wing and courtyard.

"Are you coming in?" Mr. Thompson asked.

"I'm waiting for someone."

"We'll see you inside, then."

Lia nodded and ran her hands up her arms, twisting on the sidewalk to see if Evan was coming. As her eagerness gave way to a strange trepidation, and the goose bumps on her arms seemed more from nervousness than from cold, she hoped this wasn't a mistake. She hoped he would come with the requisite suit and respect for these kinds of events, not to mention the humility it would take to apologize to Kyle.

But a small spear of panic shot through her when she realized how unlikely that was. Her best navy clutch bumped against the sequins of her dress as she rubbed her arms more furiously. *What had she been thinking?* Evan was not Drew. Drew would show up with his hair neatly parted, his suit neatly pressed, and would shake hands with all the people she told him to, even though he hated to shake hands. (She allowed him brief escapes to swath with antibacterial gel.)

But Evan didn't seem the least bit interested in selling himself. He was more likely to show up and embarrass her with his suspicious, sullen behavior in front of important people like Mr. and Mrs. Thompson.

While she had jumped at—well, okay, sort of *manipulated*— the possibility of spending another evening with him and his sexy arms, she now realized her ridiculous attraction to a

rough-around-the-edges, secretive, intensely roguish man might
have clouded her usually good business judgment.

"There you are." His deep voice came through the dark.

She whirled to see him step up from the marina docks,
circle a bird of paradise bush, and shove his hands in the pockets of a dark blue suit with an ocean blue tie that matched his
eyes. His hair still came down over the starched white collar,
but he'd slicked it back in a debonair look. He didn't greet her
with a smile—more of a look of dread—but a breath of relief
still escaped her lungs.

"Hey there," she finally managed. He even had dress
shoes on.

"Hey."

"You look great."

"You clean up pretty well yourself." His eyes made a quick
sweep of her dress, which happened to match his suit almost
exactly. He stalled slightly at her breasts, but then cut his gaze
away and cleared his throat.

"I was hoping you didn't change your mind," she said,
scrambling for the small talk she was usually so good at.

"No, but I have ten pretty solid reasons I shouldn't be here,
so you're going to have to do some clever convincing." He was
already scrutinizing the festival banners.

"Okay." Another shiver went through her. "Let's get inside
and get at least one bacon-wrapped shrimp in you to help
me out."

They entered the museum courtyard through a bright green
shrubbery arch coiled with twinkling lights, Evan taking in
everything with critical surveillance. After handing over their
tickets, they stepped into a large, pebbled patio strewn with
lace-tablecloth-covered bar tables, the cloth tied at the base of
each table to create martini-glass shapes. Glass-block vases of
hot pink orchids sat in the center of each table, illuminated with
tea lights. Lia snagged a table toward the back, one with no
chairs, where they could keep an eye on the entrance for Kyle.

Once their stake was claimed with her clutch purse, she
grabbed two champagne glasses off a passing tray and set one
on the table in front of Evan. Her confidence was back, her
work hat back on. "So ten reasons why you shouldn't be here.
We'll count backwards. Number ten: Go."

He took a sip with the bandaged hand. "I hate crowds."

"Yeah," she said, leaning in. "Why is that, anyway, Captain Betancourt? Is that why you live on that boat all by yourself?"

"I didn't think this was an interrogation. I thought I just had to tell you my reasons."

"Well, we only count them as valid if I can't counter them."

"So how do you counter the fact that I hate crowds and you've just invited me to a party?"

"As far as crowds go, this one's pretty small, you have to admit."

He glanced around, looking none too certain.

"It's fifty people max," she insisted. "And you know two of the attendees already. And, if you're going to ease yourself back into society, this might be the way to go."

"What makes you think I'm easing myself back into society?"

"Aren't you?"

"No. I'm back on the boat as soon as my engine's fixed."

"So why did you stop here, anyway? Was it to see Drew?"

"Just to fix the engine."

"But why here?"

He looked away, letting his gaze bounce around to the other patrons. "It was just to fix the engine, Cinderella."

A tray of hors d'oeuvres passed by, and Lia took a few spears of prosciutto-wrapped asparagus on cocktail napkins and set two in front of Evan. "Certainly you could have stopped in San Diego, where I'd think you knew the marinas better. I think you pulled in here, whether consciously or subconsciously, because you really wanted to see Drew again."

He ignored the appetizers she'd set in front of him and stared at her from under his eyebrows. "Let's move on."

"Okay, well 'crowds' is negated because there are less than fifty people here. And besides, I'm here to protect you from all the crazy extroverts. I can hold my own with any of them." She smiled and popped her asparagus spear in her mouth. "Reason nine?"

"I hate dressing up."

Her perusal snagged at his biceps, which strained the navy fabric sleeves as he leaned across the bar table. "Well, you should try it more often. You look great."

Better words than "great" leaped to her mind—*powerful, sexy, hot, virile, lickable, jumpable*—but she knew she needed to watch her mouth tonight. This was no time to blurt out what she was really thinking.

"I wouldn't have pinned you for a suit-in-the-back-of-the-sailboat kind of guy," she said diplomatically. "Where else do you wear it?"

"We're not interrogating, remember?"

"I just want to know where you wear all that gorgeousness. Looks like Armani."

"Funerals."

Lia blinked. Her cocktail napkin slid to the floor. The jazz guitarist struck up a new number in the corner of the patio surrounded by twinkling lights and Japanese boxwood plants, and she used the musical distraction to pick up her napkin and regain her composure.

"I'm really sorry to hear about your wife," she finally said, her voice only loud enough to be heard over the guitar. "How long ago did you lose her?"

Evan shook his head. "We don't want to talk about death at a party. Sorry I said that. Let's move on."

"No, I want to know."

A strand of hair had escaped his carefully slicked-back style and fell across his eyes. "Two years ago. But that's all I'm saying. Let's move on."

"Do you not like to talk about her?"

A scowl crossed his forehead. "I love to talk about her. But it just doesn't seem appropriate right now. Next topic."

"What did she look like?"

He shook his head and laughed a little. "You do your own thing, don't you, Lia? Don't take direction very well?"

"As I said, it's not my strong suit." She took a sip of champagne and looked away from his dimple. "So what did she look like?"

He stared at his glass stem, twisting it. "She looked a little like Avery, actually."

Lia's eyes widened. *Avery?* Really?" She reran all the looks Evan had given Avery, and viewed them through a new filter. "Is that why you were all over her?"

"All *over* her?"

"Well, you know, the touching, and all that . . ."

"I wasn't touching her."

"Well, you know, holding her in the galley when she stumbled into you, and letting her hold your arm at the club, and being alone with her in the den at the end of the night . . ."

Meeting Evan's confused stare, Lia bit her tongue. She realized she'd just catalogued every pass she saw between the two of them and how obsessed it made her sound.

She took a nervous sip.

"Well, I thought she was pretty, but I wouldn't say I was attracted to her exactly," Evan said. "And I certainly didn't think I was 'all over her.' She made me uncomfortable, actually."

She watched Evan spin the stem of his champagne glass and was suddenly struck with the fact that he was opening up. The enormity of the gift, and the enormity of his loneliness, hit her full center in her chest.

"I might think seeing a woman who reminded you of the wife you lost would be a good thing," she speculated. Though her sudden curiosity spike was followed by an embarrassing twinge of jealousy toward Avery.

"You'd think," he said. "But it wasn't."

As embarrassing as the twinge of jealousy was, so was the next wave of relief.

What in the world was wrong with her? Did she think she was going to fill the terrible void in his life? She shook off the absurdity and began to formulate her next question.

"We're moving on now," he said quietly.

But she wasn't done. Her lips formed into the *W* for her question—she was filled with curiosity—but he shot her a stern look.

"*Seriously.* Move on."

As annoying as bossy men were to her usually, Evan, for some reason, was maddeningly sexy. Long-dormant tingles in all of her favorite body parts came to the surface, shocking her and horrifying her at the same time. Lia averted her eyes quickly, caught her breath, and realized she had quite possibly lost her whole sense of self.

"Give me reason eight," she muttered.

"I'm not crazy about jazz."

"Aw, this guy's pretty good."

Evan glanced over his shoulder at the guitarist but didn't respond.

"Okay, I suppose that's legit," she said. "Everyone is entitled to like what they like. What kind of music do you like?"

"Interrogation?"

"No, it's part of my counter reply."

"How is that? Are you going to make it magically appear?"

"Maybe I can request something."

He gave her his first double-dimple smile of the evening. "I'll give you a pass on that one—out of your control. What are we on, now? Seven?"

Lia tore her eyes away from his dimples and tried to get her heart to stop pounding so embarrassingly. "I believe so."

He picked up, then put down, his glass. "Number seven is that this champagne is terrible. Can I get us something else to drink?" Without waiting for her answer, he turned to look for a bar. "What'll you have?"

"I'm good."

He nodded and went in pursuit solo.

While he was gone, Lia fluffed the neckline of her dress and tried to air out the perspiration she could feel dripping down the center of her bra. She took another few breaths to recover from that last sweet smile of his, and the soft voice asking about her drink preferences that sounded something like a regular date, something she just decided would be an awfully sexy thing to have. What did Evan do at the end of a date? Did he kiss at the door? Invite himself in? Push his date back into the entry hall while undoing her zipper down her back?

Lia fluffed her neckline another seven times.

This was not a date. She had an almost-boyfriend. She should not be having tingling lady parts over this guy. . . .

Another wave of embarrassment washed over her when she realized she hadn't thought of Forrest once all night. At the sudden realization, she yanked her cell phone out of her purse and scrolled for messages. There were none from him, but he had another social media post that seemed as strange as the last nine: *There is more wisdom in your body than in your deepest philosophy.—Friedrich Nietzsche.*

"Looking for messages from your boyfriend?" Evan's voice startled her.

She shakily clicked her phone off and shoved it back into her clutch. "I'll look later."

"I notice he didn't call much when you were sick. Or at all." He set a glass of water down in the center of the table.

"Water?" she asked.

"I want to stay sober."

"Long drive?" She smiled.

"I just think I need my wits about me tonight," he said, avoiding her eyes. "So what's with the never-calling boyfriend?"

"It's . . ." She shook her head. She didn't think it was fair to discuss Forrest when he wasn't there.

"Are you very serious?"

She shook off the question again. She and Drew had had this discussion so many times. She didn't like the idea of people tying each other down, or keeping each other from traveling, or doing whatever they wanted. She always kept things light with boyfriends, not wanting to place demands and not wanting demands placed on her. But Drew said that's why she'd never been in love: If you didn't jump in with both feet, committing your heart wholly and completely, you would never experience true love.

Either way, she didn't want to discuss this with Evan.

"Dinner's almost here and you need six more reasons to avoid it," she said.

"Number six is that I don't like pretentious people, and these kinds of things tend to be filled with them."

"Well played, Captain. I'll counter with Exhibit A, Exhibit B, and Exhibit C." She nodded across the patio at each uttered letter. "Exhibit A is Mr. Rossmoor over there. He's on the board of trustees for the Marine Mammal Search and Rescue and gave up a lucrative legal career to join forces with the MMSR and save abandoned baby seals in the area. Exhibit B is Ms. Gomez. She's a former Assistant U.S. Attorney who quit her job to offer free legal counsel to environmentalists in the area who want to keep the oceans clean. She donates tens of thousands a year to the Ocean Museum. And Exhibit C is Carissa Delgado. She's a past president of the American Cetacean Society who donates forty hours a week to make sure fishing lines are pulled up properly so as not to harm the whales." She took a sip of champagne. "These people are the real deal."

His eyebrow raised while he studied each of her exhibits. "How do you know them?" he asked with a new note of respect in his voice.

"Elle has been representing most of them for years. I come to a lot of the events for her. These charity ones are my favorite because I like to see people doing real things, and making a difference."

"Does Elle donate, too?"

"Yes, but she's a bloodsucker. She's in it for the money."

He smiled. "Is that why you call her a vampiress?"

Lia's eyes widened. "Did I say that when I was out of it?"

"Something like that." He gave her an understanding smile.

"Oh my God, I can't believe I let that slip. Don't say anything."

He frowned and shook his head. "So why don't you tell me more about why you want to see Paris so badly?"

"I—" She shook her head. She didn't even know where to start. It had been so long since anyone had asked about her dreams and goals.

"First, why don't you tell me your last five reasons for not wanting to be here?" she skirted. "Although—"

A figure caught her eye over Evan's shoulder. Her stomach fell. "You might have to tell me later. Kyle's coming our way."

"Ah, then here comes reason five right now."

CHAPTER

Seventeen

Evan watched the color drain from Lia's face as Stevens came into his peripheral vision. The jazz guitar slid into a slow chorus.

"Kyle!" Lia said with a smile that looked gorgeous and fake at the same time. Or maybe gorgeous because of the fakeness. When it came to Stevens, Evan supported fakery. Maybe she was finally starting to be wary of that guy.

"How are my two favorite boaters?" Kyle schmoozed in an already-one-too-many-vodkas voice. His black eye had faded to a light purple and he sported a small bandage over his nose.

"Stevens." Evan nodded.

"Listen, I'm actually glad to see you both here. I hope our fun the other night wasn't taken in the wrong way. Lia, how are you feeling, darling?"

Darling? Evan ground his teeth together.

"I'm doing much better," she gushed. "Thanks for sending the roses, and the medic, and *everything*."

Evan raised an eyebrow at her easy agreeableness. His first instinct was to jump in and help her, maybe give Kyle a dressing down, or at the very least save her from seeming too easy-going around a leech of a man, but he remembered how much she hated that. He took a few gulps of water to keep his mouth shut.

"I'm feeling great now, but I've had to do some fancy foot-work with Elle," she said, the smile never leaving her face.

As Evan watched her over the rim of his glass, he almost saw the exact moment her affability turned into some sort of shrewd marketing skill.

"Really?" asked Kyle. "About what?"

"She's under the impression I caused you to pull the char-ter, and I think she's seconds away from firing me."

"No, no," Kyle said, looking away.

Evan leaned back and smiled. Now he was ready to watch this with interest.

"I'm sure you wouldn't mind talking to her again, Kyle?" Cinderella said, with the sweetest expression. "Setting her straight?"

Stevens's gaze darted around the crowd. "Well, the truth is, Lia—"

"I know you didn't mean to get me *fired*." She laughed a little.

Stevens paused. Stared into his glass. Swirled his drink.

Good job, Lia. Let's see him get out of this one.

"Fact is," Stevens said, "I *was* thinking of pulling the char-ter. I wasn't sure Captain Betancourt here would have me."

Evan had sort of guessed he'd be Stevens's scapegoat for this one. But he sure as hell didn't have to let it play out.

"I'm good with it," Evan choked out in Kyle's general direction. "Sorry about the . . ." He lifted his bandaged hand.

"Really?" Stevens looked at him.

Evan nodded. He wasn't truly sorry for interrupting Kyle's behavior that night, but he definitely didn't want to get Lia fired. He'd do the charter. He'd just make sure Stevens didn't pull any more funny stuff. And maybe he'd hide the liquor just to be sure.

"Well!" Stevens looked boyishly grateful. "Let's do this, then." He looked between the two of them. "Monday at nine."

"Your father is coming, too, right?" Lia asked.

"Right."

"We'll see you then, Kyle." Lia dismissed him with the sweetest, most courteous smile Evan had ever seen.

"So, reason five averted," she said over her champagne glass as her smile broadened. "What's reason four?"

"That was brilliant."

"Thank you."

"You *are* good at your job."

She bobbed her head. She knew. "So what's reason four?"

"Reason four is no longer valid. It was that I'm lousy at apologizing."

"Is that why you're having trouble with Drew?"

The next jazz guitar number started and gave him an excuse to look away.

"Evan?"

He looked back into Cinderella's perceptive eyes.

"Are you having trouble apologizing to Drew?" Her voice was understanding, accepting, probably perceiving much more than he wanted to give her credit for. She certainly had his number on the pulling-into-Sandy-Cove thing. He hadn't even thought of it himself—he honestly thought he was here just to fix his engine. But she was right. He could have stopped in San Diego.

"Maybe I can help," she added softly. "He listens to me, and we have a good connection."

Evan turned his glass between his palms. He *did* have some questions regarding her and Drew. . . .

"What exactly is your relationship?" he asked.

"We're friends; I told you."

"But . . . was there ever anything more?"

She frowned. "No. Why do you ask?"

Relief swept through him. "Just curious."

"We might have kissed once."

As quickly as the relief had come, jealousy set in. Evan pictured his brother kissing this beautiful woman and let the heat fire up around his ears without looking up. He cleared his throat and stared at his glass. "You kissed?"

"Once. But it was silly. We both cracked up. It wasn't right."

His lungs managed to fill again.

"But anyway, I can get you two to talk," she said. "Maybe I can arrange something for this weekend. We can meet on the boat, or you and I can go to Drew's house."

Evan nodded. It was a possibility.

"You did all right with Kyle just now," she nudged.

He couldn't help but smile at that. "Thanks to you. Nice job, again, Cinderella. I didn't even have to grovel."

"I can't see you groveling anyway."

"I would've, for you." He hadn't meant to let the admission slip, but now that it had, he reluctantly met her eyes. Her face softened into an unspoken thank you, her eyes never leaving his, her lips parting.

Evan shifted. Every body part on him that had been dead for much too long began perking up again and pulsating its protest: his groin, his heart, his veins, the arteries of his neck. He could even feel the blood pounding through his arms, and had to resist stepping forward and wrapping them all the way around this woman, who was soothing him and turning him on in a strange sort of out-of-control way. He wanted to move closer, but knew it wasn't a good idea. He settled for a half step, even as a mayday distress signal sounded through his head.

"What's reason three?" she asked, her voice cracking. She twisted her champagne glass.

"Reason three is I didn't want to see you in this dress."

A pucker creased her brows. She glanced down. "*This* dress?"

"Or whatever dress you were going to wear."

Her frown deepened. "Why did you not want—?"

"Because of reason two."

Her yellow hair shimmered as she shook her head. "Which is . . . ?"

"That you make me forget about my wife. You've made me forget for entire days. And you're the first woman who's ever done so."

The heat around his collar moved toward his face, making him feel raw and vulnerable. This was why he kept things to himself—spurting out how you really felt always brought a rawness that was unbearable.

But she stepped closer.

Dangerous.

She put her hand on his arm, which was more dangerous still.

By the time her lips parted and her eyes softened, she had put herself in complete peril. Of him.

He didn't know what possessed him next, but within seconds he had his bandaged hand in her hair and was pulling her toward him, enveloping her into his body, bending down toward her, covering her mouth with his. Her lips were soft and giving, kind and hopeful, understanding and open, just as he'd imagined they'd be. Her fingertips came to his chin, soothing and gentle, and he let them play along his jawline, up to his ear, relishing in the warmth that overcame him for the first time in two years, as his body relaxed and became taut at the same time. She tasted so sweet—like vanilla and home. And when he closed his mouth deeper over hers, he caught the tease of her tongue—flickering and promising, just the tip— and a heat shot through his groin. He pressed into her, wanting more, wanting to take her right there. He wanted her naked, wanted to feel her soft skin, wanted to feel that softness beneath her breasts and between her thighs that he knew would be silken—the highest vulnerability. A long-dormant need for that vulnerability felt like it was splitting inside his chest—that need to be open, exposed, trusting, and ultimately one with another human being who would be careful with it. He desperately stepped farther into her, pressed his tongue deeper, but as soon as he felt the table behind her back— realized he'd pushed them both into it—some kind of miraculous sense came into his brain and he shoved himself away, panting.

He stepped back and sent about twenty swear words through his head.

"And that would be reason one," he managed to get out. "I didn't want to do that."

Lia resisted the urge to press her fingertips to her lips, to preserve that kiss somehow, and instead tucked her hair behind her ear, smoothed her dress, and glanced at the table beside them. Luckily the next patrons over hadn't seemed to notice their inability to keep their hands off each other here in the corner of the patio.

The jazz guitar fell into relaxed notes as Lia caught her breath and touched the stem of her empty champagne glass.

"More?" A waiter swept in beside her.

Yes, please was her first thought. *More of those kisses, more of Evan's fist in her hair, more of his body draped over hers, more of that promise of how much more intensity he had wound inside that body of his. . . .*

The waiter motioned to her glass.

"No thank you," she squeaked.

She had a boyfriend. Didn't she? Not that she and Forrest were exactly committed to each other. . . . And not that he called once in eight days to find out how she was. . . . And not that he had *ever* kissed her like *that*. Not ever.

She glanced up at Evan, who was staring at the table. He ran his hand down his face.

"I'm really sorry," he said gruffly. "Won't happen again."

Well, that's too bad.

She straightened the neckline of her dress and nodded politely.

She had Forrest. And smart, nearing-thirty women were supposed to date to marry, weren't they? They were supposed to look for stable men who would be good fathers, who had good jobs that matched theirs, and made at least as much money as they did. Who were reasonable and polite, and wanted to be equals in a relationship. Who were urbane and had good manners, and who ate the continental way and knew what to wear to an expensive club.

She moved her empty glass around the table, glanced at Evan again, and wondered why, then, her breath was coming in short rasps every time she looked at this guy.

"Tell me you forgive me," Evan said, low.

"For a guy who isn't good at apologies, you sure have a lot of them in you."

Several clumps of hair had fallen over his eyes. He shoved them back and gave her an embarrassed glance. "I should be an expert by now, eh?" He looked back over his shoulder. "Can I get you some water? Or something stronger, maybe?"

"Water would be good."

He bolted toward the bar.

Lia took a deep breath and rummaged in her clutch for her lipstick and compact. When she saw her swollen lips in the mirror, her lipstick smudged and feathered from that amazing kiss, another tingle shot through her, straight between her legs.

Dang.

She was in trouble.

And that was with clothes on. As her mind began to drift to what Evan could do to her without clothes on—

Another deep breath followed the first.

She needed to push away these thoughts, push away this tingling, push away this guilt. . . .

To distract herself, or perhaps to get her thoughts reassembled, she checked her messages again. Another twenty had come through, several from work, including four from the Vampiress. But still nothing from Forrest. He had posted another social media message, though: *The unexamined life is not worth living.—Socrates.*

What the hell was up with Forrest?

Feeling guilty, she dashed off a quick text to him: *"Hi, Forrest. Hope you're having fun. Haven't heard from you at all and just wondering how things are going."*

She reread it and realized it sounded like she was talking to a cubicle-mate, but it would have to do.

She glanced up for Evan. He was nowhere to be seen. Maybe he was trying to slip out the back door. While she waited, she pretended she was looking at her messages, but in reality her mind was drifting back to the conversation that had led to the kiss. *Did he say she made him forget about his dead wife? And that she was the first woman to do so?*

At the memory, a warmth curled in her chest, warring with the tingling that was moving out to all of her extremities and causing a near-spontaneous combustion of some sort.

She wiped her brow.

"Telling on me to your boyfriend?" Evan's voice rumbled over her shoulders.

"Of course not." She shivered and threw her phone back in her purse.

"I wouldn't blame you." He set her water down on the table and stepped all the way around to the other side.

She watched his tanned hands, pictured them in her hair again, pictured them touching her jaw as he kissed her again, pictured them running alongside her naked breast . . .

"I'm really sorry, Cinderella."

Her head bobbed several times to make up for her vanished voice.

"I don't know what came over me," he said. "That was a lousy thing to do, to both you and him. Tell him I'm sorry. What's his name, anyway?"

"Forrest."

He nodded. "It's good I know his name. So am I forgiven, or would you like me to leave, or what?"

"You're forgiven." She refused to look into his eyes again, for fear of the spontaneous combustion. She couldn't even look at his hands now. Instead, she focused on the orchid floating in the glass block in the center of the table and noticed that Evan brought a scotch back this time.

She wanted to ask so many questions, like was it true what he said about her making him forget about his dead wife, and what was her name, and why did he say "funerals"—plural? But something told her she was walking a fine line here. She had a long history of blurting out whatever was on her mind. And if she did that here—and admitted that that was the most passionate and memorable kiss she'd ever received in her twenty-nine years—she would be betraying the only boyfriend she'd ever had that seemed like marriage material.

And since that was the only sure thing in her life these days, as sad as that seemed, she thought she'd hang on.

He turned to watch the jazz guitarist he pretended to like, and she did the same.

Dinner went on forever, although it was as good as Lia had promised.

It was held in the next room over, inside the newly funded Ocean Museum, and there were plenty of things to look at and focus on, thankfully, to keep his mind off his boorish behavior and the way the light hit the sparkles of Lia's dress and accentuated every one of her curves.

There were speeches, a short documentary, plenty of applause, four courses, too many utensils, tanks of starfish and seahorses lining the back wall that caught his attention, a whale skeleton that hung from the ceiling and demanded his scrutiny when he was being good, and—of course—Lia's curves when he wasn't.

As dinner ended, she pulled out a checkbook and scrawled out a hefty donation from her company.

"Ready to go?" she asked.

"Yeah." He should've left two hours ago. Sometime before that kiss.

They said good-bye to Stevens, verified the time of the charter, then stood awkwardly as Stevens introduced them as "the captains" of the upcoming charter to four or five silver-haired patrons who were, apparently, going to be aboard. The patrons all acted impressed and asked good questions about the whales, begging Evan to tell them what he knew about Valentine and walk them through an explanation of the ceiling skeleton. Evan gave them longer answers than he probably needed to. Their silver-headed nods and serious expressions were strangely comforting. He sometimes forgot that other people really loved the ocean as much as he did.

By the time he and Lia headed up the sidewalk along the marina shops in the cool night air, he had to admit to himself that he'd had a good time.

Except the kiss.

That had made him feel guilty.

"You don't have to walk me to my car," she said. "I know where it is."

"Chalk it up to military training."

She stiffened as they marched toward the parking lot.

"I promise I won't try another kiss when we get there," he said, glancing once to make sure she took that as a joke. "Sorry again. It was a stupid impulse."

She gave a perfunctory nod.

The wind whipped off the water and blew the banners into a bit of chaos—all shouting "Whale Festival!" from every light post along the marina.

"This place is going to be crazy tomorrow." Lia shivered as she walked against the ocean breeze.

Evan slid his jacket off. "I remember how it gets. Here." He held the jacket open.

"It's okay." She pushed it away. But then, as another gust came up through the narrow rows of shops, she succumbed, letting him settle it over her shoulders.

"It's probably even bigger than when you saw it last," she said. "Are you going to be okay with these crowds, doing the weekend tours? I'll be coordinating Drew's booth, and I'll take any help Douglas or Cora want to give, but I don't plan to be on the boat. But if you need me . . ."

The phrase rang through his brain like a distress call. "Need" was something he hadn't thought of in a while, and the "need" going through his mind right now, relating to this woman, was surprising him. And probably not what she was talking about.

Why couldn't he have experienced this with someone else? Someone, maybe *available*? And damn it, how about someone Drew didn't know?

"I'll be fine," he lied.

"Here's my car," she said. "Do you have a place to stay tonight? They'll be watching the harbor closely for sneak-aboards with this many people around."

He shoved his hands in his pockets and nodded.

"You're staying at the motel?"

"Yeah."

"Do you want a ride?"

"I have to go back to my boat first."

"Do you . . . Do you want to stay at my place?"

The idea buoyed him for a flash of a second, but then he noticed how carefully she avoided his eyes.

"Given the circumstances, I don't think that would be a good idea," he admitted.

She nodded her agreement.

He watched her get in the car—her curves, her yellow Cinderella hair, her understanding eyes, her delicious lips, her upbeat attitude that was lifting him in ways that suddenly and mysteriously now called to mind the word "need."

And then he watched her drive away.

He might have just screwed up the best thing that had happened to him in two years.

Eighteen

Lia awoke the next morning and planned her day in her head as she stared at the late-February light across her ceiling.

After she'd returned home last night, as she'd slithered out of her sequined dress and tried not to think too much about Evan's eyes sweeping over it, she'd left a message with the Vampiress, announcing that the charter was still on.

While she'd wiped her makeup off, she'd verified with Douglas, Stewey, and Cora that they could make it onto the *Duke* for the weekend tours and would each work the booth for a few hours.

Then she'd left a message with Mr. Brimmer about his website, fed Missy, and left two more messages with clients to catch them up until Tuesday.

So today could be all about the festival.

She watched the white winter light play across the ceiling and let her mind color in the lines from the evening before: Evan stepping around the bird of paradise bush in that gorgeous suit; the way his eyelids had lowered when he'd told her she made him forget about his dead wife; the feel of his arms around her; the scent of mint and longing on his breath; . . . and . . . glory, *that kiss* . . .

Lia sighed at the way his velvet lips felt, the way his bandaged hand came up around the back of her neck, the way he seemed to unleash a torrent of emotion that he'd been tamping down for so long. She'd had many kisses in her life, but that was different. That was passionate. That was *aching*. That was pain and longing and lust and memory and hope and grief all tied up at once. She reran it like a movie until Missy leaped onto the bed and pushed her head under Lia's palm.

"You hungry, Miss?"

Lia crawled out of the covers, sad to leave the Evan movie behind, and padded into the kitchen to start the coffee.

But Evan kept returning. First every delicious physical part of him—his lips, his arms, his hands, his . . . um . . . private areas that were still hovering in her memory. And then the dead wife he loved, the protectiveness he learned in the Coast Guard, the obvious longing to reconnect with Drew that he didn't even seem to recognize, the loyalty that went with all those things, the emotion he'd kept bottled for so long, the surprise he showed when it surfaced . . .

She jostled the thoughts out of her mind, stabbed with guilt because of Forrest. Her coffee sloshed over the rim of her cup.

She fed Missy, then took her coffee, rattling on a saucer, into her room to get ready for the day. It was best she wouldn't see him much this weekend. They might pass each other when he was boarding the first tour at noon, but she assumed he'd sleep in and stay away from the early morning festival.

Forrest. Marriage material. Who she didn't spend nearly this much time thinking about. In fact, she'd forgotten to check her messages again, but she'd do it right after her shower.

While the hot water steamed up the bathroom, she forced herself to think about work, pushing thoughts of Evan aside every time they tried to resurface.

Which was an embarrassing number of times.

While getting dressed, she caught sight of the newest shoe boxes in the entryway and thought that might be a good distraction.

As Missy darted around her legs, she tried on one set of blue high heels after another. She'd bought every width, height, and toe shape in every shade of blue. She just didn't have time to wander around a mall. And even if she did, the last thing she'd wander a mall for were high heels. Especially these dyed-satin ones. The Vampiress required that the women and men in her office dress up every day—the women in high heels, the men in ties. Period. Lia spent what felt like half her paycheck on heels that were well made enough to be comfortable, then kicked them off as soon as she got home, wishing she could spend the money on plane tickets instead.

But these bright blue shoes were particularly loathsome: mostly because they went with the bright dresses that served as some kind of alarm in her head that the days were ticking toward her thirtieth birthday, a date when she thought she'd have white bride's heels in her closet, not more bridesmaid colors.

She buckled a pair of strappy ones and sauntered around the living room. She hadn't even realized how much she'd wanted to get married until recently. As her thirtieth birthday loomed, and the bridesmaid dresses started piling up, she realized she was off her original "schedule." She'd always assumed she'd be married by thirty. Or thirty-one, at the latest. She thought she'd have two babies by the time she was thirty-five. She'd imagined an adoring husband, a great career, nannies, beautiful children, a lovely home with a lamp-lit walkway through bright green grass, a Christmas tree in the front bay window, a jogger stroller to push around the neighborhood, and nice comfy walking shoes lining her closet so she could chase around after children all day.

But she was as far from that as she could imagine.

Her career wasn't even close to set. She wasn't even in the right number of digits for a down payment on a house. She had never had a boyfriend for longer than a year. And her doctor had stopped smiling when he asked if she was thinking of having any children anytime soon.

"You know, your eggs are best before the age of twenty," he'd begun saying, clicking his pen calmly, as if he hadn't just turned up the alarm on her biological clock.

Forrest, in the last six months, had appeared as a glimmer of hope. He was urbane enough for her sensibilities. He made a good living. He wanted kids. He liked being around family. He liked the idea of a big house, and a Christmas tree in the bay window. He liked feeling settled. He wasn't wild and crazy, or passionate and sexy, but he'd be a steady father. He was the Norman Rockwell painting of "family man" Lia had always imagined.

She tossed the strappy blue shoes back in the box and tried on a pair of simple royal blue pumps. As she wandered around her living room, her phone sang out a Gershwin tune she hadn't heard in some time. *Forrest!*

She scrambled for it. "Hello?" she said, leaning over another three shoe boxes against the entryway table.

"Lia!" His voice crackled over the phone.

"Forrest! I haven't heard from you! I was getting worried."

"Yes, I know. I hope . . . *static, static* . . . going . . . *static* . . . byway." Or did he say "my way"?

"Forrest, it's hard to hear you. I can't make out what you're saying."

"Yes, the connection is . . . *static, static* . . . always, so we've encountered . . . *static.*"

"Can you call me back?" she shouted into the phone. "I can't make out half of what you're saying."

"Yes, I'll call . . . *static* . . . if you could . . . *static* . . . text from the messages. Did you . . . *static, static.*"

"Call me back!" she said.

The phone went dead.

She stared at it, disappointed she didn't have a fonder reaction to his voice. She'd hoped to have a soaring in her chest when she heard his voice again—something like they would show in a Lifetime movie. But right now, all she could think of was that his voice sounded so thin.

The royal blue pumps went back into the box and she dug out the next pair, glancing intermittently at her phone. They were a high-heeled robin's egg Mary Jane. They pinched her toes immediately, but she gave them a spin, Missy in tow. Then they went into the "no" pile and she looked at her phone again.

By the time she got through all the boxes, had them separated into "maybe's" and "no's," and had checked her phone about a billion times to no avail, it was time to get to the festival.

No text from Forrest.

She tugged on her sandals, slipped on a cute floral dress she loved, and headed out the door, trying to ignore the buoyant feeling she got every time she thought of seeing Evan in a few minutes.

Man. She was a disaster.

Evan padded down the misty dock in his bare feet, one set of clothes in his arms like some damned vagrant, and leaped onto his boat through the morning fog.

He'd made his way down the hill from the motel, weaving through early morning runners who were participating in the "It's Not a Fluke" 5K; past the syrupy scents of flapjacks in a booth near the start of the race; and around a series of floats, horses, tuba players, Boy Scouts, and clown cars that were apparently getting ready for the "Whale of a Tale" parade. The sticky scent of cotton candy already permeated the air.

Closing his cabin door to the cacophony, he threw his clothes into a corner and crawled on top of his sheets. The boat rocked gently. It would be good to have one morning in his own bed.

He woke again a little after ten, to the sounds of bands and cheers and Model A cars honking.

And to the sweet memory of another dream about Lia.

He rolled over and tried to figure out which was insult and which was injury.

His arm lay heavily over his eyes while he let himself remember the real previous night, especially the shimmering, sequined hourglass shape of her body, which had later become a key feature of his dream.

But, as horrified as he'd been last night at his boorishness, and the fact he'd kissed her so hard he'd practically had her bent over a cocktail table, there was one detail he hadn't let himself think of until right now: She'd kissed him back.

He sat up and rubbed his face. Sure, she'd looked a little stricken. Sure, she'd looked a little insulted. Sure, she'd accepted his apology and had straightened her dress and reapplied her lipstick. But in the moment—when he'd had her pinned against the cocktail table—she was kissing him back.

A shock of disbelief swam through him. A Model A car honked its *a-ooogah* from high up on the hill, as if snapping him out of his foolishness. He rubbed his face again and let the guilt fill his chest. Even if Lia did feel something back, he shouldn't be noticing. Renece was dead only two years. He'd let her down in a horrible way. He'd let her *and* Luke down. And now he was just going to go on with his life? What kind of asshole did that?

Finally rousing, he yanked the covers aside and talked himself into the day. He needed to talk to Joe the Mechanic about getting a new water pump. His boat wasn't moving at all now. But once the charter was finished on Monday, he needed to hightail it out of there, away from Lia and her ability to make him forget Renece; away from everything she was reminding him he wanted; away from Drew and memories of how much Evan had screwed up. Evan just needed to sail the fuck away.

Twenty minutes later, Evan popped his head into Joe's shop. A boy sat behind the counter.

"Joe here?"

"He's at the festival," the boy said. He was about thirteen, with a mop of long surfer hair and a beanie keeping it secure. From the looks of his long nose and close-set eyes, he must be Joe's son. "Why aren't *you* there?" the boy asked. "Everyone in Sandy Cove is."

Evan shook his head. "Not my thing."

"Me neither."

At the boy's conspiratorial glance, Evan felt the stab. The one that hit him every time he thought of his dead son. This was what he was going to miss—relating to Luke, having things in common, understanding him on a level only another introvert could. When Evan had seen Luke sitting off to the side of his classmates, coloring by himself, a ribbon of recognition and understanding had woven around his heart. His boy was just like him, and they'd be bonded forever.

Except not forever.

Evan tried to catch his breath. He wanted his son back.

He wanted more kids.

The last realization hit him like a forty-knot gale, and he stepped back, into a rack of Sandy Cove sweatshirts.

"You okay?" the kid asked.

"Yeah. I'm . . ." Evan waved his hand to dismiss the concern, then turned and stared at the sweatshirts.

"When will your dad be back?" he asked gruffly.

"Probably not until late—sometime after the band tonight."

"There's a band?"

"Band in the Sand. Starts at seven. Goes 'til about eleven."

Swell.

"All right, thanks. I'll catch him later." He threw a pack of beef jerky and a couple of bottled waters onto the counter and paid, then headed back into the noisy marina and escaped to his boat.

Sandy Cove was making him think strange thoughts.

He really had to get the fuck out of there.

Lia handed out brochures and whale-shaped bookmarks to visitors who came by the booth, chatting with several about Drew's whale-tooth displays.

Kids came by with festival sweatshirts tied around their waists—it ended up being one of those warm February days. They jumped up and down at the huge bowl of blue and white M&Ms, and she scooped small piles into their hands, asking how many whales they thought came by Sandy Cove every year.

When the last set of children passed under the bright midday sun, Lia scooted her chair farther under the shade of the booth umbrella, smiling at Cora.

"You look good," Cora said, offering her a bite of sno-cone.

She shook her head at the sno-cone and smoothed her dress. "Thanks for the compliment. You sound surprised."

Cora laughed and took a bite out of the brightly colored treat. "I don't usually see you looking so relaxed, is all."

"As far as work days go, this is a good one."

"I've missed having you on the boat," Cora said. "I think someone else did, too."

"What do you mean?"

"I mean a dark, brooding, tall drink of water might have missed you, too."

"Douglas?"

Cora laughed. "Dougie might be a short, stubby highball glass of water, but he's all right, too." She wriggled her eyebrows.

"Cora! You have a thing for Douglas?"

Cora offered a wink that belied her sixty-something years.

"Why don't you say something to him?" Lia asked.

"Oh, it's not that easy."

"Sure it is!"

"No it's not."

"It is!"

Cora threw her a stern look to knock off the obvious nonsense.

Lia sighed. Cora was right. She should know. Lia was the most emotionally constipated woman in Southern California.

"But, to my point, I think our resident captain might have missed you," Cora said. "He brooded a lot more when you weren't there."

"He did?"

"And he was worried about you when you were sick. He kept begging me to make soup for you."

The thought warmed Lia all the way to her toes. She wriggled away the pinpricks under the table.

"I haven't seen your business-suit beau around in a while," Cora went on. "Does that mean the deck is clear for Captain Betancourt?"

"No!" Lia's vehement reaction startled even her. "I mean . . . No, my business-suit beau, Forrest, is still on the scene. He's in Bora Bora."

"Without you?"

Cora was about the fifth person who had said that now, and it was sinking in to Lia how incongruent it must have seemed. Lia was open about the fact that she'd always wanted to travel, yet never had. And now her very own almost-boyfriend had gone off to Bora Bora without her. Maybe that was sort of rude. Of course, Lia had always told Forrest she appreciated distance, so he was just following her wishes. But still . . . maybe it wasn't right how happily he'd done so.

"Seems you're only half-committed, Lia," Cora said. "When you meet the right one, you'll be fully committed. You have to throw yourself all the way in. You can't fall in love until you give your whole heart."

"That's what Drew always says."

Cora nodded sagely.

"But I don't want to be completely dependent on a man."

Cora lifted an eyebrow. "Maybe dependence isn't entirely bad."

Lia laughed. "Dependence is bad." Her mother had told her that a million times.

Cora brushed stray sno-cone ice off her shirt. "Why is dependence necessarily bad?"

Lia gaped. Did she really need to answer this? Didn't Cora know?

"It makes you weak, Cora. Vulnerable. It's not what women should strive for. Women should strive for independence."

Cora didn't seem fazed. "What if the positive side of dependence is deep trust? And it's *shared*? And that's what gives you *both* strength? Maybe you've been running away from the wrong thing all these years."

Lia held her breath. Could that be true? She tried to imagine the kind of trust you'd have to have to rely or depend on someone wholeheartedly—it would be extreme. She'd never even come close to that kind of vulnerability. From where she stood, it seemed like tumbling into a deep, dark abyss.

"Aaaaand speak of one of our devils," Cora whispered, looking past Lia's shoulder.

Lia's heart leaped when she thought of which devil it might be—and fell again when she saw it wasn't the one she'd hoped.

"I'm here, reporting for work, Cap'n." Douglas threw a grin Lia's way.

"Thanks. Is it almost noon?" That meant Evan would be here soon. Her stomach made a funny flutter.

Another group of small kids came up to the table and asked about the M&Ms and the whale teeth. Since Cora was giving Douglas a shy smile—the first time Lia had noticed such a thing between them—Lia attended to the children to give Cora and Douglas a few minutes alone.

She had fun teasing answers out of the kids about killer whales while giving them an M&M for every right answer. She got so swept up in her game, she didn't notice Evan sauntering up the marina sidewalk. Only when she heard his rough voice greet Douglas—and felt the responsive butterflies throughout her belly—did she realize he'd arrived.

"Lia." He nodded an awkward hello in her direction.

He looked good today. Again. He had on a short-sleeved

navy T-shirt that showed off his body much more than Lia wanted to notice. Blue jeans and boat shoes rounded out what must be his winter wardrobe.

His careful distance—along with the use of her real name that sounded almost formal now—made her realize they might be on some new, uncomfortable ground.

"Evan." She nodded back.

Cora looked back and forth between them. "So, who's ready for a tour?"

"I'll stay here and man the table," Lia said, shooing them off. "You guys are doing great together."

"Why don't Douglas and I stay here, and you go aboard for the narrative?" Cora gave her what was probably supposed to be a meaningful nod.

But Lia wasn't biting. Even though it might be nice to give Cora and Douglas some time together in the tiny booth, she didn't want to take any chances being near Evan. The decision felt immature and childish, but a man who made you forget you had a boyfriend was a dangerous man to be around.

"You guys go," Lia said firmly.

She couldn't help but notice how relieved Evan looked as he bent to help Cora with her bags of homemade chocolate-chip cookies. He guided her down the dock to follow Douglas.

Once they were all gone, Lia began to relax. She sat back in her chair, kicked off her sandals, sipped her water in relief, and looked for more kids to entertain.

CHAPTER
Nineteen

Evan lifted the binoculars to see if he could spot any more grays. They'd seen four already—nice for the festival passengers—and he'd even pointed out two fin whales in the distance, which Douglas had repeated over the microphone.

Evan turned into the wind and pushed his hair back. He was glad Lia didn't come aboard. The guilt about forgetting Renece, kissing a woman with a boyfriend, and all around behaving like some kind of lout came firing back at him as soon as he saw her at the booth. It would be best to just stay away. His thoughts of "need" and attraction were now swirling into uncomfortable storm patterns, and he knew it would be best to ride off on Monday. Alone.

The crackling of the radio interrupted his escape plans: ". . . *Pod of dolphins heading southwest . . .*"

Evan lifted his mouthpiece. "Captain Betancourt here, from the *Duke*. Where is the pod now?"

"*It's in Laguna, Betancourt, off Thousand Steps beach. Where are you?*"

"We're almost there."

"*Have you seen a female humpback down that way?*"

"No. What's up?"

"We thought it might be Valentine."

"Valentine?"

"Yes, but we couldn't tell if she was really tangled. She was a little out of our range, and now we don't know where she is, but she's somewhere between us. If you get up this far, give her a check."

Evan calculated how long that would take. They'd remained back a bit to look at the four grays, and he still wanted to travel northwest to give these passengers the experience of seeing a dolphin pod.

He clicked the radio back on. "I won't make it this trip, but maybe I can come back. She's got a baby with her?"

He figured as much, since that's the only way they knew the females.

"Affirmative."

"Wilco. Out." Evan threw the throttle, hoping he might make some good time in that direction and catch a glimpse of what the captain was seeing, but within ten minutes, he could see dolphins to the north and knew he needed to complete this tour first.

He clicked to Douglas about the dolphins' position, listened to Doug come onto the microphone to begin his description, and thrust full speed to catch the pod and ride in with them.

But as magnificent as the dolphin pod was, Evan couldn't get Valentine out of his mind. Huge nylon commercial fishing nets often came unhinged from the sea floor and floated away, trapping large mammals in their tight weaves. And the more the animals struggled, the more the nets would tangle.

As soon as the trip's passengers disembarked with their cookies and new stories to tell, Evan yelled for Douglas.

"You think Drew would mind if we took the boat back out?" he asked.

"Why?"

"A Newport boat might have just spotted Valentine, just south of Newport Harbor."

A flash of worry crossed Douglas's face. "Was she tangled?"

"They couldn't tell. I want to check her out."

Douglas's brow crumpled into regret. "I can't, Evan. I'm plannin' to visit Drew now, in fact. But I don't think he would mind if you took the boat. Especially for a disentanglement. I'll put in a good word for you. But ask Lia. Or take her with you. She can be a good deckhand when her ankle is working."

"I don't know."

"She'll be helpful."

"Ahhh . . ." Evan shook his head and looked away.

Douglas's frown turned into something that had a quirk of awareness. "I recommend her." He winked.

Evan put the binoculars away. Yeah, that's all he needed—to be stuck alone with Lia on a boat for a couple of hours. Just enough time to become more mired in guilt and make more of an ass of himself.

He sighed. Maybe Cora could serve as a helper. . . . Or maybe even Joe the Mechanic's kid.

"I'll go find her," he told Douglas. He had to at least ask for the boat. "Leave some of this for me." He motioned in the direction of the work that needed to be done and leaped off the cat.

The marina had become even more crowded, if that were possible. Evan edged between the festival crowds up the winding path that led through grassy picnic areas.

At the far end of the row, he came upon Lia sitting alone in the booth. The light that had seemed to surround her and her shiny hair and feminine dress earlier was gone, as she shrank into the shadows, staring at her phone.

"How'd it go?" he ventured.

She sniffled and brushed at her cheeks. "Fine." She tossed her phone into her purse that lay in the grass and bent to put her sandals on. Although she kept her face averted, he caught a glimpse of her red-rimmed eyes and rosy nose.

His stomach clenched when he saw the grief that clouded her usually sunny face, and he took a step forward. But then he stopped himself. They weren't on that kind of ground. He'd just promised to keep his distance.

"Something wrong?" he asked from a few feet away.

"No, I'm fine." She summoned a fabricated-looking smile then turned her head in the other direction as if she were looking for more booth customers. She leaped up, pretending to fuss with the brochures on the table.

Evan didn't really know how to handle this kind of thing. Normally, he was one who liked directness, but he could appreciate a person's need for privacy, too. And he and Lia were on a weird kind of shaky ground now—he was obviously attracted to her, and she obviously didn't want him to be.

"I, uh . . . I wanted to ask a favor of *you* this time," he said.

She turned her head slightly while she busied herself with a box of bookmarks. "What is it?"

He stepped closer. "It seems there's a whale up north that might be Valentine. A female with her baby. Got a radio call. I wondered if Drew would mind if I took the boat back out to make sure she's not tangled?"

"By yourself?"

He shrugged. It wasn't impossible to handle the boat by himself; it would just be easier if someone else were there, especially if the whale really were in trouble. "I can handle it."

"What are you going to do?"

"Just want to check. See if she's stuck. I'll radio for help if I find her."

"How long will you be?"

"Two hours? Maybe three?"

She glanced nervously at her phone. "Maybe I should call Drew."

"That's fine."

She averted her face, and took another swipe at her cheek.

Evan was surprised at the anger that surged through him when she wiped away tears. Who had upset her? What had upset her? He wondered if it was that crazy boss of hers, or maybe even that absent boyfriend. Either way, it was making the blood speed through his veins.

But this was none of his business.

She was none of his business. . . .

"Drew?" she said into the phone, then began talking in low murmurs.

Evan sort of wanted to hear what was being said but he refrained from eavesdropping. He was used to being on the outside of everyone's regard. He could handle another couple of days. He stared past the crowds at the ocean.

"Is Douglas available?" she shouted toward him.

"No."

She returned to the call. He took pains to focus on a treasure hunt being played in the grass behind them, but snippets of Lia's conversation forced their way into his awareness: *"I'm not sure. . . . I don't want to go. . . ."*

When the call ended, he heard her footsteps brushing through the grass.

"He said you can take the boat, but he thinks you should bring someone along," she said. "Drew said it can get dangerous out there with whale disentanglements."

"I'll be fine."

She smoothed her clothes uneasily. She had on a cute short dress—kind of a flowery thing—that let him see way more of her legs than he wanted to.

"I guess I can go," she said, looking at the grass.

"I heard you say you didn't want to."

She winced. "I didn't mean it like that. It's just . . ." She waved her hand as if the answer were hovering near them.

But she didn't need to tell him. He knew. The kiss. The boyfriend. There was something new changing between them that neither wanted to acknowledge.

"How about if I go, but we agree on a few limited topics of conversation?" she asked.

He thought that over for a second. "That could work."

"How about: I don't have to tell you what's wrong, but you must tell me the story between you and Drew?"

He squinted at her. "Seems like everything's in your favor."

"You get the boat."

He hung his hands on his hips and assessed the damage that could be done with that arrangement, but he didn't have too much time to think. "All right, let's go. We might have to hurry. If that whale is caught, we don't know how long we have."

She cleared the booth in a flash, shoving the whale-teeth exhibit into his arms, then handing him the box of bookmarks and six batches of brochures. She whipped the tablecloth into a bundle and carried the enormous jar of M&Ms to the booth next door.

Within two minutes, they were scurrying down the

marina—Lia taking one more swipe at her cheeks and Evan trying not to notice.

Lia surveyed the ocean for the area Evan pointed out, leaning over the edge of the starboard side with the set of binoculars.

"See anything?" he shouted from the bridge.

"No."

She lowered the binoculars and scanned the horizon again without them.

It was easier to sit separately, on the lower deck, so she didn't have to talk about—or, more likely in her case, blurt out—why she'd been crying.

Forrest had broken up with her.

There.

Yanked off like a Band-Aid.

She just needed to accept it, say it to herself a few times.

He'd sent a text, saying he'd been trying to reach her but the phone connections were very bad there, and relaying that he cared quite a bit about her, but he'd decided to stay in Bora Bora. He'd found religion. He'd shed his materialistic belongings and wanted to start over. He thought he might be back in five years. . . .

Lia hadn't even known how to respond. She'd simply stared at the phone, wondered how he'd get along without the Italian loafers he so cherished, and then realized her own life's trajectory had, once again, hit a curve.

She'd cried for the loss of her plan, she realized, more than for the loss of him. And that made her cry even more. Perhaps she'd wasted another six months of her life.

"Anything yet?" Evan shouted.

She lifted the binoculars. He'd told her to look for the slick or the top of the whale's back about a mile offshore. She scanned all the way up and all the way down.

"Nothing," she shouted back.

Although Evan was the first person to approach her since her life had changed course, she didn't want to tell him about Forrest. After all the heat that had been generated between them last night, swirling with her own confusion about her life and where it might go, she knew she'd be incapable of making smart, rational decisions. She worried she'd find herself in his arms, in his bed, in his life in a way that was probably not the most responsible choice.

So she sat way down here.

Away from all his testosterone.

A slight mound in the distance caught her eye, and she brought the binoculars back up.

"I see something!" She stood abruptly, bumping against the side of the boat. Excited, she readjusted the lenses.

Yep, it looked like a whale. She could see the back. She stared for nearly a minute through the binoculars and didn't see any movement at all—it looked like it was just floating, with no apparent blow.

She scampered back up the steps to the bridge, where Evan had noted her focus and was leaning into the helm, seeming to push the boat with what seemed like all his might. Concern carved lines around his mouth.

"Is she moving?" he asked.

"I don't think so," Lia whispered, staring out to sea.

They traveled quickly, not speaking, the wind whipping icy jags across Lia's face.

When they arrived within forty feet, Evan turned off the motor, and they floated in silence, staring at the enormous figure, which hadn't moved and hadn't spouted at all. Finally, Evan dropped his head.

"I'm going into the pod to see if I can identify her tail," he said reverently.

Lia stared at the poor, dead whale until Evan came back up.

"It's Valentine," he said.

They gave it another two minutes, listening only to the water slapping the side of the hull, then Evan picked up his radio: "This is Captain Betancourt of the *Duke*. I found the whale you identified earlier. It is Valentine. Affirmative. She's dead." His voice trailed off for a moment. He took a deep breath. "She's about twenty miles off . . . uh . . . Crystal Cove, I believe. No sign of the baby, which is strange. I can see some netting in the water. I'll call NOAA."

He dropped the radio to his side and leaned against the rail, his eyes never leaving the whale, his shoulders slumped.

They stood in silence for a moment, each lost in their own

thoughts and wishes for poor Valentine, who had become almost a symbol of Sandy Cove.

Finally, Evan moved into action.

He puttered the boat closer, then cut the motor and vaulted down the steps, leaning over the side of the cat so he could grab some of the nylon netting. He pulled as much as he could onto the deck, whipping a Swiss Army knife out of his pocket to sever the remainder. His jagged movements had a desperate, frantic motion. His hair swung violently across his eyes, his mouth twisted in grim determination. After he struggled for about five minutes to cut as much as possible, flinging the slippery white netting behind him onto the deck, Lia stepped forward and touched his arm.

He pushed her away. "I should have come sooner," he said through gritted teeth.

"Evan."

"They're so vulnerable out here—they don't know how to get out of these lines." His movements, sawing at more of the net, became more and more furious.

"Evan."

"She needed help."

Lia tentatively reached out for him again. "Evan."

"I let her down, Lia." His head whipped toward her, his eyes frantic. "How could I have let her down? This mother and baby . . ."

Lia reached for the knife but he shouldered her back and slashed at the net.

"How could I have let them down . . . both of them . . . so *badly*?"

The pain in his grim expression, the desperation in his voice—needing to understand himself, but needing someone to understand him, too—gripped her like a vice. She knew who he must be talking about. Not just the whale, of course. The pain in his voice was too great, too raw, too untouched for her to mistake whom he meant.

She managed to reach for the knife. "Evan, let's . . . let's pull this aboard now."

He shook her off with his shoulder, leaning forward to cut more savagely into the net. He slashed seven or eight more times, severe slashes tackled with grunts, then, finally, his shoulders slumped. He leaned on the edge of the boat.

She slipped the knife from him—his fingers relaxed reluctantly—and he stood, frozen.

"Let's get all this pulled up," she said.

He dropped his head, breathing heavily. She let him pause, let him absorb what he needed to absorb, didn't try to fill the silence with meaningless words. She closed the knife and put it away. And finally, together, they tugged the rest of the cut netting aboard. The nylon was sharp and cutting against her fingers. The dead whale bobbed about ten feet away, then eleven, then twelve, as they pushed the stiff netting across the deck for the next fifteen minutes and untangled themselves from it.

After the net was in a white heap in the center of the cat, he stopped, hanging his hands off his pockets and scowling toward the ocean. He wouldn't meet her eyes. "I just . . ." He made a feeble motion toward the water. "I wish I could have saved her."

"I know."

She stepped toward him. The urge to soothe him came on strong—this enormous man, who seemed strong as a mast, yet had these same vulnerabilities like mere mortals: a desperate love, an enormous loss, a feeling of guilt, an uncertainty about going on. . . .

She put her arms around him.

First he stiffened, pushing himself away. But she hung on. Then, within another fraction of a second, she felt his resolve weaken, his spine loosen, his arms go loosely around her waist.

They stood that way in the deep ocean, swaying with the rocking boat, the only sound the light rise of the waves. They comforted each other for a full, quiet minute, mourning Valentine; mourning Evan's lost wife; mourning their inability to make life go the way they wanted; mourning their inability to save who they wanted to save; and mourning old lives they were going to have to leave behind.

Lia thought she felt a tear slip down her shoulder.

CHAPTER
Twenty

Lia glanced up at Evan, sitting in the bridge as they rode quietly back to shore. One of his feet was up on the rail, his arm flung over his knee and the other loosely touching the wheel. His head was permanently turned away from her, his sunglasses pointed toward the sun on the horizon. He was clearly lost in thought, lost to her, lost to everyone for a while. . . .

Lia stayed on the lower deck, cleaning up as much as she could in her dress and sandals, but soon she couldn't stand it any longer. She wanted to make sure he was okay. Such a quiet man, who had been sailing around the world alone for so long, must have experienced a lot of his grief alone, maybe not talking it out with anyone. She watched his averted face, his limp hands. He seemed trapped in a silo of guilt.

"I wanted to see if we could find the baby," he mumbled when she crawled to the top. He leaned forward, his face still turned away. "It's unusual for the baby to leave so quickly."

His sudden worry and something he'd said earlier hit her with full force. "Evan, when we were pulling up the net, why did you say you let 'them' down?" she asked quietly.

"Sorry about all that, Cinderella. I don't know what came over me."

"Probably grief."

He didn't even turn in her direction.

"Maybe grief you haven't let yourself express."

He watched a family of pelicans skim the ocean's surface. For a second, she thought he was going to let her in. Maybe open up to her a bit, like he had at the charity event. But then a shadow crossed his face and he looked out toward the horizon. "This wasn't on our approved topics list," he said.

The pelicans flew in a swift dip, then a rising arc over the quietly lapping waves.

She took a seat on the bench next to him and thought maybe she could find another way in. "Speaking of our approved topics, you never told me about Drew," she said.

Evan stood. "I don't see the baby anywhere. But we're getting pretty far out." He pulled the boat wheel all the way around.

"Is it a long way back?"

His biceps strained against the wheel as he pulled them all the way around, the wind pushing them back, making Lia clutch one of the rails. Once they straightened, Evan stepped back to join her in the seat.

"Long enough that I can tell you the whole story, if you insist."

Lia took in his puckered eyebrows, his grim mouth, his worn expression, and knew she could give this to Evan as a gift. He needed someone right now.

"I'll make us some coffee."

Evan didn't really want to knock around stories about him and Drew, but it beat acknowledging all the feelings that were stirring about Renece and Luke.

The feelings had overwhelmed him when the murders first happened, so much so that he learned to ram them down, somewhere deep, somewhere they couldn't have an effect. And he'd been okay that way—the pain had never gone away, but it wasn't allowed to surface.

But meeting Lia had stirred everything: interest, intrigue, want, need.

The "need" that had surfaced yesterday was exploding into

something that felt much larger and more complicated than he'd first imagined, solidified by how good it felt to simply hold her, and be held by her. To be somehow absolved. To be somehow understood. By this tiny woman who stood bravely when she needed to, and who only saw positive things. But letting himself feel anything at all meant facing the painful feelings, too.

"So you were watching Drew's friends get on the boat . . ." she prompted, handing him a cup of coffee. "This isn't going to be as good as Cora's, but it'll do."

He took a sip. It was terrible. But the warmth felt good. "Yeah."

"And then what happened?" She scooted to the side of the captain's bench to give him space. She had one of Drew's jackets pulled over her shoulders.

"I noticed a girl he'd invited." He finally took a seat next to her.

"A girl?" Lia grinned over the top of her coffee. "Now we're getting somewhere. So who was this girl?"

He reached forward to tilt the wheel with his other hand.

"Renece," he said. It felt weird to say her name casually, without the pain that normally jabbed his chest.

"Was that your wife?" Lia asked on a whisper.

Evan nodded. "And it turned out Drew was in love with her."

Her brows furrowed. "I think I missed something."

Evan told her about their childhood, keeping his eye on the horizon. He told her how he and Drew were separated in the divorce, how he'd missed key things like the fact that his brother was crushing on a certain girl ever since puberty. He told the whole story, ending with the black eye and wedding and the silent treatment Drew had given him ever since.

"So he's never forgiven you for stealing who he thought was his girl?"

"I guess."

"Well, that doesn't seem fair. I mean, he *introduced* you. And he hadn't said he was serious about her."

"That was my take."

"I can't believe he'd still be mad about that."

"Well, then for letting her die." Evan's shrug belied the difficulty of admitting that.

Lia's lips parted. She lowered her head and stared at her empty coffee cup. "I'm so sorry, Evan. How did she die, if you don't mind my asking?"

He did. But he'd come this far now. Somehow it felt good to tell Lia this. He didn't know why, but Lia was looking at him through this falling afternoon light with an understanding, a kind of verification that maybe Drew had been unreasonable and maybe Evan wasn't such a jerk. And Lia's understanding was unfolding into a type of forgiveness that he'd never been able to give himself.

"She was murdered. In a mass shooting."

Lia's eyes went wide.

"She was in a fast-food restaurant with our son."

Lia's lips opened into an O as if she were going to say something, but then she pressed them together. Her hands shook as she smoothed her dress. He didn't mean to shock her, but there was never any other way to say this.

"You had a *son*?" Her voice was strangled.

This was the part that always caused the lump to form in his throat, so he forced himself to skim over it. "Yeah. Luke . . . Luke the Duke." He tried to smile at the nickname. "He was five."

Lia swallowed several times and stared at the ocean. He could see her mind putting together the name of Drew's boat and Drew's nephew—could see the exact moment the levels of sadness, the degrees of loss, probably occurred to her.

"I'm sorry," he said. "You said you wanted to know."

"Thank you for telling me." Her words came out scratchy. She cleared her throat. "I feel . . . honored . . . that you told me."

"Honored?"

"That you trusted me enough to share."

He nodded. It did feel good to tell her. It did feel good to tell someone who wasn't judging him. Even his parents, his cousins, his closest friends from boyhood—they all knew Drew, too, and he always sensed they took his side. It made him feel as if he were the devil incarnate. But Lia knew Drew also, and wasn't looking at him like that at all.

"Is that why you took off for the open sea?" she asked.

"Yeah. Drew and I had just inherited some money from my grandfather, and Renece and I were going to buy a house in

San Diego. I'm sure Drew used his money to buy this." He waved his hand over the deck. "So when . . . everything happened . . . I just pulled the money back out and bought a sailboat and took off. I wasn't sure . . . I just wasn't sure how to handle anything. It was easier to be alone."

"Is that why . . ." Lia swallowed. "Is that why you sleep with that gun?"

He looked up sharply at her. He'd forgotten she saw that. It felt desperate and weak, and he had to look away. "All boat owners keep a firearm on board, Cinderella."

"Do you feel guilty because you think her death was your fault?"

He wanted to be irritated that she was seeing right through him, but for some reason it felt like a relief.

"I was used to protecting people. I spent eight years in the Coast Guard, saving lives every week, and the two lives I most wanted to protect . . . I wasn't even there."

"But Evan." Her hand slipped over his forearm. He stared at it because it felt good. But she seemed to notice his attention, and moved it away. "It was a senseless and unpredictable crime. What could you have done?"

He shook his head. No one really understood this part. "Just have been there. It took me four days to get back in from Alaska. Her parents had to identify the bodies. I was her *husband*. His *father*. And yet his *grandparents* had to identify them. . . ."

The afternoon light hit the water in a way that sent golden rays across the tiny whitecaps.

"Thank you for telling me," Lia said quietly. She stood abruptly and headed down the stairs.

As quickly as the relief had come moments earlier, now came embarrassment and regret.

He watched Lia retreat down the staircase and remembered why it was better to keep things to himself.

Lia pulled Drew's jacket over her shoulders and used the long brush to sweep some of the excess water from the netting to the deck drain the way she saw Douglas do.

She couldn't believe Evan had lost a son, too. Just five years old. . . . She could feel the tears welling up, and had made a quick retreat before she burst into tears and made him feel even worse.

No wonder he'd looked so terrified of the children on the boat this week. No wonder he'd stared a hole into Avery's forehead, and gawked at her little boy when he almost fell from the bridge. Lia thought back to the picture frame Evan had shoved into his drawer in his cabin that first morning, the gun, the scotch bottles on the floor. . . . Tears threatened again and she swiped beneath her eyes and then swept harder with the broom.

She wasn't going to tell him about Forrest breaking up. Her little problem seemed so small compared to his loss. But the more she was learning about him today, and the more she remembered his comment before he kissed her, the more she wanted to be with him.

Would it be so terrible?

For two people who were *not* interested in a relationship, would a single night—a simple temporary comfort—be so wrong? One night of absolution in each other's arms? Comfort between two strangers who had shared an emotional week?

Lia sighed. She'd never had a one-night stand. She didn't even know how this worked. Sex had always been a way for her to express emotion, although she had never had the crazy sort of passionate sex she'd seen on TV. She'd never even had an orgasm like she'd seen on TV. She thought that might be for pole dancers, or something, or maybe yoga instructors. They must possess some kind of gene or G-spot she didn't have. Or maybe they just didn't have the control issues she had. She could never relax enough to enjoy herself.

Yet—she had to admit—every time she looked at Evan, and every time he gave her that half smile that revealed that deep dimple, as if he were thinking about something he didn't want her to know, she felt that rise in her blood temperature that she associated with pole dancers. Maybe she did have the gene. Maybe she'd just been with the wrong men.

"Lia!"

She stepped into the orange sun to look up at the bridge.

"Leave that," he yelled, not looking at her.

But she ignored him. She wanted to help. She wanted to do

any little thing that might help in any small way. Getting rid of today's loss—the netting and the reminder of the death of Valentine—seemed like a start.

She resumed her sweeping where he couldn't see her, pushing the puddles as quietly as she could to a starboard drain.

"Lia!" he yelled again.

She stopped but didn't go into the sun this time.

"Get up here!"

His bossiness could really be annoying. She quieted her movements but, within minutes, the motor stopped, and Evan's footsteps fell heavily on the narrow stairwell behind her.

Seconds later, she felt the broom being lifted out of her hands.

She whirled on him.

"Did you *hear* me?" he asked. The deck was now bathed in gold and reflected in his sunglasses.

"Of course I heard you."

"*I'll* do this."

"I want to help."

"I don't want you sweeping."

"Why not?"

His teeth pressed together as he seemed to search for an answer. "You don't even have the right shoes." He frowned at her open-toe sandals, which were, indeed, getting too much saltwater sloshing through them and probably ruining them forever.

But she could buy more shoes. She yanked the broom back. "I want to help. And I'm tired of you telling me what to do." She resumed her work.

The gentle sound of sweeping water became rhythmic after she sent long strokes of water off the deck. She could feel him practically vibrating behind her.

"Why are you so stubborn?" he asked through clenched teeth.

"Why are you so bossy?"

He sighed and pulled the broom back over her head. "Maybe because you don't listen to me."

"This isn't the Coast Guard, Evan. You don't need to boss everyone around."

"I don't boss everyone around."

"You do me."

"That's because I want to protect you. And I know I can't."

The admission seemed to surprise him as much as it did her. He backed away, about a foot, as if he were backing away from his own shocking comment. The ocean water lapped the fiberglass as they both stilled.

"You don't need to protect me," she whispered.

"It's my nature."

Lia could see that now. She could see that Evan's impulse to help was not *judgmental*, which was how she'd been reading it. It wasn't about the person he was helping. It was about *him*, and the way he simply reacted to life. He wanted to protect wildlife, kids, his wife—the people and things he loved.

When she suddenly realized the wonderful company she was in, her heart began to race. Having this simmering man stare down at her like this—this 180 pounds of pent-up passion, whose jaw muscle was dancing and whose chest was heaving, who was fighting guilt against a lost wife but finding Lia desirable enough to challenge it—was causing her knees to want to buckle. Lia locked them just in case.

Evan yanked off his shades, bringing his fingertips up to press the bridge of his nose.

"Look, Lia." His voice dropped to a strangled whisper. "I feel guilty for every feeling I have. I feel guilty for every minute you make me forget about my wife. And it's been a lot. Of minutes, that is . . . It's been hours . . . days. I don't know what it is about you, but . . ." He shook his head and stared at the ocean for a minute. "I haven't even thought about anyone else since she died. I've had a deadness in my chest." His hand went there. "I *like* it there. It reminds me of where she is. It keeps me with her, in a weird way. But when I met you . . ." He shook his head.

Her hand went up toward his jaw. "It's okay," she whispered.

But he caught it and dragged it away. "It's not. I'm trying to do the right thing here. I don't even know what the right thing is anymore. I'm just damned glad you have that boyfriend."

Her mind raced, for a second, about whether or not to tell him. The confusion and pain etched into his face made it seem as if she were causing him more grief than good. But then she took one more look at that chest she wanted to touch, one more glance at the lips that had feathered her lipstick last night, and one more glimpse of the passion she wanted unleashed upon her right now.

"The thing is, Evan . . ."

As if he sensed what she was about to say, he looked up at her slowly. "What?"

"I wasn't going to tell you because it seemed so petty, and then . . . well, it wasn't on our agenda or anything . . . but . . ." She took a deep breath and decided to just blurt it out: "Forrest and I broke up this afternoon. That's why I was crying earlier."

He didn't move for the longest time, just stared at her from beneath the hair that had fallen down his forehead. Several emotions seemed to play across his face, which she watched almost like a movie reel: awareness, skepticism, worry, pain, then something that looked like resignation.

"You okay?" he asked. Anger now replaced worry, etching a line between his brows.

"I'm okay. I think I might have liked the idea of him better than the actual him."

He nodded and seemed to think that over, staring at the deck tape. "On a scale of one to ten, how okay are you?"

"What's a one?"

"You're so upset you want me to get out of your way and take you home right now."

"I'm a nine, then."

The corner of his mouth quirked up. A family of seagulls squawked overhead as he seemed to think something over. "Then can I do what I've been wanting to do for the last several days?"

The ocean felt quiet and private beneath them, as the boat rolled gently. She took in his hooded eyes, his stubbled jaw, the full lips that were waiting for her answer. . . .

"Yes," she whispered.

And Evan's mouth covered hers in a kiss that sent her back against the cabin wall.

Evan's hand was in her hair, his other shoving Drew's jacket off her shoulders, then roving her body, his lips taking hers, before he could even think about what he was doing.

With all rational thought now overboard, all he could concentrate on was getting under her dress, touching those peaked breasts he'd glimpsed while she was sick, feeling that backside he'd watched sway away from him one too many times, lifting her and wrapping her shapely legs all the way around him—preferably naked.

He pushed her back against the cabin, breaking the fall of her head with his palm, and using it to steady her so he could kiss that mouth of hers, which turned him on in ways he couldn't even begin to understand. His erection pressed hard against his jeans as he explored her lips, her tongue, and tried not to crush her against the fiberglass and—*God, it had been so long since he'd touched skin so soft*—his other hand skimmed along her curves from her thigh to her breasts, desperate to get inside her dress and touch the body he'd been staring at for five days, as if her clothes might miraculously fall off if he'd stared hard enough. He groped for some kind of entry at her top, and—*damn, she didn't have a bra on, sweet holy God*—made his way over her hip, to cup that beautiful ass of hers and see if she still had that thong on, and—*fuck, she did*—and there was only a tiny thin fabric between his hand and that bare bottom. His fingertips went down to find the hem of her skirt, and . . .

"*Evan?*"

She was talking. She wasn't pushing him away, but she was talking. He struggled to wrap his mind around the first point while ignoring the second, because all he wanted was more touching, more skin, more breasts, more of that flickering tongue that was doing some damage here, but she suddenly sounded urgent.

"*Evan?*" she asked between kisses.

He backed away about an inch, trying to get his brain to function again, embarrassed that he'd just lost his mind. He breathed into the narrow space between their chests. "What?"

"Who's . . ."

Her fingertips were at his chest. He wanted to rip his shirt off and give her better access, but he was trying to concentrate on what she was saying. "Who's *what*?" he asked, impatient.

"Who's navigating the boat?" she whispered.

He spent another fraction of a second getting his brain to

start whirling again, tearing away from her body, moving his hands from the softest skin he'd touched in ages, moving away from her rosebud mouth.

"I should get to that," he managed.

"You should." Her chest was rising and falling, too, her breath coming in gasps, her lips all rosy and swollen.

"Give me ten," he choked out.

He took the steps two at a time to the bridge. The boat hadn't gone off course—thank God he'd killed the motor earlier—so he fired the cat forward, pulled hard on the wheel and got her back strong and steady. But damn. How embarrassing. Stupid. Irresponsible. Adolescent. *What was wrong with him?* He shoved his hands through his hair and looked around for his shades, but realized he'd left them down there. Probably flung them somewhere in his mindlessness.

He glanced out of the corner of his eye to see where Lia had gone, or what she was doing. She probably thought he was a sex-starved idiot. Which, right now, didn't seem like an unfair assessment, but still. . . .

He didn't know what had come over him.

Well, he sort of did.

A sassy mouth. Thrown back shoulders. Nerve. Bravado. Two perky breasts. Lush lips. Curves for miles. Great legs. *That* had come over him.

But he didn't know why her. And why now. Not when he still felt like he needed to mourn Renece.

He turned the boat toward the marina and let the guilt wash over him again.

"Hey," he heard from behind him.

He could hardly look at her. "Hey."

"You forgot these." She held his shades toward him.

"Thanks. Did I throw them on the ground in my overzealousness?" He wiped them on his T-shirt and shoved them back on. "Sorry about that, Cinderella. I don't know what's come over me."

"It's been a while?"

He couldn't help but laugh. "Yeah. It's been a while. . . ."

"So between the driving, the steak dinner, and the kissing, what's been the best thing to get back to?"

"Ah, that's easy. That steak dinner was something else."

She laughed and slid into the bench behind him. "If it makes you feel better, it's been a while for me, too."

He lifted an eyebrow. "Thought you had a boyfriend."

"Well, we've done the kissing, but not much more. And he doesn't kiss like . . . *that*."

Evan wanted to puff out his chest at that comment. But then he realized he was an idiot. Because a guy who'd only been with one woman his whole life shouldn't be feeling bravado when faced with a little spitfire like this. Though that detail that she'd never slept with her boyfriend intrigued him. . . .

"What was up with you and your boyfriend?"

"What exactly is your question?"

He smiled. "Why were you not letting your boyfriend touch that beautiful body of yours?"

The jetty was on the horizon. Thank God. Because he didn't know if he could keep talking to her like this, with an ongoing erection he hoped wasn't too noticeable, without doing what he really wanted to do.

"I thought maybe he was The One, and I wondered if maybe abstaining from sex until we got married might be good for the relationship."

"I take it that didn't work out."

"No."

The motor revved louder as Evan tried to get the cat to the marina faster.

"But we failed for other reasons," she went on. "It just wasn't a strong relationship."

"You don't seem too broken up about it."

"I'm not. I just want to have really great sex right now. I've never had really, really great sex."

Evan swallowed a few times and leaned toward the jetty.

"What do you think?" she pressed.

"What do you mean, what do I think?"

"I mean, what do you think about us just having really, really great sex?"

He tried to swallow again around the tumbleweeds that were in his throat. "I think, if that's what you want from me right now, Cinderella, I can oblige."

"You can give me really, *really* great sex?"

"I could do my best."

"I don't want to be let down."

"I'll try."

"I want it to be like on TV."

He glanced at her. "You got any other demands for me?"

"I might have a few when we get there."

He closed his eyes and willed himself to get to the marina yesterday.

Twenty-one

As soon as the boat was snuggled into the slip, Evan galloped down the stairs, tied the lines—he just secured two; the other two could wait—then banged through the cabin door.

The guilt was still there. He loved Renece. He knew that. But he wanted Lia so badly he ached.

She stood still, leaning against the cabinetry, turned toward him. He knew his brain had gone into a sexual fog of some kind, and he was in that stage where he couldn't make a rational decision. If she gave any indication that she didn't want this, he'd back off. He needed her to think for both of them. He looked at her dumbly and waited for a clue.

For a long time, she did nothing. Just stared at him, her eyes roaming up and down. Her perusal turned him on. He hadn't felt that in a long time—or at least hadn't paid attention in a long time—and it sent his testosterone into some kind of chest-pounding overdrive. His groin followed suit, and he shifted uncomfortably, finally letting go of the door handle but not taking his eyes off Lia.

She nibbled on her lip. She couldn't possibly be imagining

what he was—her naked, moaning, under his hands, under his body, burying himself inside of her.

She shifted and blushed. Her sassy exterior was missing, replaced, now, with a shyness he didn't recognize.

He gulped for air while he waited for a signal.

Then—finally—she held out her hand.

Evan turned and locked the door.

Lia let herself swim in the kiss that melted her bones as much as the first two did. Evan's lips were demanding, promising, suctioning then soft—all in a carousel that had her sliding along the wall, his hand in her hair, his need for her pressing her into the streamlined cabinetry.

Her body was liquefying, her arms and legs already a pool of jelly.

Evan's hand moved to the side of her breast, cupping its smallness, his fingertips running along the deep neckline of her dress, searching for entry. She loved his frenzy; she loved his delirium; she loved the recklessness that drove her back behind the galley, her hands gripping the wall behind her to make sure she didn't fall.

His lips left a trail of kisses toward the inside curve of her breast as his enormous hand cradled the outside.

"Lia," he breathed heavily. "If you're going to tell me this is a bad idea, please tell me now."

"We're good," was all she could manage. Her voice was strangled and foreign.

He lifted his head. "Then help me get you out of this damned dress."

Her fingers pushed his aside and made quick work of the knot behind her head, as she panted and undid the dress, peeling it down. Evan stood back and watched her, his arms held out slightly at his sides, an animal restrained, his eyes never leaving her bared skin.

"Are you on birth control?" he asked hesitantly.

Her fingers stilled. *Dang.* Since she and Forrest had decided to wait . . . *Why was sex so hard for her?*

He turned slowly, reluctantly, backing toward the entrance

cabinet. He reached to the high shelf and pulled down the first-aid kit.

"It kind of freaked me out to discover my brother keeps condoms in his first-aid kit, but now I'm grateful." He rifled through the box, slid it back up to the shelf, and came back toward her. "Who do you think uses these?"

"Cora and Douglas?"

"No kidding?" He smiled, then parked himself in front of her, arms crossed. "Continue," he said gruffly. "Please."

The command had the reverse effect she would have thought it would have. Instead of irritating her, it sent a thrill through her fingertips. *Who was she with this man?*

She undid the hook at her waist and unraveled the rest of her dress. She felt so exposed—revealing breasts too small, hips too wide—but Evan's appreciative gaze wrapped her in warmth.

The dress fell to the ground.

Evan's eyes worshipped her for a few more seconds. "Come here," he said.

"You're still dressed," she threw back.

"Come here, Lia."

"Not until you undress."

He glanced behind her once, or maybe it was a bit of an eye roll. "Come here."

"We're not going another step further until you undress," she said.

He laughed and started toward her. "You don't take direction very well in the bedroom either, do you?"

"As I said, it's not my strong suit." She smiled, covering up her nervousness. "Does it bother you?"

"No." He stepped forward again, his fingers going to his buttons. "It turns me on, actually." He unbuttoned the rest, shuffling the shirt over his shoulders and flinging it behind him.

But she pushed him back with both hands. "You're still not undressed."

He was beautiful. Perfect V shape, from his shoulders to his waist, rounded muscles on top that gave way to tanned, ridged ones across his stomach. She hadn't had such a physical-labor, workhorse-type man before, with muscles formed under wind and rain, and callused hands from ropes and sails. The few men she'd slept with had been so urbane, with soft shapes and manicured fingernails. They'd usually be sitting on the edge of her bed by now, carefully undoing their cufflinks, tucking their loafers neatly in the corner—not smiling wolfishly like Evan was right now, his shoes coming off in a whoosh, flying to the other side of the cabin. Making rough, quick order of his Levi's buttons. Swooping off his worn blue jeans while maintaining a forward motion with an impatient, all-male body.

His animalistic approach didn't leave her enough time to look at him, enough time to appreciate the naked bullishness that was this man. She was back against the farthest wall in the cabin before she knew what hit her, his mouth again covering hers, his hands all over her body. He treated her breasts as if they were prized possessions instead of the small package they were, palming their softness, running the nipples between his fingers until they rose like little mountains, licking them to attention, kissing their peaks. She rose to her toes with each delicious tug, letting out moans that embarrassed her. Her hands clawed at his shoulders, at the wall behind her, then found their way into his hair.

"Do you want to do this against the wall or do you want the cot?" he mumbled, his hand sliding up the wall where the cot hook was.

She moaned. *Do this against the wall?* This was perhaps more than she was ready for.

But no, she was ready. This is what she needed. This is what she'd always wanted. Urbanity had been her problem. Wolfishness was where it was at.

Her legs went weak; Evan's tugs at her breasts sent her off the floor; his strong, naked body against hers drawing squeaks from her throat. Evan's biceps froze next to her ear, waiting on her word about the cot, as his kisses trailed down her neck. His other hand slid along the side of her breasts, over her hip, between her legs. She couldn't even answer. She could barely breathe.

He abandoned the hook and used both hands to pull her toward his nakedness. A groan rumbled in his throat as their bodies met and molded, skin to skin.

Maybe the wall it was.

His fingertips traced the thong band over her hip. "Take these off," he said between kisses.

"So bossy," she managed to whisper.

She could feel him smile against her lips. "So stubborn. Spread your legs."

"You're too bossy, Evan."

His smile grew wider as his hand continued between her thighs. "I could coax them off you."

He touched her through the lace and nylon of her thong until a gasp escaped her throat. He tugged it aside and slipped his finger underneath, catching her by surprise and sending her off the floor with another embarrassing gasp. By the time his finger plunged inside, pleasure spiraled through her, and she was on her toes again, sucking in air as she bucked against the wall.

"Cinderella, I know you want to run the show here, but if you're demanding really, really great sex, you need to let me take control for a while."

"I can't—*gahhh . . .*" Her protest was swallowed into a spike of pleasure as he withdrew his fingertip and parted her gently, then began circling her entrance with his thumb.

"You can," he said low into her ear. "Let go." His finger went deeper.

"Of what?" she asked around her next three pants.

"All that control."

She couldn't imagine what he was talking about until his finger plunged again, and—*oh sweetness, glory be*—she moaned, and he withdrew methodically and began that circle again at her entrance until she was light-headed, her head lolling against the back wall.

"Take these off," he repeated.

She acquiesced this time, her legs and arms barely functional, but she managed to scoot the lacy scrap down over her thighs, her knees, her ankles, then stepped out of them. He stepped back to watch her, then sheathed himself with the condom and pinned her again.

"If you let me take over, we'll both be happier in the long run." He breathed into the space between them. "As I said, it's been a while."

She simply nodded. She couldn't even speak.

He had her off the ground in one strong lift, hoisting her and pushing at the backs of her thighs until she wrapped her legs around his waist. He entered her swiftly, but only his tip. Her body seemed to clamp down, and as he pushed farther, pain shot through her.

"Wait, wait," she gripped his shoulders.

She squeezed her eyes shut. Damn. This is what always happened. *Why couldn't she have normal sex like other women?* Here was the sexiest guy she'd ever had the pleasure—ahem—of knowing, who had her in a froth just moments ago, had curled her toes, had her moaning with enjoyment, and now here they were—her body shutting down like it always did. *What was wrong with her?*

He was too big. It was his fault. He was hung like a bull. What woman could possibly—

"Lia, *let go*," he said between deep breaths.

"Let go of what?"

"*Control.* Seriously."

Her head went back against the wall and she willed herself to relax.

"Don't think of anything but pleasure," he said in a husky voice. "You're allowed."

His finger wrapped from underneath her thigh and hit that joyous spot again, and she bucked against the wall.

"There we go," he whispered.

He coaxed her open. He rubbed, he circled, he kissed her neck, he whispered dirty words in her ear, and next thing she knew, he was fully inside of her—all huge amounts of him—and thrusting her against the wall. Sometime between the velvet kisses and the fourth time he said, "*God, I've wanted you so badly . . . ,*" she came in a magnificent way—her body breaking apart, her head exploding into a shattering light, a ray hitting her brain, and pleasure throbbing to her fingernails. . . .

His biceps shook and he slid her down the wall, then stilled against her, pulling her into his chest but leaning his forehead against the wall, breathing heavily.

She closed her eyes and let the last of the rays reverberate away. "What was *that*?" she whispered.

"That was really, really great sex," he said.

"Thank you, Evan."

"Pleasure's all mine."

But Lia simply smiled. Definitely hers.

Finally.

Evan could hardly lift his head, hardly lift his arm, but he needed to get off her. He was probably crushing her with his weight.

But *damn*. But *damn* . . . Cinderella was amazing.

The first stab of guilt came when he let his mind wonder if he'd ever taken Renece against a wall, and realized he hadn't. But he shoved the guilt aside. Not now. He wanted to enjoy this. He wanted to look at Cinderella, and enjoy the first and only woman he'd ever taken against a wall, and push her hair over her ear, and revel in the fact that she was who she was. And maybe that was okay. He wanted to look at her, kiss her forehead, take his time backing away from her, and—

A frantic rap at the door shook the thin catamaran walls. "*Evan?*" came a man's voice.

Lia met his eyes with her own saucer-sized blues.

"Evan, you in there?" the deep voice came again.

His brain couldn't get synapses firing into place.

"Douglas!" Lia whispered, filling in for him.

Damn. Adrenaline shot through him, helping him move away from her, helping him find his jeans, yank them on.

The rap sounded again. "Evan? You okay?" A key began scratching at the lock.

"Just a minute," Evan yelled toward the door. He threw Lia's underwear at her, yanked her dress off the floor, and began pushing her toward the head.

But the key jiggled just the right way and the door swung open—Lia halfway to the head, her dress clutched in front of her, frozen in the deep sun rays that shot through the galley.

Along with Douglas's frown.

And, right behind him, Drew's shocked expression from his wheelchair.

"Fuck," Doug whispered, slamming the door shut.

Fifteen minutes later, they all sat crammed in the dinette—Lia dressed, Evan with his pants buttoned back up, Douglas avoiding their eyes, and Drew scowling at all of them.

"So is anyone going to explain what's going on here?" Drew directed the question around the table.

"It's exactly what it looked like," Evan intercepted. He didn't like how Drew was glaring at Lia.

"You're fucking my friend, on my boat, while the lines are half undone, and netting is all over the deck?" Drew looked at him incredulously.

Evan sat back and did his best to formulate a sane response. "Look, Drew, I'm sorr—"

"Douglas was just at my place, telling me how much I could trust you now," Drew went on, his voice shaking in a holding-on-by-a-thread voice. "And I arrive to see how the disentanglement went, and see *everything* to the contrary. You know how much it . . ." Drew's hand waved in the air toward the back of the cabin where Evan had just been naked with Lia, and his face went a little white. ". . . *freaks me out* to have your . . . *germs* . . . all over the . . ." He motioned again, seemingly unable to even finish the sentence. He stared at the offending area as if he were imagining how he might bleach it down.

"And there's fish netting all over the deck?" he went on, sweeping his hand back toward the door. "And the *fucking lines aren't all tied*?"

Evan looked away, embarrassed. What had he been thinking? He couldn't remember the last time he'd been so stupid.

"And Lia, what the hell? Didn't I ask you specifically *not* to get close to him?"

"Leave Lia out of this, Drew," Evan said, although his thoughts dragged over that last comment.

"Evan, you don't need to speak for me," Lia said.

"And Evan, damn it, can you not leave *one friend of mine* alone?" Drew's hands clenched, and his breathing was labored. If his legs had been fine, he'd certainly be pacing now.

Evan would let Drew vent, have his piece. The main thing he felt bad about was that the lines weren't all tied. That was irresponsible. He'd truly lost his mind, there. But the rest was just Drew being Drew. Evan was used to his brother's outbursts, his overreactions, his phobias. He'd wait it out, like he used to, then maybe get to the part where he could apologize for the things he *really* wanted to apologize for. He'd wanted to have this discussion for some time. He just didn't think he'd be doing it after being caught with his pants down. Literally.

"Drew, you need to stop yelling at your brother," Lia said. "Especially for being with me. It's not like I was an unwilling participant."

"And what about that, anyway, Lia?" Drew said, turning to her. "What about my simple request: to *stay away from my fucking brother?*"

"And why did you ask that? That was a ridiculous request, with no explanation whatsoever."

"Can't you just do *one* thing I ask you?"

"Not without a good explanation."

"She doesn't take orders well," Evan threw in.

He resisted the urge to smile at her. He liked her more every minute. Normally he'd jump in with his brother yelling at a woman like this, but Lia was holding her own, and the two of them seemed like they'd done this a million times.

Douglas moved his bottled water around the table and

looked like he wanted to be anywhere but there. "I'm just going to . . ." He gestured with his thumb toward the door.

"No. Douglas, stay," said Drew. "You were vouching for him earlier. I need you to see why I have a hard time buying into the fact that he's someone I can trust."

"I'll vouch for Evan, too," Lia piped in. "We all like him. He helped us out tremendously this week, Drew. He's smart, and he's a good captain, and—"

"He can navigate a boat—I get that," Drew snapped. "I never had any issue with that. I'm more worried about the damage he can do to people."

"I'm sitting right here," Evan murmured.

"I didn't want you to get hurt, Lia," Drew said. "That's why I wanted you to stay away from him."

"Evan's not hurting me."

"Yet. He hurts people. He only thinks of himself."

"Evan's *not* hurting me," Lia said more forcefully.

"I'm sitting right here," Evan repeated.

"He just fucked you," Drew said to Lia, "probably with no thought of—"

"That's enough, Drew," Evan said, louder.

". . . with no thought of you and your boyfriend," Drew went on, "and he'll never look back. I imagine he'll be leaving any day now."

"*Knock it off.*" Evan shoved out of the dinette. He'd heard enough.

Drew looked up at him with surprise. Maybe he thought Evan might hit him. But Evan wasn't going to hit him, as tempting as it was. They were through with their competitive boyish tumbles of the past.

"You know he's been sailing the world, right?" Drew asked Lia, but he kept his eyes on Evan. "Who knows who he's been with? Or what diseases he's brought home? I hope you used a condom."

"You don't know anything about me, Drew." Evan was getting pissed now.

"I know you take what you want."

"That's not true."

"So you *don't* just sleep with whomever you want? I must have been mistaken."

"You are. And this is bullshit. I'm not going to discuss my sex life with you. Or Douglas." He motioned to the poor guy.

"What about Lia?"

"I'll discuss it with Lia if she wants to, in private."

"We used a condom," Lia blurted. As soon as she said it, she leaned back against the dinette in a brazen way, but then she glanced at Douglas and her fingertips fluttered to her collarbone.

Evan smiled at her. He was really beginning to love everything about her—her directness, her bluntness, the cute expression on her face when she said something she didn't mean to.

"Forrest and I broke up anyway," Lia added, waving her hand.

Drew frowned, his concern playing across his forehead lines. "Oh. Sorry about that, Lia."

The smile Evan had just had on his face slid away as he watched the interplay between Drew and Lia, the clouds of old-time guilt gathering and hovering over his head. Drew really did care about her. Maybe Drew *was* just looking out for her. Evan could see how Drew could feel protective. He slid back toward the dinette bench. Maybe he should cut his bro some slack.

"But the fact that you had a boyfriend probably didn't matter to Evan," Drew said. "That never stopped him before."

Or maybe not . . .

"Watch it, Drew," he said under his breath.

"He's using you," Drew told Lia.

"You don't know what you're talking about," Evan said.

"So you're *staying*?" Drew threw back at him.

Evan glanced at Lia. Well, sure, he was leaving. But she knew that. He certainly didn't see himself as *using* her—

"Evan's right." Lia turned angrily toward Drew. "I have no illusions here. I'm not dating him, and I don't expect him to date me. Or stay. We're just two adults. And we can handle ourselves. It meant nothing."

Evan snapped his head up. He knew that's how she felt. He knew that going in. In fact, it was every man's fantasy to have such a willing partner with no strings attached. But it still gave him a ridiculous tug in his chest to hear her say it. He stared at the table.

Douglas moved his bottled water around and stared at the porthole as if he hoped it would suck him through.

"You didn't even know her," Drew said quietly toward the tabletop. "You just wanted her because she was mine."

The sound of the water lapping the side of the boat was the only sound for half a minute.

"Are we talking about Renece now?" Evan asked.

Drew had aged quite a bit in the last few years. Or maybe it was just the pain of the broken legs and DVT, but he looked haggard—permanent lines crossing his forehead, his hair receding around the temples. Suddenly, Evan was sorry he'd let so many years go by. They should have settled this years ago.

"Doug, Lia, can you give us a minute?" Evan asked.

Douglas bolted out of the booth, leaving his bottled water shimmering on the table. Lia hesitated, but finally moved out too, running her hand over Drew's shoulder almost maternally.

When the door closed, Evan slid into the bench across from his brother. "Let's have it."

The haggard lines in Drew's face went from anger to fatigue. "What do you want me to say?"

"I guess we both have a lot to say. And we probably should have said it a long time ago. Do you want me to start or do you want to?"

"You look like shit."

"Thanks, I was going to say the same about you."

A reluctant smile crossed Drew's face. He stared at his own water bottle as he twisted it between his palms.

"So you made it all the way around?" Drew finally asked.

"Yep."

"How long did it take you?"

"Two years."

"What was the hardest part?"

"I hit a crazy storm near the Maldives. And the Panama Canal was a bitch to get through. But I don't think this is what we need to talk about."

As the boat rocked gently, Drew's smile was replaced by a terrible sadness. "I can't seem to stop hating you."

The words were delivered in almost a whisper, without

malice, matter of fact, but they held so much honesty Evan couldn't help but recoil.

As many problems as he and Drew had had as kids, they'd always loved each other. There had been fistfights and silent treatments, toothpaste wars and demolition derbies on bikes, but that had all been just normal brother stuff. There had also been the time little Drew had stood guard over Evan's aquarium when some younger cousins came to visit, or the time he'd collected signatures at school to get Evan voted as junior campus police. Once, Drew rode his bike all the way into the next city to tell Evan he was going to get in trouble if he didn't come home by five, and another time Drew had made a terrible "carrot soup" for Evan when he stayed home with the flu and their mom had to go to work. It was just boiled water with carrots in it, but Drew had thought he was helping.

Evan stared across the table at the little brother who had always loved and admired him, and realized how much he'd really hurt Drew when he'd left with Renece.

"I'm sorry," Evan finally said. "Look, Drew, I didn't know you were in love with her. It had never come up between us, and you introduced her to me on the boat. I honestly thought you were introducing her to me as a possible date."

Drew looked up at him quizzically. "You're insane."

"That's how it looked from my perspective."

Drew stared through the porthole and seemed to consider that for a second. "That's stupid. I'd invited her there because I'd had a crush on her for a million years."

"You never told me that."

"Why didn't you back off once I *did* tell you?"

"We'd already gone out every day for two weeks. I fell hard, man."

Drew looked up with surprise. "You fell in love with her? You didn't just sleep with her?"

"Who do you think I was? I was a geek. I didn't sleep with girls. She was the first. She made me feel like I mattered to someone."

"She was the first?"

Evan just shrugged.

"I thought you were a dog, man."

"What made you think that?"

"You got *everything* you wanted."

"What are you talking about?"

"Your own bedroom, a normal life with no OCD, your own boat, you got to live with Dad, he *took you with him*—I was just the 'disappointing kid.' "

"I was always jealous that you got to stay with Mom."

They both stared at the table. A patrol boat sounded a horn in the marina, and the festival crowd erupted.

"Well, whether or not you're trying to take everything from me, I don't want Lia or my boat to be part of the collateral damage," Drew said.

"*What*? I don't want to take everything from you. And I would never use Lia that way."

"Why did you come here, then, Evan? Why are you on *my* boat? And why *her*, of all the women in the state?"

Evan looked away. That, he didn't know.

"I didn't know why I came here, to be honest," he said, deciding just to answer the part he understood. "Lia thinks I secretly wanted to apologize. And she's probably right. I know I pulled into Sandy Cove when I could have easily gone to San Diego. And I know it's late to apologize, but now that I'm here, I just want you to know that I never meant to hurt you."

"And why Lia?"

Evan shook his head. His first instinct was to say nothing about Lia, but keeping things to himself when it came to Drew had gotten him into this mess in the first place.

"I know it looks bad," he said, "but there was no intent there, to go after her because she's in your life. I even asked her if she ever dated you. A few times, actually."

"What'd she say?"

"She said you kissed once, and that was it."

Drew snorted. "Yeah, that was a disaster. But seriously, man, I've always been half in love with her."

Evan looked up sharply. "What?"

"Yeah. So to see you two together . . . I just . . . I can't figure out why *you* always get the girl. And to think you're doing it just for kicks—or just to *use* her to pass your time here—kills me."

"Wait, you're in *love* with her?"

"Well, not anymore. Exactly."

"She said you have a girlfriend."

"Yeah, I've moved on."

"But you still hang around with her?"

Drew shrugged. "We have the same friends. And I've come to terms with the situation. I know she has a type, and it's not me. It's not you, either, by the way. Usually suits, guys with lots of money—I get that. I just want her to be happy. But to see her with *you . . .*" He shook his head. "And you're just using her."

"I'm not using her."

"You're fucking her until you leave in a few days? With no plans of a future? I think that's the definition."

Evan looked away. "I had no idea you felt that way about her," he said instead. "I really didn't mean—"

"You didn't mean to come here and steal one more thing that might be mine?"

"Of course not."

"Then leave her alone."

Evan's back pressed against the upholstery in the dinette. It sounded like a simple solution. He'd just met her, after all, and he was leaving in a few days anyway. And she'd just said their really, really great sex "meant nothing." Of course. Yet his heart did a strange thud when he imagined saying good-bye.

"I'll talk to her," Evan said.

"There are plenty of other women," Drew said.

Evan nodded. Of course.

"How long are you staying?" Drew asked.

"Few more days."

"She knows that?"

"Yeah."

"Where are you heading?"

"Might go up north to see Mom and Dad. Or maybe south, for another loop around."

"Really? You're going again?"

"I might."

"Where do you start?"

"Panama to the Marquesas, usually."

Drew nodded. "Well, talk to Lia. Make sure she knows. I'm serious, Ev. If you hurt her—if you screw this up—I'll seriously never forgive you."

"Got it." Evan took a deep breath. He wasn't sure what he

was getting himself into, but he knew he didn't want to hurt Lia, either. And he didn't want to screw this up. He wasn't a man who didn't care. At least he hadn't been, in the old days. Renece and Luke's death had changed him, sure, but he didn't want to be changed into a man who had no feelings for people who really mattered.

"So a few more days?" Drew asked. "You still up for the charter on Monday? Everyone seems to think you're the best captain ever."

Evan didn't miss the eye roll. Or the jealousy in Drew's voice. He didn't mean to take over his boat, too, though. Or his staff. He'd be sure to make this all right. "Sure."

"I'd appreciate that. I have someone coming on Wednesday, but can you handle things until then?"

"Sure."

Drew didn't seem completely comfortable with the idea, but he wasn't frowning anymore. "I might join you on the charter," he said.

"You don't have to do that. I can handle it."

"I know. But I just want to . . . *be* there. It's important. Kyle Stevens is—"

"I know about Kyle Stevens." Evan didn't really want to hear his name anymore.

"He might want to invest."

"You need an investor that badly?"

A sadness crossed Drew's face as he nodded.

Evan sighed. Damn. He didn't know Drew was this bad off. But he didn't want to harp on it right now—his intent wasn't to make Drew feel worse.

He moved Douglas's bottled water around on the table and thought about something else that had been bothering him.

"You named the boat after Luke," he said.

The words flew out of nowhere. He worded it as a statement, but in reality it was a question. If Drew had never forgiven him, and couldn't even bring himself to go to the funeral—still a thorn in Evan's side—why had he named his boat after Evan's son?

"I saw pictures of him," Drew said. "Mom showed me. He looked just like you *and* Renece. He reminded me of you, but he had her smile—that smile I remembered." He looked out the porthole for a minute as the boat swayed. "I wish I had met him, Ev. I'm sorry I didn't. I know you'll never forgive me for that. And I was always sorry about your loss. It's hard to imagine. I just couldn't go to the funeral, you know? But I wanted to honor him in some way."

On the list of things they had each grown to resent in the other, Drew's not attending Renece's and Luke's funeral was at the top of Evan's.

But they were breaking this cycle now. . . .

"I appreciate the gesture," Evan finally said.

Drew's hand slid across the dinette for a shake. "Move on?"

Evan stared at it for only a second before taking it. Yes. They would move on. The pain was still raw for everyone. They both still missed Renece. Evan would never stop missing his son. Drew would still feel the pain of being betrayed in his mind. Evan would still feel the pain of Drew missing the funerals. They might not learn right away how to stop feeling jealous of each other and what the other had. But in a world where things could be taken from you in a flash, Evan was learning that—despite the heartache and misunderstandings a family could bring—you had to hold on to the people you cherished. Although there had been numerous misunderstandings between them, Drew was still the little brother who had made him the carrot soup.

"Move on," he said, shaking Drew's hand.

The smile that stole across Drew's face was tired, not entirely certain. But the relief there was unmistakable.

But quickly the smile disappeared and his eyes turned as dark as a night ocean: "And *don't* hurt her," he added.

Evan finished the shake and nodded.

He suddenly had his priorities rearranged.

Lia tugged on the net from one side, but Douglas came up behind her and nudged it out of her hands. "Evan and I can get this later, sunshine."

"I want to help."

Douglas looked up and down the deck. Fluffy navy purple clouds, tinged in pink from the bottom, lined up across the blue sky like baked goods, promising dusk in a couple of hours and possibly a little rain. Sounds of the festival—a distant rock band, children laughing, a clown's horn—bounced down the hill from Sandy Cove and across the marina.

"Do you do windows?" Douglas asked.

"Sure."

"Can you give them a quick swipe? Don't spend too much energy—it might rain. We just need a quick rubdown to get the saltwater off." He set her up with a barely filled bucket and a sponge squeegee, then picked up the deck hose and began hosing down as they listened to the distant strains of a Neil Diamond impersonator from up the hill.

"Think they'll be okay in there?" she asked, nodding toward the galley and taking a few quick swipes at the closest window.

"They should be. Family's all you got, you know?"

Lia thought about her sisters, and how she often missed their events because of work. She'd felt especially bad for missing Coco's first school play, and one of Coco's surf meets that Fin helped with. And she had felt really bad for missing Giselle's first wedding dress shopping day. She'd also missed a pet fair that Noelle had put on and had been really proud of. And her mother had been sick with pneumonia once and Lia had never been able to get up to see her in L.A. because Elle kept her late every night.

The guilt curdled in her stomach as she soaped up the next window.

"Do you have family, Douglas?"

"Little boy in Vegas."

Lia's arm froze mid-circle. The fake Neil Diamond launched into "Sweet Caroline."

"Is that why you always go out there?" she asked.

"Yep. He's eleven," Douglas said over his shoulder as he continued sweeping. "He was a late-in-life one. But I love him like crazy. His mother I have a problem with, but the kid's terrific. I'm trying to save enough money to go live out there, but my work has always been on the ocean. I'll have enough saved right about the time he leaves home." He chuckled. "But you've got to try."

Lia continued soaping the window. *Yes, you've got to try. . . .*

She glanced toward the galley and felt immeasurably proud of Drew and Evan.

"I heard you and Cora are sort of an item," she said, ready to change the subject.

"*What?*" Douglas turned off the hose. "Did Cora say that?"

Lia turned her face toward the window so he couldn't see her smile. "Not exactly. I just assumed, by the way she looks at you."

"*Looks* at me?"

"Douglas, you men can be so daft."

He looked out at the ocean for several seconds, then turned the hose back on. "I won't argue with you there, sunshine."

As she rounded the last curve to get the front windows, she came face to chest with Evan. "Ooooh!"

With one glance at the chest she'd just been running her hands over—and the arms that had just been holding her, naked, against a wall—a ray of tingles shot throughout her body like some kind of fireworks show gone awry. If she'd been worried before that she didn't have the gene to enjoy sex properly, she knew the worry was over. The secret, apparently, was not being a yoga instructor or a Cirque du Soleil performer. It was having a large man with very soft lips pressing you against a very hard wall, kissing you like he was drinking water after a long, long drought.

She smoothed her dress and looked away so he wouldn't see her blush. Then she wondered for about the twentieth time who she was around Evan Betancourt.

"Hey," she said to his third button. She couldn't quite bring herself to lift her eyes to his face.

"Hey," he said in a voice that reminded her of slow, sweet syrup.

"How'd it go?"

"It went okay." He took the bucket from her hand. "You and I need to talk, though."

"About what?" She had seen the way Evan shot a look at her when she said their little . . . um . . . encounter "meant nothing." Could she have actually hurt his feelings?

"Drew," he answered.

"Oh."

Of course he wouldn't have been hurt. That was a silly thought. These Neil Diamond songs must be putting romantic notions in her head.

"Douglas and I are almost done here," she said. "Want to get something to eat?"

"You *are* done here," he said, taking the squeegee out of her other hand and dropping it into the bucket. "And I don't know if my brother is quite ready to see us walk off this boat together. Maybe you should get home. Big day again tomorrow."

She started to protest. She wanted to be with him. She wanted to talk more. She wanted him to kiss her again, and maybe have a round two of that "really, really great sex." She wanted to give him someone to talk to and let him vent about Drew. She wanted to be there for him, and help him sort out all his relationships. She wanted to hold his hand, and sit there with him in the falling dusk, and tell him that he was inspiring her to be a better sibling.

But then she realized, with a degree of horror, that she was about to beg. So she pressed her lips together. "You're right," she said. "But let me help." She reached for the bucket.

"Go home, Cinderella."

His gaze tore away from her and went over her shoulder. She followed it to see Douglas carrying Drew back to his wheelchair. Fake Neil Diamond crooned "Love on the Rocks." The scent of popcorn drifted down from the festival booths.

"Let me walk you off," Evan said in a voice that sounded strange and distant.

She was surprised he was pushing her away so quickly. And *sheesh*, the way he was holding her elbow to steer her off the boat felt like their perp walk by the harbor patrol the other night.

"I thought we'd at least get to spend a little time together," she found herself saying.

His glance first looked nervous, but then it relaxed into something more like amusement. He slowed. "All right. You do need to leave now, for Drew. But . . ." His low voice tickled her ear. "If you want to come by later . . ."

Lia smiled to herself and let him guide her the rest of the way off the boat.

Yes, yes, yes . . .

Twenty-three

The chaos of the festival erupted around them as they saun-tered through the grass in the twilight. They'd played the ring toss and water-balloon gun shoot, and had picked up hot dogs and funnel cakes for dinner. Evan snuck up and squirted the last of his ketchup onto Lia's hot dog. She squealed and squirmed away.

He laughed and resisted the urge to tackle her in the grass—she was getting sexier and cuter by the second, and was lifting the weight of the world off his shoulders. She was reminding him what it felt like to laugh again; and just act stupid; and, quite frankly, to live.

He watched her hair swing around, and his memory shot him back to just hours ago, when she'd leaned against the fiberglass, breasts and belly and thighs all bared to him, hands behind her back, waiting for him to ravish her. And he wanted to be back there right now, doing it all over again.

But damn, he needed to talk to her.

"So Drew was concerned about why you came back here?" she prompted, balancing her red-checked paper hot dog boat to point to a picnic table on top of a grassy knoll beneath a lantern that had just popped on.

He followed her to the top. She'd been pushing him to describe his conversation with Drew. Most of it he wanted kept to himself—he and Drew would have to tread lightly into working out their own differences—but he knew he had to tell her the part that involved her. He'd need to back away from her slowly, but he wanted to give her a reason.

At the table, they laid out their dinner spread, set down their drinks, and crawled into opposite benches.

"He seemed to be under the impression I was here to steal his life."

"Steal his life?" Lia frowned across the table. "That's crazy." She leaned over and snagged one of his French fries. "Although, I guess if that's how he interpreted your past with Renece, maybe that makes sense."

A spear went through his lung as he struggled for air. There it was. Her name again. He hardly ever heard it anymore, and Lia said it so casually. He focused on his French fries a minute while he pulled himself together, then stared out at the view. The table was perched at just the right angle that they could see the marina through a narrow patch of trees. Sandy Cove sprawled like a glittering half moon.

"He seemed to think I was moving in on his boat, his clients, his life here . . . you," he said.

"Me?"

Evan nodded.

"But I'm not part of his 'things.'"

"He has a lot of affection for you." He didn't want to say more than that. It was Drew's story to tell, Drew's feelings to reveal or not to reveal. But Evan had to make the next point.

"He wants me to back away from his life, including you," he said.

Lia frowned. "But he has no right to ask that."

"He sees it differently."

Lia seemed to think that over as she stared at her food. Children's laughter drifted up over the hill, and a slew of kids came running through the grass, shooting each other with fluorescent water guns they must have won at a booth. Evan thought about how Luke would play like that. He'd loved watching Luke laugh, play, run. There had been nothing in Evan's life that had prepared him for how much he'd love being a dad, but he had. He glanced up at Lia and had a strange, distant curiosity about whether she wanted kids someday.

"I'm a little suspicious," Lia finally said.

"Of what?"

"This sounds like a 'wham, bam, thank you ma'am.'"

Evan frowned. "What are you talking about?"

"Your way of explaining to me that the bang was good, but you're done now."

"I didn't say anything remotely like that, Lia. We can still . . ." He motioned toward the boat but then wasn't sure what he was offering. They could still what? Fuck a few times? But make sure no closeness was involved? How nice.

"I mean, we can do whatever you want," he said.

A smile curved her lips. "I think, what I want, is more of that 'really, really great sex.'"

He chuckled. At least she wasn't the helpless victim Drew seemed to think she was. And how awesome that she might be open to a physical relationship that didn't have to go anywhere. But even so . . . He had to be sure.

"Drew thinks I'm using you," he reiterated.

"So 'use' me."

Evan smiled. She was getting better and better. "He thinks I'll hurt you," he added.

"You would only be hurting me if I had feelings for you."

The same tug from earlier dragged a hook through his chest. Damn. He looked away. He was turning into a sap. He knew she *didn't*. Have feelings for him, that is. But maybe part of him thought she was starting to. And maybe part of him hoped she would.

"Yeah, no worries there," he said.

"I don't mean . . . I mean, of course I have *feelings*." Cinderella waved a French fry around. "I *like* you and all. But it's not like we're going to get *married* or anything." She laughed.

Evan remembered Drew's comment that Lia had a distinct type—usually suits, guys with lots of money. Guys like her Forrest, probably, who left for Bora Bora without her. Guys like Kyle, undoubtedly, who had Harvard degrees and watches that needed to be insured. No wonder she was rolling her eyes at the prospect of him right now.

He concentrated on the ketchup and resolved to dismiss the burning jealousy around his ears.

"Well, Drew has more affection for you than you might realize," he said. "And it might hurt him to see us together."

"So we won't let him see us together."

"He might be joining us on the charter."

It was her turn to raise her eyebrows. "All right, we'll play things off on the charter. But we still have today and tomorrow."

Evan nodded, then gathered their trash. Walking over the slight hill and back in the cool evening air did him good. *She didn't need this to mean anything. She just wanted great sex.* He could get on board with that. If his heart was starting to bleed, he'd just close it up. Lia was being clear about what she expected out of this. He'd just enjoy the sex and walk away.

He shoved his hands in his pockets and pushed away any stray guilt regarding Renece: *It was normal to want a woman. Renece wouldn't expect him to be celibate. This was perfectly normal. He didn't need to feel bad. . . .*

Then he shoved aside any remaining guilt regarding Drew: *He'd made Drew's worries clear, and Lia was making her own decisions.*

When he came back down the hill, she was ready to go, looking up at him from the long drag she was taking on her milkshake.

"I think I have enough fuel in me now to beat you at that water-balloon game," she said.

He let himself watch her full, beautiful lips; let himself stare as she sucked hard; let himself close his heart a little about how much he was growing to like her. He'd just concentrate on the sex. *Those lips could do some damage. . . .* He let his mind go to all the body parts he'd like to have those lips on and then cleared his throat before finally looking away.

"Lead the way," he choked out.

Lia galloped from game to game, feeling flirty and strangely comfortable in the blue stilettos she'd worn. The shoes had arrived today as yet another wedding option—complete with sparkly hardware in a "buckle" pattern across the top—and she'd been surprised to actually like them. Plus they didn't look bad with the sundress she wanted to wear tonight for Evan. She'd thrown them on with the hope of breaking them in. She'd tossed some sandals in her bag just in case, but so far these were great. Maybe they'd be her lucky shoes.

She tugged Evan beneath the bright festival bulbs strewn across the fairway, and he followed behind her, his hands in his pockets, his mouth in a constant quirk of amusement.

Harry James had set up a harbor patrol booth with a spinning wheel game near the marina entrance, planning to stay until seven with his deputy Steve, so Lia and Evan decided to wait to slip past him and get to the boats. They didn't want to give any indication that Evan would be a sneakaboard tonight. And maybe Lia. If she could summon the courage, that was.

This kind of behavior was not like her at all. She was not the type to sneak aboard boats. She was not the type to sleep with men she'd known for only five days. She was not the type to stare at a man's body as he leaned over a wooden gun rack and shot at moving cardboard ducks.

But she *was* with this man.

And she liked it.

And she liked him.

Plus, he *wasn't staying*. It was such a rare, delicious opportunity to spend time with a sexy man without any fear of growing too attached. They could just have this incredible few days—help each other over a hard time—then go on to live the lives they were probably meant to live.

Evan won two games for her and handed her a stuffed dolphin and a pewter goldfish ring. They talked to some of her friends from the Ocean Museum. Then she won the Ping-Pong ball toss and handed him a pair of oversized sunglasses. Every time she heard him laugh, she couldn't help but feel a sharp sense of accomplishment. His laugh sounded rusty and reluctant, which gave her an extra dose of joy.

She still couldn't believe he'd lost a son. A wife. Her memory opened to the gem she'd kept carefully tucked away: his comment before he kissed her the first time, *You make me forget about my wife. And you're the first woman who's ever done so.* . . . That awareness brought her the greatest joy of all. She tucked the gem back into the furthest recesses of her memory, the furthest recesses of her heart, where she knew she'd pull it out again and again over the next several years. She hoped she could help him for just a few days at least and make this memory a rich one.

The band struck up off to the edge of the marina where the beach was. "Band in the Sand!" Lia clapped. "Let's go listen!"

"Harry should be leaving soon." Evan glanced toward the harbor patrol booth hopefully.

"It'll take him at least fifteen minutes to clear it out. Let's listen to the band."

Without waiting for his protest, Lia grabbed Evan's hand and dragged him toward the beach. He offered a trace of resistance, but still had that quirk of amusement around his mouth and seemed to hold her hand tighter. She pictured him on his sailboat, wind in his hair, alone for two years, and wondered how long it had been since someone had simply held his hand.

About a hundred people had staked claims with their low beach chairs around the stage. Spotlights lit the makeshift amphitheater, where five middle-aged men in Hawaiian shirts crooned "Surf City" like the Beach Boys. Although the beach-chair crowd had settled their places carefully, most were already up out of their chairs, twisting to the beat in the sand, or doing impressive "swim" moves to the music.

Lia shot a smile over her shoulder as she dragged Evan closer. "Wanna dance?"

"Absolutely not." Evan looked mortified.

"C'mon, dance with me."

"How about if I sit over here and watch you instead?" He pitched his behind into the sand. His jeans were already sandy as he made himself comfortable, leaning on his side, propping himself up on one arm. He looked sexy enough to jump, but Lia got ahold of herself. Her sweep of his strong thighs and flexed triceps probably lasted a beat too long, but she bit her lip and turned toward the band. She loved to dance. She tugged off the blue shoes, wriggled close to the edge of the stage, and let loose her joy.

After the first number, she returned to Evan and fell next to him, panting. He actually had a smile on his face that looked like it had lasted longer than a nanosecond.

"I enjoyed that," he said.

A blush heated her cheeks, which were already rosy, she could tell. Strands of hair were already plastered to her hairline. The fake Beach Boys went into "Surfin' Safari." The cold sand felt good.

"Go for it." He nodded toward the band. "I'll watch again."

His obvious enjoyment, and the rumble in his voice, gave her goose bumps. She ran her toes through the night-chilled granules. "How about if you get to watch for three songs, but you join me for the fourth?"

"I seriously don't dance."

"Then you seriously don't watch, either."

He lifted an eyebrow. "You drive a tough bargain."

She stood and brushed the sand from her hands. "I'm going to dance way over there unless you change your mind."

He grabbed her wrist before she could even take a full bare step through the sand. "I want to watch." His smile was embarrassed.

"Fourth song."

Without letting go, he stared at her for eight beats of "Surfin' Safari," then gave a nod of acquiescence.

Lia bounced back to the edge of the dance floor, bobbing to the smooth, summery music, and found a cluster of dancers who were as enthusiastic as she was—one was Vivi's hairdresser on Main Street and another she thought was Mr. Brimmer's daughter. They welcomed her into their fold and danced through the rest of "Surfin' Safari" and then "Barbara Ann." Lia threw her hands in the air with wild abandon, and shook her hips with joy. One of Xavier's friends saw her from across the "floor" and shimmied toward her for "Fun, Fun, Fun." Before that song was even finished, she felt a hand at her back.

"She's mine," Evan said to Xavier's friend. He smiled and drew her away from the group.

Startled at the interruption, at Evan's words, at the way this caveman behavior was thrilling her instead of insulting her, Lia started to open her mouth to protest. But when she caught his wolfish gaze, her breath caught. He pulled her toward a lone palm tree in the dark, away from the crowd.

"I'd better keep this proper," he said, lifting her left hand in his right. With his other hand, he touched her back lightly in a waltz pose. "Is this right?"

"That's perfect."

They did a sort of waltz to "Little Surfer Girl" far away from the others, their feet barely shuffling through the sand, mostly rocking in a light circle in the shadows. Evan was a terrible dancer.

Lia bit back a smile.

"When's the last time you danced, Evan?"

"It's been a while."

"I see."

"Can you tell?"

"A little."

The embarrassed grin that swept his face was too cute.

"Like the driving and the steak dinner, the kissing and the sex, it's been a while?"

"Hmmm."

"Were you faithful to Renece?"

He looked startled at the question. Or maybe at the mention of her name. His face seemed to go a little white whenever Lia said it. But she could tell there was some guilt clouding his enjoyment of their kisses, and even their "really, really great sex," and Lia figured it was because of his wife. Maybe he hadn't quite mourned her. Maybe he hadn't talked about her enough. Maybe Lia could help him remember her, honor her, have respect between them. But Evan must know that his wife would have wanted him to move on—certainly she would have wanted him to have joy again.

"Of course," he said.

"Some men aren't into monogamy."

"I was."

For the first time, Lia let herself imagine Evan as a husband. Perhaps he had been a good husband to Renece. The thought filled her with a strange warmth.

"Did you two have a good marriage?"

"We did."

"Did you have good sex?"

He smiled. "Lia. We're not going there."

"You told Drew you'd talk to me about your sex life. In private."

"I meant the parts that concern you."

"Like how many ports you'd visited?"

He chuckled. "Exactly. Drew's an idiot."

"You weren't sleeping with prostitutes at every port?"

"Not even close."

"Have you slept with anyone since Renece?"

Drained face again. His smile slid away. "No."

"No one?" She leaned back to peer into his face.

"There were two close calls, but I couldn't go through with them: Once I was too drunk, and once I was too aware."

"Aware of what?"

"Aware that she wasn't Renece."

"So . . . earlier today, with me . . . ?"

He leaned down and kissed the part in her hair. "That was a first."

The warmth that had been sweeping through her continued, turning her legs into linguini noodles. Maybe, even though she thought none of this meant anything between them, it did. Maybe it meant something to him. And, judging by her linguini legs, maybe it meant something to her. Maybe it meant more than she was acknowledging. She concentrated on hanging on to him and realized she was the lame dancer now.

He shuffled through a few more notes of the song, then stared over the top of her head.

"Harry's gone." He strode to where her blue shoes were, then scooped them up and handed them to her.

"You don't want to dance anymore?"

"This conversation is reminding me of what I really want to be doing." He grabbed her hand and began trudging through the sand with his long strides.

Lia took a deep breath of relief. Yes. This was only about really, really great sex. She'd said so, and he was agreeing. They were back on common ground.

"Hey!" She hopped and skipped to keep up. "I feel like you didn't complete your end of the dancing bargain here."

"Did I mention I never got the bacon-wrapped shrimp the other night?"

"The prosciutto-wrapped asparagus was good."

"It wasn't bacon."

She laughed and tried to keep up with him in the sand.

Evan's boat at slip ninety-two was just as messy as the last time she saw it. She glimpsed inside from the doorway, but he pushed her gently back with an apologetic smile, then went on a scramble, snatching clothing off the bed, shoving boxes aside with his foot, closing the motor door and moving a set of dumbbells off to the side. "Okay. I think you can make your way in here now."

"You sure are different than Drew," Lia couldn't help but speculate, stepping over another box. She had the shoes back on, and they were making her feel very sexy.

"We shared a room when we were kids, but my mom realized that wasn't going to work. I drove him to the brink of insanity by the time he was eleven: He'd start crying if any of the socks or clutter from my side even crossed the clothesline onto his side."

"You actually had a clothesline?"

"Oh yeah. All the way across the room. But it didn't work. My mom gave me my own room, in our attic." He moved a box of greasy boat parts off the dinette chair. "Drew was spoiled."

"What were you like, as kids?"

"Jealous." He laughed. "Drew was pretty coddled. I was jealous of him all the time. I thought he had everything."

"Maybe he thought you did."

Evan looked thoughtful about that for a second. "That's what he said. . . ." A cloud passed over his face.

Lia wanted to kick herself. *Way to set the mood, girl. . . .*

She scrambled to recover. Her fingertips sought his T-shirt, but he didn't notice and leaned just out of her reach toward the dinette. He swept a handful of crumbs off the seat. "Do you want something to drink?" Worry etched lines between his eyebrows.

"I'm fine." Lia stepped toward him again, but this time changed her mind. She needed to be even more direct. She went all the way around him and made her way down the narrow entrance toward the bed.

He looked immeasurably uncomfortable, and passed her before she could get to it, snatching a few more shirts off the navy comforter. The scent of cedar, which lined every hard surface, from the bedframe to the cabinetry, was heavy in the air. He closed one of the curtains and opened a window. The sound of the festival trickled in as she sat primly on the edge of the bed. Lia could hear a distant "Wouldn't It Be Nice" from the fake Beach Boys.

Evan headed back to the front part of the cabin, dimmed the lights, and came back. "Harry will have to think no one's here."

"Of course."

She watched him slow as he came toward her, looking her up and down, then he leaned near the door frame.

"Aren't you going to sit down?" Her voice was sort of shaking.

"This is definitely okay with you, Cinderella?"

"Am I making you nervous?"

"Drew's going to kick my ass."

"Only if you hurt me."

He nodded.

"You're not hurting me." She smoothed the bedspread nervously. "You're simply giving me the great sex I've never had before."

A quirk of his mouth followed that—pride, maybe, or more relief. "Are we talking orgasms here?" he asked.

"Yes."

"You don't normally orgasm?"

"No."

His eyebrows rose. "Seriously?"

She nodded.

"You did okay earlier."

"That's why I'm back."

He didn't smile at that. Just studied her carefully. "Come here, then, Cinderella." His voice sounded husky.

"This bed seems nice."

"Come here."

"Are we going to go through this bossiness thing again?"

"Do you have any complaints about last time?"

Her memory only had to get through three flashes of how it felt to be stripped down and held against a wall by this man before her breathing became shallow. She shook her head.

"Then come here. And leave those shoes on."

CHAPTER

Twenty-four

Lia approached Evan tentatively, but he didn't have "tentative" anywhere about him. He drew her toward him, pinned her hands against the wall, and worked his way down her body with his lips, his tongue, his fingertips. He peeled down her dress, keeping the shoes on, and explored her breasts, her stomach, her hips—first in a gentle way, then in a way that felt more desperate—and traced a fingertip down to her panty line, where he hooked it and got on one knee. She knew something lovely and raunchy would follow. He didn't disappoint.

By the time all the sounds fell away from the festival—after the laughter had subsided, the guests had driven away, the booths had been packed up, the band had packed away its last instrument—Lia and Evan lay soaked in exhaustion and perspiration across his navy sheets, Lia facedown, having tried at least three new positions she'd never even heard of before, and Evan on his back. The comforter lay in a crumpled pile on top of the shoes somewhere.

"That was . . ." She struggled to lift her cheek off the mattress, but found the effort too taxing, and let it fall back. . . . *Incredible. Fantastic. Phenomenal. Stupendous* . . . She let him fill in the proper word because she couldn't even make the effort at this point. And she didn't even care what word he used. For her, it had been *all of the above*. And her worries were truly over. . . .

Cirque du Soleil was unnecessary.

All you needed was a manly man.

And the courage to be vulnerable, and let him take over, if that turned you on.

And, apparently, for her, it did.

The boat rocked gently as the sounds of quiet waves lapped the side of the hull.

"Drew's going to kick my ass," Evan said into the quiet air. He rolled toward her and touched her hair, stroking it off her shoulder. "If he had any idea what I was thinking . . ."

"Which is what?" she mumbled into the sheets.

His hand ran down her back, over her bottom, between her thighs. "About five more ways I'd like to 'use' you before I leave this week."

Lia giggled and found the strength to lift herself and turn toward him. "Permission granted."

His face lit up. "To board?"

She laughed and pushed at his chest. "Give me a minute, dude. Sheesh. I thought men were the ones that needed recuperation breaks."

"It's been a while, remember?"

"That's your excuse, huh?"

He chuckled while Lia moved slowly toward the side of the bed—a sloth came to her mind—and finally managed to snatch one of the blankets off the floor. She rolled back toward Evan and threw it at him. She'd love to explore those five more ways. And she meant to do so later in the week. But, for now, she needed to leave. She wasn't in the habit of spending the entire night with a man—it smacked of neediness and dependence—and if she left any later, she'd be like a sloth trying to drive a car, draped over her steering wheel.

She inched her way to the side of the bed.

"Where are you going?"

"I need to leave." She found her underwear on the other side of the cabin.

"You don't need to leave."

"I do."

"Lia. It's dark and it's late. Just stay here."

"I don't make it a habit to spend the night."

"You also said you don't make it a habit to orgasm. And you broke that rule. Four times, I might add."

She hurled a pillow at him, and he caught it and grinned.

"So tell me about this," he said.

She found her dress and stepped into it. "Tell you about what?"

"Why a beautiful, sexy woman like you is not out there having great orgasms. . . . Outside of this cabin, anyway."

He caught a second pillow and chuckled.

She didn't quite recognize the lightness and the teasing in his voice—she hadn't, until now, heard him speak in a way that hadn't sounded like he was weighted down by a ton of bricks—but she liked it. A lot.

"Maybe you were right about that control thing." She found her dress belt.

"Lia, come back to bed. Take off your clothes. Let's explore this."

She laughed but tugged her belt through the loops.

Damn. If she took one look at him, she might very well stay. That had been incredible. And fun. Evan was a great lover. But she didn't want to "explore" why she'd never found that kind of joy out of sex before. Maybe it was because she dated men that were too urbane. Maybe it was kind of sexy that Evan took control. Maybe she kind of liked being vulnerable. Maybe she liked being protected. . . .

She pushed those last thoughts away. That couldn't happen. And damn, *where was her cell phone?*

"Lia." Evan sat up in bed. "Stay."

"I have to feed Missy."

"Missy will be fine. She has the extra bowl of dry food in the laundry area."

Lia bit back a smile at Evan's memory. "Well, I'll take your card and swipe it through the exit gate for you so you can stay here all night. Harry James will think you've left and will be none the wiser." As she finished buckling her belt, she glimpsed her purse and her phone sticking out, and made a move toward them.

"Lia."

She didn't want to look at him. If she turned around, all she'd see—even through the dark—was a man who knew exactly what she was doing right now.

They were two people who were staying removed, who both knew how to do it, who had both perfected the maneuvers—Evan probably since his wife had died, and Lia all her life. They both knew that if you opened your heart a crack, you could let too much emotion come in. And Lia knew that if the emotion began flowing, you could become dependent on someone else, lose your footing.

But Evan was in her camp on this one. He didn't want to get too close, either. He probably wanted someone to stay who understood all this. Who he could hold all night, the way he'd held his wife, but who wouldn't read too much into it the next day.

And Lia might enjoy that, too.

They could both—with their simultaneous understanding—possibly bring each other peace, and one night of a feeling they both wanted. Temporarily.

"Yes?" she asked, her hand still on the back of a chair, her phone still untouched.

"Please stay." His voice had now dropped into something husky and embarrassed.

As the water lapped the sides of the boat and a fog horn sounded somewhere in the far distance, Lia ignored her phone and took off her clothes in the darkness, under Evan's watchful gaze, and crawled back into his bed. He wrapped his arms around her, kissed the part in her hair, and pulled her toward his chest.

"Too tired for another go-around?" he whispered.

"I am pretty tired."

"It's okay." He stroked her hair in a way that felt more comforting than sexual. "I just want you to stay."

"Good night, Evan," she finally whispered.

"Good night, Cinderella."

And Lia, for the first time ever, fell asleep in the arms of a man, who rested his lips against her temple and breathed softly into her hair.

The next morning, Lia awoke to the sounds of a marching band drifting from a distance, followed by distant applause and toy horns blowing. The scent of pancakes and cotton candy seemed to float into the bed around her, but—more immediately—she could smell coffee. When her eyes peeled open, she sat up with a start, remembering she was in Evan's bed.

It was Sunday. No work today . . . She repeated the mantra about five times, until her heart started beating normally.

She looked around the cabin. Evan was nowhere to be seen.

She wrapped a sheet around herself and padded into the galley, which was also empty but where the glorious scent of the coffee originated. A single cup steamed in a tiny coffee-maker for one. Through the open galley door she spotted him, out on the fog-filled deck, fully dressed, a beanie pulled onto his head and morning stubble still across his jaw. He wound a rope around his arm and stuffed it into a bag.

While she admired his masculine movements, at peace with the world as he moved deftly through the fog, he spotted her and came shuffling back in.

"Mornin'," he said.

"Good morning."

"Coffee's for you."

Her hand reached thankfully for the single cup. "We can share."

She took a life-affirming sip and handed the cup to him. He smiled and took the second sip while his eyes took in her toga-style bedsheet. "Now, that's a nice sight in the morning." He handed the coffee back.

"What are you doing out there?" She nodded toward the deck.

He didn't seem able to look away from her sheet, but finally tore his eyes away long enough to glance down at the bag he'd just filled. "Just getting together some things to take out today in case we spot Valentine's baby and she's tangled." His gaze went back to her shape. "But now I'm regretting getting up so early."

He dropped the bag into the dinette bench and moved toward her, yanking the beanie off his head and removing the coffee cup from her hand to set it on the counter. "You have to be anywhere this morning?" His trajectory was still coming right at her.

Lia giggled. "I just need to get ready for the festival booth today."

His fingertips tugged the sheet out of her hand. "We have plenty of time for that."

Lia made it down to the booth around nine-thirty, a half hour late, and mumbled her apologies to the folks sitting to the left and right of her, even though they certainly didn't care.

Evan plopped the box of bookmarks into the grass, along with the whale teeth they'd had to pick up from the *Duke*, since that's where they'd left them in what was starting to feel like her trail of irresponsibility.

Lia caught him grinning at the way she offered apologies, but he didn't say anything. Instead, he set up the tables and chairs and adjusted the awning so the sun didn't beat right on her.

"Beautiful day today," she said too loudly to the folks in the next tent over. They were an older couple, there to sell rubber ducks for the Rubber Ducky Derby to be held in the ocean that afternoon, and Lia had the strange feeling they could see straight through her clothes, straight into her most vulnerable self, straight into her secrets. Although she didn't know what secrets she was afraid of people seeing. That she'd finally had an orgasm? That it was with that pirate-looking guy back there? That she was falling into some kind of weird traditional female role, admiring a man using a screwdriver to adjust awnings, even though her mother had always told her to "be her own man"?

The older couple nodded and went on to set up their own booth, stacking yellow ducks, while Lia adjusted her dress and began setting up the bookmarks. Luckily she had changed clothes last night and no one would recognize she was wearing the same thing. Cora would be there any minute. And luckily she'd had the sandals in her bag, which she tugged on this morning for the festival. Unfortunately, she'd left one of the blue shoes on Evan's boat in her haste to scoop up her discarded clothing, but she'd get it later. She was always going to think of those as her "sex shoes." Break them in, indeed.

At noon, she and Evan took the last weekend tour out on the cat. They left Cora in the booth, despite the fact Lia had wanted to leave Cora and Douglas alone together. But Evan needed Douglas to help with the deckhand duties. Lia felt a bit superfluous, but Evan insisted her narration was terrific. Once or twice, he turned to grin at her. "Very good, Cinderella," he'd say, low, so it couldn't be picked up in the microphone.

Much to her surprise, her knees went a little weak each time.

The only time Evan seemed distant and unreachable was toward the end of the tour, when he went about ten minutes off course.

Lia pulled herself up the steps to the bridge to check.

"The baby." Evan thrust his chin out toward the horizon. "I thought I saw her, but maybe not."

"Are we off course?"

Evan glanced down at the gauges. "Not really. We'll be fine. I just thought I saw her. . . ."

"We should get back, Evan."

He nodded absently and lifted the binoculars, seemingly forgetting she was there. But after another minute, he pulled the boat around and grinned at her as if he'd just remembered.

After the tour, she, Douglas, and Evan spent a couple of hours cleaning up the boat—they needed to do a good job for the charter the next day. Evan kept trying to get her to take off, but she insisted she wanted to help. The physical activity, out in the bright sun, with the seagulls cawing overhead, was strangely edifying.

In the evening, once the booths closed up, Cora joined them, and the four of them grabbed dinner at the festival after wandering through the sandcastle-building contest.

After they said their good-byes to Douglas and Cora near the grassy knoll, Evan grabbed Lia's hand and tugged her back to his boat just as the sun set, where they enjoyed two more of the five positions, to the distant sounds of the new Band in the Sand, which was supposed to sound like the Rat Pack.

"I really need to go home this time," she said, as "That's Amore" came drifting down the cove. Her head hung over the side of his bed.

"Why?" He rolled toward her and ran his hand down her backside.

"The charter is tomorrow, and I have to get ready—at least wear fresh clothes, feed Missy."

"You look fine."

"Fine enough to fuck?"

Evan raised an eyebrow.

"I'm sorry." She waved her hand. "I didn't mean to say that. Sometimes my mouth filter doesn't work."

"You do have quite a mouth on you, Cinderella."

"Not very Cinderella of me, is it?"

"It's not."

"Does it bother you?"

"Not at all. I think I love it, in fact."

The word "love" fell so beautifully from Evan's lips, so naturally, so right for him, that Lia rolled over and stared. Although the word sometimes gave her the heebie-jeebies, and she knew he didn't mean it in a serious way, Lia felt a strange, sudden bolt of jealousy toward the wife who heard this from him for real. She rolled away from him.

Her head lolled toward the drawer where she remembered Evan shoved that photograph that first morning.

"Evan, what was Renece like?" she whispered. "Can I see her picture?"

He hesitated for what felt like an eternity while the boat rolled gently. Finally, he leaned over to open the drawer.

Lia lay flat and held the silver frame between her palms. She stifled a gasp—she hadn't expected Luke to be in the picture. He looked exactly like Evan—adorable, with Evan's blue eyes and high cheekbones. His hair was a tumble of curls, like his mom's, but the color of Evan's. He had his mother's smile. Lia let her gaze slide up and down over Renece's face. Avery did look quite a bit like her—Evan had been absolutely right about that.

"They're beautiful," she said when she found her voice. Tears pricked the backs of her eyes. "He looks just like you." She tried to smile.

Evan nodded. Words seemed beyond him.

"What was he like?"

"Happy," Evan said. "Energetic. Curious. A little introverted, but once he trusted you, he was so loving. He'd throw his arms around your neck and cling like a monkey. He liked to draw. He loved animals."

Evan leaned over again and pulled a piece of notebook paper out of the drawer. "Here's his drawing of Valentine. We used to see her in San Diego."

Lia took the paper with the crayon drawing. Luke had even gotten her flukes right, with a heart drawn right in the center. The whale was smiling with red crayon lips.

"This is lovely." Tears threatened again, and Lia laid the drawing on the tabletop. "We should get you a frame for that, so you can keep it out."

Evan's eyes had become gentle. He nodded.

"What was Renece like?"

Evan took longer to answer this time. He tenderly tucked Luke's drawing back into the drawer. "I'm not sure what you want to hear."

Lia sat up. "You don't have to worry about what I want to hear. I'm not competing with her." She laughed, but her laugh sounded hollow, even to her. "I just get the sense that you don't talk about them very often. But it's probably good to talk. It helps people heal."

Evan's mouth was set in a line that made it clear he didn't think so. But Lia wanted to help. Part of the obvious guilt he carried around, and carried into the bedroom, was probably the assumption that any woman he took to bed would want him to *forget* Renece. But Lia didn't. She thought it was good that he remembered.

"Was she talkative?" she prompted.

He thought that over while the waves lapped the dock pylons outside and the boat rocked slowly. "No," he said. "She was quiet."

"Not like me, huh?"

He chuckled. "Not like you."

Bolstered by the answer, Lia shifted onto her elbows and tried again: "Was she funny?"

He shrugged. "Not in an overt way, but she made me smile."

"Was she fun?"

"Yes."

"What did you love most about her?" Lia held her breath. And, when she did so, she realized that she was asking these questions for herself.

She had to suck in some extra air and look away toward the pillowcase once the realization hit. *She wanted to know what*

Evan loved. And, more importantly, *she wanted to know how close she came to that description.*

The shock of it all—the fact that the word "love" had come into her awareness with this man—made her want to jump out of the bed, jump out of her skin. But her curiosity kept her firmly in his bed.

She stared at the pillow seam and waited for his gravelly answer. And she knew, suddenly and without warning, that she was waiting to see if Evan Betancourt could ever fall in love with her.

"Let's do this another time." He took the frame out of her hands and put it back in the drawer.

Disappointment warred with relief in her chest. On the one hand, she could start breathing again. But on the other hand, she really wanted to know.

She knew she had crossed a very dangerous line in what she wanted from this man. *She wanted him to love her.*

But she didn't know why. She frowned into the dim cabin. He wasn't staying, and she couldn't ask him to. They were just too-different people. She was filled with ambitions he would never understand, and he lacked any ambition at all, which she would never understand. . . .

With the picture tucked back into the drawer with the drawing, and the door slammed shut, he turned toward her.

"You don't want to talk about Renece anymore?" Lia asked into the silence.

"If I'm going to 'use' you, I'll be damned if it's going to be as a shrink."

Lia couldn't help but laugh.

Then Evan gave a low chuckle that seemed to come from deep down within his chest—a laugh she hadn't had the pleasure of hearing until just now—and wrestled her backward until he pulled the top sheet away. And, for the rest of the night, Lia made sure he had as much fun as he'd ever had with Renece.

CHAPTER
Twenty-five

The morning of the charter had finally arrived.

Lia's stomach was a mess.

After another wonderful night with Evan, where she'd been able to forget about the entire outside world for nearly twelve hours, she'd gone home to feed Missy and change—despite Evan's assurances that she looked fine the way she was.

She now stood on the deck of the catamaran in her favorite boating clothes—her white and navy pants and sweater—hoping the rain clouds in the distance would take their time coming in, hoping this seventy-degree weather would last a little longer, and hoping she wouldn't throw up.

She glanced down the dock, waiting for the arrivals.

The Vampiress would be coming. Evan had said he wanted to meet her, but that just made Lia want to throw up even more. She wondered what Elle thought a whale-watching trip would entail, what she would do around J.P. Stevens, and what she would think of the job Lia had already done. . . .

Lia's stomach flipped again at the thought of Kyle arriving, and how he'd get along with Evan—if there would be any left-over grudge stares—and if Kyle would see fit to invest in Drew's boat.

Then it did an impressive backflip at the idea that Drew was coming aboard, and how he'd get along with Kyle, and if he'd harbor any leftover anger toward Evan.

And she glanced at Evan and wondered what *all* of these people would think if they knew she was doing Captain Betancourt. . . .

"You all right, sunshine?" Douglas asked as he stepped toward the back of the cat. He and Cora were the only ones who seemed happy that Lia and Evan were together. He frowned and gripped her elbow. "Here, sit down. You look like you're going to pass out. Did you eat breakfast? You can't be a good seafarer without a hearty breakfast in you."

"I'm fine, Douglas, really. I—"

"*Cora?*" Doug yelled, twisting toward the galley door. "You got something for breakfast for Lia?"

"No. I already ate," Lia lied. "I'll be fine. I'm just nervous about all our g—"

"What's wrong?" Evan barked, flying down the bridge steps as Cora banged the galley door open.

"I'm *fine*, everyone." Lia put her hands up to ward off their approaches. "Let's just do this. I'm fine."

They all looked at her skeptically, but eventually backed off, each going back to their assigned tasks.

Evan hesitated in the stairwell, although he pretended not to. He looked amazing today. He wore one of the boat's bright blue logo'd polo shirts that Cora had found somewhere in the back. Lia guessed he was only wearing it to help Drew and make the crew look professional. But he looked damned good. The blue matched his eyes perfectly, and the band around his arms was just tight enough to show off his biceps. The shirt tapered to his waist, where he was wearing khaki Dockers that hugged him in all the right places. He came closer to her now, and hung his hands on his hips.

"Are you checking me out, Cinderella?"

Lia smiled and looked away. "Don't flatter yourself."

"I know it's going to be hard, but you're going to have to keep your eyes and hands to yourself when Drew gets here."

"Worry about yourself."

"I already am."

"*Halloo!*" came a voice up on the dock.

As if they'd conjured him, Drew rolled down toward the plank. "Get Doug!" he yelled.

Douglas and Evan managed to get Drew out of the wheelchair and into a side seat just as the other passengers started to arrive. They folded his wheelchair and set it next to him. Lia asked Drew if he wanted to do the narration himself—she could stretch the microphone cord around the galley. He glanced up at her to answer, then scowled between her and Evan, looking suspicious. Evan moved farther away from Lia's hip.

"No," Drew finally said. "You can do it. Everyone says you're good."

"Thanks!" Lia couldn't help the smile that overtook her face. She wondered if he meant Cora or Douglas or Evan, and felt a flush that any of them would say such a thing. Evan glanced at her with a grin and then returned his attention to securing Drew's wheelchair.

She took a deep breath, told her stomach to relax, and began greeting Kyle's charter guests, who were all dressed up a little more than the average whale-watching guest and whose hair seemed excessively styled for a trip that would involve mist and wind.

But the guests were nice, and very polite as they seated themselves and struck up conversations about companies they worked for or the latest stocks in Orange County. Lia recognized a few of the guests from the VIP event. Some asked for Evan, remarking how well he had explained the whale bones to them, and Lia pointed him out.

Elle arrived fifteen minutes into the seating. She donned a Versace blouse underneath a white, fur-lined puffy vest (Lia hoped to God that was fake fur), over white pants and too-high heels, on which she wobbled onto the boat while clutching Douglas's beefy forearm.

Lia probably should have mentioned that boat shoes would have been more appropriate. Drew's eyes practically rolled into the back of his head when he saw the spiked heels the female guests were wearing on his fiberglass deck. But this whole trip was going to have to be thought of as an investment.

Kyle arrived shortly after Elle, looking cool and collected in cabana-styled clothes. Lia was happy to see he made a bee-line toward Drew, commented on his accident, then sat down with him.

Kyle's father arrived not much after that. Lia had no problem identifying him. He looked just like Kyle, fast forward twenty years. He had a beautiful close-cropped haircut, loose-fitting yacht clothes that skimmed his trim frame, and strode with his hand in his pocket the same way Kyle did. The major differences were the gray in his hair and the extra lines around his eyes when he smiled. He greeted Lia with the effortless charm that men of his position were so good at. She let herself watch him for a good five minutes as he made his way through the crowd.

"So that's your type, huh?" she heard from behind her.

She whirled to see Evan. "What? Who?"

"I guess you're not going to have too much trouble keeping your eyes off me today." He smiled to convey the joke, but the smile slipped away too quickly.

"He's just . . ." Lia waved her hand to see if any words would fall into the sentence. "He's the client Elle is going after today."

"It's okay, Cinderella." The smile made a weak return. "Are we ready to leave?"

Lia felt silly trying to defend her staring. But protesting too much might be worse.

"They have the boat the whole day," she said instead, "so why don't we let them mingle for a few more minutes? Say fifteen?"

Evan nodded brusquely. "I'll be above. Fifteen minutes and I'll start the motor."

Lia almost reached out to stop him, to make sure he knew how handsome she thought he was, but she caught Drew's hard stare from across the deck and turned away.

Instead she focused on her job: She chatted with the guests, first the ones from the VIP event then a few others she recognized from the Orange County society pages or various charity events in the area. Kyle came to greet her and join in a conversation she was having with the developer of a new seaside mall. Lia made sure Elle was happy, and sitting near J.P., and that everyone had a comfortable place from which to view the whales. Kyle had ordered several trays of hors d'oeuvres and champagne, and Cora helped uncork and pour.

So far, the charter seemed to be off to a good start.

After fifteen minutes, Lia felt the motor rumble beneath her and took to her microphone.

"Welcome, everyone!" She went into her routine. "We hope you enjoy your visit today on the *Duke*. My name is Lia, as some of you know, and I'll be narrating for you today. We have Captain Evan Betancourt navigating our ship; Coraline Jones offering hors d'oeuvres, champagne, coffee, and soft drinks in the galley; Douglas Kendricks is our deckhand today; and we have a special visit from Captain Drew Betancourt, owner of the *Duke*, who is sitting up front nursing a motorcycle injury, but who came aboard today to meet all of you and answer any questions you may have. We're all excited to share the great sea life of the Pacific with you. We've been seeing plenty of gray whales, humpbacks, some fin whales, lots of dolphins, and even a few blue whales, which are the largest mammal to ever live on Earth. So take a seat as we jettison out of the jetty, enjoy some champagne and sunshine, keep your eyes peeled on the horizon, and we'll walk you through our sightings today. . . ."

The wind blew back her hair as they picked up speed through the jetty. She glanced at the stairway that led to Evan and knew how good he must look right now. She wanted to join him—it occurred to her that this might be their last tour together, if she had to work tomorrow and he was leaving Wednesday—but knew she should stay down here.

Once they got past the jetty, Lia began her speech about the sea lions that lounged on the buoys. After that, they saw a small pod of common dolphins and she went into her description. Drew glanced over his shoulder and gave her a thumbs-up.

Out on the ocean, Lia encouraged the guests to enjoy more hors d'oeuvres and champagne, and to be sure to visit the viewing pods down below. She answered questions about the whale teeth, then heard Evan's code clicks from above. Without needing to ask, she could see the slick he must be gunning toward and stood to identify the whale. She could see it was a fin whale. . . . Another female, there with her calf. Lia launched into an explanation of all she knew.

After a wonderful afternoon spotting two more fins and three grays, plus two small pods of dolphins, Lia sat back and took a deep sigh. A few rain clouds were rolling in now, but they would be heading back any minute and would beat them. Kyle had mingled appropriately but had spent the majority of the trip laughing with Drew. Elle looked confident, with a champagne flute in her hand and the wind blowing her shiny bob in a strangely perfect way, standing there laughing with J.P. And the guests were all oohing and aahing at the pods, at the whales, at the dolphins, and complimenting Drew on a fabulous boat.

Everything was going so well.

But after a while, Lia realized they still hadn't turned around.

She glanced at Drew to see if he'd noticed, but he was engrossed in his conversation with Kyle. She looked for Douglas, but he was in the galley, helping Cora keep up with the champagne. Finally, she ventured up to the bridge.

"Aren't we turning soon?" she asked Evan.

"I saw her." Evan was staring through his binoculars into the distance north.

"Who?"

"The baby. She's caught."

"Evan, we can't go find the baby right now. We have to get everyone back."

"She's not far."

"But what will we do once we get there? We don't have time to disentangle her. The rain is coming in, and J.P. has a plane to catch." Lia stepped forward, her hand going toward the controls for some reason. A panic began rising in her chest.

"It'll only take a minute." Evan's hand kept hers from the controls. His other lifted the binoculars again. He seemed to be in the same trance he was in earlier.

"But what will we do when we get there?" The panic was playing out in her voice now, which she could feel slipping into squeak status.

"I'll radio it in. Tell Drew."

As she made her way down the narrow stairs, she could hear Evan sending out his coordinates to fellow captains. She didn't know why she was heading down to tell Drew. What was he going to do about it? But she made her way through the clusters of passengers—they were still drinking champagne but beginning to shiver now with the coming clouds. She slid into the bench beside Kyle and Drew.

"Evan thinks he spotted the baby whale," she said, low.

"Hey, beautiful. What baby whale?" Kyle asked.

Drew frowned at Kyle—perhaps at the endearment—then turned back to Lia. "He's not going back for her, is he?"

"He seems to be."

"We don't have time for that. Have him radio it in. We've got passengers who need to get back. Don't you need to get back, Kyle? Or your father? You guys have a plane to catch, right?"

"Yeah, but what's this about a baby whale?"

"They get caught in commercial fishing nets sometimes. Ev found the famous whale Valentine dead in a net the other day, but the baby was missing. We wondered if she was caught, too."

Kyle's eyes grew round. "I've heard of Valentine. Damn, let's go find the baby."

"But your father has a—"

"It's okay. We can reschedule." Kyle strained to look over the rail in the direction they were heading.

The boat picked up a speed Lia wasn't used to. Even some of the other passengers seemed to notice, as they gripped the side rails and eyed the rain clouds they were zooming toward.

"Tell him to turn around," Drew said. "I feel bad about the whale, but this has to be a business decision."

"No!" Kyle interrupted. "I'm your client, so your business decision is now full speed ahead." He had a giddy look on his face, leaning in toward the wind. "I'll tell him."

"Kyle!" Drew reached for him as Kyle whirled toward the bridge stairs, but he missed. He looked back at Lia, his own panic starting to show on his face. "We can't do this. Have you ever seen a disentanglement?"

"Just the other day when—"

"But she was dead."

"Yes."

"When they're alive, and fighting, they can be dangerous,

even the babies. We can't do this with a tour boat, for God's sake. Go tell Evan. I'm still the captain of this boat. And I say turn it around. Send Douglas over here."

Lia ran into Douglas coming the other way. "Drew wants you."

"Where the hell are we going?"

"Evan spotted Valentine's baby. She's caught."

Douglas glanced up toward Evan, then at the horizon. "It's too dangerous with a tour aboard."

"That's what Drew says. He needs you to convince Evan."

"But the whale might die." Douglas dropped his head.

"Drew doesn't want to take a chance with the guests."

"No good way out of this one, sunshine. I'll talk to Drew." He pushed behind her.

Lia headed back up the stairs and pushed herself into the tiny space between Evan and Kyle, who were both leaning into the wind, sharing the binoculars, like they were best buddies all of a sudden.

"We can save her!" Kyle said, turning toward Lia, joy and excitement splashed across his face.

Lia ignored him. "Evan, Drew says we have to go back."

"No! We can save her," Kyle insisted.

"Hold on, cowboy," Evan said, looking through the binoculars. "It's not that easy. They sometimes fight. Lia's right. They don't always understand what's going on. Did Drew really say that?" He turned toward her.

"Yes."

Evan looked disappointed, to be sure. He took one more look at the whale, who was so close now she was visible with the naked eye. She was about twenty feet long and had the mottled gray and white bumpy back typical of the humpback. Her back was arched and still at the surface, much like the dead whale they'd seen the other day, only this one had a strange, screaming sound coming from her blowhole.

"Why is she making that sound?" Lia asked.

"She's trying to breathe. She's afraid to dive back down. The nets catch other animals and start weighing them down, and they can't easily break to the surface anymore. So when they do, they sometimes stay. She's scared. But she's worn out. Did Drew really say to turn around?"

Lia nodded.

Evan reached out and pulled the wheel. The pain across his face was palpable.

"If this is about my dad, and his time, don't worry," Kyle said. "I'll take care of it. What can I do right now?"

"You know, we need to radio in all the details we gather," Evan said. "The rescue teams have trouble if they don't know many details. Go down into the pod and take a look at where she's tangled. See if it's her tail, or her pectoral fins." Evan tapped his arm to show Kyle where the pectorals were.

When Lia got to the bottom deck again, Drew had scooted to the edge of the bench seat so he could see the whale himself. He and Douglas were both watching her. When Lia approached, Drew turned.

"She's dying," he said. "Ev's right. We have to help her. Did he radio it in?"

Lia nodded, her breath gone a little from the stairs.

"Lia, what's happening?" Elle came toward her, bouncing from rail to rail on the rocking boat. The water was becoming choppier as the clouds came in.

"There's a whale. Caught." Lia gazed at the helpless animal, gripping a rail herself. She took a deep breath and prepared to get her microphone.

"But we're going back, right?" Elle peered at the whale, the corners of her mouth dropped into disdain.

"We'll be just a minute. We're going to radio it in." Lia headed toward the stairs.

"But we need to get back," Elle said in her familiar screech. "I'm feeling . . ." She gripped the side rail. She was looking decidedly greenish. The boat rocked more fervently under the dark clouds.

"Here, come sit down." Lia steered Elle toward the front of the boat, but she resisted when she saw J.P. coming the other way. Elle forced herself to stand straighter.

"What's going on, kids?" J.P. asked.

"Mr. Stevens, there's a caught whale," Lia said. "Valentine's baby. We're going to take a couple of minutes to radio it in."

"I have a plane to catch."

"I know. We'll be just a minute," Lia said.

She pushed past both of them to her microphone.

Kyle came bounding back up from the pod and then took the bridge steps two at a time to report back to Evan.

"Ladies and gentlemen," Lia said into the microphone, "we seem to have come across a baby whale in distress. We think it's the calf of Valentine, who we found, unfortunately dead, the other day, after being trapped in netting. We're stopping for a moment to radio in the details about this baby calf and make sure she can be saved."

Many of the guests had drifted toward the starboard side to see, and were leaning over the rails in their Yves Saint Laurent clothes, holding their champagne glasses so they wouldn't spill. The sky grew darker. Waves rose higher and pitched against the side of the boat. The guests clutched the sides but refused to move away.

"We need to get *back*," Elle kept repeating. One or two other guests nodded their agreement, but the couples from the VIP event crowded her back and leaned toward the whale with concern.

"Lia, we have to get back," Elle's voice rose. "What kind of idiots have you found here to run—"

Lia clicked the microphone off in a panic.

"Just a minute, Elle!" she whispered. "It'll only be a minute."

"But J.P. has a plane to catch! And I . . . oh, God, I don't feel well." She gripped the rail by the bridge steps and leaned her head against it.

"Maybe you should sit down."

"I don't want to sit down. I want you to turn this boat back! Why can't you get anything *right*?" she screeched. A few of the passengers turned to stare. "You said your little Sandy Cove friend Drew could handle this with his boat, but obviously he doesn't know what he's *doing*." Her voice made an upward pitch at the end of every sentence and seemed to match the roll of the boat. Her face continued to take on a ruddy coloring as she gripped the stair rail with both hands. "And if I can't count on you for *anything*, then how am I going to send you to *Paris*?" Another stifled scream.

"What's going on?" Evan came down from the bridge.

Elle glanced up at him. His face was set in stone as he surveyed the situation.

"Are you the captain?" Elle asked.

"I am."

"My employee here does not know what she's doing, and she—"

"I think your employee is doing fine."

"Evan, let me handle this," Lia said, putting up her hand. "Elle, let's go sit down." Lia gripped Elle's arm and tried to shuffle her to the side.

"I don't *want* to sit down," Elle said. "I want to—"

The boat pitched, and Elle let out a scream, bouncing away from the rail and gripping the cabin wall. Lia lunged for her at the same time Evan did. He flew down the last four steps and found her elbow first.

"Evan, I've got her. Let me handle this," Lia said sternly.

"Don't you want to *steer the boat*?" Elle screeched.

"You must be Elle," he said.

"Evan, I'll handle it." Lia pushed him back up. "Elle, do you want to come inside?"

"I do, but I feel so . . ." Her fingertips tried to grip the fiberglass wall. When the next wave of nausea seemed to pass, she recomposed her features and glanced at Evan. "My employee here is failing to tell you, but we need to get *back*. J.P. Stevens is a very important man, and he has to—"

"I know who J.P. Stevens is," Evan said impatiently. "And we're going to head back. And your employee is doing fine. She's doing a great job, in fact, and—"

"Evan!" Lia interrupted.

He closed his mouth but continued to scowl.

"Go do what you need to do." She gave him a gentle shove. He was just going to make everything worse.

He stared at both of them for another beat but finally launched back up to the bridge.

Lia clicked the microphone back on. "Sometimes commercial fishing nets lift from the sea floor and accidentally trap animals they aren't intended to trap: sharks, sea lions, and other marine mammals," she explained to the guests. "Sometimes they entangle whales, and prevent the whales from diving properly or coming up for air."

"Why is she making that noise?" an elderly gentleman shouted back to Lia.

"She's trying to breathe," Lia said into the microphone.

The crowd offered a collective gasp and pushed closer.

"Five degrees starboard!" Drew yelled up toward Evan.

The boat puttered to the right, though Evan kept the motor to a minimum.

Kyle careened down the stairs, toward Drew, and Lia strained to see over the heads of the passengers. She could see Douglas and Kyle both leaning way over the edge, Drew holding on to Douglas's shirt. Her heart throbbed into her throat.

"Lia, get control of this situation!" the Vampiress whispered harshly.

Lia dropped the microphone and climbed the stairs to Evan.

He was standing near the bridge rail, leaning slightly so he could see Drew's hand gestures.

"Did you radio it in? What did they say?" Lia asked.

"They said they'd be here in an hour. Not sure she'll make it. Kyle said both her pectorals are bound, as well as her tail—possibly two different nets. Can you tell the passengers to step back a little?"

Lia scrambled for the upstairs microphone as the clouds ahead blackened. "Ladies and gentlemen, if you could please step back a little, it'll give our captain and deckhand a chance to assess the situation. We've radioed this in, and another boat will be here in an hour."

"She won't make it!" yelled someone from below.

Evan glanced at Lia and nodded as they heard the whale make the screaming noise.

"Captain!" the same voice yelled from below.

Evan leaned over the edge of the bridge.

"We can help! I'm ex-Navy, and my buddy here is ex–Coast Guard, and we've done this before."

Kyle moved out from the crowd at the front of the boat. "That's right! Ed, Manny—come here and lend me a hand!"

"Kyle, get out of there!" J.P. said, stepping forward.

"Dad, we've got this. Just let everyone work."

"You don't know what you're doing!"

"These guys do. I'm helping."

"You're going to get hurt, son. Move back!"

"Dad, relax."

The first raindrops began to fall as the ex-Navy Ed stepped between Kyle and his dad. "J.P., you're not going to let this poor whale suffer, are you?" Ed clapped him on the back. "If you're going to run for senator, you don't want news like that out. Kyle, help out the deckhand there."

Kyle turned back toward Douglas and watched as Doug grasped a handful of red netting and began to pull it toward him. The rain came down harder, and some of the passengers went into the cabin, trying to squeeze themselves in. But many of the elderly men from the VIP event stayed out, all looking like former marines, not even caring now if the rain was soaking their cabana shirts. They helped Drew and Evan keep the boat in place by shouting positions up to the bridge. Douglas, Kyle, Ed, and Manny managed to get a small buoy attached to the whale in case they lost her again, then they used Evan's curved knife and another one they found in the emergency kit, leaning forward and cutting at the netting that circled the whale's bumpy gray body. The whale was staying at the surface and still making that terrible screaming noise through her blowhole.

"Can you hold this?" Evan asked Lia, pointing to the wheel. He looked longingly toward the rescue.

"What? No! I can't navigate a boat!"

"I've switched off the motor. You just have to hold her steady with the wheel."

"Okay." Lia shoved a wet wisp of hair out of her face and pushed the rain out of her eyes. "Okay, just come back up here if you feel we're drifting too—"

He was halfway down the stairs before she could even finish her sentence.

Twenty minutes later, Evan and Kyle—both with wet hair swinging across their faces and their shirts plastered to their bodies—had the whale's first pectoral fin freed, as it slapped happily into the air. Douglas came up and sat with Lia to make sure the boat didn't turn, and asked if she wanted to go inside where it was dry, but she didn't. She wanted to watch the rescue. She wanted to watch Evan, and watch the joy and relief on his face as he freed this baby.

When the second pectoral fin came loose, Evan and Kyle high-fived, rainwater splashing everywhere, and the whale dove. She came back up, though, right beside the boat, as if she knew what was happening and wanted more help. The guys leaned forward again and hauled up as much netting from the back of her as they could.

"I think it's just her tail left," Evan shouted.

"Looks like both flukes," Drew agreed.

Ed and Manny pulled the netting up while Kyle and Evan used the knives. The tail was so powerful, Douglas pointed out, they had to be careful the whale didn't slap it and pull them all in, but they systematically cut and pulled, cut and pulled, under Evan's direction, and finally—after many shouts and screamed directions later—they all yelled and threw their hands in the air as the last of the netting seemed to come free. Lia could even hear the shouts from inside the cabin below, and knew all the society ladies must be watching through the portholes.

The guys hauled the last of the nylon netting aboard while the freed whale dove down, leaving the surface strangely still.

All the passengers seemed to hold their breath, peering over the side of the boat, waiting to see what she'd do. . . .

The water was still and black. . . .

Finally, about fifty yards out, she breached. Her body rose into the air, spun around, and slapped the water as she dove back down.

The entire boat let out a cheer.

The whale breached about forty times, getting farther and farther out, slapping her pectorals against the ocean water, slapping her tail. When her tail came up out of the water, they could see she had the same marking as her mother—another heart shape, outlined in white. Every time she breached, the entire boat yelled again, toasting one another with their champagne glasses, slapping one another's rain-soaked backs.

The baby whale was clearly thankful, clearly full of joy, clearly free.

And, as Lia looked at Evan through misty eyes, high-fiving Kyle and Drew, she knew someone else was, too.

CHAPTER

Twenty-six

The ride back to the marina was wet but wonderful.

Evan navigated, his polo shirt drenched against his chest. He caught Lia's eye while he was talking to Ed Harper up on the bridge, and threw her a smile she hadn't seen on him yet—one of peace. Lia couldn't help but grin back.

All the men kept clapping one another on the back, cheering for the baby whale they were now calling "Valentine II," while the women joined them with clinks of their champagne flutes. Lia mingled with the crowd downstairs, some venturing out to the wet deck. They had taken on a feeling that they'd all gone through something together, and spoke in voices too loud with emotion, hugging one another, hugging Cora, and holding their glasses out for more champagne.

Drew sat at the front of the boat, talking excitedly to Kyle. They waved their hands in the air as if they were drawing large arcs, and Lia had the feeling they were also drawing large plans. She hadn't seen Drew smile that much in ages. Kyle motioned his father over and introduced him to Drew, and somehow Drew's smile got even larger.

Only the Vampiress looked uncertain: Her faux fur was matted from the rain, looking like she had a weasel around her neck, and her bob had lost its aura of control, wisps of wet black strands sticking out all over. She finally sprang loose out of the cabin.

"Lia!" she hissed, grabbing Lia's arm. "Is this a *disaster*? Or a *boon*?"

Lia glanced again at the cabin filled with champagne toasts and damp hugs. "It's not a disaster, Elle."

Elle looked around uncertainly but finally gave a hesitant nod. "J.P. seems happy."

Lia scanned the crowd herself. "Janice Peterson is toasting with Carmen DeLeon. Haven't they been chairperson rivals for eight years?"

The Vampiress gave a rare laugh. "They have."

"I think everyone had a good time. People feel like they made a difference today. And did it together."

Elle nodded, then turned toward Lia and looked her up and down.

"You ready to talk about Paris?"

Lia thought her jaw was going to hit the deck. "What?"

"Paris. You still want to go, right?"

For some reason, a flash of Evan went through Lia's mind—Evan lying on the sheets this morning, his hair tousled, running his finger along her shoulder. Lia blinked the image away. *What was that doing there?* Evan had nothing to do with Paris. Evan had no business whatsoever being in her future flashes. She shoved him away—more forcefully this time—and replaced him with her old, familiar images of the future she'd always dreamed of: success in Paris, working, looking out her window at the Eiffel Tower, being her own woman. . . .

"I do," she said, trying to keep her voice in a pitch that sounded professional rather than like a young girl who just got a pony for Christmas.

"Let's talk. We'll go over specifics." Elle gazed around languidly, lifting her eyelashes with some degree of interest toward the other guests. As if she were discussing the weather. As if she weren't just changing Lia's life.

Lia nodded, trying to breathe.

Evan shook hands with Ed Harper and nodded good-bye as he left the bridge. Ed had just offered him a job, which he politely turned down. But as he watched Ed walk away, he started to wonder why he'd said no.

He'd never thought about staying *anywhere* permanently in the last two years, but Sandy Cove was starting to grow on him. He'd never thought he'd say that. People had grown annoying and wearisome to him in the years since Renece's and Luke's deaths, and connecting had seemed pointless. Why connect when people just let you down? Or betrayed you? Or abandoned you? Or died?

But these charter guests had proven to be okay. And Kyle had turned out to be okay. And Drew was coming around. And Evan respected Douglas and Cora. And Joe the Mechanic was doing a great job, and his son was all right.

And then Evan scanned the crowd for his favorite Sandy Cove resident of all. . . .

He saw her from the back, shaking hands with a few of the guests, her rain-dampened ponytail over her shoulder, a drenched sweater giving testament to what a trouper she was.

And she'd been something else these last couple of nights. He'd never had so much fun—in bed or out of it. She was nothing like Renece, but that's part of what he loved about her. Or part of what he *liked* about her. Or loved. Whatever . . .

He rubbed his hand over his neck and watched her again.

Where had that word come from?

He'd thought he'd never love anyone after Renece. He'd assigned himself the penance of never loving again. He'd had his chance. He'd let her die. And now he needed to roam the Earth, knowing he'd let his wife and son down, and wait for his turn to die, too.

But something was definitely happening with Lia. His heart was cracking, opening up, letting her in. She made him laugh. She made him worry. She made him angry sometimes, and made him nervous. She made him feel protective again, and made him hard. She made him smile. She just made him *feel*. . . .

He wanted to tell her, but he was afraid to put himself out there again. She wouldn't feel the same way. She was attracted to men like Forrest. Men like Kyle, or J.P. Stevens. Men who fit in with her definition of "success." He got that. And he could never give her that.

So maybe he should just keep his mouth shut. . . .

He descended from the bridge, standing near the base of the steps to wait for all the guests to disembark.

"Evan!"

His body went on full alert at her voice. Just as he sensed, she was bounding right toward him. He opened his arms just in time to catch her. And, as soon as he wrapped her toward him, the feeling of rightness overwhelmed him.

He resisted the urge-to-kiss-her part, since Drew was still around, and looked into her face instead. "What is it?" A feeling of tenderness warmed him—coiling through his chest, his lungs, his heart.

"Evan, you'll never guess what! Kyle offered to invest in Drew's boat!" Her eyes were wide with joy.

"That's *great*."

"We're going to go out and celebrate tonight—you must come!"

While Evan would have said no without a thought just a week ago, it sounded kind of nice all of a sudden. . . . "You're sure?"

"Yes. You *must* come. Drew said so. Did he tell you he got his captain for tomorrow?"

"Yes, he mentioned that." Another tug pulled at Evan's chest.

"So tonight we'll celebrate. Doug will be there, Cora—we're all going. You can meet our other friends, Xavier and Fin and my sister Giselle. Please come! And there's more good news: Elle wants to talk to me about Paris!"

Evan looked up sharply. "Paris?"

"The promotion I wanted—remember?"

"Oh."

"It's all I ever wanted."

"Is that right?"

"So will you come out with us?"

Suddenly the urge to go out with everyone—to talk, to laugh, to connect—slid right out of his veins. "That's okay, Cinderella. I'm pretty beat."

"C'mon, Evan! It's your last night."

"I really don't want to."

Lia grabbed Evan's collar. "Listen, buddy." She shoved him

back toward the cabin wall, much to his surprise. And, immediately following that, his amusement. This woman could
probably turn him on every day of his life, if she wanted to.
He smiled and accommodated her by stepping back against
the cabin, focused on how warm her hands felt.

But he looked immediately for Drew.

"I know you have an image to uphold of being the sad,
angry dude who's just going to sail around the world until he
dies," she said, his polo shirt still bunched in her fists, "but I
think you're much more than that."

Evan lifted an eyebrow. Had he become that much of a
caricature of himself? A heat formed around his neck and he
had to look away.

"I think you're a gentle, caring man," she said, with three
little shakes.

The words suddenly felt like bullets riddling his chest.
What started out as playfulness turned into something painful
and unbearable, as the heat in his ears moved upward and the
bullets seared a new heat in his chest cavity.

"And you have a lot to give." She gave one last shove, then
let go.

The bullets ricocheted around and hit various arteries. The
blood started oozing out and his chest wanted to cave in. He
opened his mouth to say something, but no sound came out.
He'd been that once—that gentle, caring man she was
describing—but he knew those parts of him had shriveled up
and died. It shocked him that Lia could still see them somehow, buried under all the darkness and gray and suspicion.
And here she was—resurrecting those descriptions, resurrecting those possibilities. His chest was trying to fill with air, but
he was having a hard time breathing.

"You've got to get back in the game, man," she said quietly.
"You could make a woman very happy again someday. And
you'd make a great father."

Not enough air . . . The bullets were causing blood to seep
all over. *Make a woman happy again someday? Make a great
father?* Images flooded his mind and terrified him: a woman
to love again, her hair on his pillow, her head nestled under his
chin, a newborn baby, holding him the way he used to hold

Luke. . . . The blood felt like it was seeping into his lungs and he might be drowning. He kept trying to breathe.

One look at Lia's flashing eyes, though, and he realized—with a certain degree of horror and yet a feeling that it was something he always knew—that she was the woman. She was the one whose hair he could see across his pillowcase. She was the one he wanted to tuck into his chest. She was the one handing him the newborn. . . .

Air was in short supply now, but he found a gulp on a salty-tasting breeze and sucked it down.

His first instinct was to stop the waves of feeling—shut her down, shove his sunglasses on, mumble something about Drew seeing them, and walk away to try to get his breath back. But then he took a deep inhale and took a chance:

"You could come," he choked out.

"What?"

"You could come with me." He almost couldn't get it out the second time. *What was he doing? Was he making the biggest mistake of his life?* But he knew he wasn't. She was the one. She was the one on the pillowcase—it was her Cinderella hair. She was the one to make him feel again, to give him something to live for. Images began flashing of how wonderful it would be—to do the whole circumference again, but *feeling* this time. To share it all with her. To take her around the world she so wanted to explore. . . .

But Lia stiffened right before his eyes. He could see the exact moment her walls came up.

"Me?" she asked, frowning.

He'd made a mistake. She didn't want him. . . . The blood gushed harder, into his lungs, into his chest cavity.

He nodded anyway.

"I didn't mean *me!*" She laughed a little, but sounded terrified. The ocean wind swept down the deck through the gap between them. "I meant . . . well, I meant *another* woman. A really *great* woman. . . ." She waved her hand. "I mean . . . you know, someone who could be good for you. I have . . . well, I have a *job*. Some of us can't just sail around the world when we want to. We have to be providers. And make something of ourselves. And be successful . . ."

She was stammering in a way that was already familiar to him—nervous, backing away. He would normally find it kind of cute, the way she reacted to things that scared her. Except that this time it was him.

"I can't um—" Her hand went into the air again, as if she were hoping to sweep back the right words.

"It's okay, Cinderella." He tried to smile to reassure her, but he couldn't make his mouth form the right shape. He didn't want to scare her any further, so he looked away.

"Hey, everything okay here?" Drew came around the corner in his wheelchair, being guided by Douglas, who was helping to make sure there weren't any obstacles. The chair barely fit in the width of the side deck.

"We're fine," Evan grumbled.

Damn, even if he could revive Cinderella here—who looked like she was going to pass out—and talk her into at least *one leg* of the sailing tour, what was he going to do? Take off with her while Drew watched? Again? . . . He'd have to make friends with never speaking to Drew again.

Drew looked between the two of them. "You're sure?"

Evan glanced down at Cinderella, who didn't look fine at all. Her face had gone white and she was staring at the decking tape.

"You don't look fine, Lia," Drew said. "You want to come with me and Doug?" He threw a look of daggers Evan's way.

"No, no. It's fine."

"Lia!" Her boss came around the corner. Elle looked terrible—her hair matted to her head, the strange thing she had around her neck all damp fur. "We need to . . . Oh. Hello." She glanced at Drew, Douglas, and Evan. Her look was one you'd give the help. "Kyle is preparing your tip," she said with an efficient lift of her chin. "Lia, let's go back to the office. We have a lot to plan and discuss."

"Now? It's five forty-five."

"Yes, it's going to be a long night. We have a lot to do—to make *plans*." Her voice left on an upswing that seemed like it was supposed to generate enthusiasm, but Lia looked less than enthused. "Paris!" She grabbed Lia's arms and shook them, but Lia stood stiff as a statue. "We're going to swing by my house on the way so I can get cleaned up, and then we'll pick up some coffees and head back in. I have to go over everything with you. You'll be leaving this week."

"This week?"

"Of course."

"I thought it was in July?"

"No. I just decided I want to launch early. Come along." She shuffled down the deck, tripping in the ridiculous shoes she was wearing.

Lia looked up at Evan. "I have to go," she whispered.

Her eyes were begging. Clearly, she wanted to be free. Of him. Of his moment of honesty. Of his need for her. Of all the emotion that was spilling out of him right now.

He looked into her eyes one more time, to see if there was even a slight sense of hesitation there.

But all he could see was a woman who wanted to escape.

He nodded and cut her loose.

She hustled down the deck behind her boss, glancing back only once. The blood spilled out his heart, through his innards, clogged in his stomach. He wondered how long it would take for it to harden around his organs again and shrivel them up so he could stop feeling.

He glanced down at Drew.

"You asshole." Drew shoved the wheels of his chair and followed to the edge of the cat. Douglas fell in step behind him, throwing Evan a sympathetic glance.

For another ten minutes, Evan stared at the redness of the setting sun bouncing off the decking tape until it turned duller, darker, then a deep purple. He willed his heart to shut down again.

Then he shoved his sunglasses into the front of his shirt and dragged himself to the edge of the boat. His body felt like it was a hundred years old again. Joe the Mechanic's kid was standing there at the edge of the dock.

"Hey, Mr. Betancourt. Your engine's ready."

Evan meant to say thanks but he couldn't get words out of his mouth. Instead he nodded, and the kid walked away.

Just in time, was all he could think.

CHAPTER
Twenty-seven

What the hell was that? was all Lia could think as she shuffled down the dock behind the Vampiress, trying to keep up. *And why did she clam up like that?*

Why couldn't she have said what she had really been thinking? Why couldn't she have told Evan that his stunning proposal—to travel around the world with him, to see all the countries she'd ever wanted to see, to wake up every morning with a man who made her feel sexy and alive—was about as glorious an idea as she could imagine? But the song her heart had wanted to sing couldn't come out of her mouth. Just like usual.

She had gone immediately into practical-person mode. Which had shut off her emotions. The practical side of her said it was a stupid idea. How would she make money if she were on a boat for a year? What kind of job would she have when she came back? How would she ever be a success if she drained all of her savings like that? And how could she be a success with a man like Evan, who seemed bent on living only one day at a time? It didn't fit into her worldview at all.

But, then again, *Evan* . . .

She couldn't help the schoolgirl sigh that escaped. And although its dreaminess embarrassed her, it felt kind of good.

Being with a man who made her laugh every day, who could make her smile just with a quick glance, who could give her that kind of passion in bed every night, who could bring her out onto the ocean with the wind in her hair and make her feel so alive, who would stand up for her and protect her when he wanted to just because he *wanted* to . . .

Her heart quickened at the idea of that kind of life.

"Let's hurry," said Elle. She dug a brush out of the depths of her tote bag and yanked the wet mink from around her throat. "I have a car waiting."

"I have my own car, Elle. I'll just meet you there."

"No, I need you to help me. Here. Carry this." She turned and handed Lia her tote bag.

"Elle, you don't need me to carry your bag."

"Of course I do. Now let's talk. Can you be ready to go to Paris this week? I already have an office space, and wanted to send someone ahead to make sure everything's correct. I can send James with you. . . ."

"I have a dress fitting for my sister's wedding on Friday."

"Oh, I'll need you to leave before that."

"But I can't just—"

"And once you're there, I need you to stay there until July. I already have a flat rented that you can use."

"Well, I have a few things I have to be back for, with my sister getting married. I'm a bridesmaid, and—"

"Oh, you'll have to delegate all that, Lia."

"But I can't delegate supporting my sister!"

"Of course you can. She can handle it. Doesn't she have friends?"

"Well, yes, but . . ."

"Then it's settled. I'll send you and James on Thursday. Here's the car. Let me make a call. . . ."

Lia accompanied Elle back to her penthouse apartment, her mind whirling the whole time Elle was on the phone about how she might explain this to Giselle and Fin, how she might make the arrangements with the clients she was handling pro-bono, how she'd help Drew finalize whatever he needed for his boat, whether she could bring Missy to Paris, what she would pack, and—most of all—how she *absolutely* had to go back to Evan's tonight and apologize.

She couldn't leave him feeling like he was anything but special. She'd made a terrible mistake, not saying what she was feeling. She needed him to know he was a special man, and that he was truly going to make a very lucky woman happy someday. And she wished it could be her. . . .

The sigh escaped her again, and she glanced quickly at Elle to make sure she hadn't heard. Elle continued talking. Lia took a deep breath and stared out the window. She'd get over there to tell him the moment Elle was done with her.

Back at the office, Lia and Elle flipped on the fluorescent lights of floor twenty-three and sat in the middle of the otherwise-darkened space. Lights popped up all over the city as night fell. They spread papers across the desks and rearranged files to launch the new campaigns in France. Elle went over the campaigns in detail, showed Lia the new blueprints for the Paris space that she wanted Lia to make sure were carried out, quizzed Lia on her French and signed her up online for refresher French lessons, then pointed to a few boxes she would be shipping that she wanted Lia to look out for. While they were setting up the new administrative files, Lia checked the time again on her cell.

"You've looked at that phone about fifteen times in the last twenty minutes," Elle said.

"Oh, I just . . . There's someone I need to see."

"Where's your work ethic? You usually stay here late with no problem."

"It's not a problem. There's just someone . . . He's leaving tomorrow, and I just need to . . ."

Lia gave up. Elle wasn't listening anymore.

"Listen," Elle said, bending forward to stare at a computer monitor, "if you want to be like me, you're going to have to give up a few things. You have to get your priorities straight."

Lia lifted an eyebrow and let her eyes slide across Elle's desk. Elle had seven crystal-framed photos across the top, but each was a picture of her and a politician—no family, no friends. Gifts and cards lined her sideboard, but none was a little crayon drawing from a niece. A beautiful bouquet of flowers erupted from a crystal vase on the right side of the desk, but Lia happened to know that Elle had them shipped to herself once a week: tulips one week, daffodils the next. A closet door stood slightly ajar, packed with the clothing Elle kept for when she spent the night in the office, and lined with high-heeled shoes, but not one was an ugly pair of blue to wear while she stood up for a friend or sister in a bridesmaid dress. . . .

Lia's heart started racing. *Is this what she was going to become?*

"Um, Elle . . ."

Elle hardly looked up, but instead handed Lia a folder. "Here, why don't you start on this? Can you get us some coffee? This might take a while."

"Um, Elle, I don't think I can go to Paris."

Elle finally looked up. Her chair creaked as it turned toward Lia. "What?"

"I can't go. I have to stay here to help my sister, just until July. And then I have two friends getting married in August and September. And I can't work late anymore. I have friends and family and a niece whose events I've already missed too many times, and I'd like to spend time with them. And I can't even stay this minute." Her heart thundered as she reached for her purse. "I have someone very important to me who might be hurting because of something I said—or didn't say—and I need to go to him right now. Will you call the car around?" Lia set the folders aside and backed toward the hallway, staring at Elle's eyes, which darkened and narrowed.

"*What*?" she screeched. "Lia, this is crazy. We've been planning this for—"

"No, Elle, we weren't." Lia could hear the shaking in her voice, but she needed to stand up for herself. Evan was right. Sometimes people took advantage of you when you always tried to be nice. "You originally said July. And I've been working my butt off for you, working toward that July date, but you've been taking advantage of me. I need to go." Suddenly she felt she couldn't wait another second to see Evan. She whirled toward the doorway and snaked her way through the rows of desks.

"Lia! Don't you dare leave!" Elle's voice zinged off the darkened walls. "If you walk out this door, you might not have a desk to return to!"

"I'll take my chances." Lia flew into the hallway and banged the elevator buttons.

Lia wanted to see Paris with someone she *loved*. She wanted to spend more time with her sisters, spend more time with her mom, spend more time with her friends and her little niece, and *live the life* she was working so damned hard for.

She also, in this moment, desperately wanted to see Evan. Maybe she would leave with him, if he could wait until after the wedding. It wasn't like her to be so impulsive, but she had a crazy amount of money saved up, given all the vacations she never took. She could introduce him to her friends—they'd all love him, especially Xavier and Fin. And she could help him with Drew. And maybe she could join him to see his parents. . . .

She'd be helping him heal.

And he'd be helping her *live*.

Because what was success without the friends, family, and passion to enjoy it?

The elevator finally dinged and she slipped inside and jabbed at the lobby button.

When the car finally dropped her off back in the marina parking lot, she flew out the door, bypassed her own car, and hustled down to the docks.

The lamps sputtered as she picked up speed, running down the ramps, imagining how strong and warm Evan's arms would feel. She pictured his smile when he saw her—it would be tentative at first because she might have hurt him. But she'd assure him immediately that she was so, so sorry. And she'd tell him that he was the most amazing man she'd ever met. And that he was kind, and caring. And that, as crazy as it sounded, she might have just fallen in love for the first time. With him. With Evan Betancourt.

The dock planks disappeared beneath her feet, one by one, as she ran all the way to the end, past the sputtering light and then around the last T-shaped dock.

But as she came to a halt around that final corner, she stopped short and gripped her purse to her chest.

Slip ninety-two was empty.

CHAPTER

Twenty-eight

The park overlooking Sandy Cove Beach was filled with wedding guests, who mingled with cups of punch under the cool July breeze.

Lia made her way between them, greeting the ones she knew, fluffing her full blue skirt out of the way when the wind blew too hard. She tried to cover her mismatched shoes so no one would see. Noelle, Giselle, and her mother were all irritated at her for losing the blue stilettos with the sparkly hardware. It was the one pair they had all fallen in love with. Noelle and all the other bridesmaids had ordered the same ones, based on Lia's recommendation, but then Lia lost hers and couldn't find the same pair in her size. Well, she didn't lose them, exactly. She lost one. And she knew where it was. It was on Evan's boat, probably somewhere past New Zealand by now. To keep everyone from being frustrated at her, she simply bought the shoes in a size too small and wore one small one for pictures. Every time she thought about those stilettos, and the way he'd seduced her that night with them still on, her bones felt like they were melting.

She let out a deep sigh.

Remembering Evan made her sad. It had been five months

he'd been gone now, without a word, and she had to simply keep shoving the thoughts aside. She'd made a terrible mistake, not speaking up when she should have and not telling Evan how she really felt. And not realizing earlier on that people were important, not the ridiculous concept of "success" she had had. She wished she could do it all over again. Drew and Cora were right: You had to give your whole heart fearlessly, or you wouldn't really know true love. You had to jump into the abyss.

And she'd been a coward.

She'd tried to find out from Drew if Evan had sailed north to see their parents. Drew called his mom and dad to ask several times, but they'd said no. He told Lia that Evan had also considered traveling south and starting his circumference again from Panama. Either way, she had no idea if she'd ever see him again. She supposed she could wait another two years, to see if he'd land in Sandy Cove again, but Drew always looked suspicious when she brought Evan up, so she might not really know if and when that happened. Would Drew even tell her?

She had quit her job with Elle. That felt good. Elle just wouldn't budge about the time off, so Lia finally garnered the nerve to quit and start her own marketing business. Her friends really rallied around her and insisted on paying her for all her work from that point on: Mr. Brimmer on Main Street, Vivi, Fin paid for Rabbit's surf camp, Xavier's boss even asked for some work. Drew came through best—Kyle had invested in his boat, and Drew was suddenly rolling in dough. He paid her probably twice what she was worth to do half as much, but he said she was worth it. Even Sharon agreed.

And Kyle—although he stayed loyal to Elle—pitched Lia's services all over, and got her another four huge accounts, two from people who had been on the charter during the disentanglement. They felt like they'd all gone through something important together with Valentine's baby—Lia included—and treated her more like a war buddy than a PR person.

Lia sighed. The work was all good. And she loved spending more time with her family and friends. But she could never shake the feeling that she let the man who could have been the love of her life slip away into the night ocean. She often lay in bed at night, trying to think of ten good reasons she needed to forget about him now—ten good reasons to just let his memory slip away. She could only ever come up with three.

Her shoes kept getting caught in the grass as she made an attempt to circulate among Fin and Giselle's guests. She finally spotted a patch of cement and leaped onto it with the comfortable foot in the right-sized shoe. The cement led her away from the guests, but right now it felt like a nice respite. She hobbled along the meandering path to enjoy the view.

Sandy Cove sprawled out like a jewel beneath her. She took a sip of her punch and took in the whole area—the marina was especially pretty from here. She glanced at the rows of boats that looked like little toys from this height and couldn't help but think of Evan again. Since he wasn't one for social media—or even a cell phone, for that matter—she had no idea. She wondered if he'd ever send a postcard, even. She wondered if she'd hurt him too much.

"Hey."

She turned to see Drew. He had the casts off but was still using a small cane he hated for balance. He'd managed to lacquer it in black so it would blend in with his tuxedo while he stood up for Fin with Rabbit and the other groomsmen.

"What are you doing here on the outskirts?" he asked. "You're usually the center of attention. Which would be over there." He motioned with the cane.

"I just needed a minute, I guess."

Drew nodded and they both stared at the Sandy Cove marina. The sun cast glittering diamonds over the waves as they rolled in gently below.

"You really miss him, huh?" he asked.

Lia was first startled that Drew read her dreamy gazing so easily. But then she knew she shouldn't be. He knew her well. "Yes."

The waves crashed below, and they watched them quietly for a minute.

"He's a good man, Drew," she finally said.

Drew didn't answer right away, studying his shoes. "Renece thought so, too."

"He told me about all that."

"About what a jerk I was?"

"He didn't word it that way."

"Then he is a good man."

The waves crashed a few more times.

"Did he tell you more than that?" Drew asked.

"There was more?"

"There was the part about you."

"The part about *me*?"

Drew nodded. "That the whole story about Evan and me and Renece was becoming the same story about Evan and me and you."

"What are you talking about? You don't have feelings for m—" She froze and turned slowly. Several memories flashed past. Drew kissing her that one time. Evan asking so often if she and Drew were in a relationship. The way Drew scowled the night he found them together.

"Do you have *feelings* for me, Drew?" She whispered the question because she could hardly form it into solid words.

"Don't worry—it's a thing of the past." He gave a weak smile. "I'm crazy about Sharon. But I did, yes. And when Evan came swooping in here, I guess it just riled everything up— my old feelings about Renece, my old feelings about you, how much I felt he betrayed me, how much I felt he disregarded me. . . ."

"He doesn't disregard you."

"I know that now. We got some things worked out. But I still asked him not to use you, or hurt you. I just couldn't bear that. It would have meant more disregard for me. And certainly pain for you that you didn't need. And then, when I saw your face on the charter that night . . . I thought he had. Disregarded both of us."

"No! He wasn't hurting me. He was actually being incredibly kind, and honest, and telling me he'd like to be with me. . . . I was the one who was doing the hurting. I should have been more honest and not so emotionally constipated."

Drew snorted. "Were you doing your 'keep me at arm's length' thing again?"

"I was. I'm an idiot."

They watched the waves below for a while.

"He left because he thought we rejected him," Drew said.

Lia nodded. "But we didn't. We should have been more straightforward."

"I've been a jerk."

"Lia!"

Lia turned to see Giselle calling to her from across the grass.

"Time for bridesmaids pictures!"

"My turn, I guess." Lia tried to smile.

She saw the other bridesmaids walking down a path toward the rocky cliffs below, but she saw that Giselle was heading toward a long set of cement stairs—probably to maneuver better in her long dress—and went to help. Together, they took the stairs slowly. So slowly, in fact, Lia had time to glance up and gaze at the marina every fifth step or so.

Giselle smiled. "Looking for Evan's boat?"

Lia looked away. Caught. She'd told Giselle and Noelle everything about Evan. It felt good to open up to her sisters again, sitting on the floor of her apartment and drinking wine and having one of their old-fashioned "whine fests." After the huge mistake she'd made by clamming up with Evan, she'd vowed not to do it anymore with anyone else. And she started with her sisters. From now on, it was put your emotions out there. So far, it hadn't resulted in the world ending. In fact, it had only resulted in feeling better and more connected than she ever had. It finally dawned on her that *that* was the feeling of success.

Giselle fluffed her full, white dress. It was a 1950s vintage-style gown that suited her Grace Kelly looks beautifully.

"You look gorgeous, Giselle. I'm so happy you found your real love."

Giselle looked up, surprised, and pulled Lia into a tight hug, despite their precarious position on the stairway. "You will, too," she whispered.

The "find" in question came into view at the base of the steps.

"Careful up there," Fin said. He stepped forward in his tuxedo and helped Giselle the rest of the way down the stairs. His wetsuit-modeling days came in handy as he smiled naturally at the wedding photographer, who appeared in the cove and got busy snapping candids of the three of them. They moved across the sand and came to a small outcropping of rocks.

"Want to get a shot of you two and your bridesmaid there?" the photographer called over the crashing waves, pointing toward Lia.

"How about a picture of me saving our bridesmaid from falling into the ocean?" Fin mumbled, reaching for Lia's hand as she tried to climb over the rocks herself.

"I've got it!" Lia slapped his hand back. "What do you think I am, some ninety-year-old lady?"

"You're as feisty as one," Fin said.

She crawled to the top of the rock, but her foot slipped, and the danged new shoe went sliding. Down. Into. The. Ocean.

"Damn it!" Lia cried. "I spent four friggin' months looking for that shoe!" An unreasonable sadness clogged her chest and she almost thought she was going to cry. Her emotions were obviously out of control.

"And I think I slept on it one night," came a voice from below the rocks.

Suddenly, the voice's head crested—*Evan!*

"You're not going to tumble down next, are you?" he asked.

Her heart started pounding.

"She might," Fin said. "But I wouldn't try to help her."

"Oh, I know better."

Evan hoisted himself onto the rock platform. He had on navy trousers and a white button-down shirt with a neat, narrow tie that swung as he lifted himself up. Lia blinked back the incongruity of seeing him standing there. Her heart pumped out of her chest.

"What are you *doing* here?" she finally managed to squeak out.

"Brought you this." Her blue stiletto dangled from his fingertip. "Thought you might need it today."

"You . . . you came *all the way back* here just to . . . to . . . bring me a *shoe*?"

"Well, and I forgot something."

The hope that had buoyed her chest when she saw him sunk. All those months of missing him, all those nights of realizing the mistakes she'd made, all those mornings of trying to conjure him at her doorway sunk like a rock in her chest. What might he have forgotten? The parts strewn across his deck? His motor pieces? His jacket? . . . Her disappointment tasted bitter in the back of her throat.

"What did you forget?" She looked away so he wouldn't see the tears threatening.

"You."

Lia's heart did a quick-and-stutter again.

He shoved his other hand in his pocket. Giselle and Fin, who were standing there gawking, suddenly seemed to capture Evan's attention.

"Congratulations," he said, nodding to them both.

"Thanks." Fin stretched out his hand. "Fin Hensen."

"Evan Betancourt."

"I've heard about you."

"Have you, now?"

"Good things."

"That surprises me."

"Why is that?"

"I think I may have made some mistakes." Evan glanced at Lia.

Fin looked between Lia and Evan for several beats, then smiled and waved his hand back toward the guests. "Well, we have to . . . uh . . . Giselle? . . . Don't we need to get back?"

Giselle was smiling at Lia. "We do." She turned toward the photographer. "Tell the bridesmaids to meet us back up there—we'll take our pictures by the gazebo."

Giselle fluffed her bouffant dress and pulled it back so she could walk more gracefully along the rocks. She let Fin reach over and hold her arm, leaning into him. Lia noted the gesture with interest. It didn't look weak. It didn't look too dependent. It didn't make Giselle look incompetent. It didn't look like an abyss.

It looked like grace and loveliness and deep, deep trust, and—most importantly—it looked like love.

Lia's eyes felt misty as she watched her buddy and sister.

"I'm sure there's plenty of food and drink for an extra guest, Evan," Giselle yelled back, watching her footing. "You should come."

"Thank you."

Giselle and Fin wandered back up the beach, hand in hand, leaning toward each other.

"Evan, I'm—"

"Lia, I'm—" he said at the same time.

They both laughed.

"You go first," he said.

"Let's sit down."

She teetered around the outcropping, heading toward a large rock where they could sit. She saw his hand jolt forward to help her, but he withdrew it quickly and ran it across the back of his neck.

After a slight hesitation, she reached back and took it. She let him help her over the rocks.

"Evan, I'm sorry," she said. "For not saying so many things I meant to that day. I went back for you."

He lifted his eyebrow. "When?"

"That night."

He looked away. They got to the lone rock and sat down. He bent forward and put the shoe in the sand.

"I'm sorry, too," he said. "I shouldn't have had such a knee-jerk reaction. I regretted leaving before I even hit Guadalajara. But by then I didn't want to turn around. I figured I didn't have anything to go back for."

"I'm so sorry. I should have said what I was feeling. I shouldn't have let Elle pull me away to work again, and I shouldn't have worked so late that night. I might have caught you. I . . . I quit, by the way."

"You *quit*?"

Lia nodded.

"Why? You said it was all you wanted—Paris and everything."

"I realized I was leaving a few things out. Like time to enjoy it. Like loved ones to enjoy it with. And . . ."

Her brain almost clamped down on the real emotion again, but she knew what it had cost her the last time. She took a deep breath and summoned the courage to say the words.

"And what?" Evan asked.

"And possibly the love of my life." She finally met his eyes.

Both Evan's eyebrows lifted this time. "Douglas?"

She shoved him in the shoulder. "*You*, you dolt."

His eyes gentled. The waves crashed around them as he tentatively took her fingers and ran them through his. "*I'm* the love of your life?"

She nodded. She seemed to have lost the ability to speak

again. She was going to have to get over this, damn it: *jump into the abyss.*

"I've been crying a lot," she finally blurted.

His eyebrows drew together.

". . . while I'm in bed. And I've been trying to make a list. Ten good reasons."

He waited, his frown deepening, rubbing her knuckles. She knew he was waiting for her to elaborate, but her throat was closing up.

"Ten good reasons to do what?" he finally asked softly.

"To forget you."

He nodded. The next wave crashed, and he watched it float close to them, but recede. A sadness took over his features, but he didn't let go of her fingertips.

"But . . ." She took a deep breath. She couldn't let him be consumed by that. He was such a good man. She needed to tell him the truth: "I could only think of three."

His mouth quirked up at the corner. "Which way were you counting?"

"Backward."

He nodded, a small smile still hovering on his face. "What are ten, nine, and eight, then?"

"Number ten was my job. I had to forget you to focus on my job. But then . . . well, I quit."

"Yeah, that doesn't work at all."

"It doesn't."

He ventured a half smile. "What was nine?"

"Nine was that you might never come back. That you'd already forgotten me."

"Doesn't work either. Obviously. I not only didn't forget you, I couldn't stop thinking about you. How about eight?"

"Eight was that I'm nothing like Renece."

His frown returned as the ocean splashed near them. "I don't need you to be anything like Renece, Lia."

"But she was quiet and pretty and shy and all the things you probably like. And I'm . . ."

He reached out to push a windblown strand of hair behind her ear. "Bossy and pushy and talkative?" He smiled.

"Something like that."

"That's why I couldn't stop thinking about you."

"Really?"

"Really."

"But you loved her, and you probably want to find someone like her to love again."

"Lia." Evan shook his head. The ocean crashed behind them as he rested his elbows on his knees, his face tightened into concentration. "I did love Renece. But I'm not looking for someone like her to have a repeat of that part of my life. I was never looking for that. In fact, I did my best to shut myself off from any memories or feelings at all. But you . . . you just wriggled your way in. You made me . . . *feel* . . . again. When I first saw you, I was irritated by your joy and optimism. But now I think I was just jealous of it. . . ." He looked at her again, as if to see if she could believe that.

"But, after being around you, it was kind of infectious. I started to see things the way you saw them. There *is* joy out there. There *are* good people. There's wonder, and beauty, and nature. There are miracles every day. There can be good memories of the people you loved. There are so many things to live for." He glanced at her. "What's that saying? 'Stay close to anything that makes you glad to be alive'?" He smiled. "It took me all the way until the Marquesas Islands to realize it, but you make me glad to be alive, Lia."

Her heart skittered over a beat or two.

"You made a difference in my life, and I just had to come back to tell you. And to see . . ." He let the thought drift off.

"To see what?" she whispered.

"If I can still talk you into coming with me. I want to show you Paris. I want to show you the world."

There didn't seem to be enough air on the whole beach to reinflate Lia's lungs, but she gulped for some anyway.

"So my ten good reasons to forget about you aren't working at all?"

"*I'm* not buying them. Ten reasons we should give things a whirl seem more doable."

"You start."

His smile was relaxed. "Ten, I want to show you Paris. Nine, I want to make you happy. Eight, I want to make you smile—just like that—every day. Seven, I want you to still have orgasms. Six, I want you to have decent coffee every day, even when Cora's not around. Five, I want you to—"

She reached out and put a finger over his lips. "I get five reasons, too."

His lips curved beneath her fingertips. His eyes flashed. She couldn't tell if he was amused or surprised or turned on, but he gave her a slight nod.

"Five, someone needs to teach you how to dance. Four, someone needs to allow you to let all those things back in your life that have 'been a while' for you."

He smiled.

"Three, you deserve love in your life again, and I want to fill your life with it. Me, Drew, your parents, friends—you deserve our love, Evan."

His smile turned more serious and he gave her another slight nod.

"Two, I want you to be a father again. You made a great dad."

Evan's eyes began to mist, and he looked away.

But Lia pulled his chin back. "And one, because I love you. You're the first person I ever wanted to really share a life with, ever wanted to rely on, and take that scary leap into the abyss for. But I could see it with you. I trust you to take care of all the vulnerability I'm handing you, and hold my hand, and we'll take the leap together."

He nodded deeply, staring at her with all the love and tenderness she'd wanted him to feel again. It looked good on him. Evan was meant to love this way—with his whole heart.

"Can we first spend some time here to give me a chance to wrap up my accounts," she asked, "and maybe spend time with Noelle and my mom and Coco, and then Giselle and Fin when they get back from their honeymoon?"

As if he finally realized she was really going with him, Evan gave her a smile of relief. "We can."

"And, before we go, spend a little time with Drew and maybe go up to see your parents?"

"I was thinking about that, actually. And I definitely want to talk to Drew." He glanced up the cliff.

"I think he'll be happy."

He looked at her sideways and quirked an eyebrow.

"Seriously. He told me about how he felt about me. And that it was in the past—he's really happy with Sharon. But he was also just telling me that he thought he might not have given you a fair chance before."

Evan was already nodding. "He sent me a telegram."

"What?"

"In the Marquesas. Shocked the hell out of me. Anyway, he told me that you were sad. And that as much as he thought I'd hurt you by leaving, he'd probably done worse to you by nudging me away."

"He didn't tell *me* that."

"He probably didn't want to say anything in case I didn't return."

"But you did."

"Of course. Are you crazy? I couldn't turn the boat around fast enough. Had to head way up north to catch the North Pacific High current to slingshot me back to the States. I never sailed so fast in my life."

"Oh, Evan." She threw her arms around his neck and squeezed until he let out an *"Ooph."*

"Drew offered me a job, too." Evan grinned.

"You're kidding."

"I might take him up on it after you and I see all we want to see. He said he could use one more investor with him and Kyle."

"Evan, that would be fabulous! You have friends here who haven't even met you yet—Fin has been asking about you, and Giselle and Noelle want to know *everything.* And Douglas and Cora were asking about you just the other day—they miss you. They're dating now."

"No kidding?" Evan's smile grew wider. "Good for them." He squeezed Lia's hand. "I'm ready. You've got a lifetime of me, if you'll have me that long. I love you, Lia."

Lia's heart felt like it stopped beating a second. She'd never heard those words before. Had never even *thought* them before. And she could hardly believe they were coming from this decent, loving man.

"I love you, too, Evan." Lia threw herself into his arms and kissed him again, hard, while a band struck up at the top of the cliff, sending some Frank Sinatra down their way to kiss to.

Lia couldn't believe Evan wanted a lifetime with her. . . . Or that she was looking forward to it. What Drew and Cora had said—you can't fall in love until you give your whole heart fearlessly—was so very true.

"You want to head up for some bacon-wrapped shrimp and champagne?" she murmured, finally breaking the kiss.

"You're not gonna trick me with asparagus again, are you?"

"I might. I can be tricky that way." She rose and tugged his hand. She could hardly wait to introduce him again to Fin and Giselle, and Noelle, and her mom. And then get him home tonight . . .

He bent over and scooped up her blue stiletto. "What about this?"

"I've been . . . um . . . thinking about these shoes quite a bit. Can we have a repeat of our adventures in them?"

He chuckled. "As I said: a lifetime of adventures, if you'll have me."

"Oh, I'll have you."

He laughed again and leaned down in front of her to guide her heel in. "There you go, Cinderella."

Read on for a special excerpt from
another Sandy Cove Romance
from Lauren Christopher

The Red Bikini

Available now from Berkley Sensation!

Giselle flung the suitcase on her sister's tropical-patterned bedspread and let out the sigh she'd been holding since sometime over the air space of Kansas. Or maybe as far back as Illinois. Or maybe even since they'd been in the airport in Indiana.

She stared at a bright red cloth napkin Lia had left on the bed, next to a note in her sister's loopy handwriting: *"It's okay. Relax."*

Giselle frowned and lifted the napkin, then felt four strings slip through her fingers.

It was a bikini. How very Lia. How very *not* Giselle.

It's okay.

Relax.

She folded the triangles and tucked the package deep into the corner of Lia's dresser drawer, amid some tissue-wrapped lingerie and a lavender drawer sachet.

"Mommy," came a breathless voice from behind her, "there's *sand*!"

Her daughter flung herself onto the bed, sending the suit-case and all their clothes bouncing and squeaking. "And Aunt

Lia left me *sandals*! Can we go to the water now? Can I put on my suit?" Little hands gripped the edge of Giselle's suitcase.

"In a minute." Giselle closed the drawer. "Why don't you help me unpack?"

Giselle's fake enthusiasm—held in a false falsetto since Indiana—sounded too breathless, but Coco seemed to buy it, and her little pale legs whisked her to the front room.

Giselle tried to take her twenty cleansing breaths while Coco was gone, but, as usual, she only got to about the seventh. Coco came bumping back through the doorway with a pink Barbie suitcase.

"I wonder how Aunt Lia knew I liked *pink* sandals."

Giselle eyed Coco's sparkly shoes and the tutu she'd worn on the plane. "Probably a good guess." She lifted Coco's suitcase onto the bed beside hers.

Lia's beachside apartment was small—not much more than a box, really—but Giselle felt a wave of appreciation that her sister had opened it to them, and on such short notice. Sandy Cove was the perfect place to escape to for two weeks. But California would have been much too expensive without being able to use Lia's apartment. Giselle couldn't use up what was left of her cash reserves.

"What was that song Aunt Lia taught you?" Giselle asked over her shoulder as she yanked closed the bedroom's palm-colored curtains.

Coco flung one of her blond braids over her shoulder and began swaying her hips. "*Stir it up . . .*" she began singing. Her toothlessness lent a lispy charm to the Bob Marley song.

Giselle smiled. "*. . . Little darlin' . . . stir it up . . .*"

Their hips moved in exaggerated sways, and soon most of Giselle's worries were tucked away with their T-shirts, shorts, Giselle's tailored slacks, Coco's sleep toy Ninja Kitty, and their sensible bathing suits.

While Giselle was sad she wouldn't get to see Lia, who was tied up with a business trip in New York, she was sort of relieved. The pitying platitudes were exhausting. Especially when coupled with the hushed tones from friends and family in Indiana: *Omygod, what will she do? And what will she do without Roy?* Giselle knew the way to make the hushed voices stop was to show everyone what she was made of—lift her chin, showcase her strength, saunter into a room with a confidence she might dredge up from somewhere. But she hadn't quite been able to do that. Maybe she just needed time. . . .

As Sandy Cove's afternoon light began calming her through the mango-colored shades, Giselle felt relaxed enough to get into Lia's tiny kitchen and bake. She'd picked up a few staples at the beach corner market to make her raisin cookies. Counting strokes and measuring ingredients always did her wonders.

While she measured and poured, Coco sat at the dining table and told knock-knock jokes until a sharp rap sounded at the door.

"Someone's here," Coco whispered.

The tightening began in her neck as Giselle wiped her hands on a towel and made her way to the entryway.

She peeked through the peephole and saw a totem pole of a boy standing on the porch.

He was young—maybe twenty—with a black rubber item folded like a tablecloth in his right hand. Sable brown hair coiled into quarter-sized curls all over his head, and a brown tuft of hair sprouted from his chin in a hippie "soul patch" style. His toast-colored eyes were close together, giving him a comical air. He brought them closer to the peephole, his face distorting in the funny glass.

Giselle opened the door a crack.

"Heeeeey," he said. His eyes took in as much of her as he could see from behind the door, but the gesture didn't feel insolent, or even flirtatious—which was good, since he seemed at least fifteen years younger than she was.

Giselle flung the dish towel over her shoulder and tucked a strand of hair back into her chignon as she pulled the door wider. He wore bright orange-and-brown knee-length swim trunks that hung low on his waist, as if there wasn't quite enough body to hold them up. He stood the same height as Giselle, but was reedier, the outline of his ribs pressing through his tanned skin. His knobby feet were covered in sand.

"You must be Lia's sister," he said lazily.

"Yes."

"You look just like her." A note of wonder hung on his words.

"Thank you." Giselle smoothed her skirt.

She was flattered—she thought of Lia as beautiful in every way—but Giselle didn't see a resemblance. She felt much older, although their age difference was only six years. But she also felt duller, and at least a dress size bigger. Despite the fact Giselle had won beauty contests throughout her teens, her confidence had plummeted when Roy had had his first affair.

"This is for your daughter." The rubber item unfurled from his fingers. It was a small wet suit. "I'm Rabbit."

Rabbit? Giselle blinked back her surprise. So this was who Lia had told her about? Somehow she'd had the image differently in her mind: She'd pictured maybe a grizzled old guru who lived on a sand dune with parrots. Or at least someone out of junior college.

Clutching the wet suit against her chest, she held out her other hand in default hostess mode: "I'm Giselle."

He regarded her hand with amusement, then shook it briefly. "Sweet. You have something cooking in there?" He tried to peek around the door.

"Oh—raisin cookies." She stepped back, and Coco popped her head around, able to stand it no longer.

Rabbit studied her as she pushed her way through the doorway. "And you must be Coco." He crouched to the ground, rubbing the tuft of hair on his chin. "I've heard all about you from your aunt. How do you feel about being a little grommet this week?"

"A grommet?"

"A young surfer. Lia signed you up for my camp. I have twelve new groms coming."

Coco's short, jilting bounces expressed everything.

Thank goodness Lia had arranged this. It would be good for Coco to escape the drama that had become their lives. All Giselle had to do in return was take pictures for Rabbit's brochure. And go out on one date with a guy Lia knew named Dave or Don or something.

Although it was a pretty close toss-up, the brochure made her the most nervous. Marketing-minded Lia had coordinated it, even though Giselle had insisted she had no brochure experience. In fact, she had no work experience at all, unless you counted posing as the perfect doctor's wife at charity balls. But

Lia had insisted that the photos Giselle took of Coco were excellent. *Your photos capture such truth and beauty,* her sister had said. Giselle had continued to protest, but Lia reminded her that Rabbit wasn't exactly a Fortune 500 company. He couldn't even pay. Except in trade. Which was where Coco benefited.

"I have a surfboard for you," Rabbit whispered to Coco. He glanced up at Giselle. "Can you come see it?"

Giselle hesitated. The unpacking wasn't done. She hadn't taken her twenty cleansing breaths. The raisin cookies had four minutes left. She needed to organize, prioritize, get their lives in order.

But she caught the expression on Coco's face—one of hopefulness, a trust in adventure—and decided she could take a few cues from her daughter. Giselle did need to learn to relax. She did need to straighten her backbone and garner some strength. She did need to learn how to grasp adventure.

"Sure," she said, shrugging as if she made impromptu decisions all the time. "But I have a few more minutes for the cookies."

"I'll wait." Rabbit grinned.

When the buzzer finally went off, Giselle loaded the entire batch onto a plate to bring to his apartment. She tucked a strand of hair behind her ear and took Coco's hand. "Then let's go."

She tried not to think of the clothing still on the bed, or the blind date with the man whose name she couldn't remember, or the twenty cleansing breaths, while she followed Rabbit next door.

Let their new life begin. . . .

A waist-high gate divided the halves of the second-story patio Rabbit and Lia shared.

When her sister had said that Rabbit lived "next door," Giselle hadn't realized how close that would be. No wonder their mother wouldn't stay here. Having their coiffed, French-manicured mother staying within shouting distance of a barely clad boy like Rabbit, who probably got stoned to the Doors and tracked sand across the patio on a regular basis, would be their mother's undoing. Eve McCabe typically chose to stay at a Hilton in posh Newport Beach several miles up.

Rabbit strode toward his wide-open door in that rubbery way lanky boys move. Music tumbled out: some kind of folk singer with a mellow, seaside sound. Soon the music swallowed him.

Giselle stalled. She peered around the doorway, but he'd already disappeared.

His place was entirely white and beige, with an empty expanse of stained carpeting. A lone card table was set up where a dining table would normally be, a smattering of potato chips and empty beer bottles littered across its torn top. Beanbag chairs were tossed about the living area, filled with boys with shaggy hair and sandy feet. One was playing a guitar to a song on the speaker.

Along the living room wall were four bright surfboards, each more colorful than the last. One showed off brilliant stripes and flames, two teemed with plant shapes, and the last was in swirls of yellows, oranges, and reds. A fifth, with a bright turquoise stripe down the center, lay across the mottled carpet. One of the boys sat on top, his legs crossed into a suntanned *X*.

"Hey," said the one on the board.

Giselle thought perhaps it was meant to be a greeting and gave an uncertain nod.

"C'min, Giselle," yelled Rabbit from around the corner.

She took a few tentative steps onto the linoleum patch that served as an entryway, her espadrilles crunching in the scattered sand grains.

A boy in the kitchen drew a bottle of beer out of a cooler and held it toward her.

"No, thanks," she said, wrapping her arm around Coco's neck and looking toward the doorway where Rabbit had disappeared.

"Are those for us?" he asked, eyeing the plate of cookies.

"Yes." She thrust the plate forward.

He took a cookie off the top and bit into it as he surveyed Coco. "You must be one of Rabbit's groms."

"I am." Coco nodded. "He's bringing me a surfboard."

"Step aside!" Rabbit's voice emerged from a back bedroom. In both hands, he gripped an enormous turquoise board.

He dipped it so it didn't hit the doorway, then gingerly laid it across the carpet. The boys moved to make space.

"This was my sister's when she started," Rabbit said.

Coco bounced around it. A wood-grain pattern ran down the center, with two bamboo shoots on either side. A row of yellow hibiscus flowers entwined through the bamboo. The artwork was faded where the hibiscus flowers began, and there were plenty of scratches and dings, but Coco's face lit up like a Christmas tree.

"My sis was a little grommet like you once," Rabbit drawled. "Now she's on the Women's World Tour and rides for Roxy."

Coco turned wide eyes toward Giselle. She clearly didn't understand any of that, but she could tell it sounded impressive.

Rabbit walked around the board. "So you can use this when you practice, but in my class we're going to use blue foam boards like the other kids, okay?"

Coco nodded.

He patted the center hibiscus. "Kick off your shoes."

Coco mounted the board with great seriousness. Rabbit's finger outlined elements of the design that would give her cues—her left toe should line up with the wood grain, while her right heel should round the curve of the bottom hibiscus.

He sat back on his haunches and frowned at her feet. "Are you left-handed, little dudette?"

Coco nodded hesitantly.

"Ah, a goofy-foot," he said. "I thought so. This doesn't look natural for you. Kino surfs goofy, too." He motioned with his thumb to a guy sitting behind him. "Let's switch feet."

Rabbit continued in his rhythmic drone while Giselle breathed in the scent of the ocean that wafted through the nearby dining-room window. The boys' chatter went on in the background—some argument about something called onshore swells. The mellow seaside singer continued to encourage love and sunshine. Giselle closed her eyes and inhaled cocoa butter and salty air, feeling a strange, sudden peace in the room full of strangers with whom she shared very little except being part of the human race.

"Now!" shouted Rabbit.

Coco pushed up with her arms to bring her feet to the cues.

"Excellent," he drawled, grinning. "That was a beautiful pop-up. Let's try it again."

Coco giggled, and he went on while Giselle noticed a beer bong in the corner of the room. Over her shoulder, two of the boys began swearing. One shoved the other, and a third threw a bottle across the room to a catcher in a beanbag.

Giselle reached for Coco's shoulder. As nice as it had been to be welcomed into this underworld for a minute, it might be time for their exit. "I, uh . . . We really need to go."

As the swearing continued, she cupped Coco's ears and began steering her toward the front door, but a smooth, firm voice came rolling across the room: *"Boys!"*

The room stilled.

"That's enough."

The voice came from another tanned, bare-chested figure leaning in the doorjamb, watching everyone, with a black rubbery tube stretched from one hand to the other. He looked older than the others, although Giselle couldn't be sure. He definitely had a more solid body, with actual muscles that looked like they would keep him grounded if a big gust of wind came through. His blond-tipped hair was pushed up as if it had just dried that way. He had on swim trunks, his wide chest boasting the dull sheen that salt water leaves, a dusting of wheat over copper.

He frowned at the boys who were swearing, then motioned with his head toward Coco.

"Sorry, Fin," one of the boys said. He gave one last quiet shove, though, like a puppy frolicking.

Giselle meant to turn her attention back to Coco, but found herself unable to take her eyes off this newest appearance, captivated by his perfect chest, his square jaw, the rock-shaped shoulders. His body was a gorgeous color—a golden brown, with tinges of smoky red at the tops of his shoulders. Giselle thought it would be perfect to paint. Her second thought was that it would be perfect to photograph. And her third was that it would be wondrous to touch.

As her mind lingered on the last thought, imagining her finger running along that ridge that defined his shoulder from his biceps, he met her gaze.

She averted her eyes. *Sweet criminy.* She pulled her

cardigan closer and smoothed her hair. She was a stay-at-home mom from Indiana. Comptroller for the PTA. A *scrapbooker*. And he was just a kid. What was wrong with her?

She clasped one of Coco's shoulders and leaned toward Rabbit. "We need to get going."

She'd had enough of the surfer underworld for one day. And this California sunshine was frying her brain—staring at a twentysomething surfer. Was she losing her mind?

Rabbit unfurled his legs. "Join us. We're cooking out."

"Can we, Mommy?" Coco begged.

Giselle ran Coco's braid through her hand. "I'll think about it." But she'd already dismissed it. Drinking beer and eating hot dogs with a bunch of sandy boys that looked barely out of high school was probably not what she and her five-year-old daughter should be doing. And she didn't need that Fin kid distracting her with his golden shoulders and strange blue eyes. Maybe she'd find a nice, clean Olive Garden nearby.

She gathered Coco's shoes, grabbed the empty cookie plate, and hustled out of the room, trying not to look back toward Fin. The other boys called out good-byes—she thought one called her "Betty"—but mostly she focused on getting Coco to the patio without any more gawking.

As she passed the doorway to the bedrooms, however, her curiosity ran rampant against her better sense. Suddenly, wildly, uncontrollably—her gaze swept back.

But he wasn't there.

She couldn't tell whether the air whooshing out of her lungs was from disappointment that she didn't get another glance at his sculpted chest or relief that she wouldn't embarrass herself any further. Either way, she gave up a prayer of gratitude that her decency had remained intact for the next sixty seconds.

After Rabbit and another boy laid the surfboard in the center of Lia's living room, Giselle closed the door and leaned her head back.

She took twelve cleansing breaths.

Starting a new life might have to come in smaller steps.

Discover Romance

berkleyjoveauthors.com

See what's coming up next from your
favorite romance authors and explore all
the latest Berkley, Jove, and Sensation
selections.

See what's new
~
Find author appearances
~
Win fantastic prizes
~
Get reading recommendations
~
Chat with authors and other fans
~
Read interviews with authors you love